# PEARL

# PEARL

WRITTEN BY
## SHERRI L. SMITH

ILLUSTRATED BY
## CHRISTINE NORRIE

An Imprint of
**■ SCHOLASTIC**

All rights reserved. Published by Graphix, an imprint of Scholastic Inc., *Publishers since 1920*.
SCHOLASTIC, GRAPHIX, and associated logos are trademarks and/or registered trademarks of Scholastic Inc.

Library of Congress Control Number: 2023943664

ISBN 978-1-338-02943-7 (hardcover)
ISBN 978-1-338-02942-0 (paperback)

10 9 8 7 6 5 4 3 2 1     24 25 26 27 28

Printed in China   62
First edition, August 2024

Edited by Cassandra Pelham Fulton
Art Assistant: November Stanley
Studio Assistant: Darlene Estremera
Jacket and cover color by Wes Dzioba
Book design by Larsson McSwain
Creative Director: Phil Falco
Publisher: David Saylor

For Rahna Reiko Rizzuto, whose
research and stories inspired this book;
for Allen Spiegel, who championed it;
and above all, for the survivors.
S. L. S.


For Jo, for always; and to
all those who traverse amongst
and between lands.
C. N.

# AMA

## PEARL DIVER

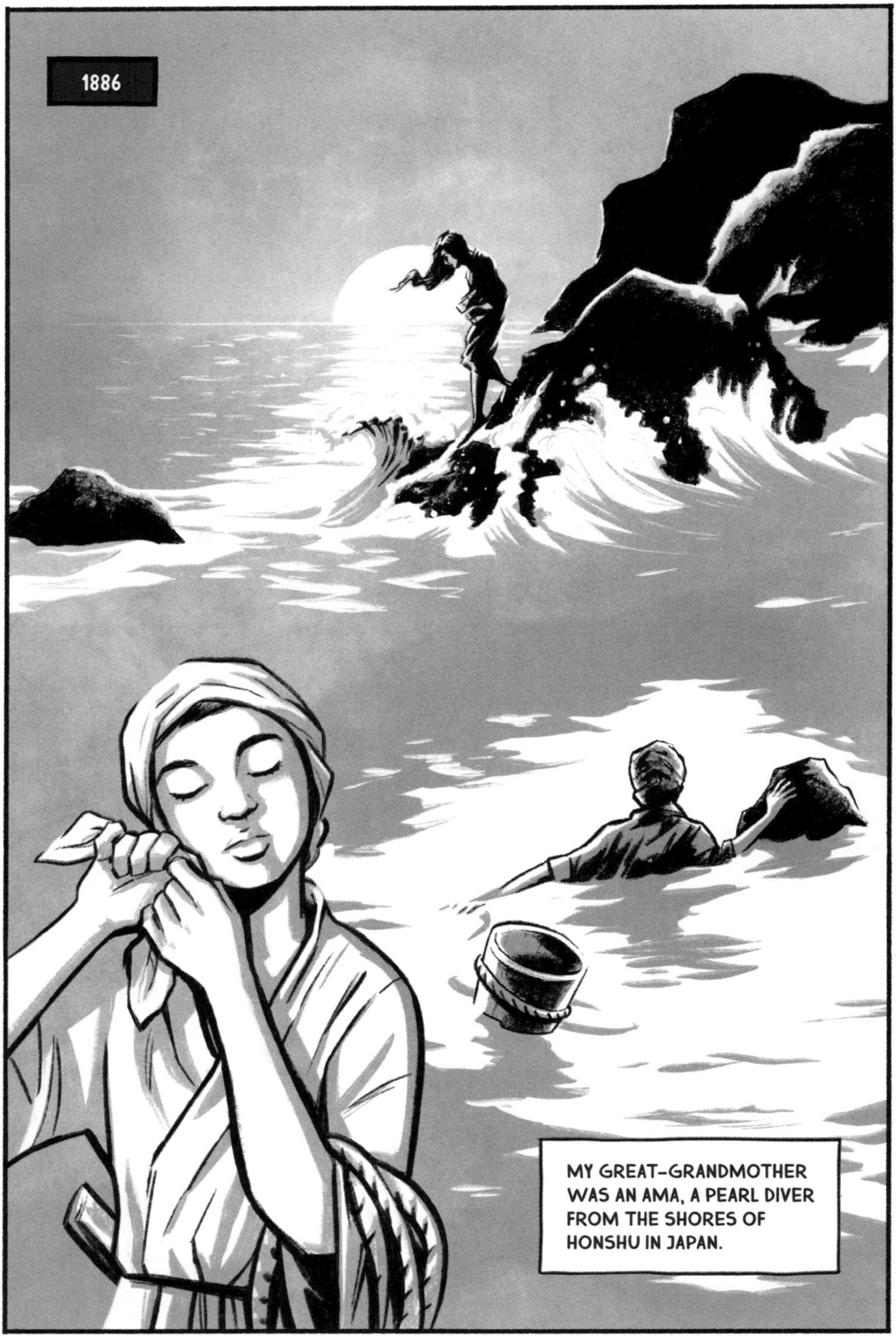
1886
MY GREAT-GRANDMOTHER WAS AN AMA, A PEARL DIVER FROM THE SHORES OF HONSHU IN JAPAN.

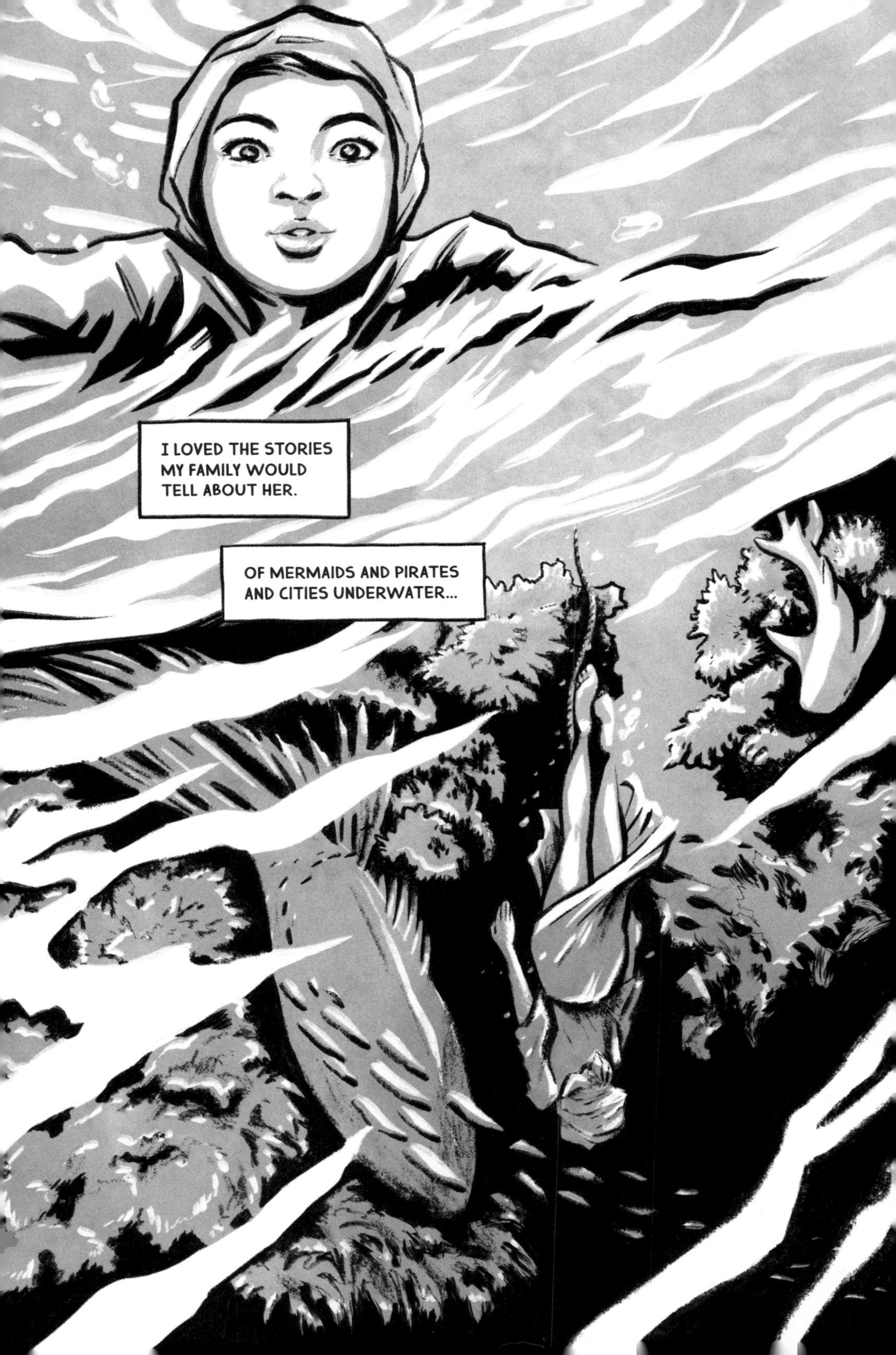
I LOVED THE STORIES MY FAMILY WOULD TELL ABOUT HER.
OF MERMAIDS AND PIRATES AND CITIES UNDERWATER...

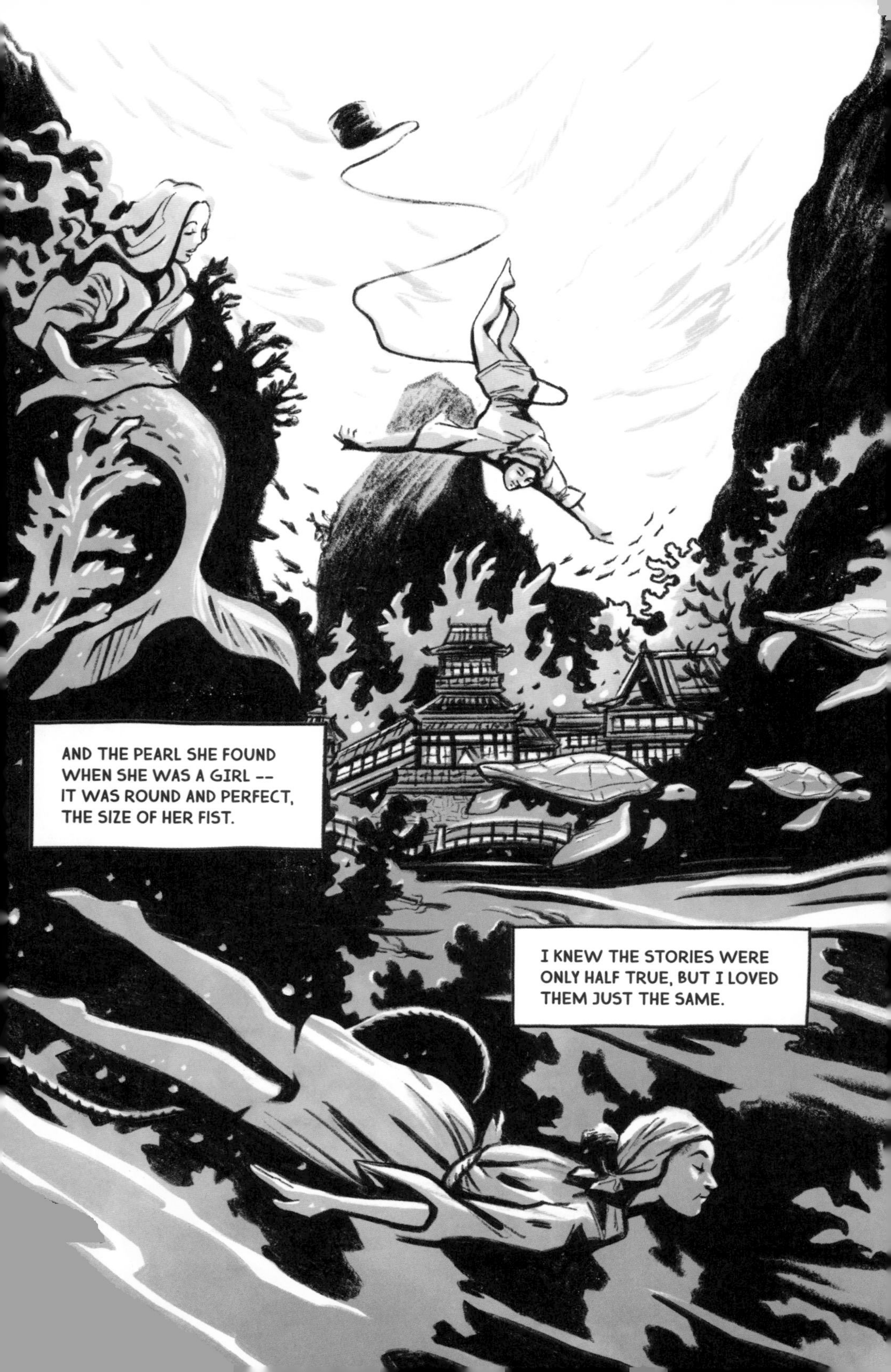
AND THE PEARL SHE FOUND WHEN SHE WAS A GIRL -- IT WAS ROUND AND PERFECT, THE SIZE OF HER FIST.
I KNEW THE STORIES WERE ONLY HALF TRUE, BUT I LOVED THEM JUST THE SAME.

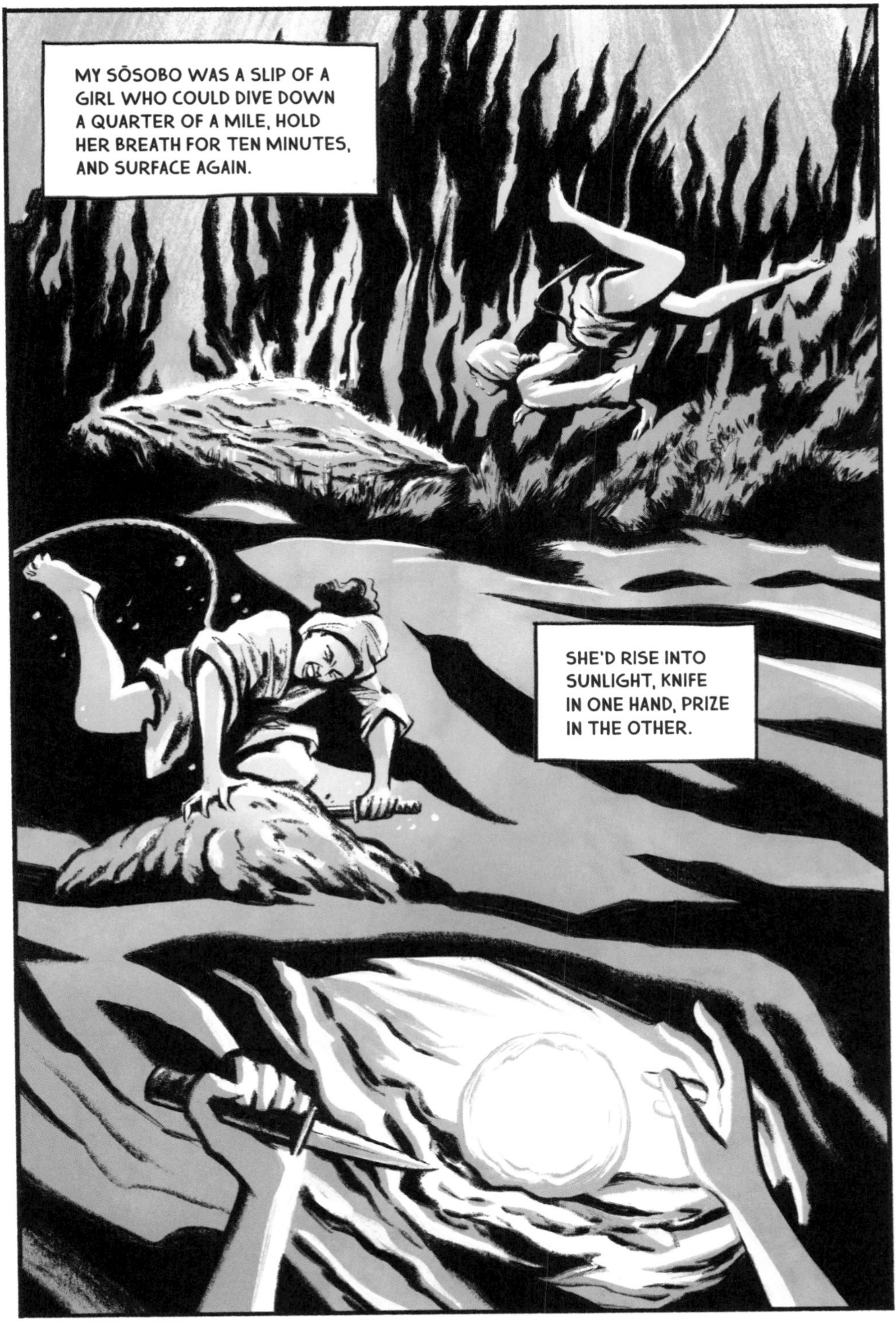
MY SŌSOBO WAS A SLIP OF A GIRL WHO COULD DIVE DOWN A QUARTER OF A MILE, HOLD HER BREATH FOR TEN MINUTES, AND SURFACE AGAIN.
SHE'D RISE INTO SUNLIGHT, KNIFE IN ONE HAND, PRIZE IN THE OTHER.

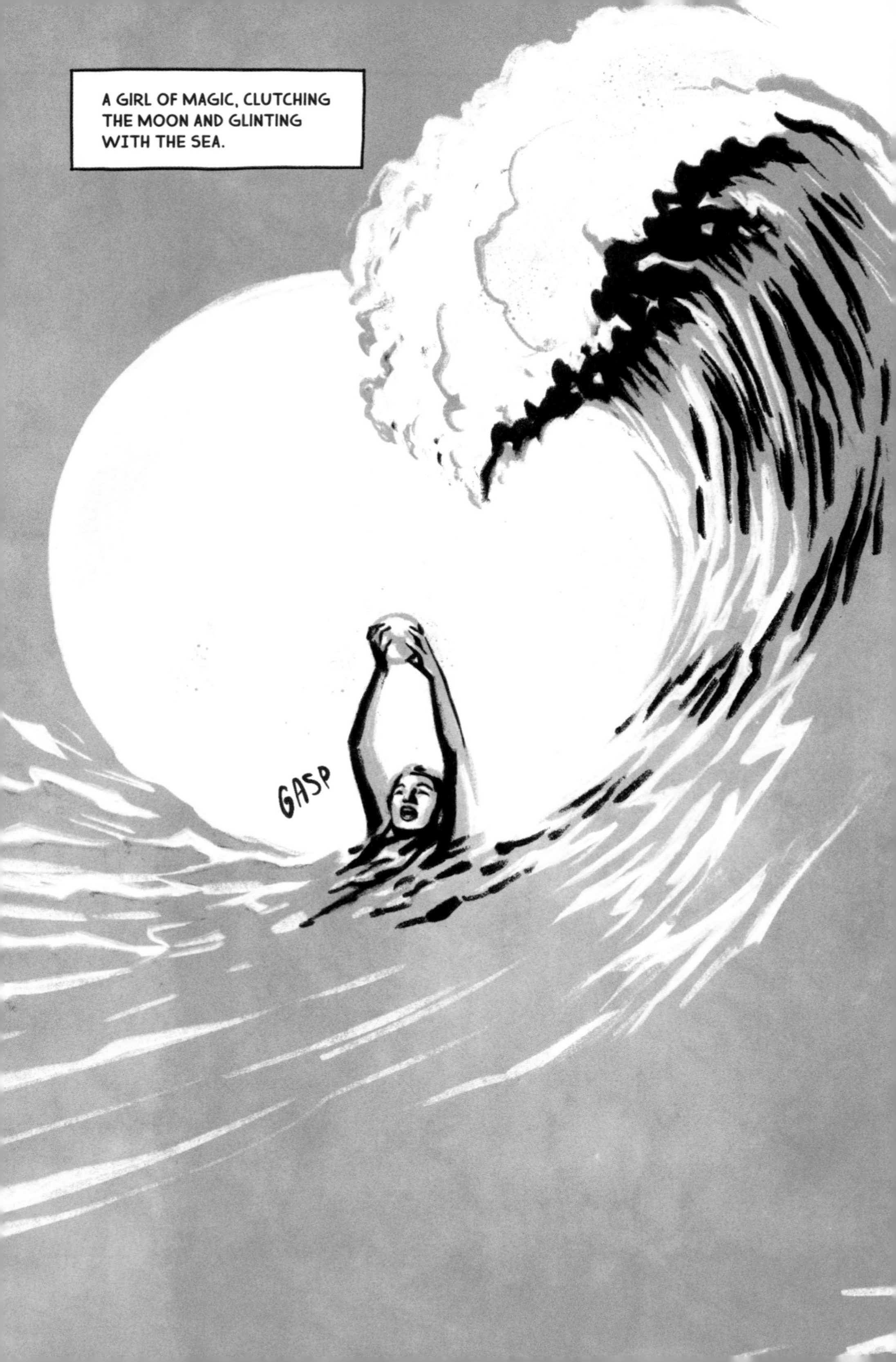
A GIRL OF MAGIC, CLUTCHING THE MOON AND GLINTING WITH THE SEA.
GASP

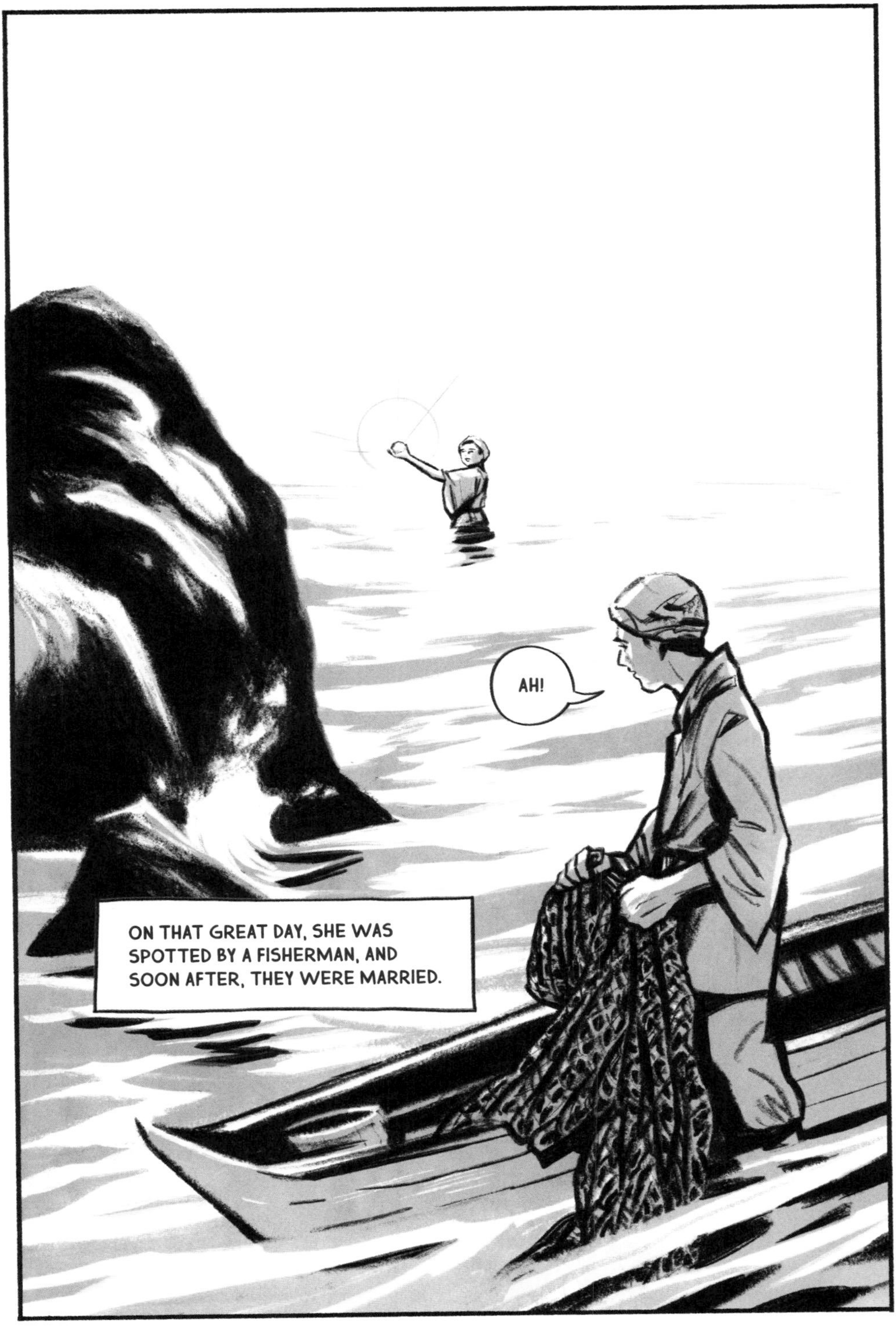
AH!
ON THAT GREAT DAY, SHE WAS SPOTTED BY A FISHERMAN, AND SOON AFTER, THEY WERE MARRIED.

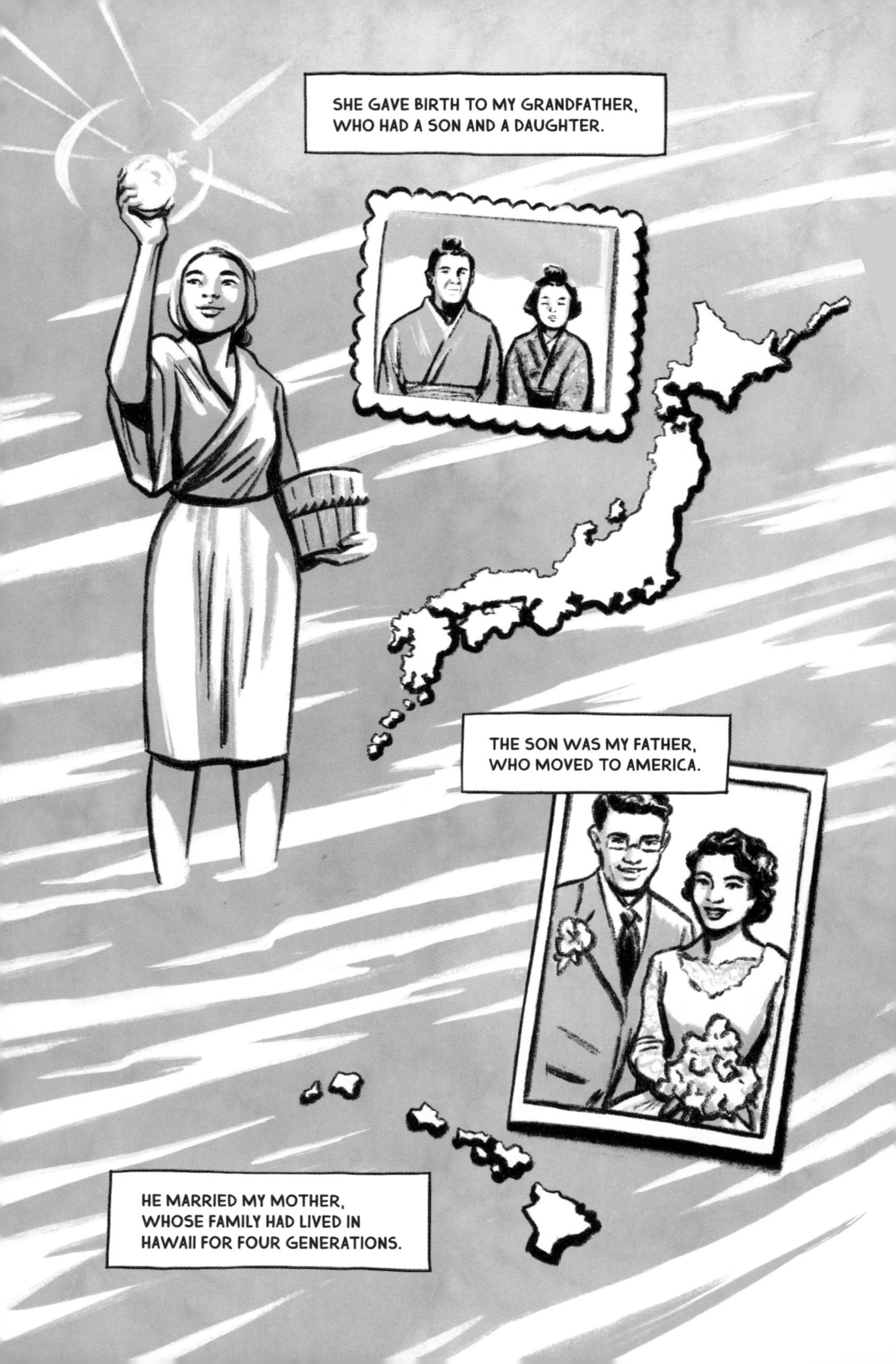
SHE GAVE BIRTH TO MY GRANDFATHER, WHO HAD A SON AND A DAUGHTER.
THE SON WAS MY FATHER, WHO MOVED TO AMERICA.
HE MARRIED MY MOTHER, WHOSE FAMILY HAD LIVED IN HAWAII FOR FOUR GENERATIONS.

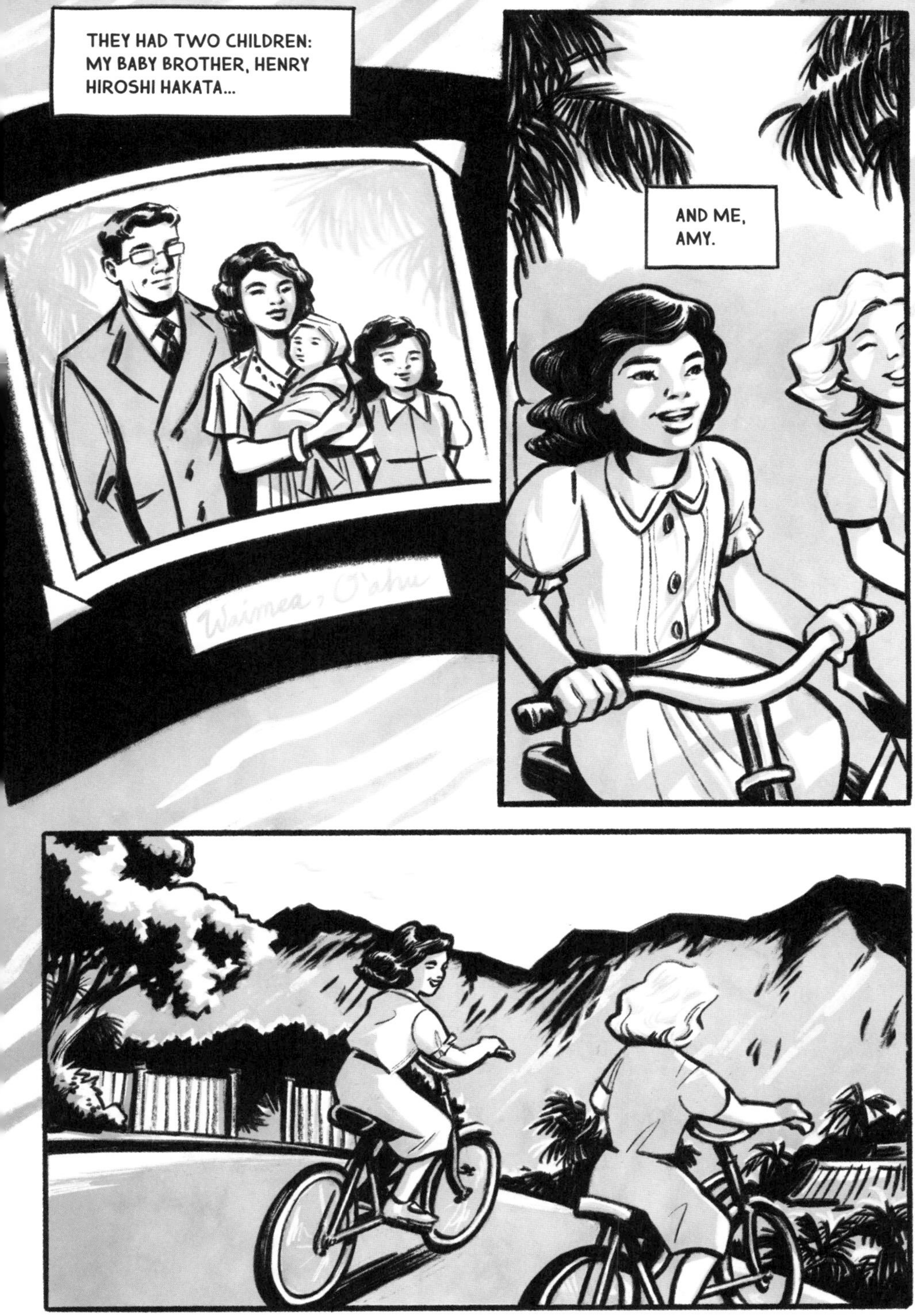
THEY HAD TWO CHILDREN: MY BABY BROTHER, HENRY HIROSHI HAKATA...
Waimea, O'ahu
AND ME, AMY.

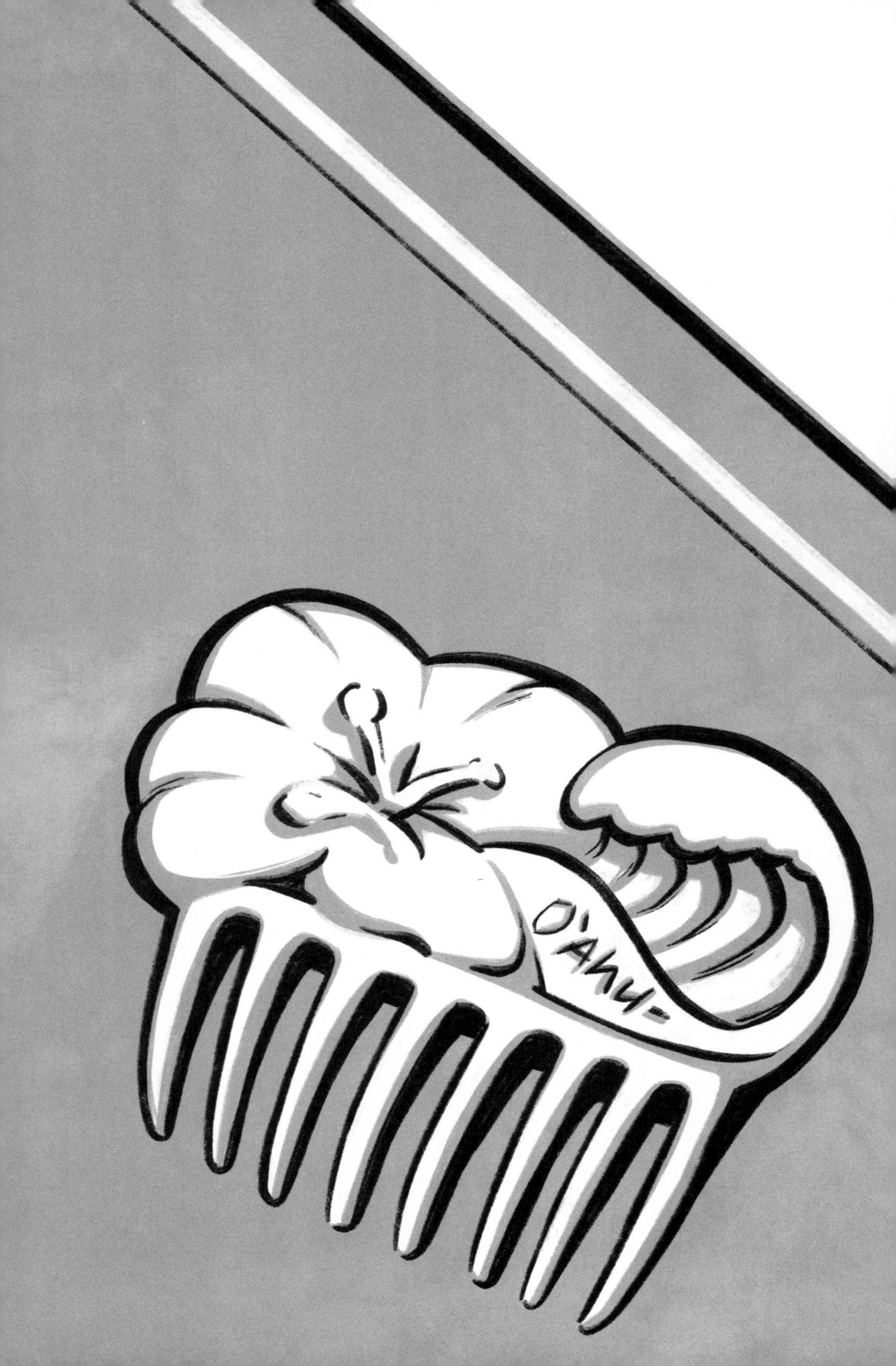
O'AHU-

# AMY

## 1941

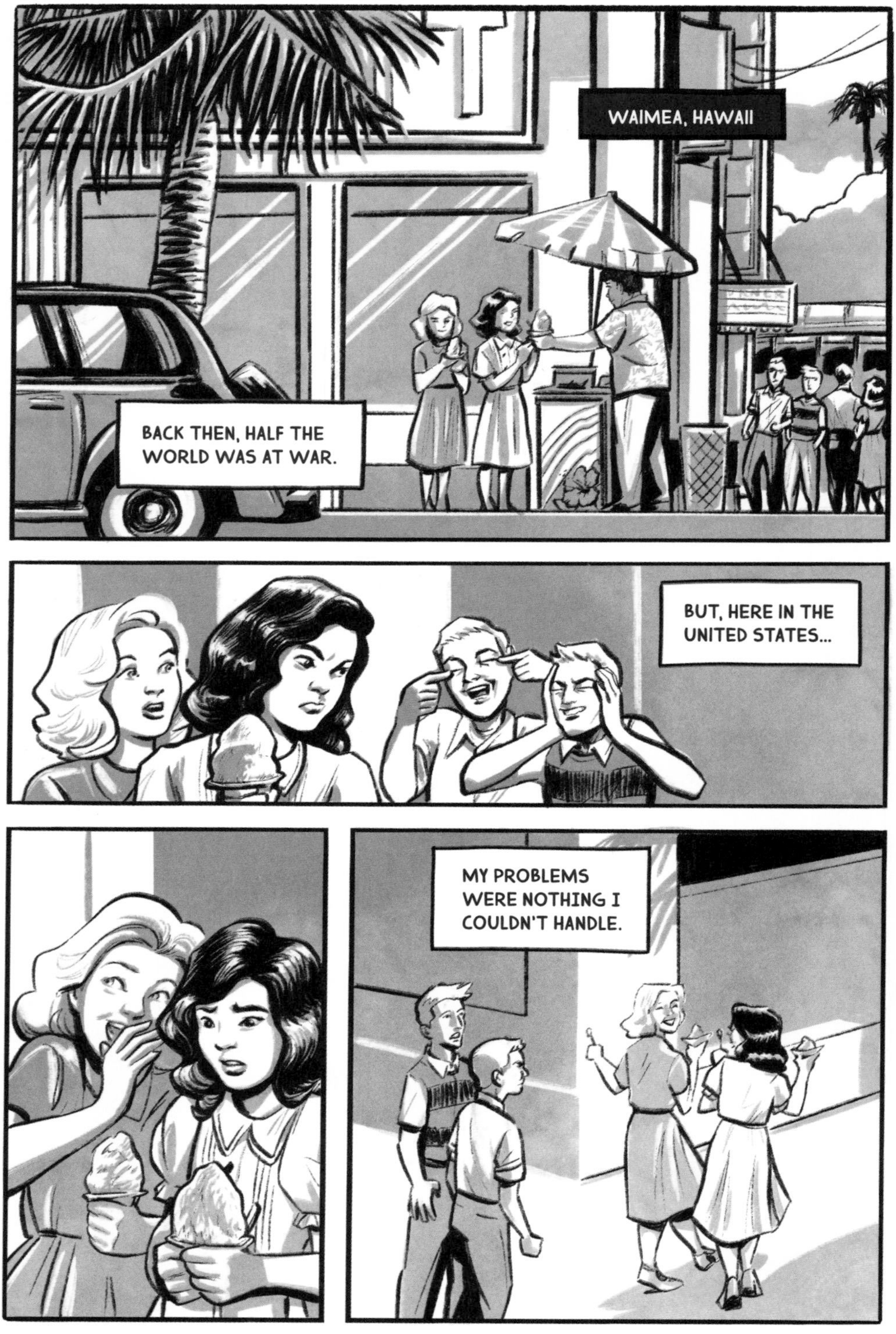
WAIMEA, HAWAII
BACK THEN, HALF THE WORLD WAS AT WAR.
BUT, HERE IN THE UNITED STATES...
MY PROBLEMS WERE NOTHING I COULDN'T HANDLE.

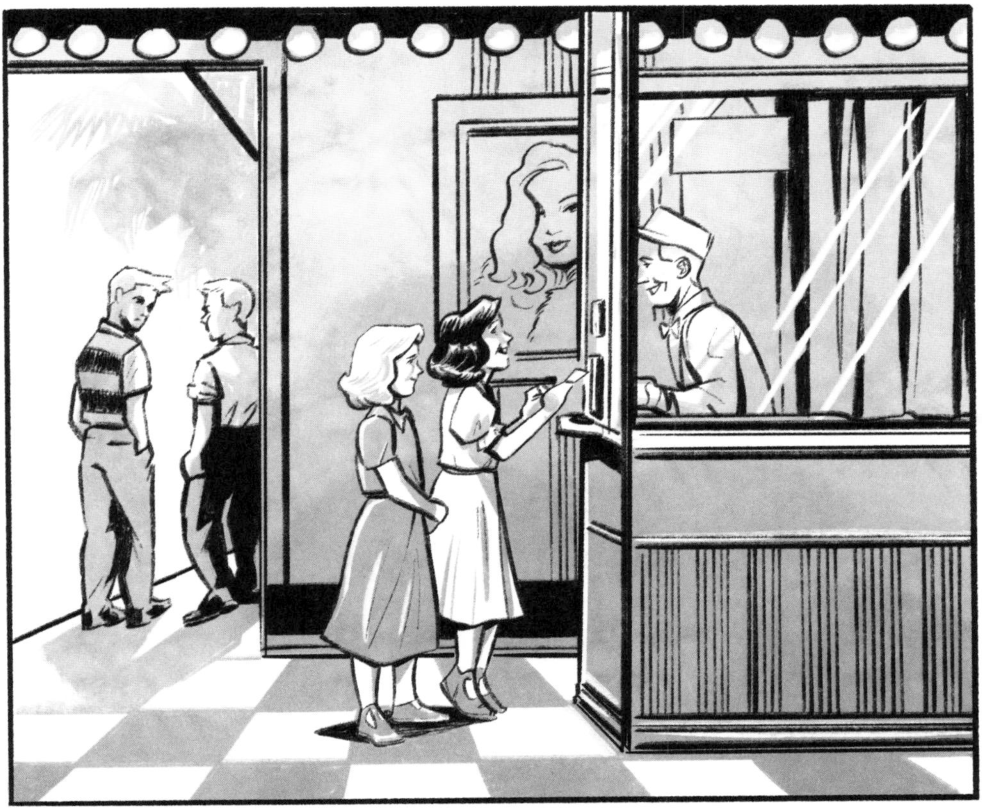

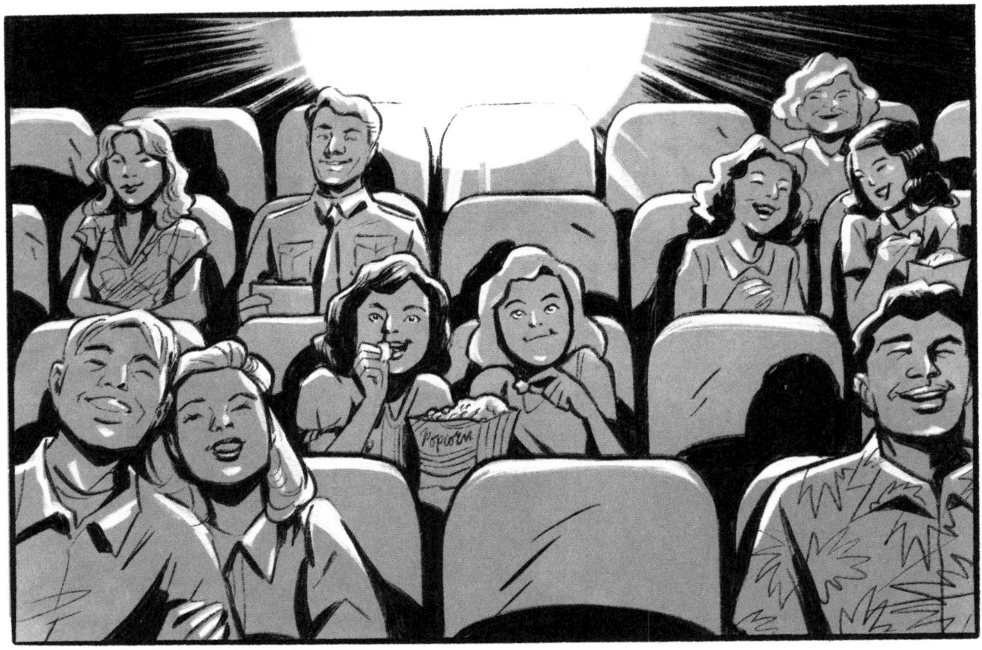
Popcorn

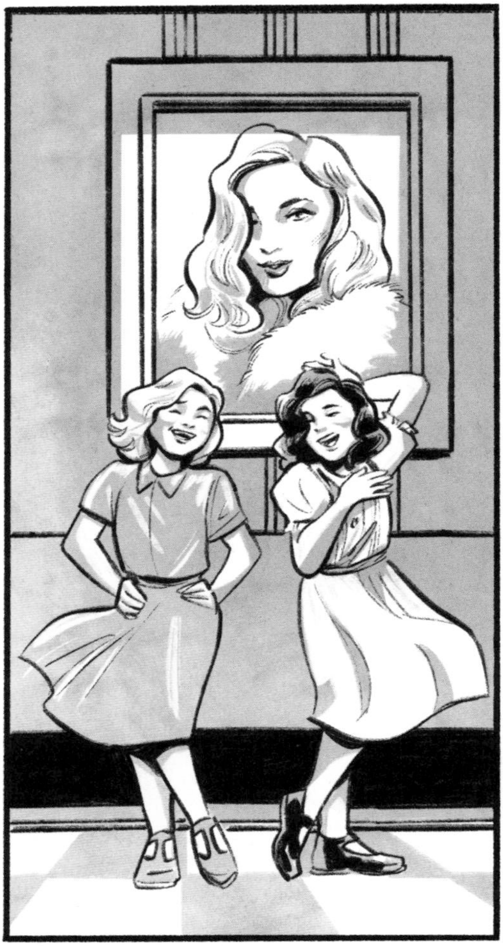

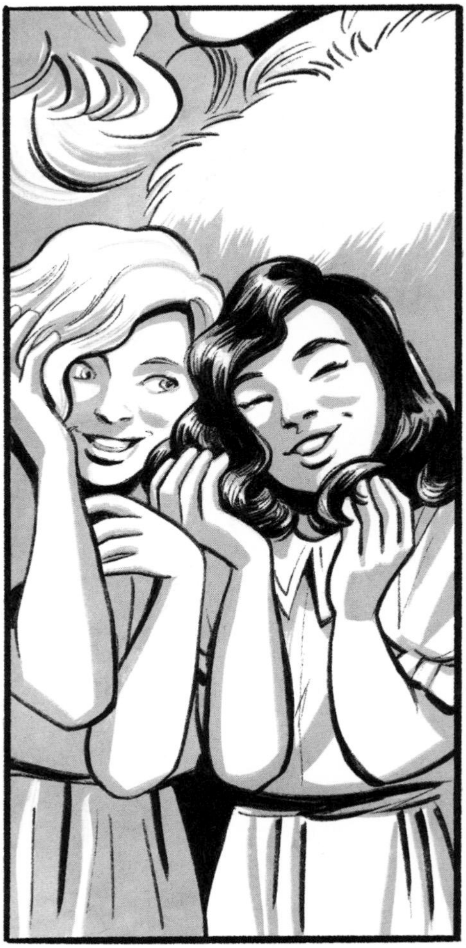

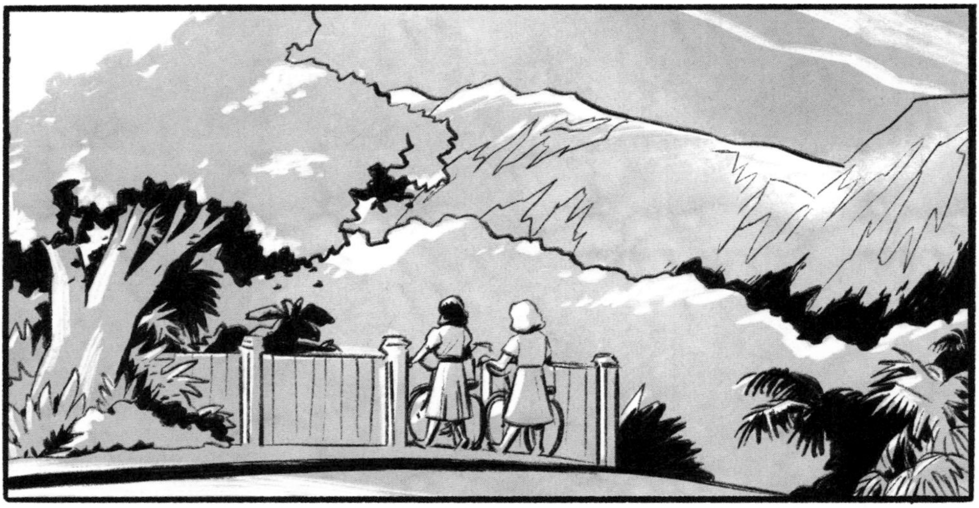

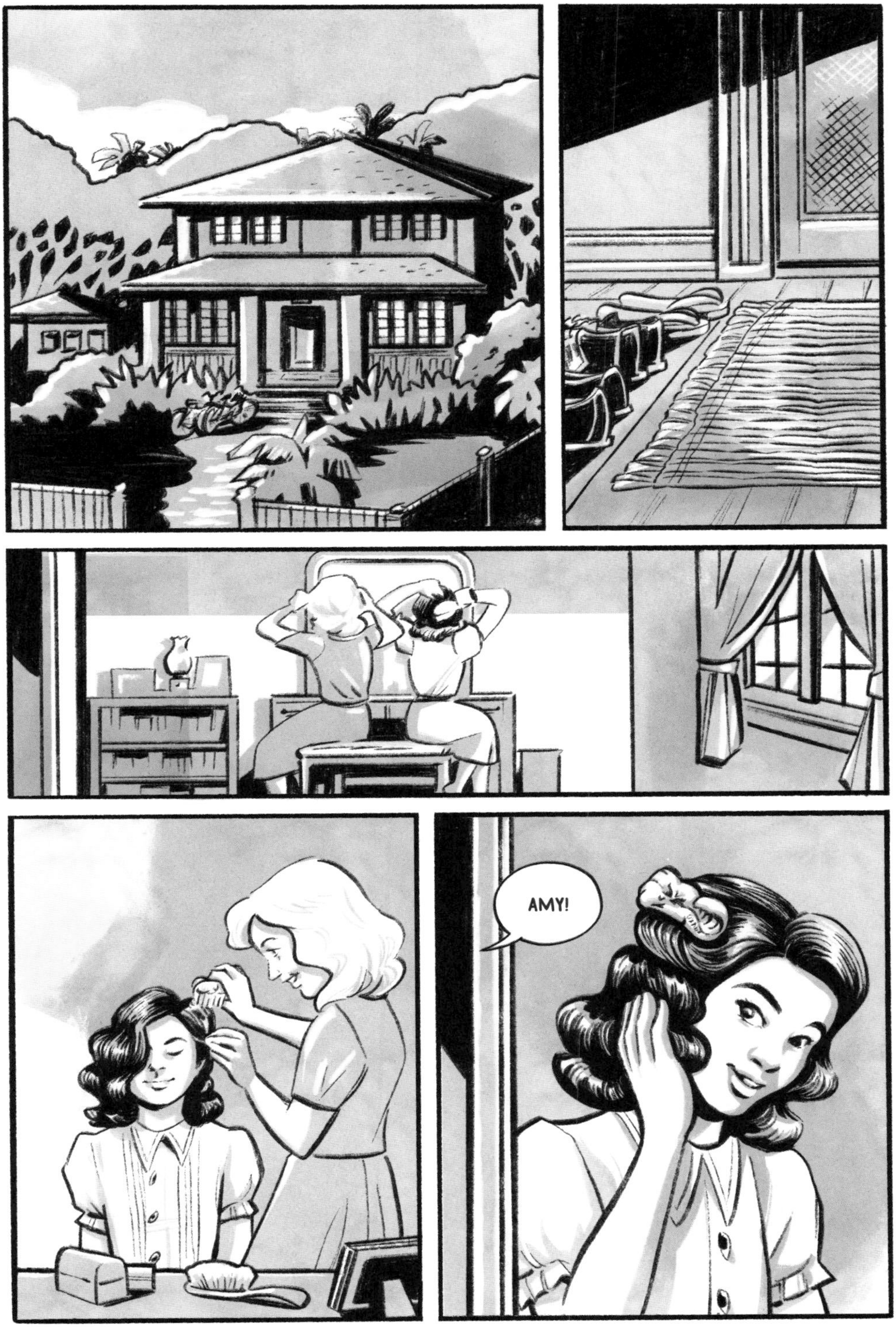
AMY!

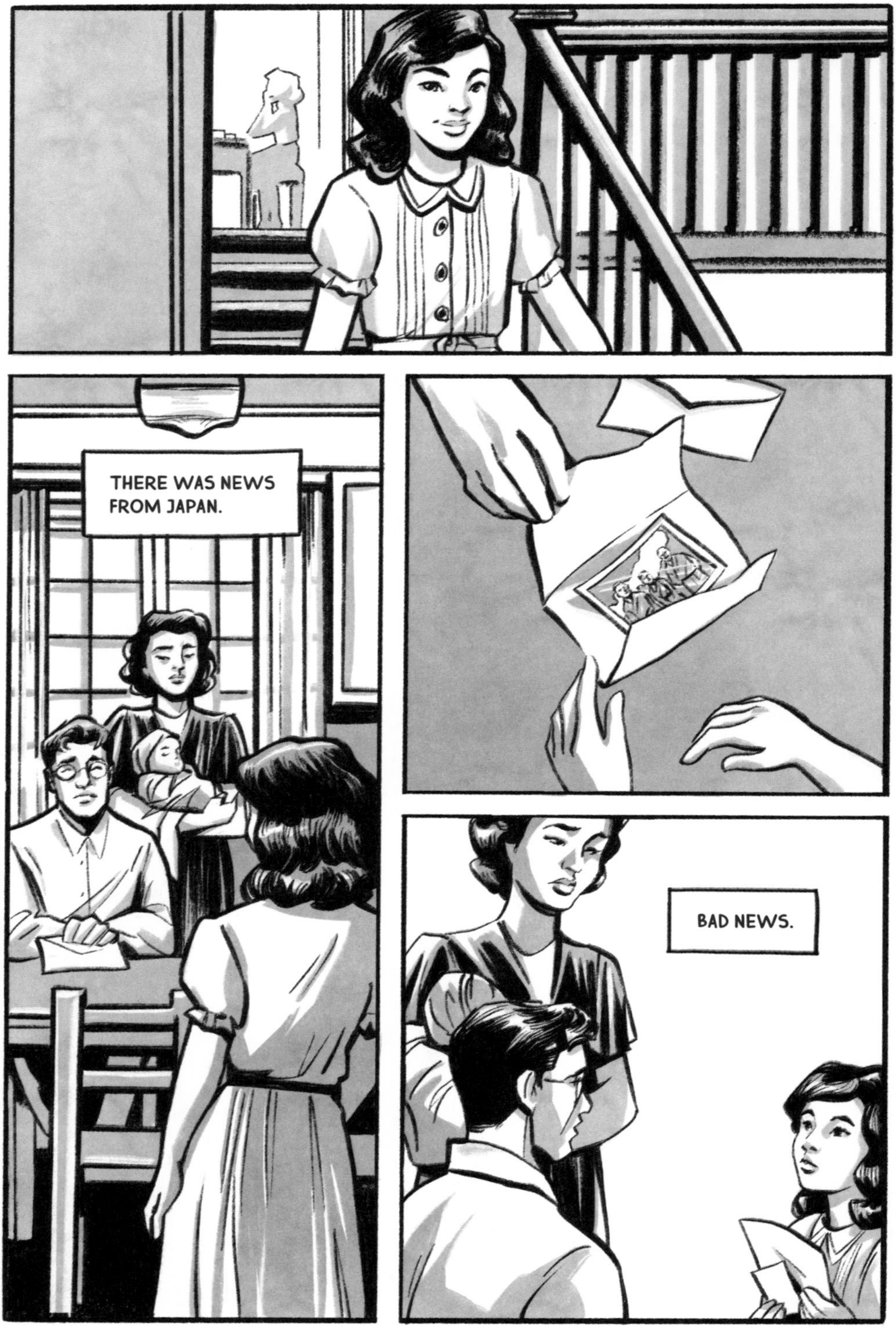
THERE WAS NEWS FROM JAPAN.
BAD NEWS.

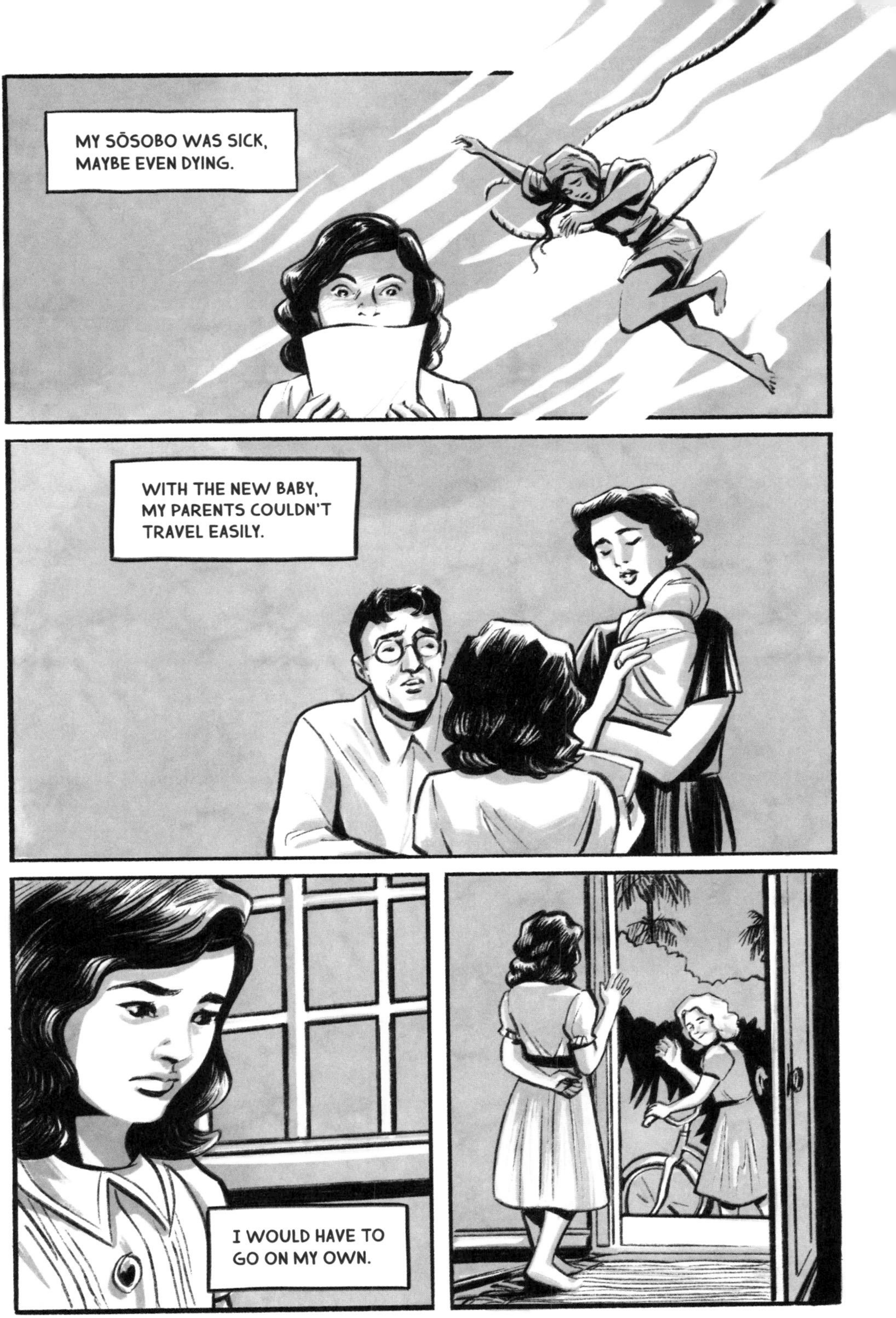
MY SŌSOBO WAS SICK, MAYBE EVEN DYING.
WITH THE NEW BABY, MY PARENTS COULDN'T TRAVEL EASILY.
I WOULD HAVE TO GO ON MY OWN.

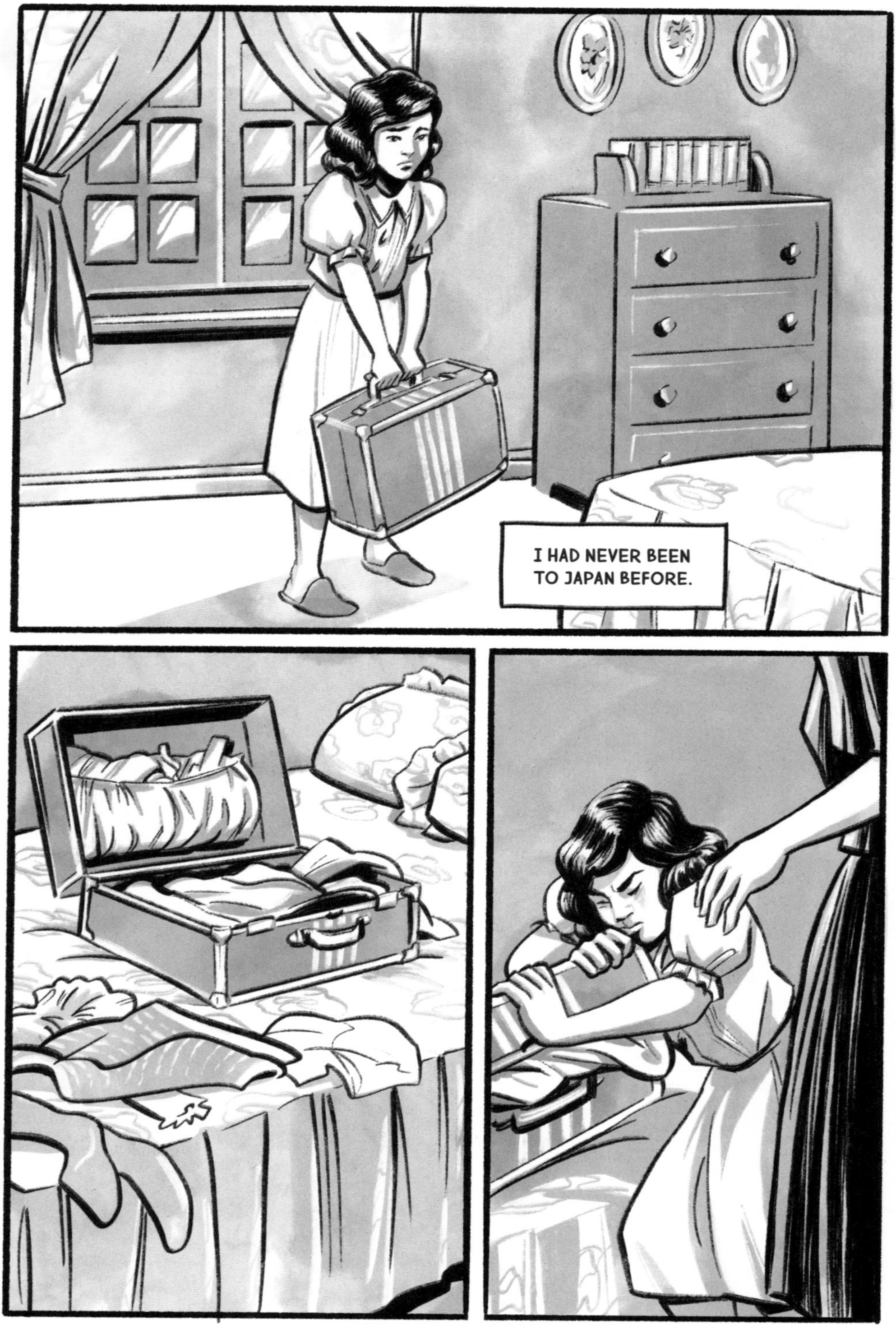
I HAD NEVER BEEN
TO JAPAN BEFORE.

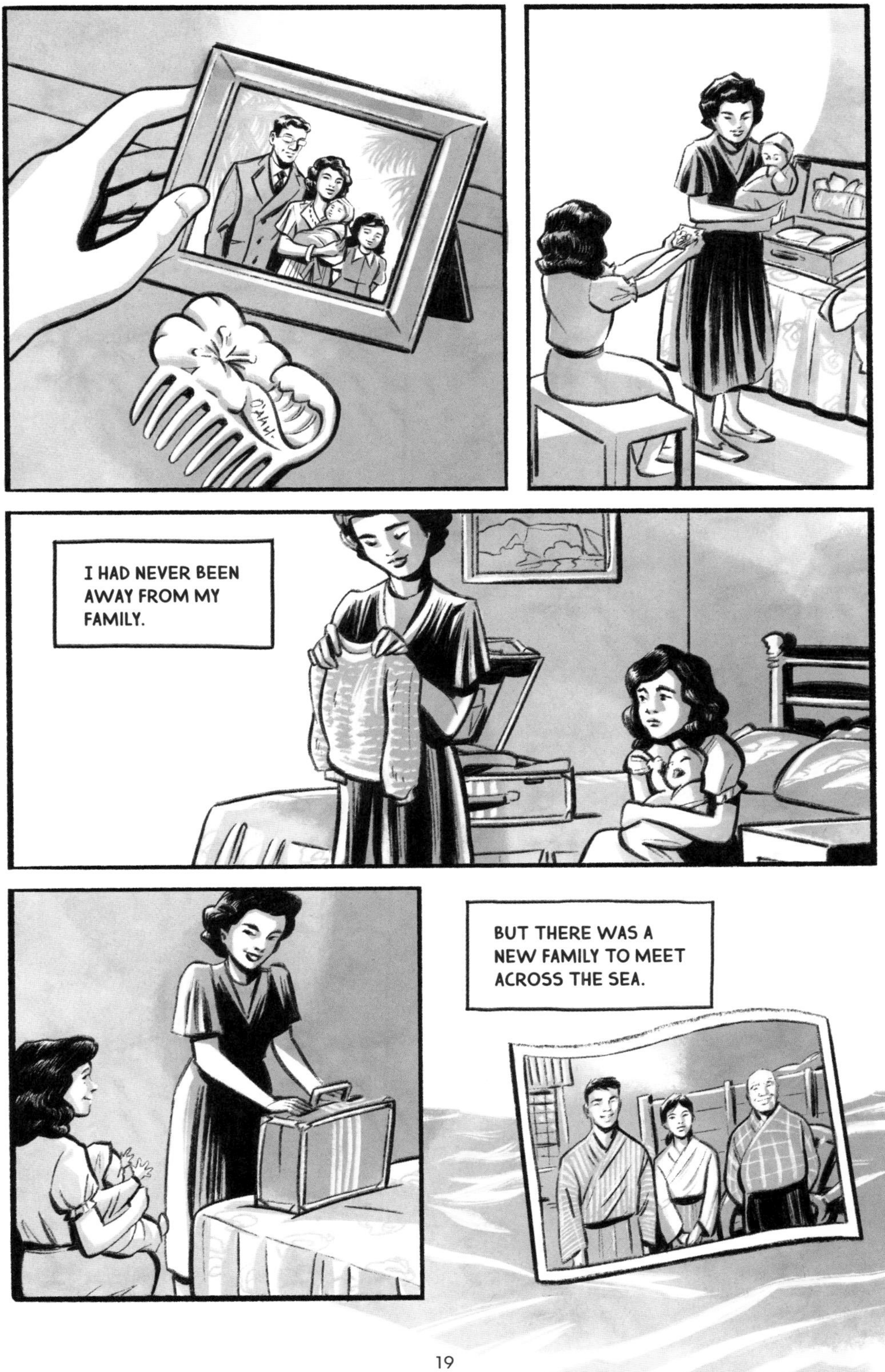
I HAD NEVER BEEN AWAY FROM MY FAMILY.
BUT THERE WAS A NEW FAMILY TO MEET ACROSS THE SEA.

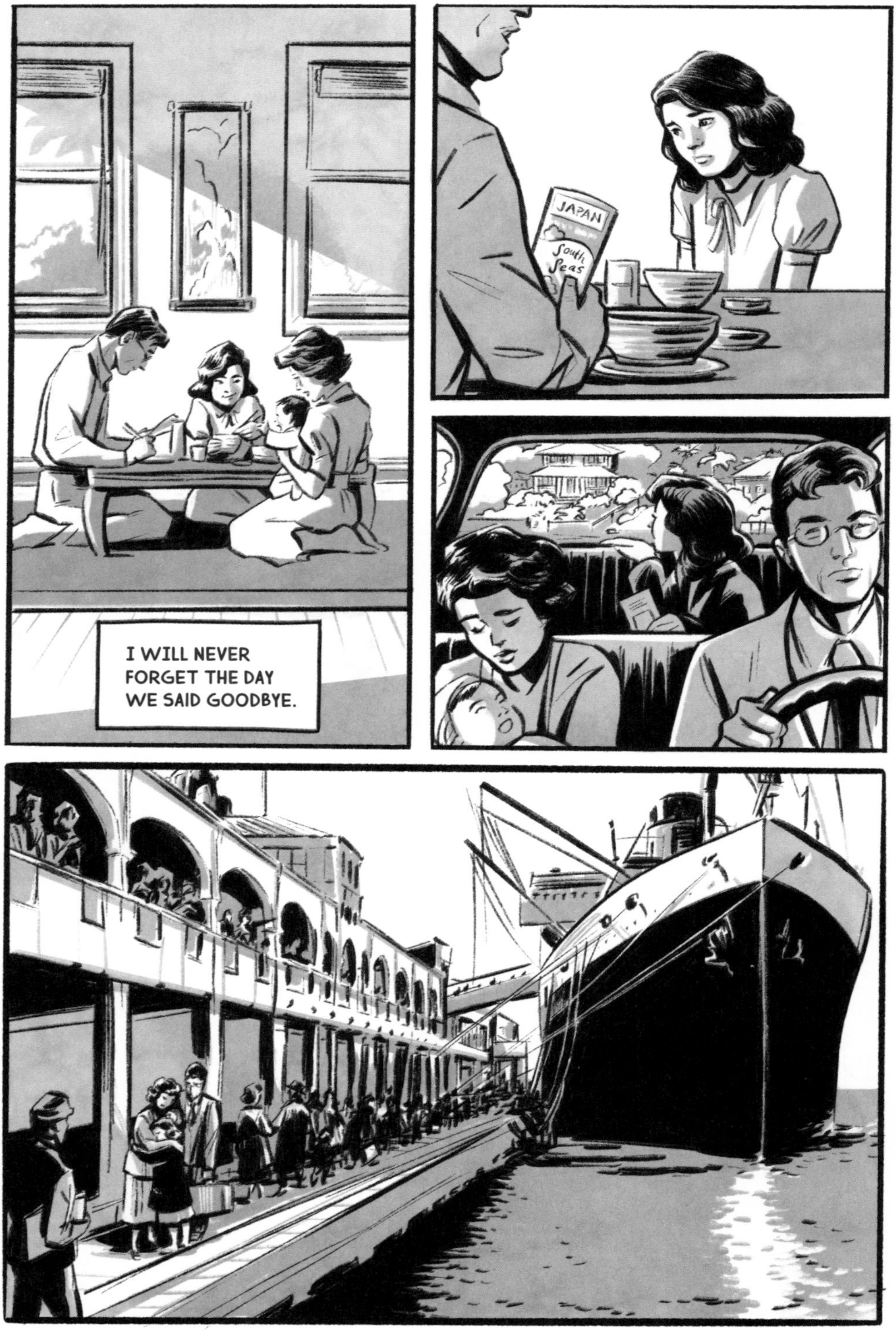
JAPAN
South Seas
I WILL NEVER FORGET THE DAY WE SAID GOODBYE.

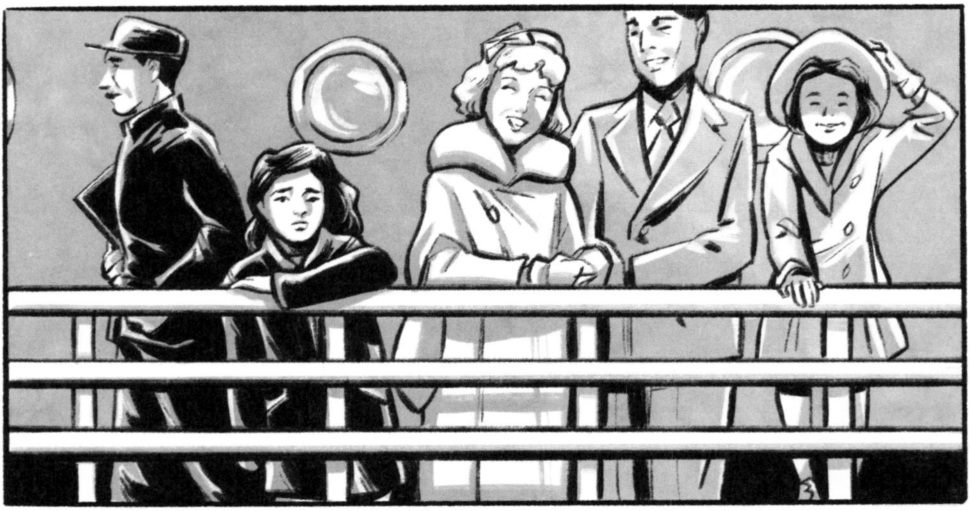
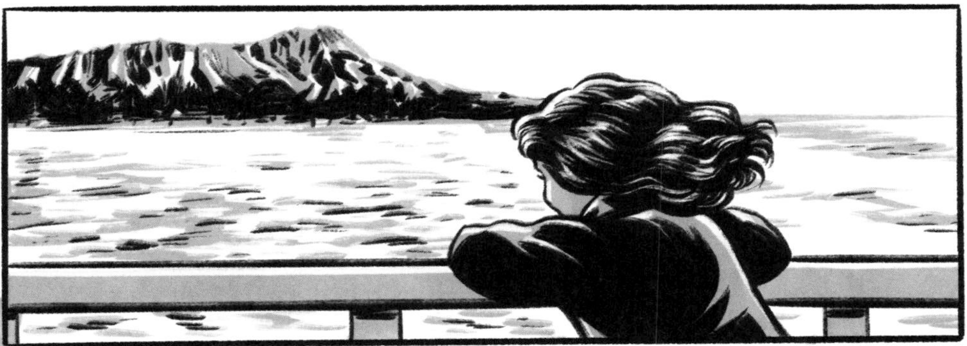
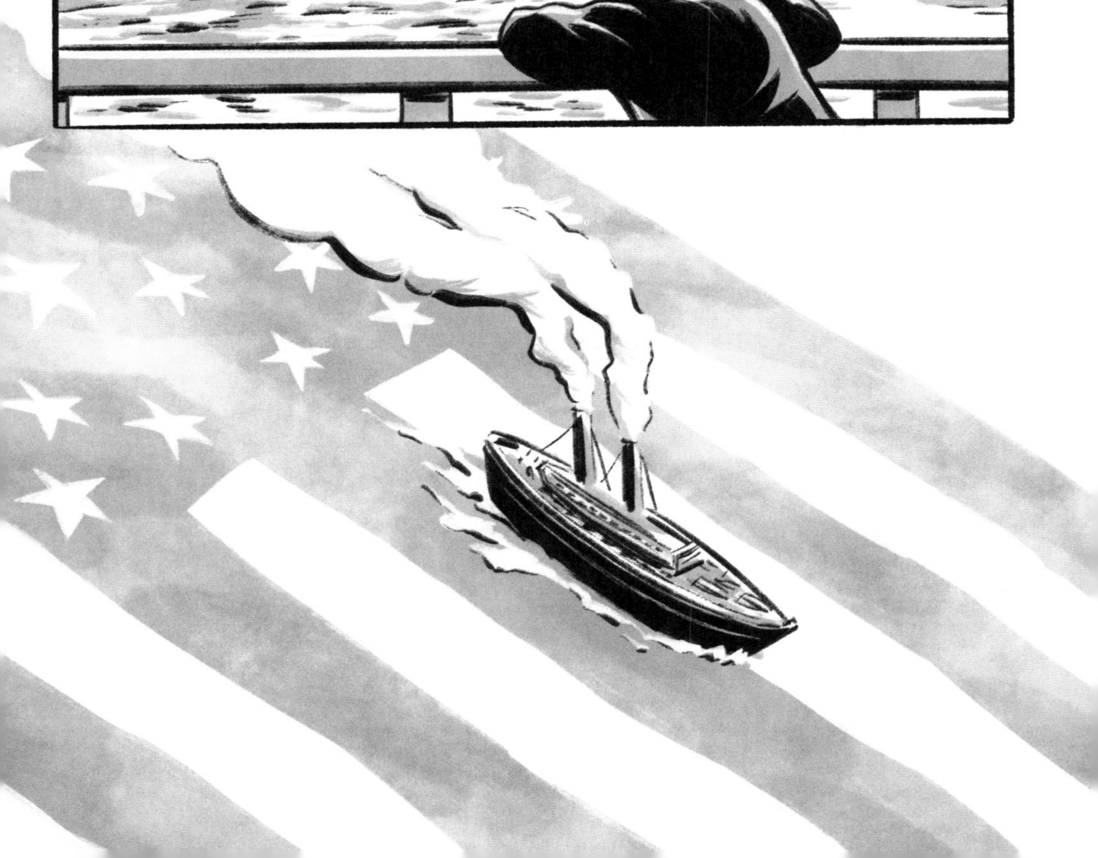

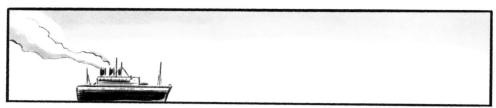

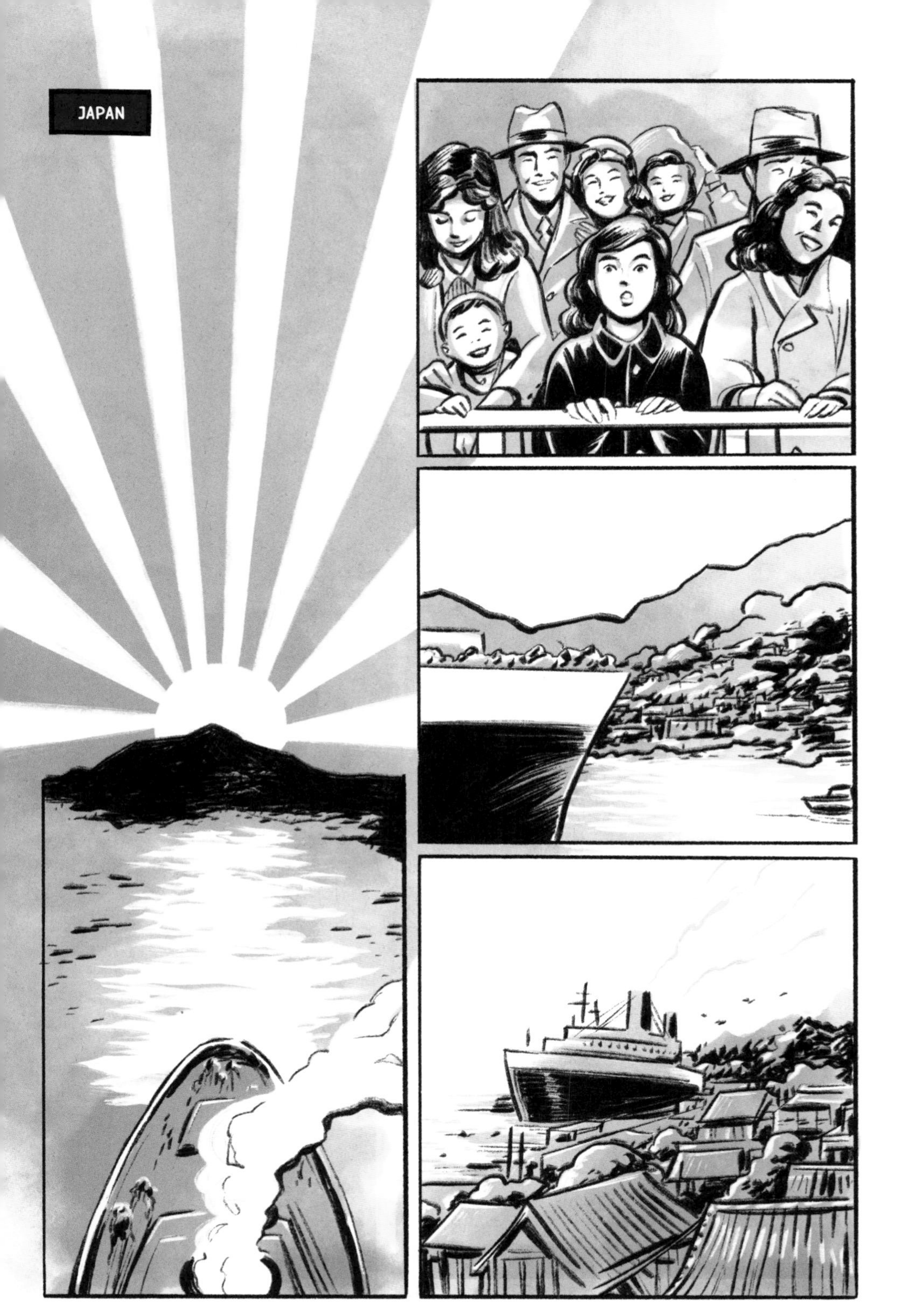
JAPAN

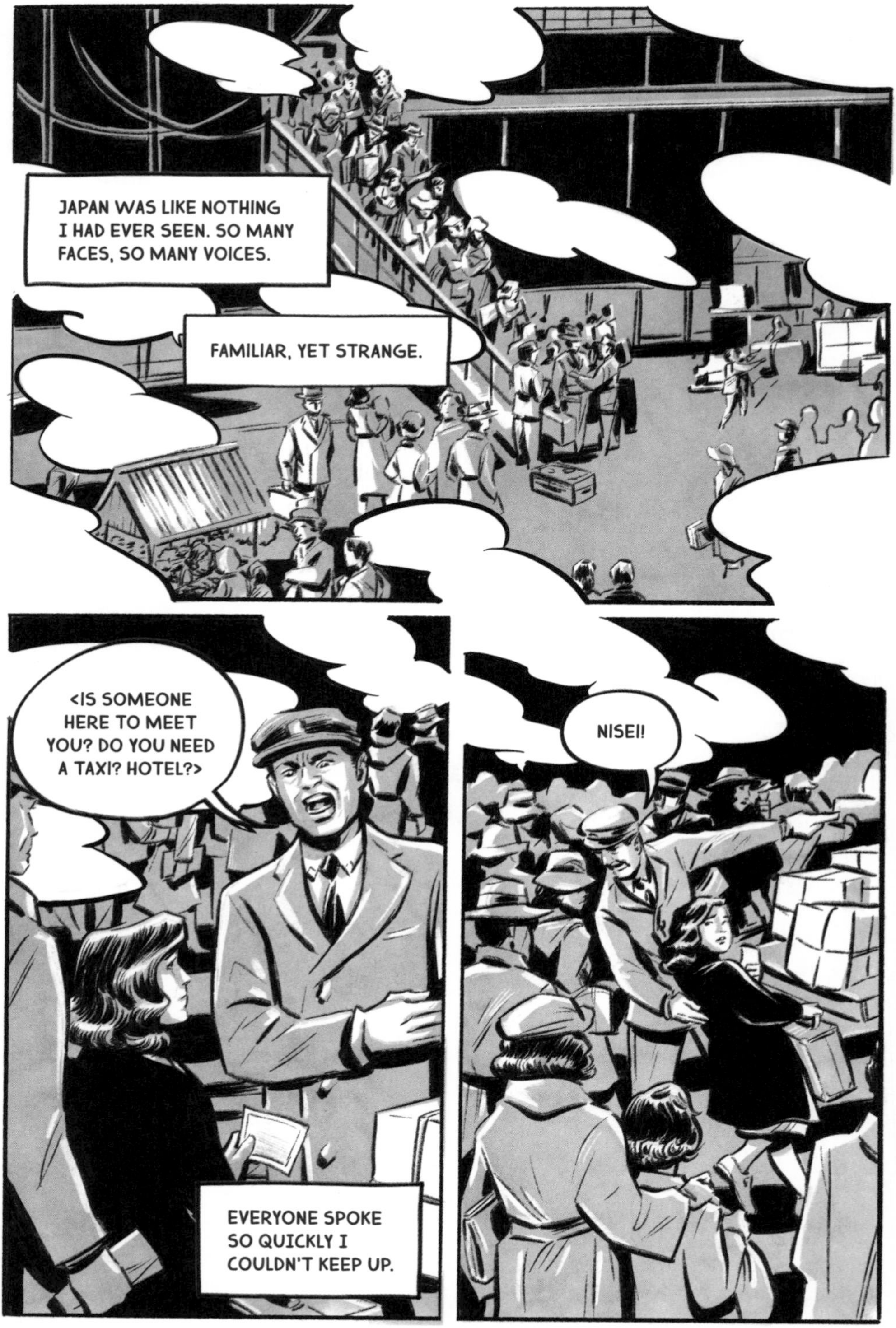
JAPAN WAS LIKE NOTHING I HAD EVER SEEN. SO MANY FACES, SO MANY VOICES.
FAMILIAR, YET STRANGE.
<IS SOMEONE HERE TO MEET YOU? DO YOU NEED A TAXI? HOTEL?>
EVERYONE SPOKE SO QUICKLY I COULDN'T KEEP UP.
NISEI!

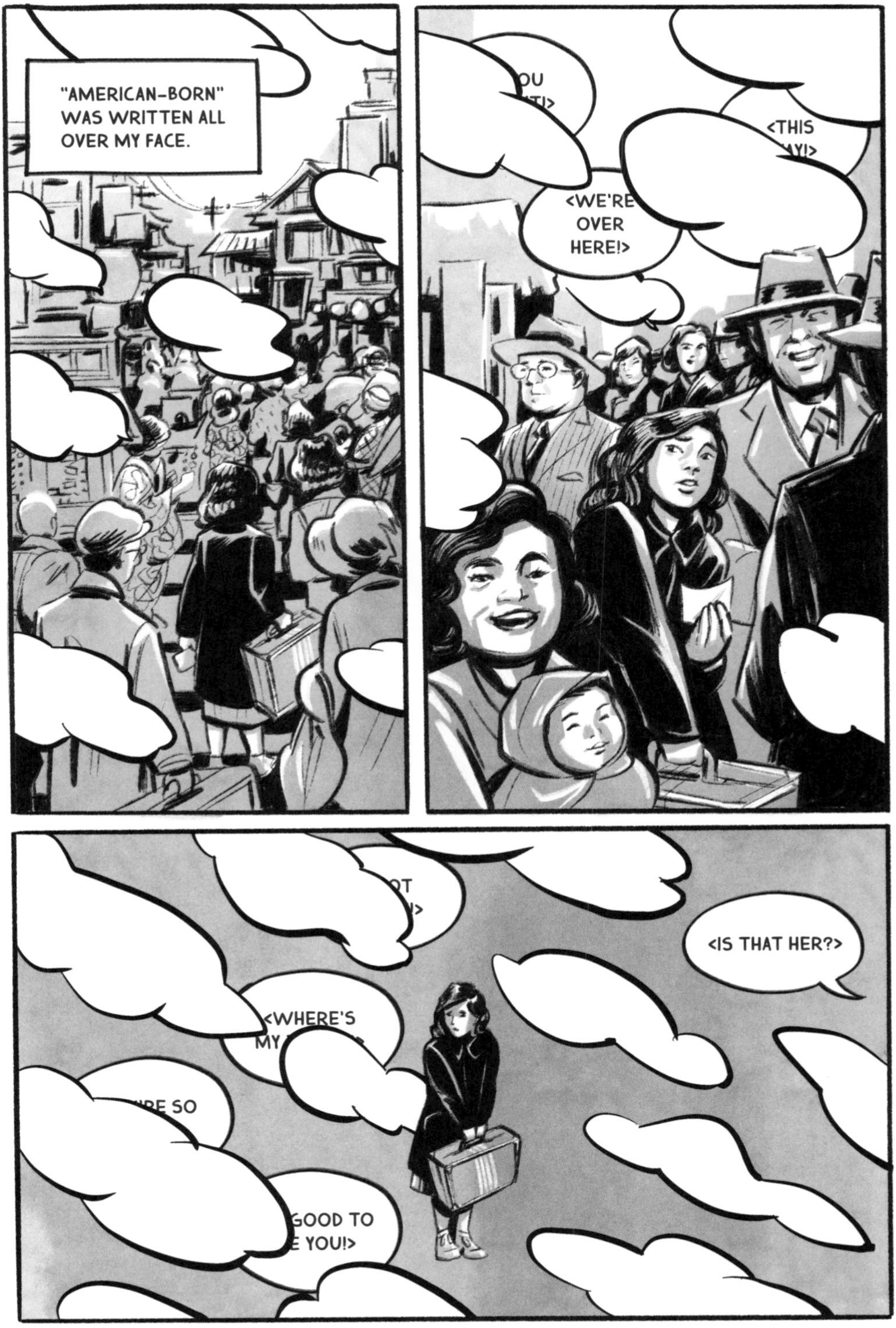
"AMERICAN-BORN" WAS WRITTEN ALL OVER MY FACE.
<WE'RE OVER HERE!>
<THIS
<IS THAT HER?>
<WHERE'S
GOOD TO
YOU!>

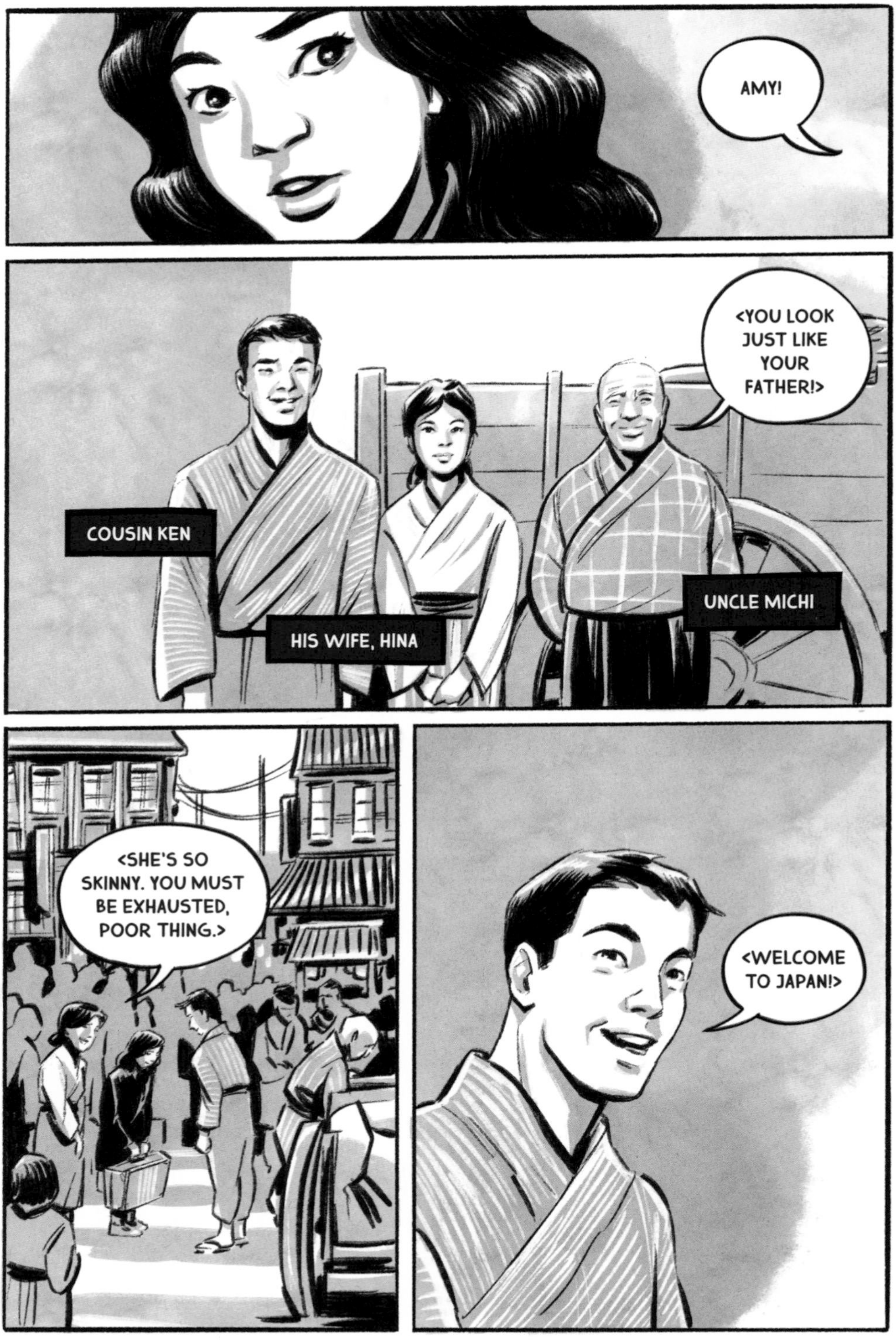
AMY!
<YOU LOOK JUST LIKE YOUR FATHER!>
COUSIN KEN
HIS WIFE, HINA
UNCLE MICHI
<SHE'S SO SKINNY. YOU MUST BE EXHAUSTED, POOR THING.>
<WELCOME TO JAPAN!>

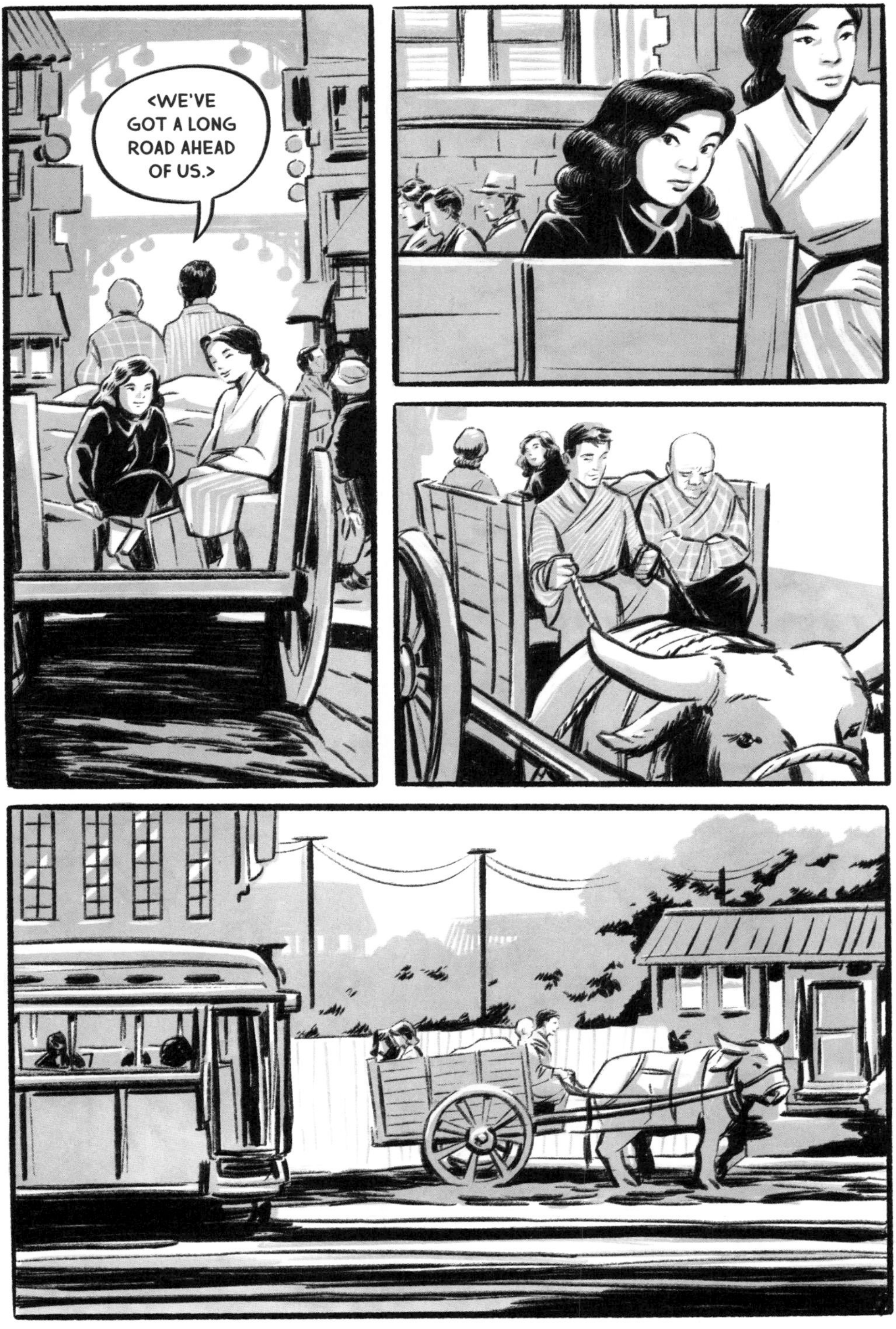
<WE'VE GOT A LONG ROAD AHEAD OF US.>

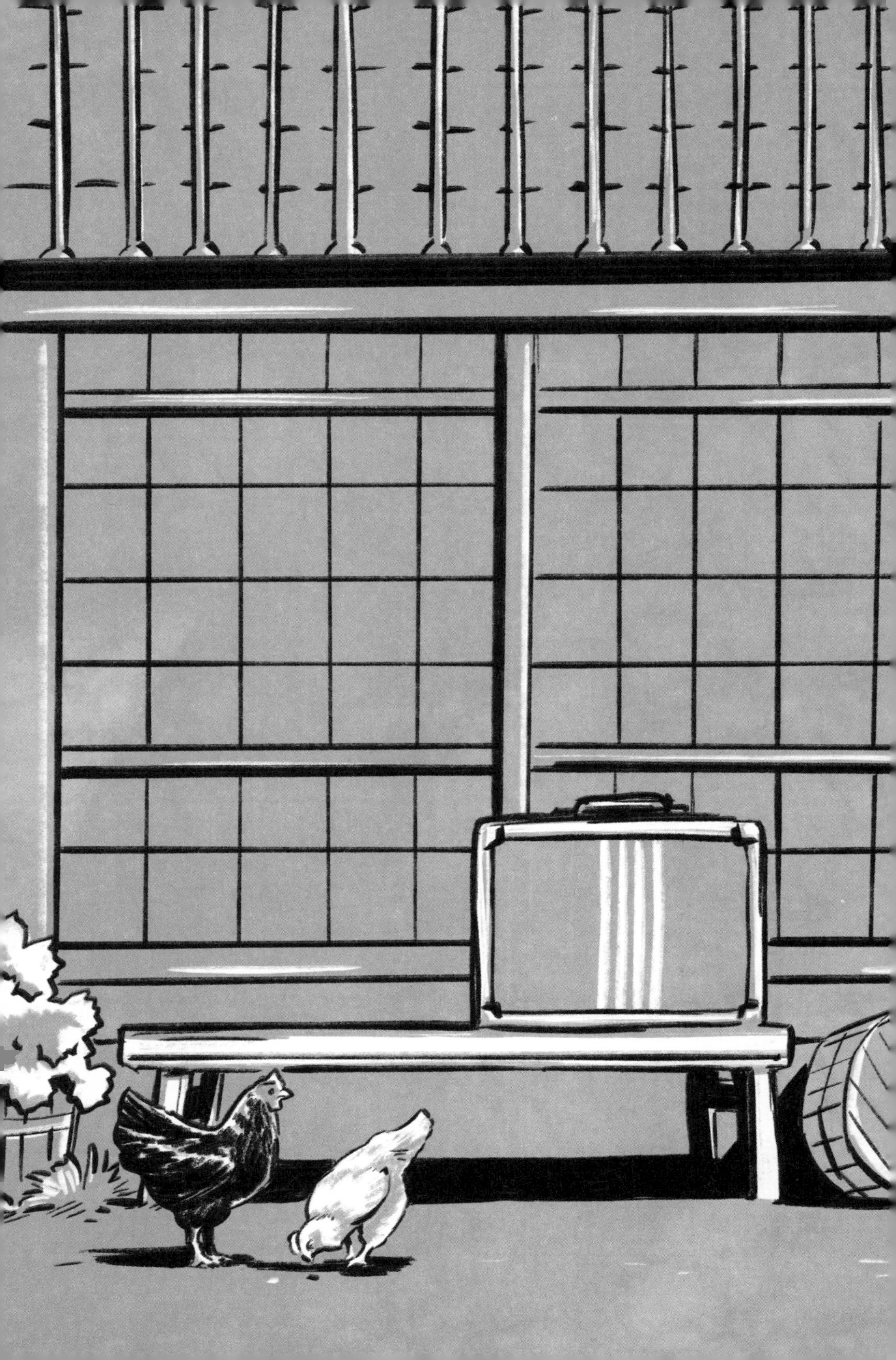

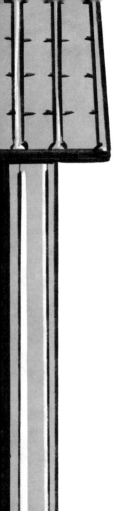

# NISEI

## AMERICAN BORN

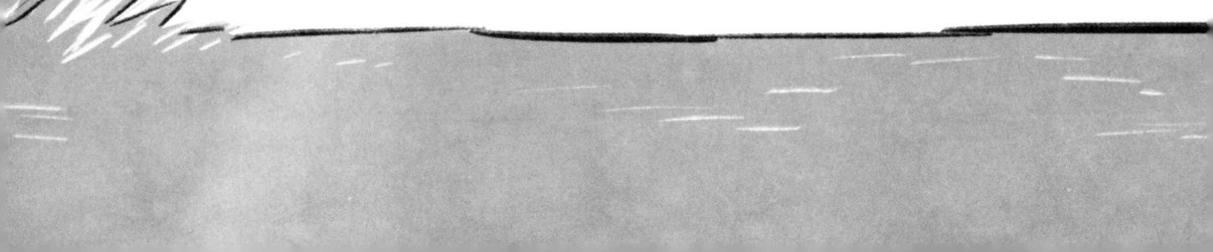

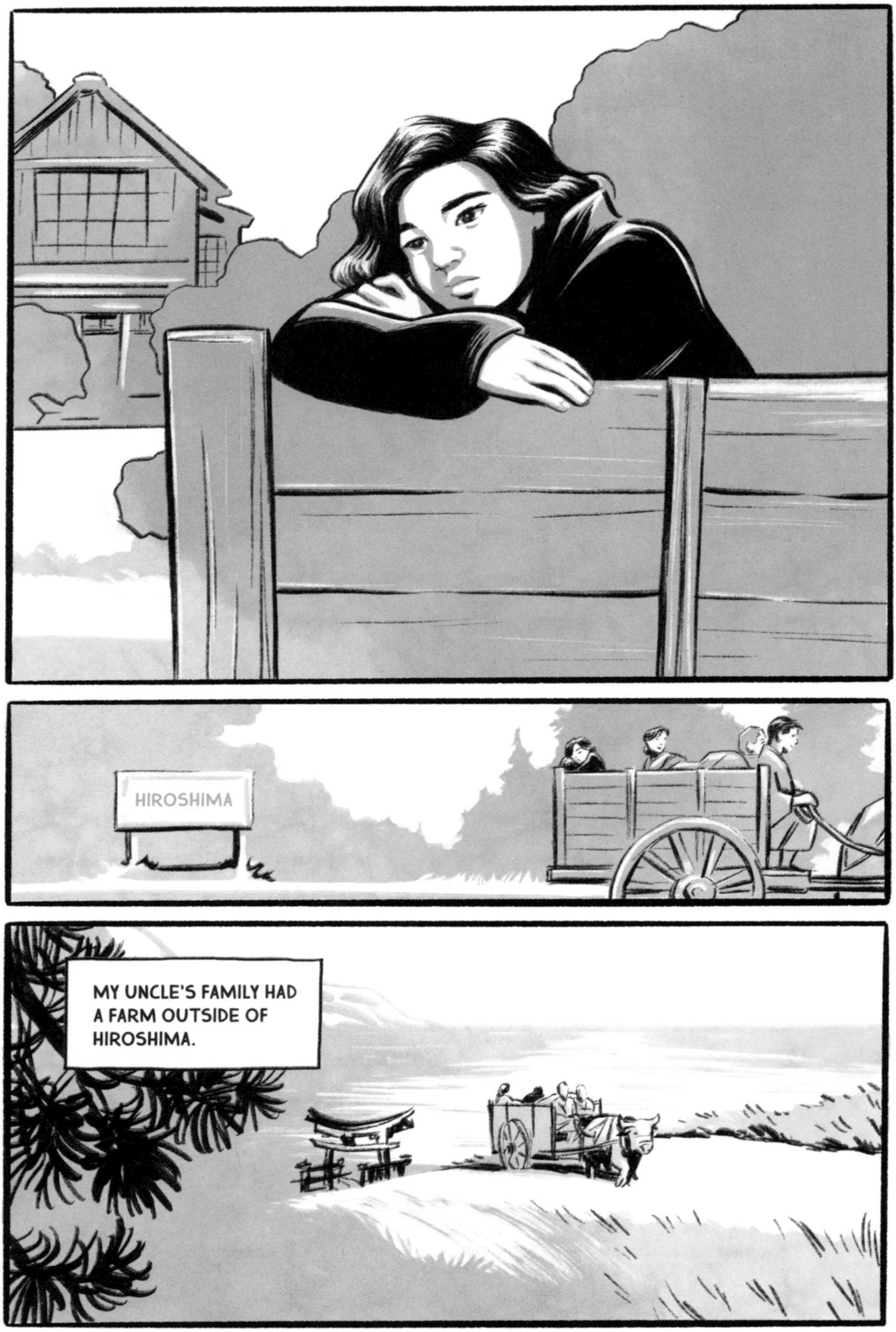
HIROSHIMA
MY UNCLE'S FAMILY HAD A FARM OUTSIDE OF HIROSHIMA.

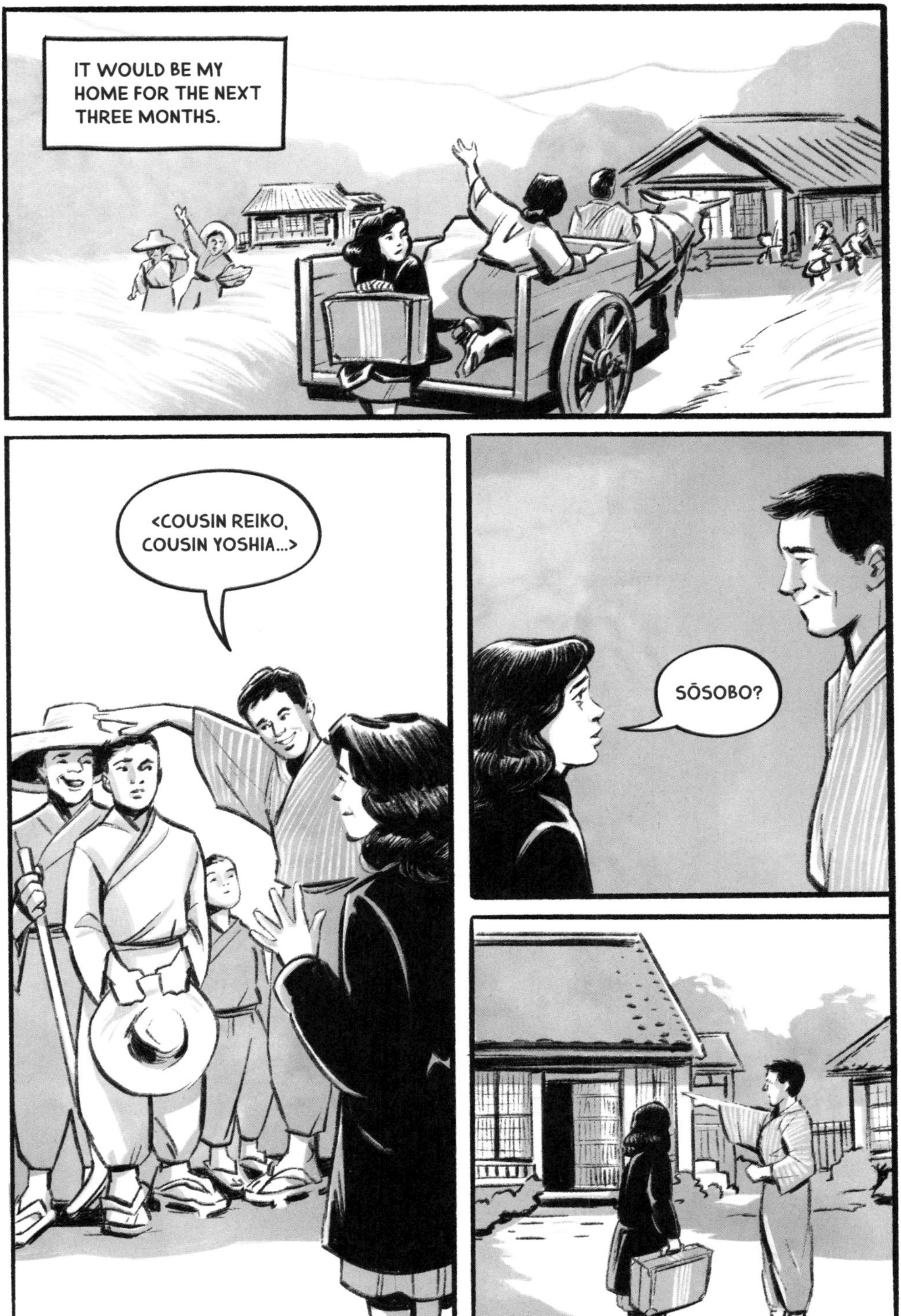
IT WOULD BE MY HOME FOR THE NEXT THREE MONTHS.
<COUSIN REIKO, COUSIN YOSHIA...>
SŌSOBO?

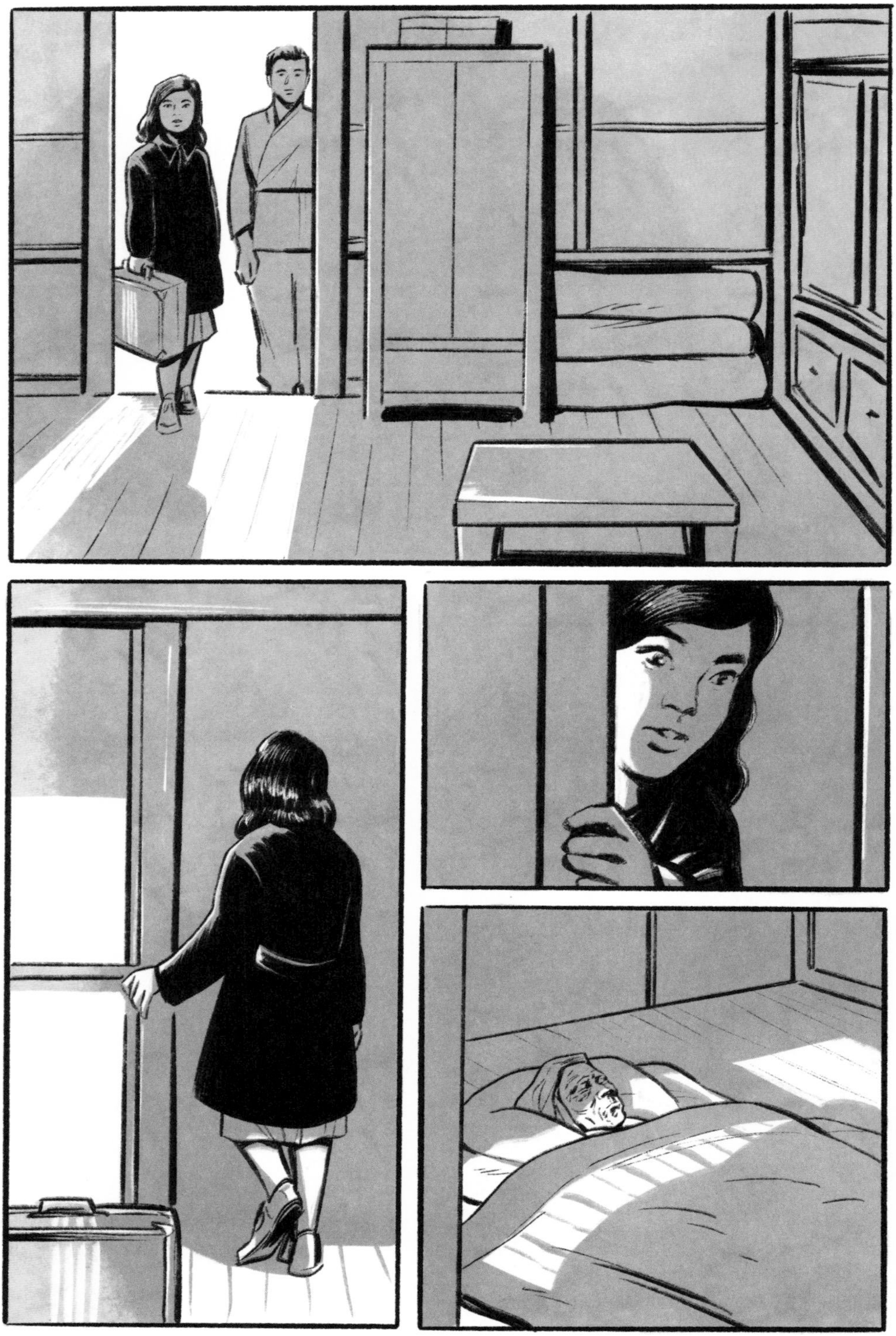

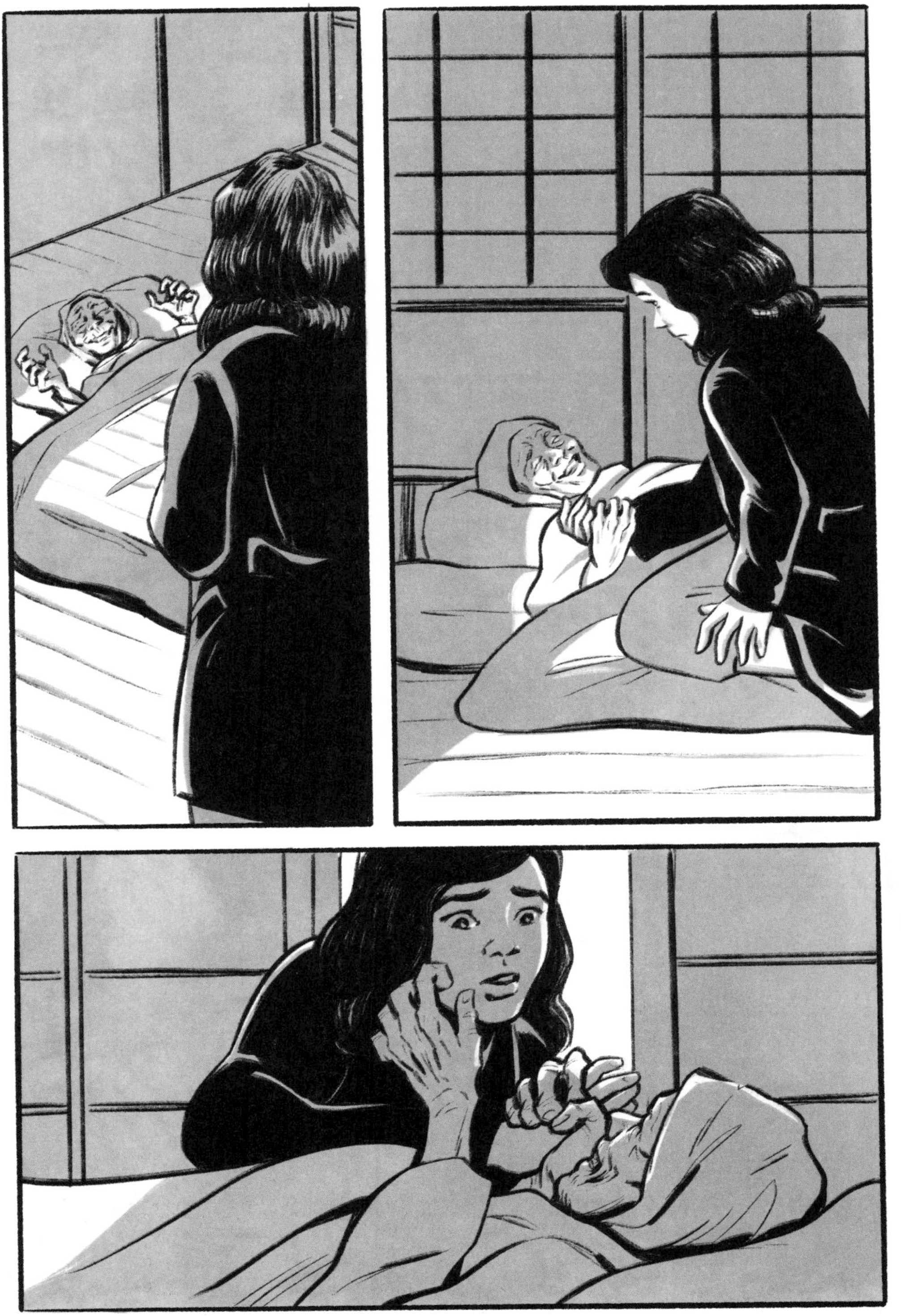

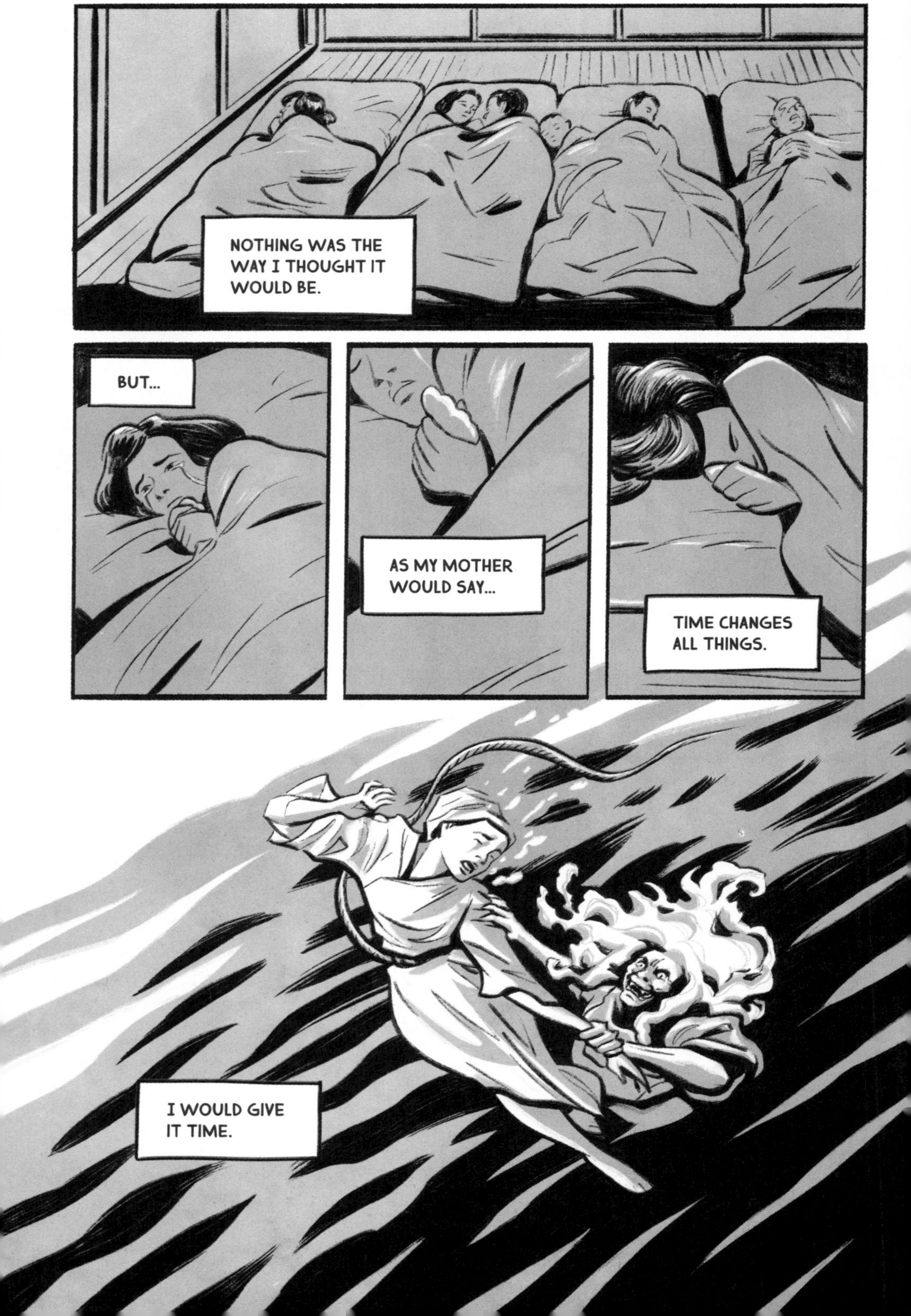
NOTHING WAS THE WAY I THOUGHT IT WOULD BE.
BUT...
AS MY MOTHER WOULD SAY...
TIME CHANGES ALL THINGS.
I WOULD GIVE IT TIME.

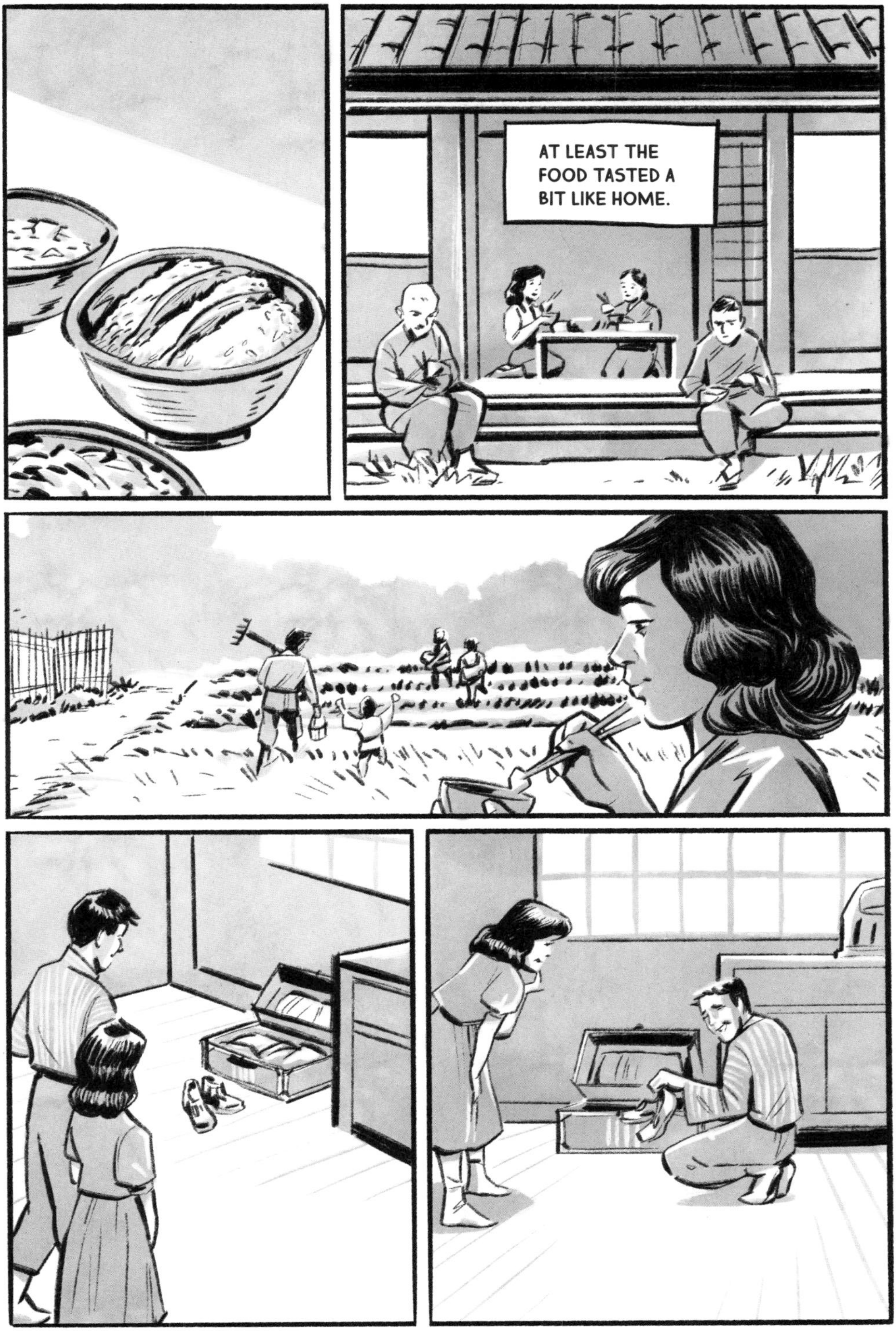
AT LEAST THE FOOD TASTED A BIT LIKE HOME.

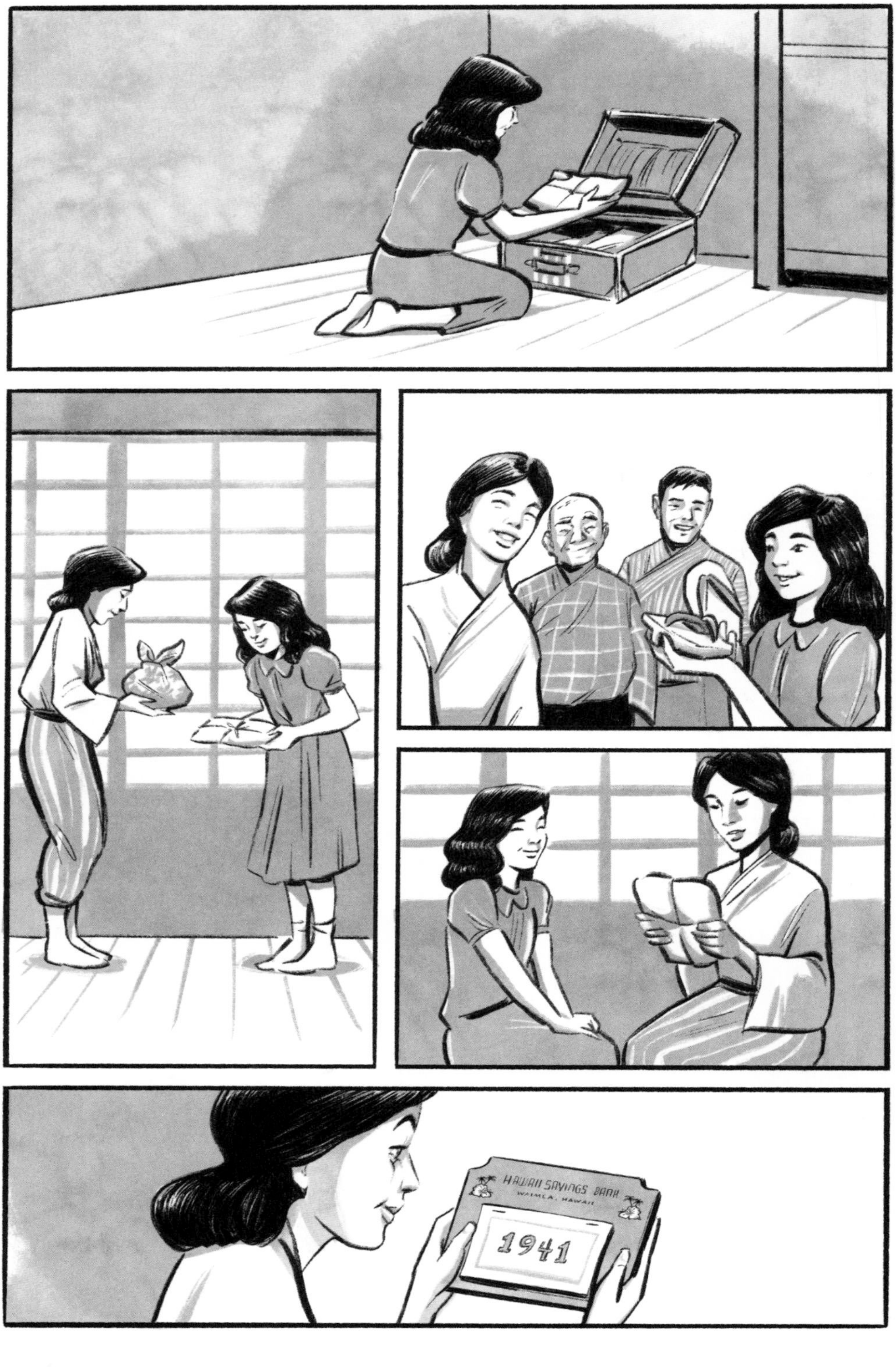
HAWAII SAVINGS BANK
WAIMEA, HAWAII
1941

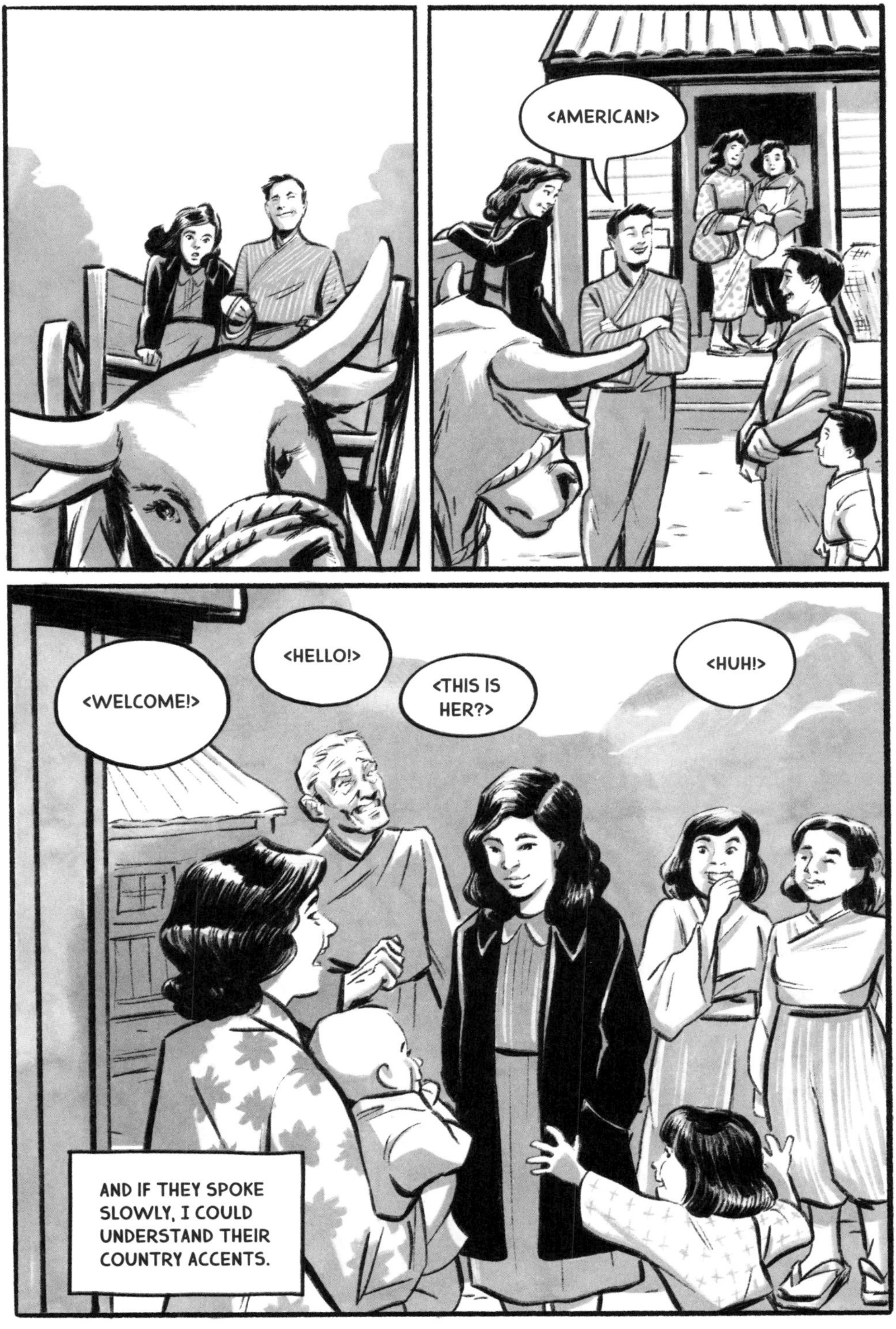
<AMERICAN!>
<WELCOME!>
<HELLO!>
<THIS IS HER?>
<HUH!>
AND IF THEY SPOKE SLOWLY, I COULD UNDERSTAND THEIR COUNTRY ACCENTS.

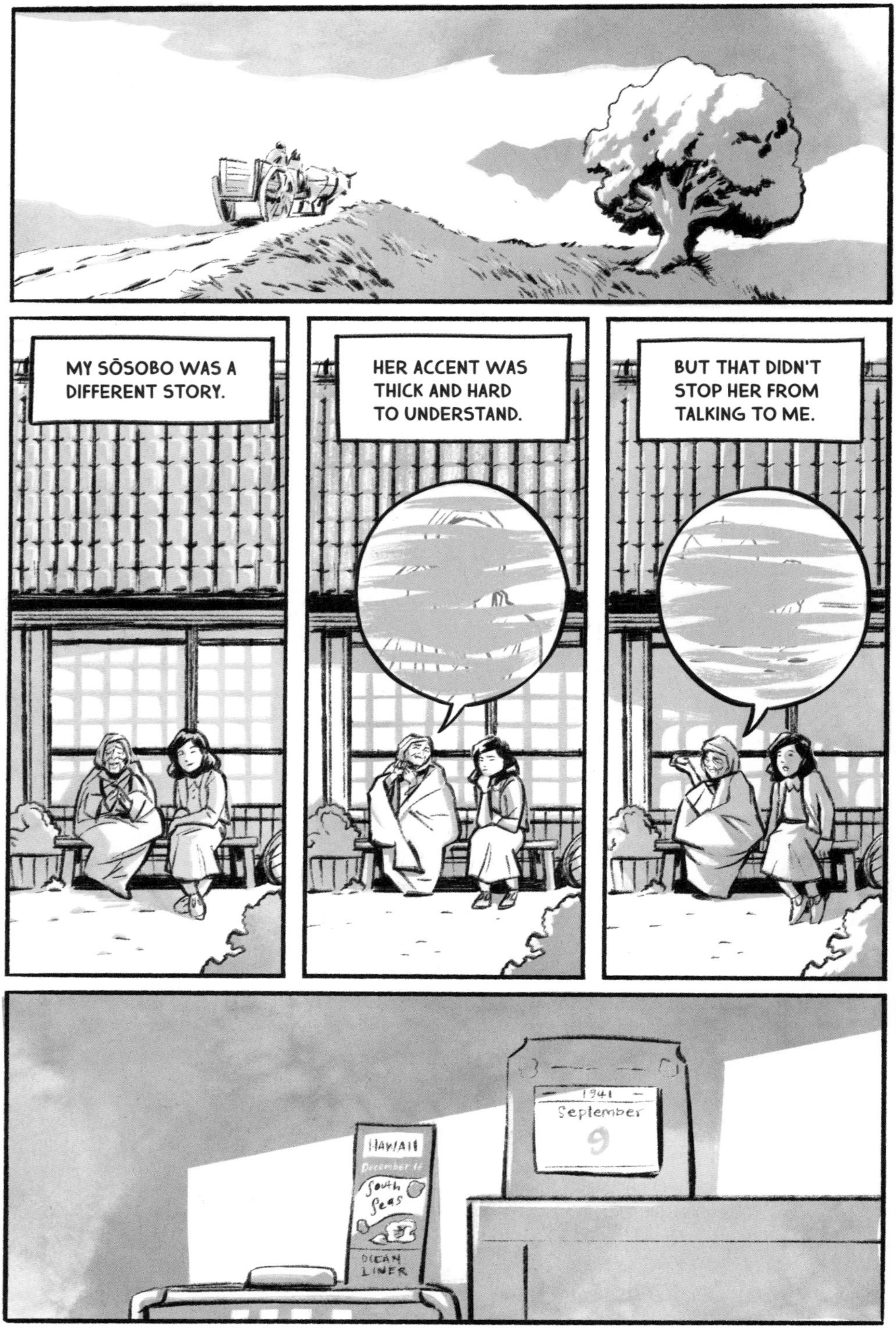

MY SŌSOBO WAS A DIFFERENT STORY.
HER ACCENT WAS THICK AND HARD TO UNDERSTAND.
BUT THAT DIDN'T STOP HER FROM TALKING TO ME.
HAWAII
South Seas
OCEAN LINER
1941
September
9

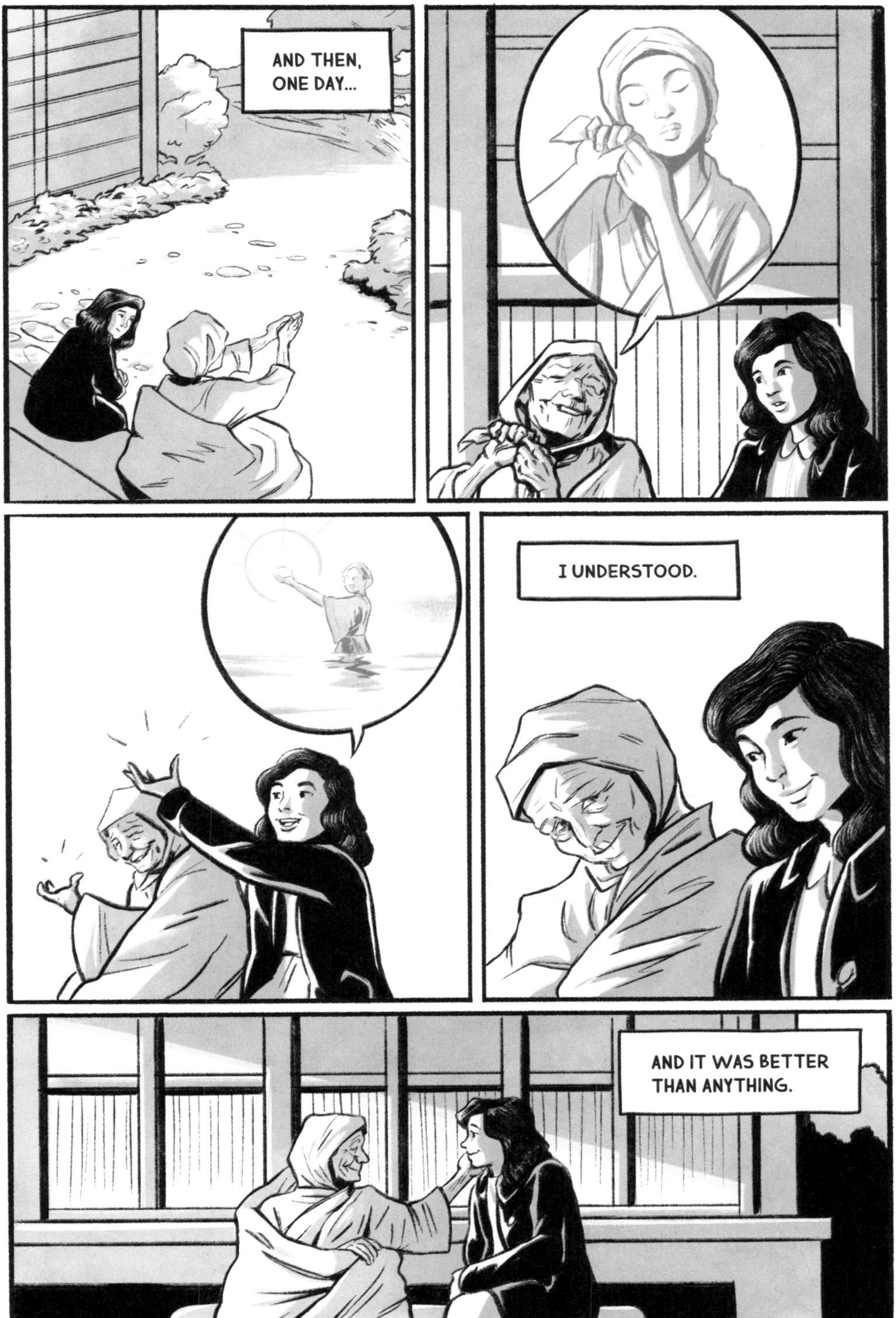
AND THEN, ONE DAY...
I UNDERSTOOD.
AND IT WAS BETTER THAN ANYTHING.

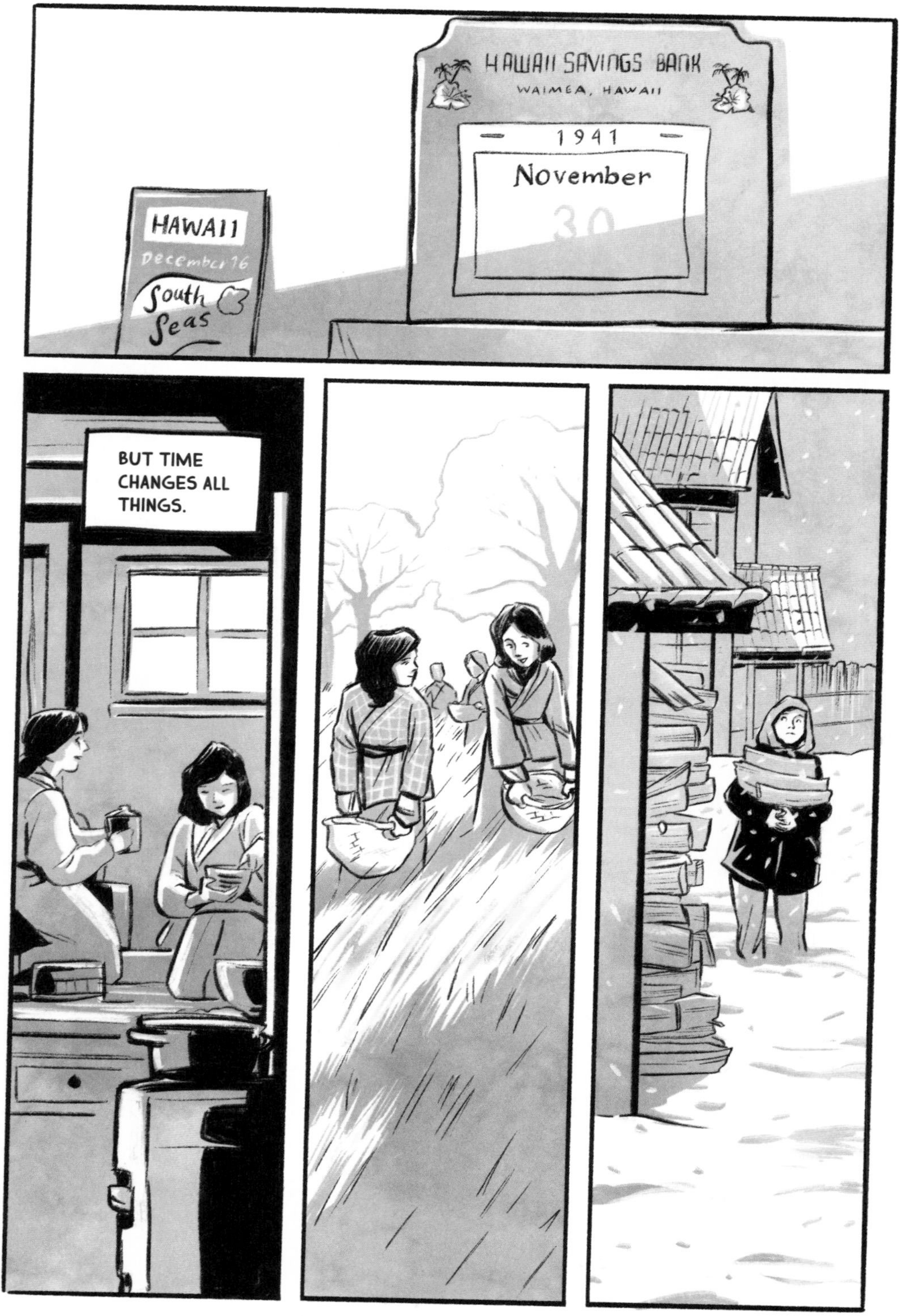
HAWAII
December 16
South Seas
HAWAII SAVINGS BANK
WAIMEA, HAWAII
1941
November
30
BUT TIME CHANGES ALL THINGS.

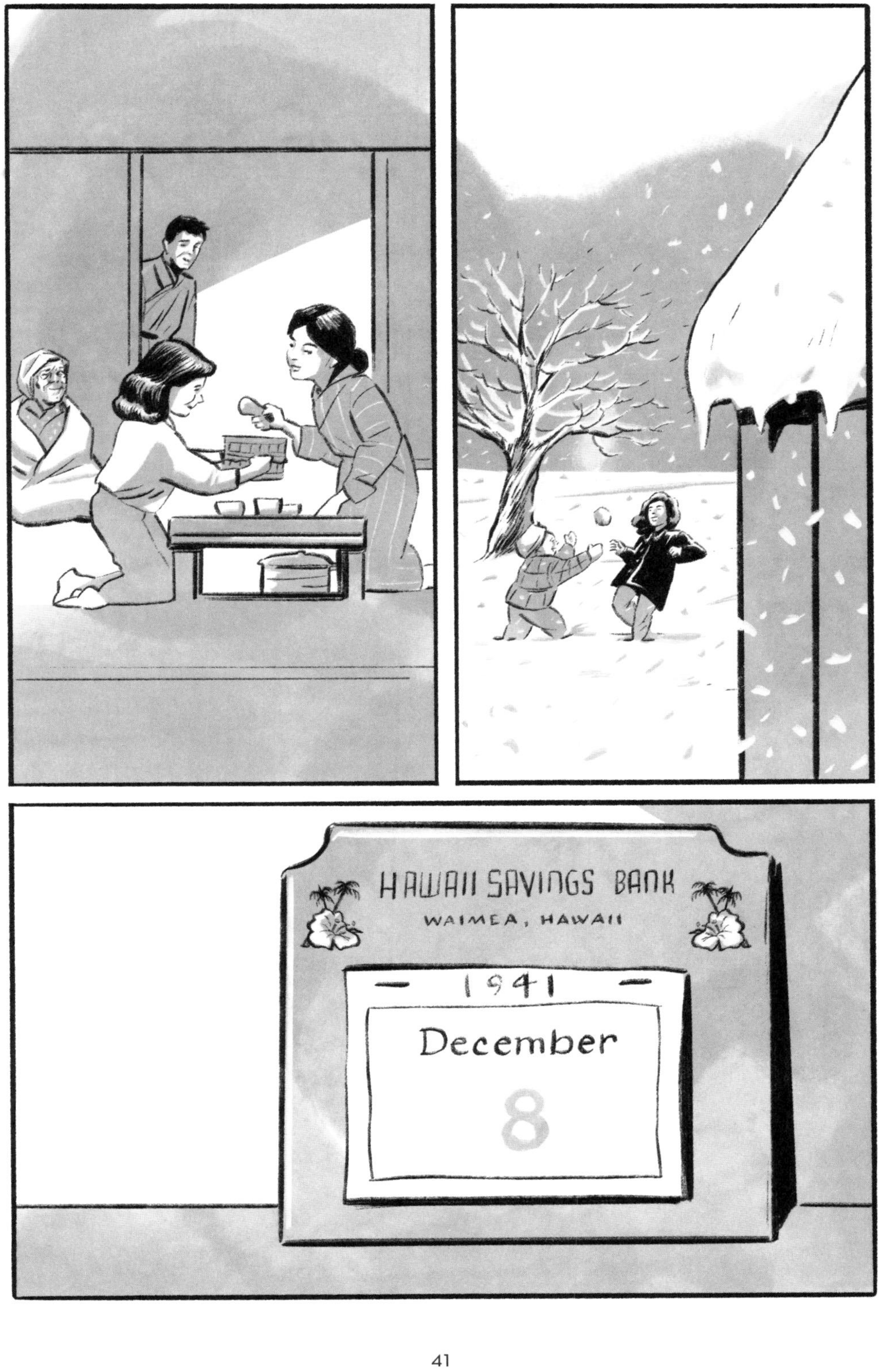
HAWAII SAVINGS BANK
WAIMEA, HAWAII
1941
December
8

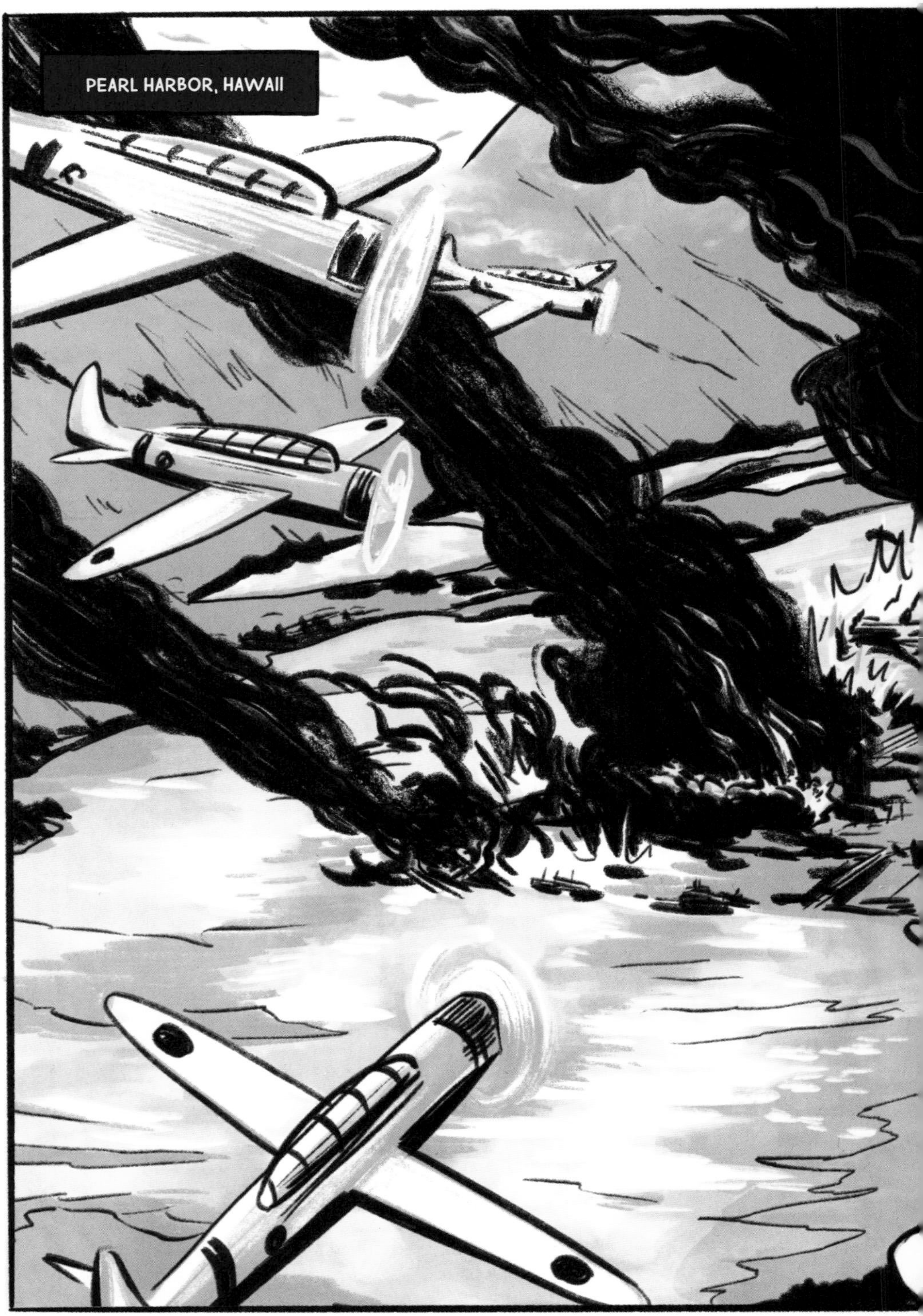
PEARL HARBOR, HAWAII

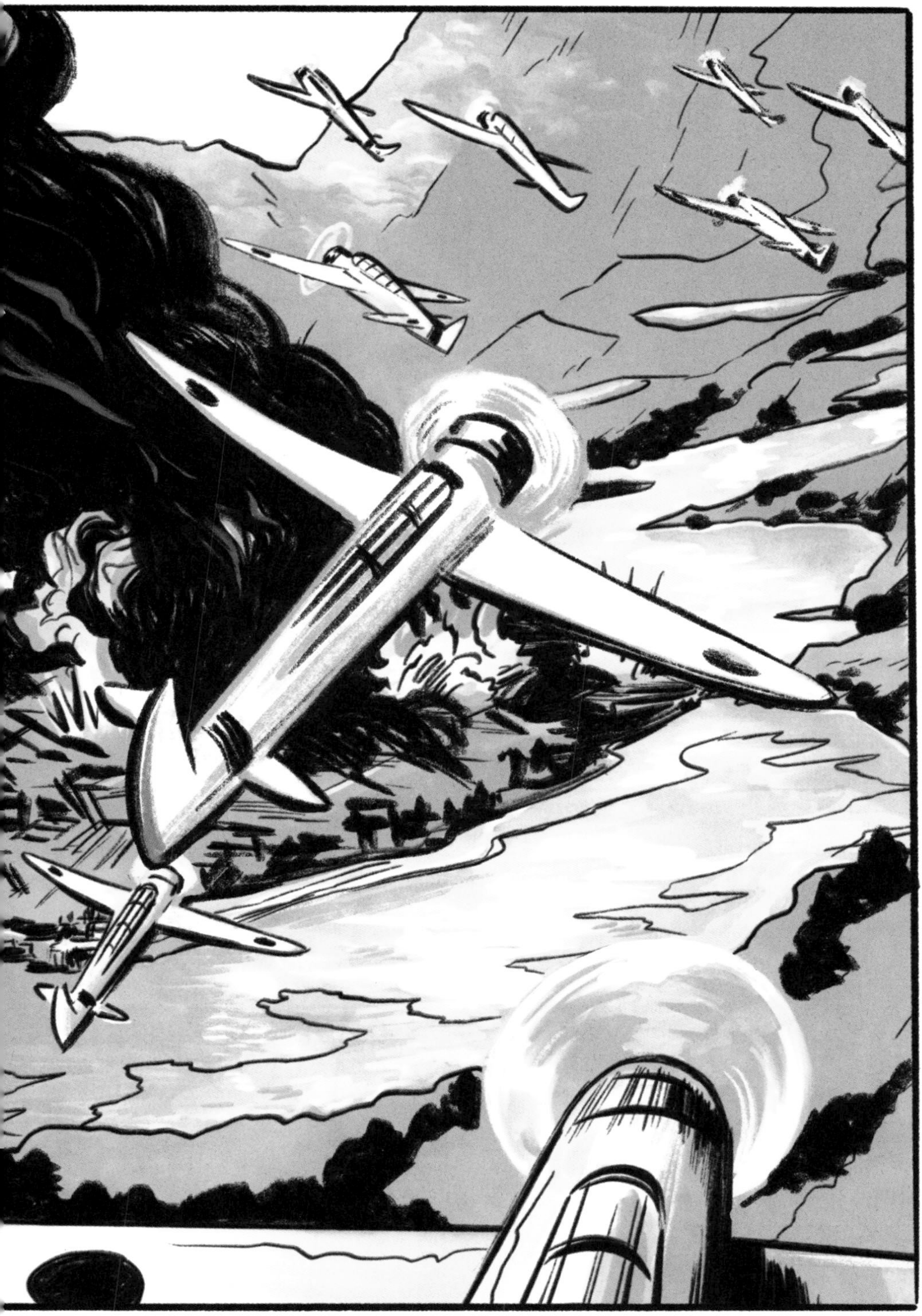

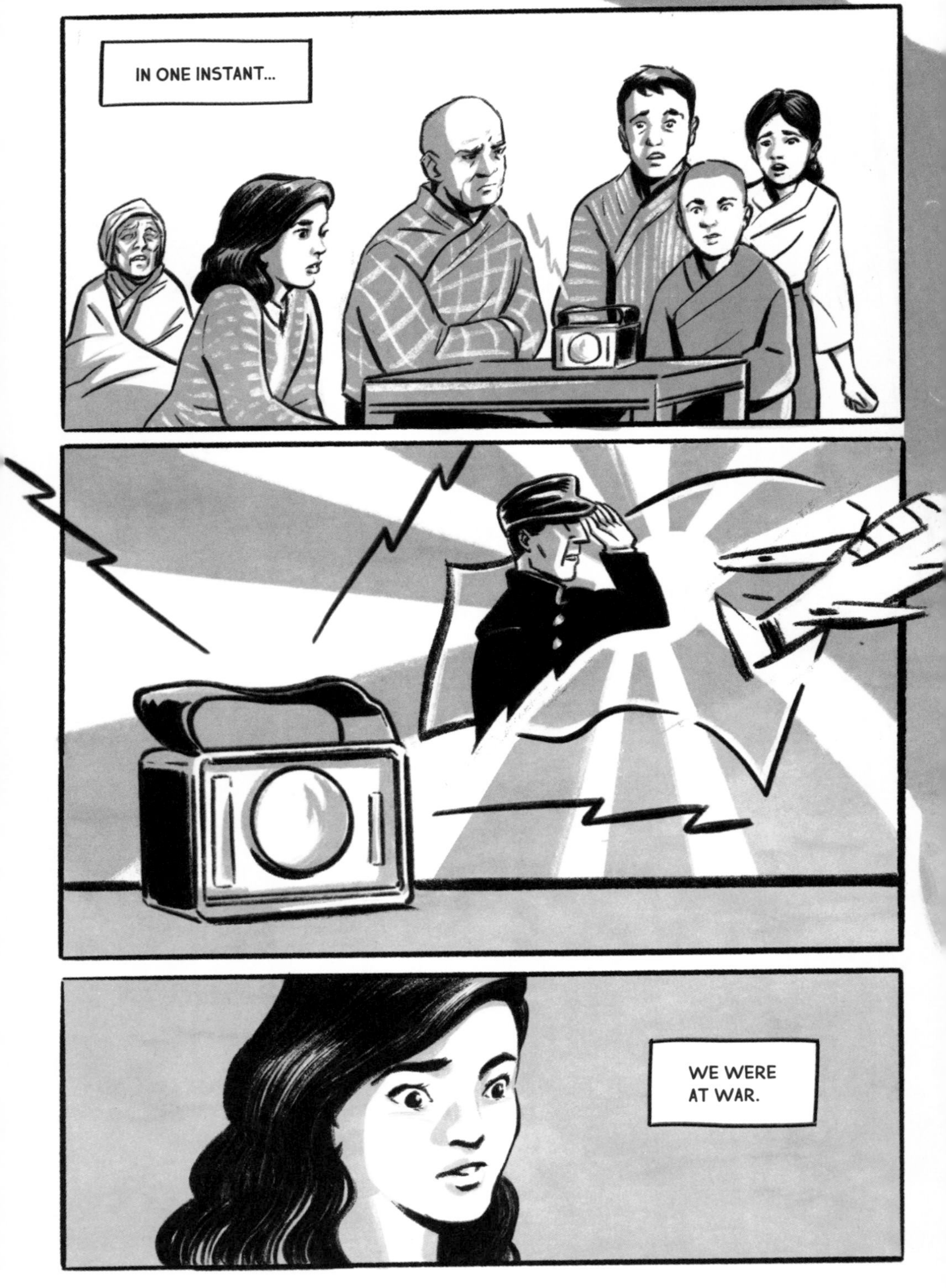
IN ONE INSTANT...
WE WERE AT WAR.

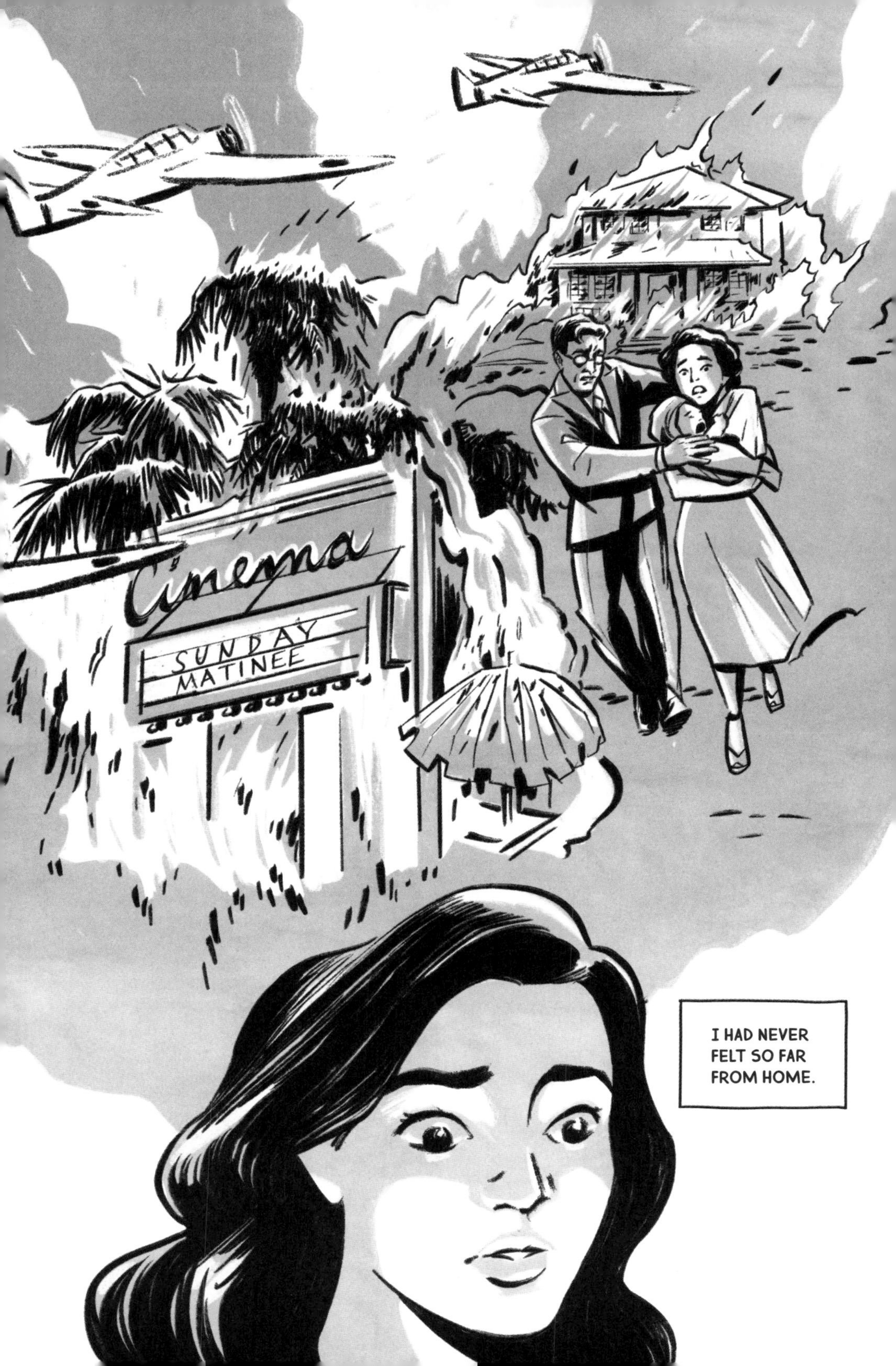
Cinema
SUNDAY MATINEE
I HAD NEVER FELT SO FAR FROM HOME.

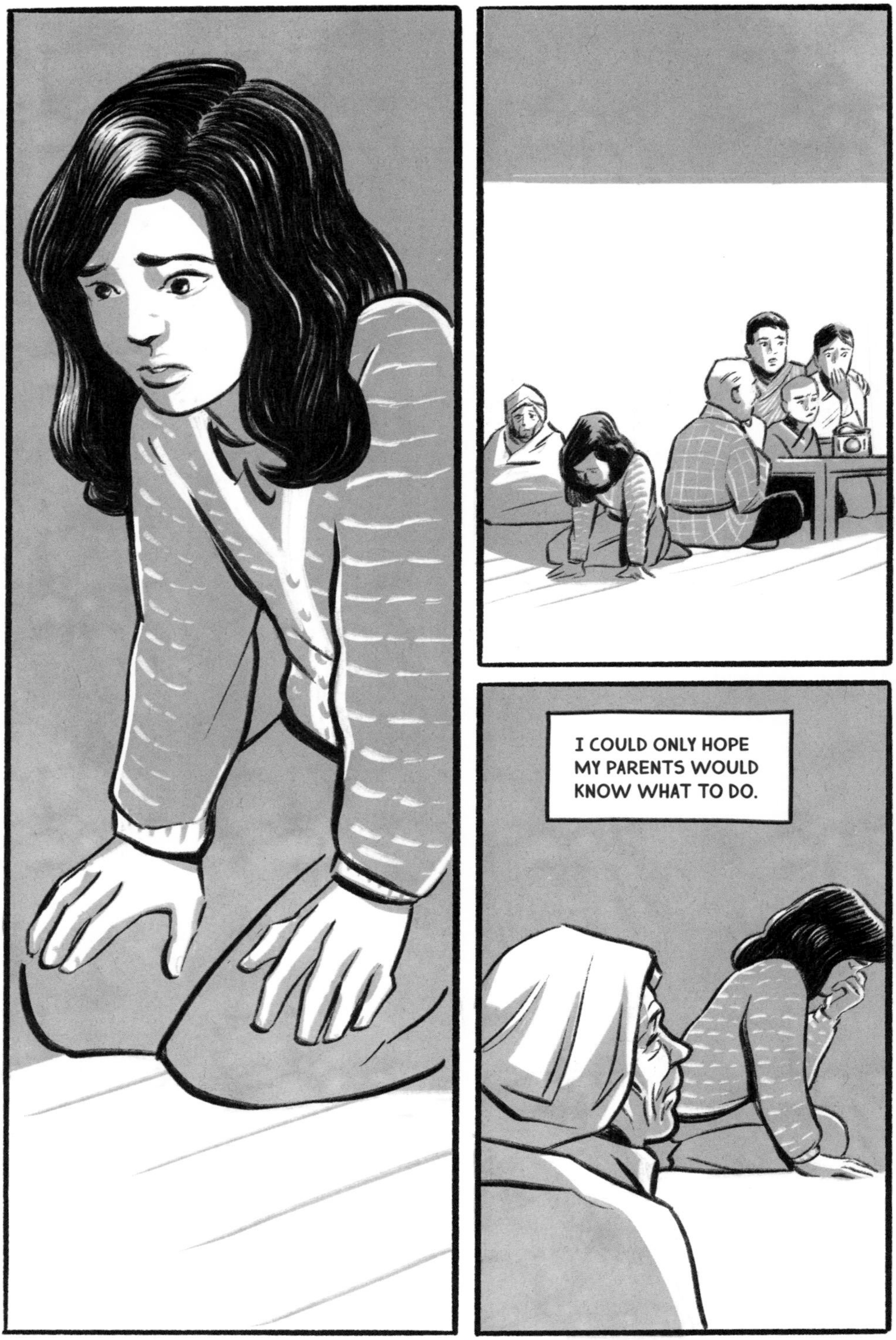
I COULD ONLY HOPE MY PARENTS WOULD KNOW WHAT TO DO.

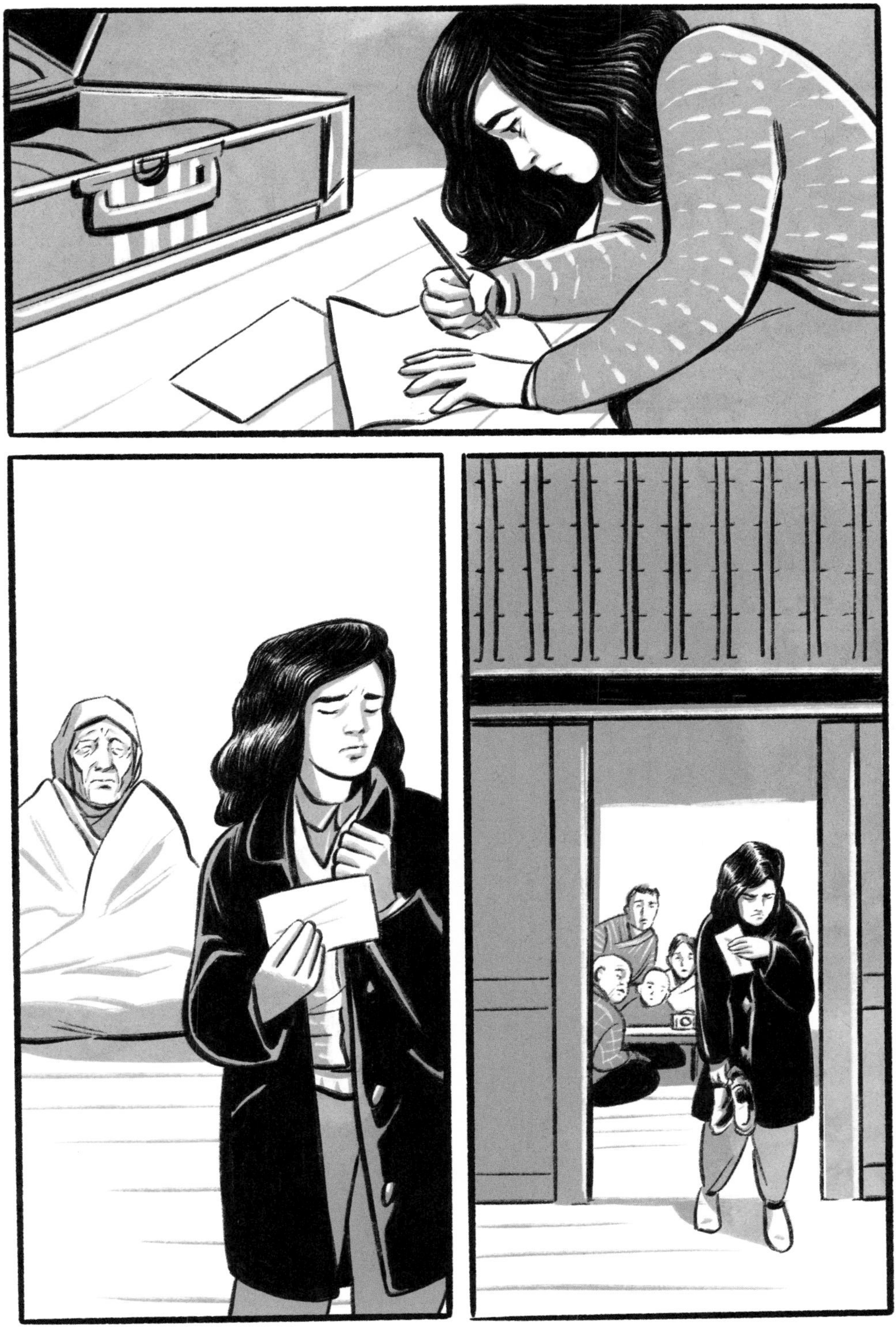

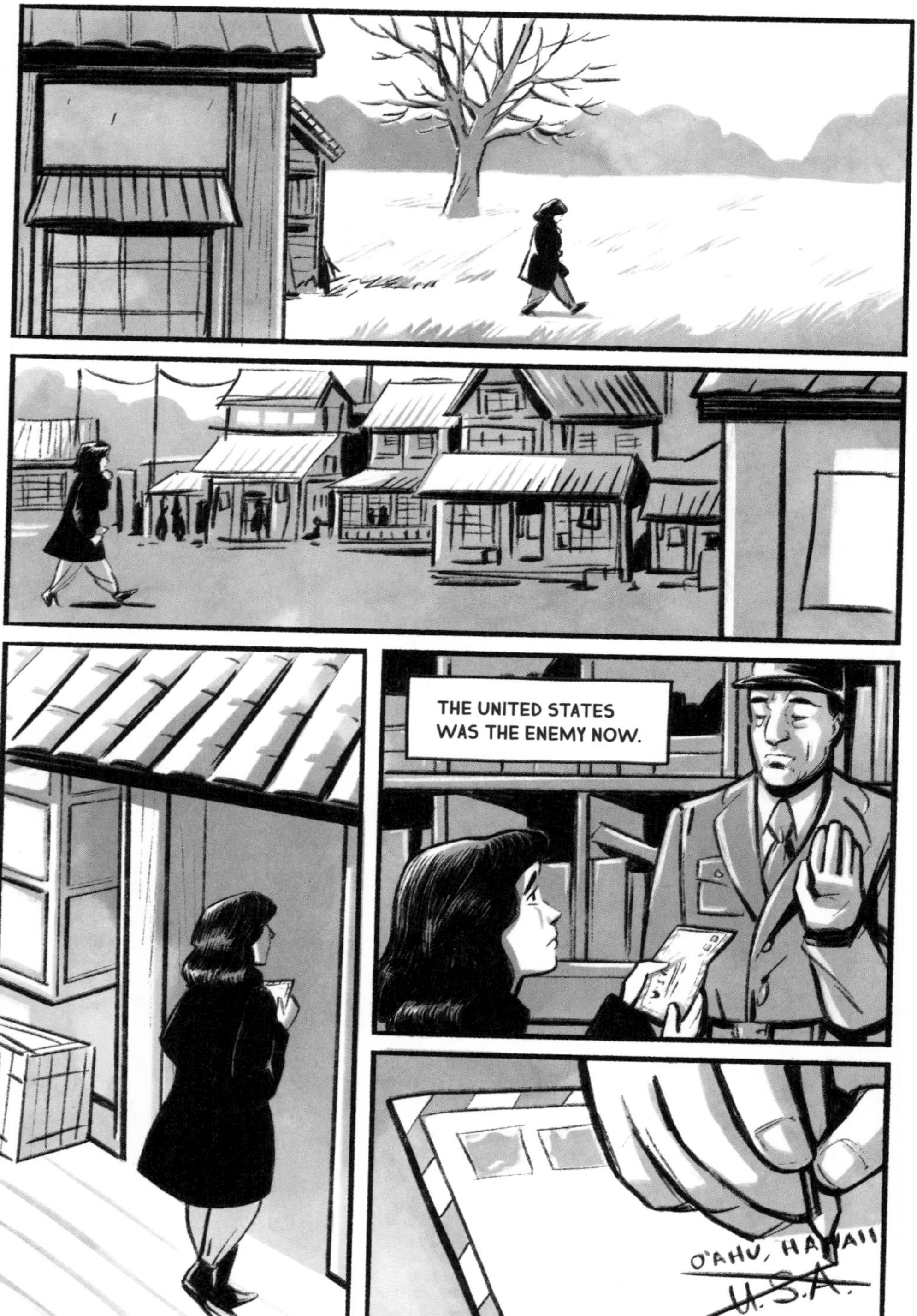
THE UNITED STATES
WAS THE ENEMY NOW.
O'AHU, HAWAII
U.S.A.

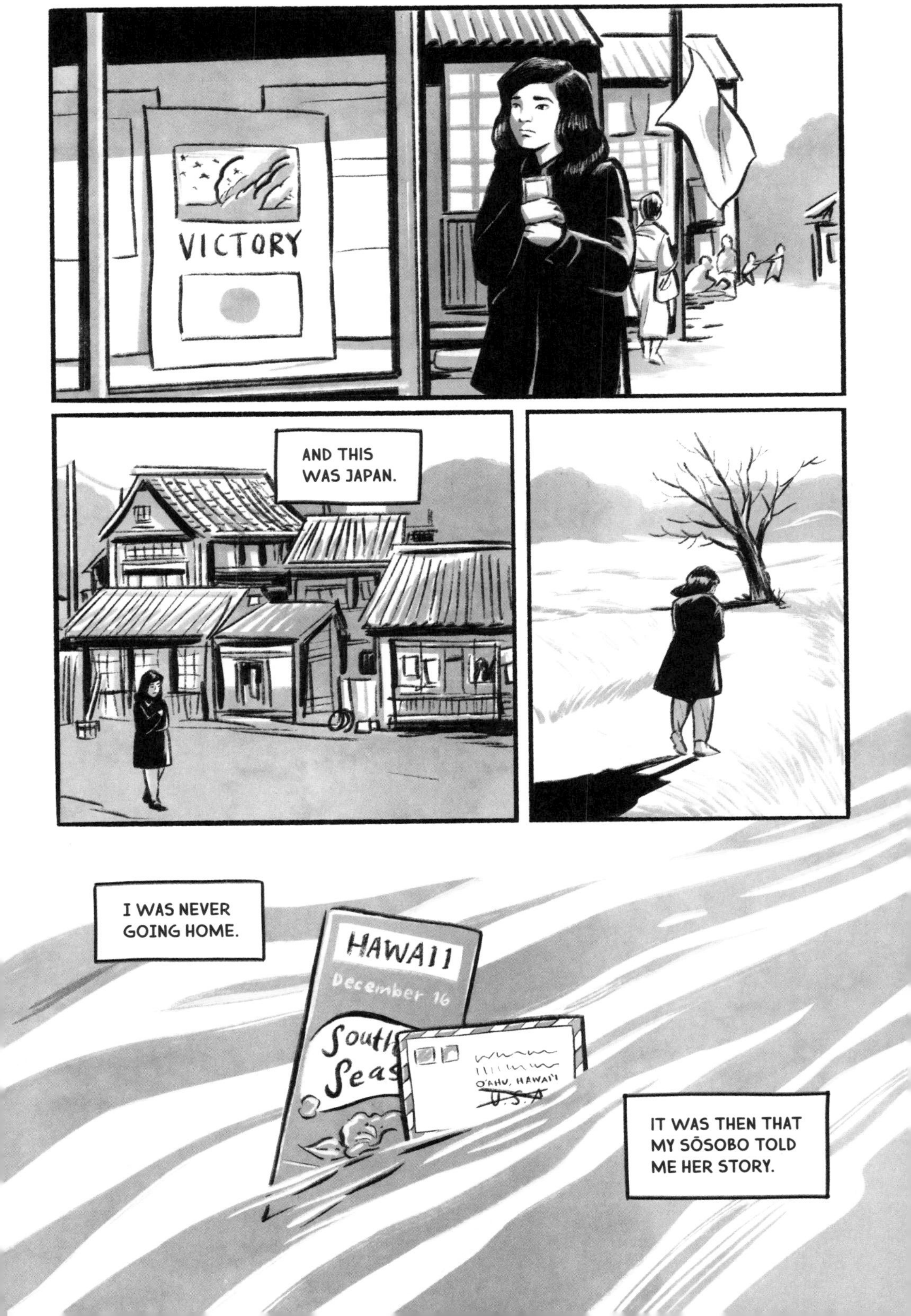
VICTORY
AND THIS WAS JAPAN.
I WAS NEVER GOING HOME.
HAWAII
December 16
O'AHU, HAWAI'I
U.S.A
IT WAS THEN THAT MY SŌSOBO TOLD ME HER STORY.

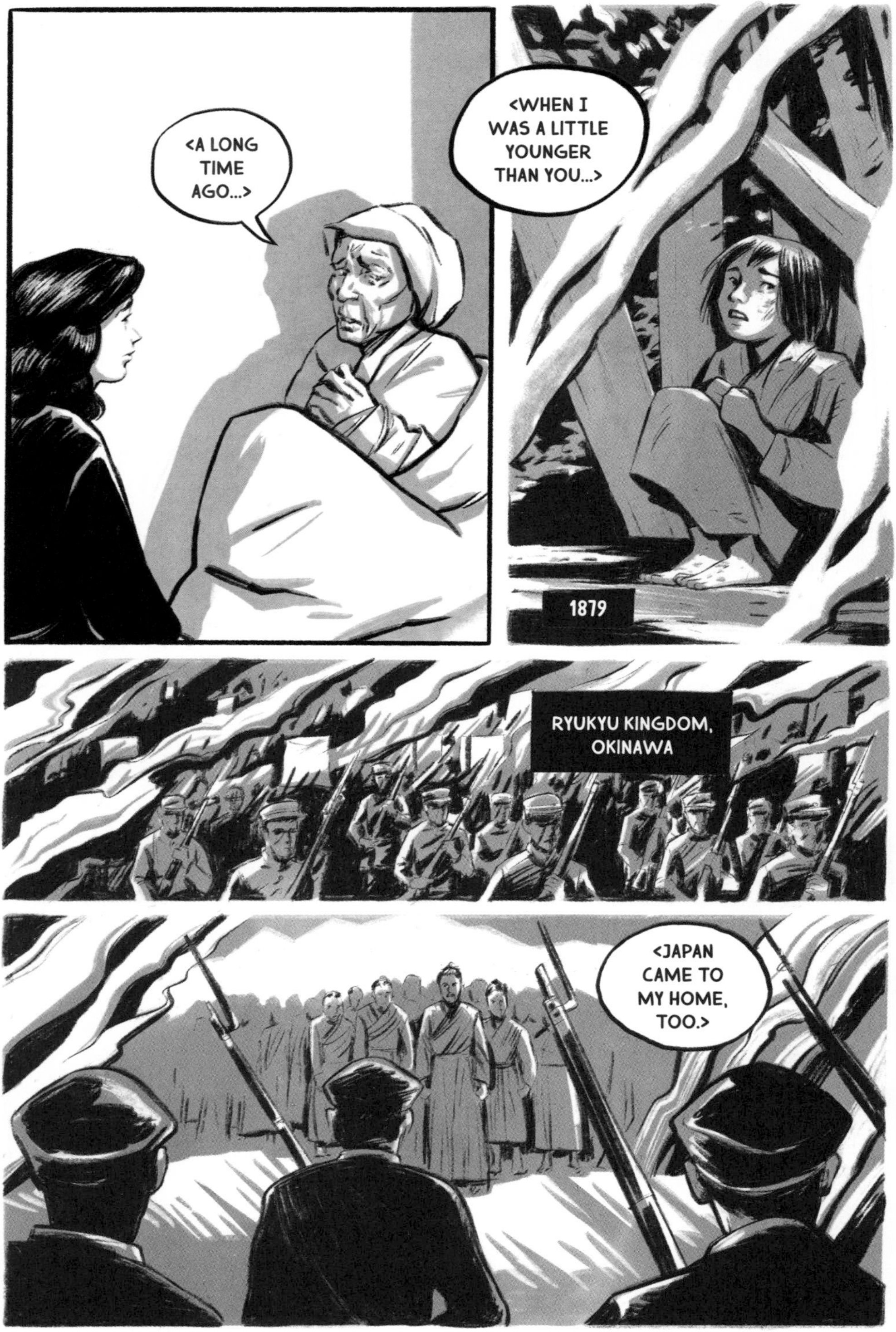
<A LONG TIME AGO...>
<WHEN I WAS A LITTLE YOUNGER THAN YOU...>
1879
RYUKYU KINGDOM, OKINAWA
<JAPAN CAME TO MY HOME, TOO.>

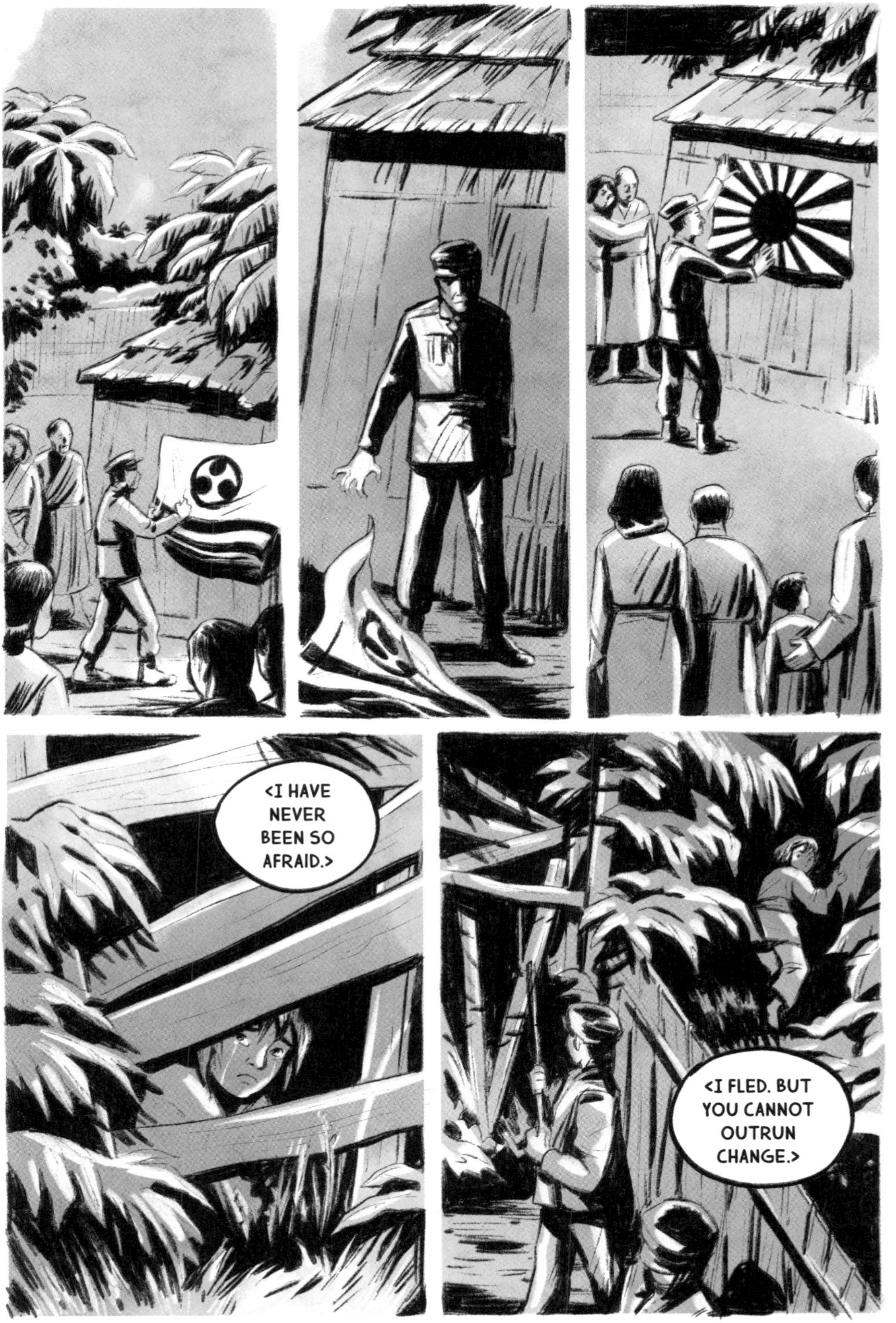
<I HAVE NEVER BEEN SO AFRAID.>
<I FLED. BUT YOU CANNOT OUTRUN CHANGE.>

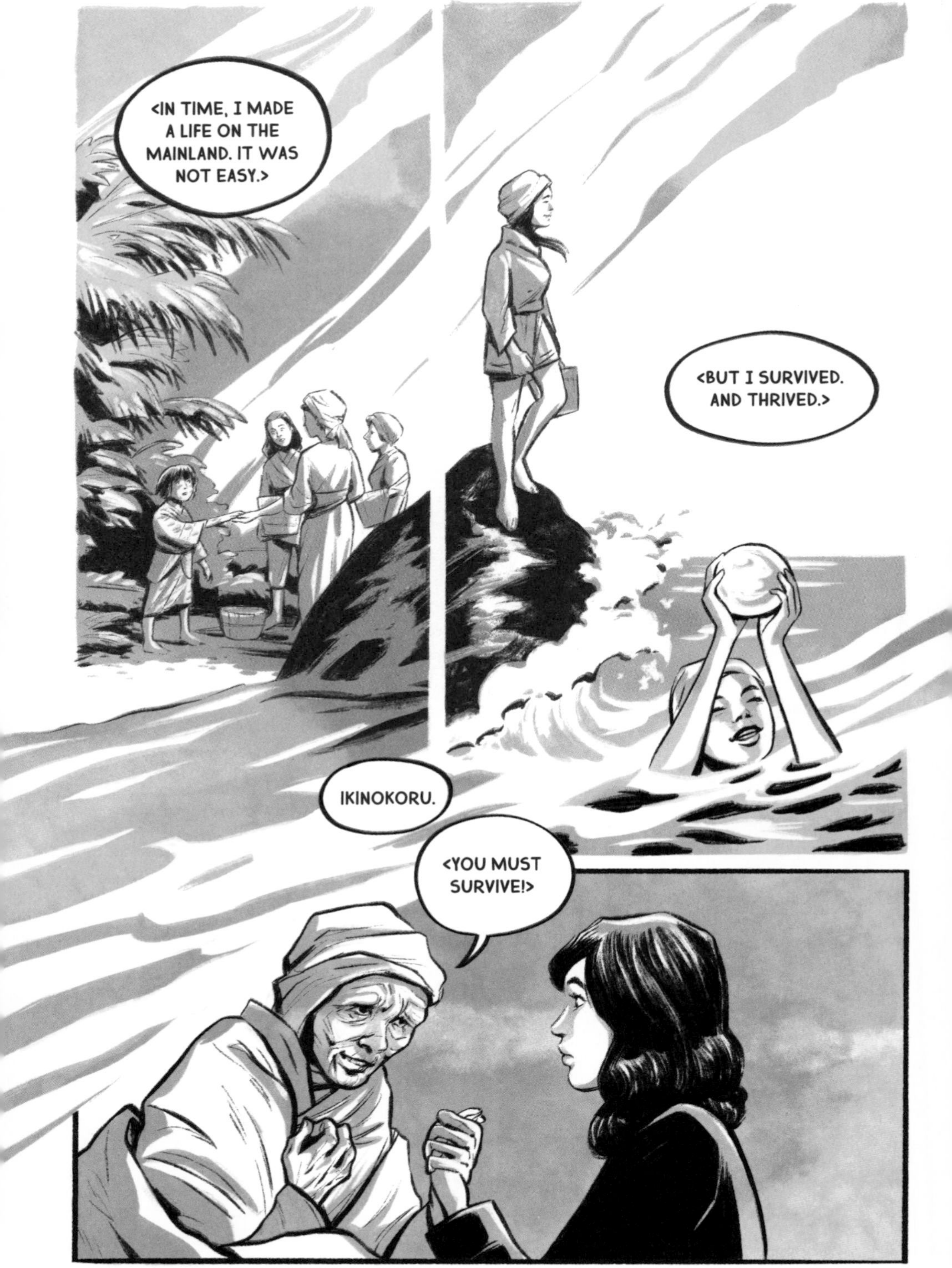
<IN TIME, I MADE A LIFE ON THE MAINLAND. IT WAS NOT EASY.>
<BUT I SURVIVED. AND THRIVED.>
IKINOKORU.
<YOU MUST SURVIVE!>

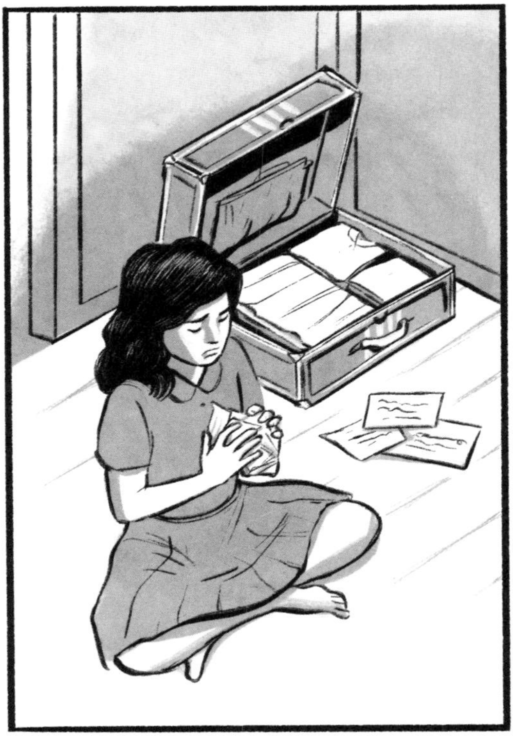
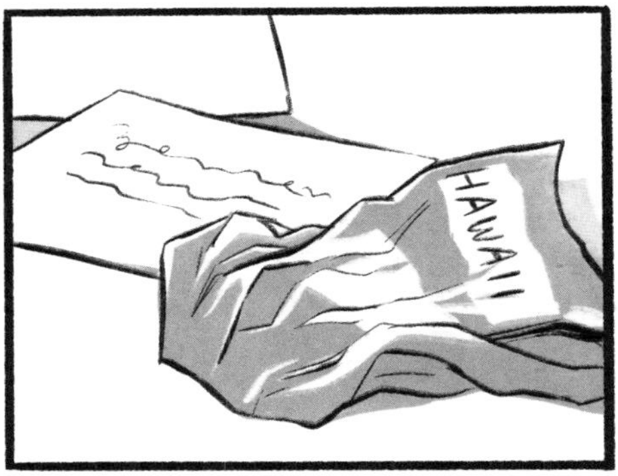
HAWAII
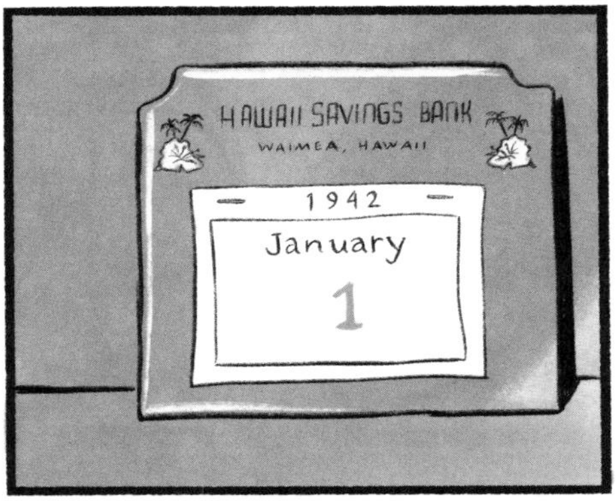
HAWAII SAVINGS BANK
WAIMEA, HAWAII
1942
January
1
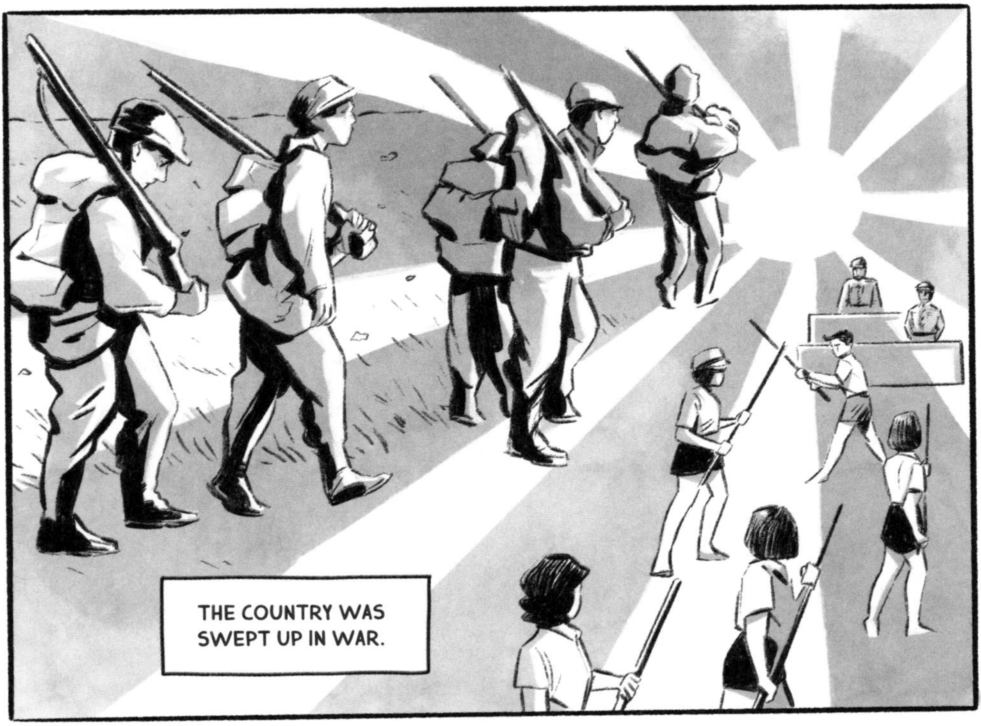
THE COUNTRY WAS SWEPT UP IN WAR.

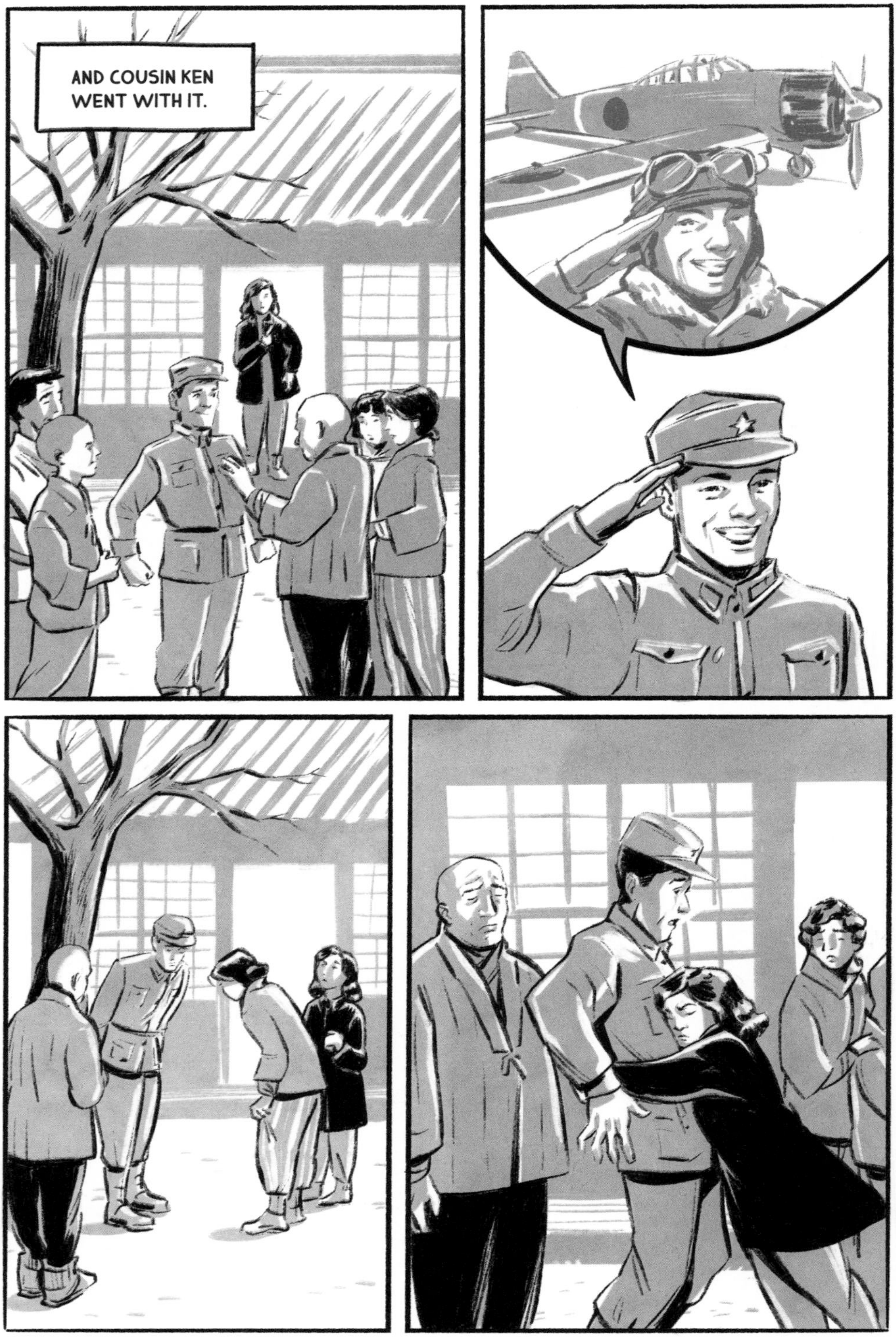
AND COUSIN KEN
WENT WITH IT.

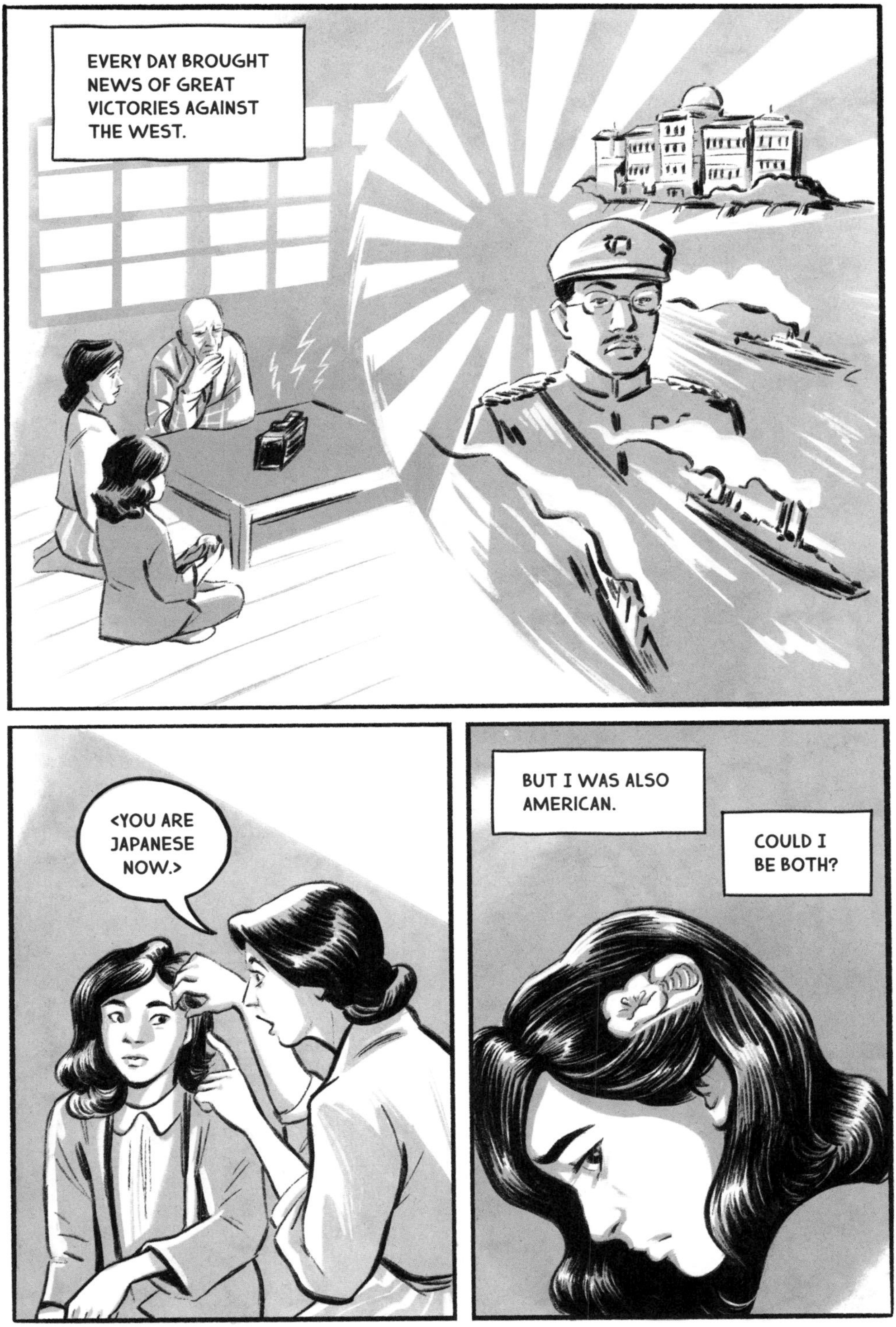
EVERY DAY BROUGHT NEWS OF GREAT VICTORIES AGAINST THE WEST.
<YOU ARE JAPANESE NOW.>
BUT I WAS ALSO AMERICAN.
COULD I BE BOTH?

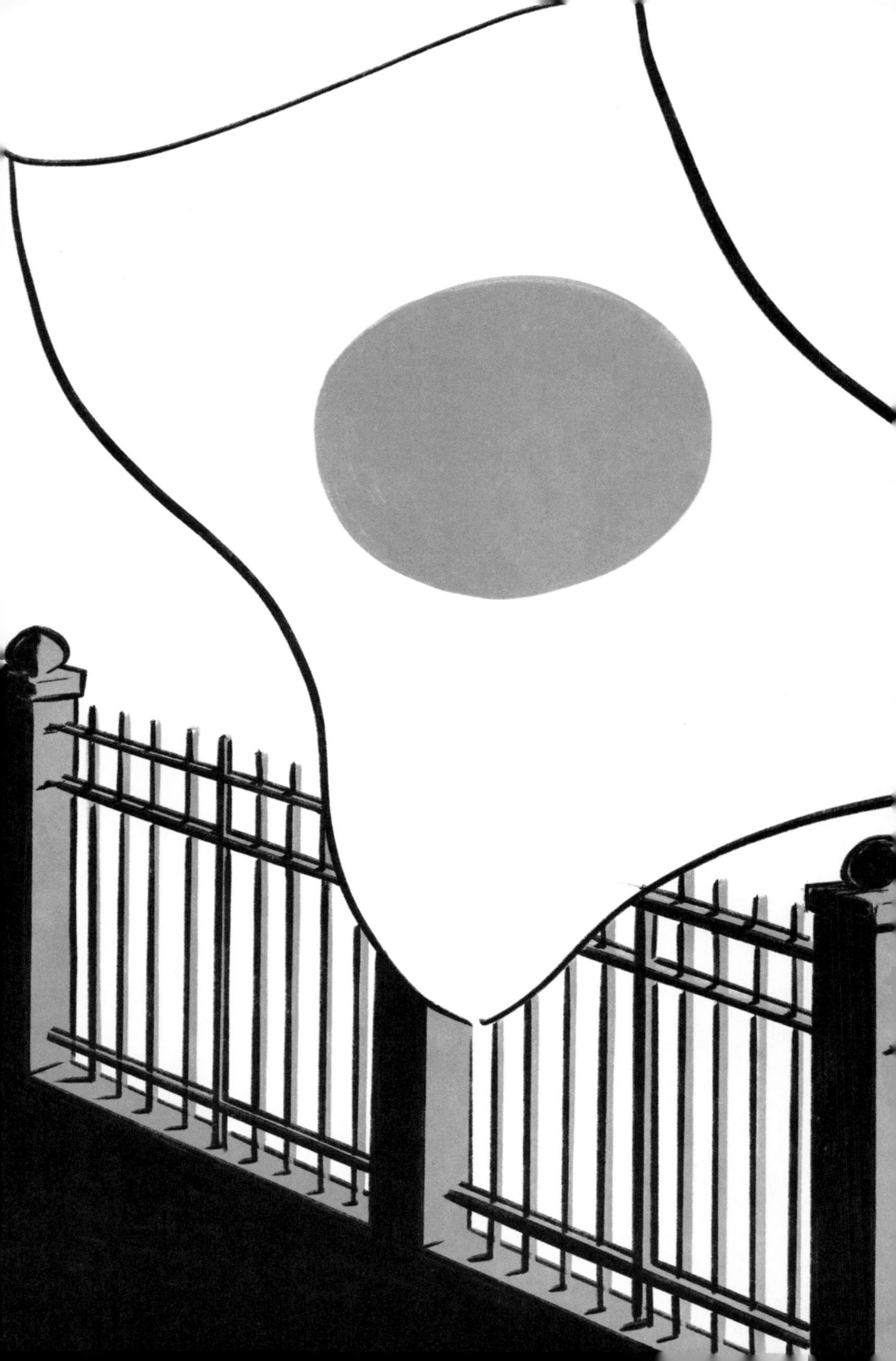

# MONITOR GIRL

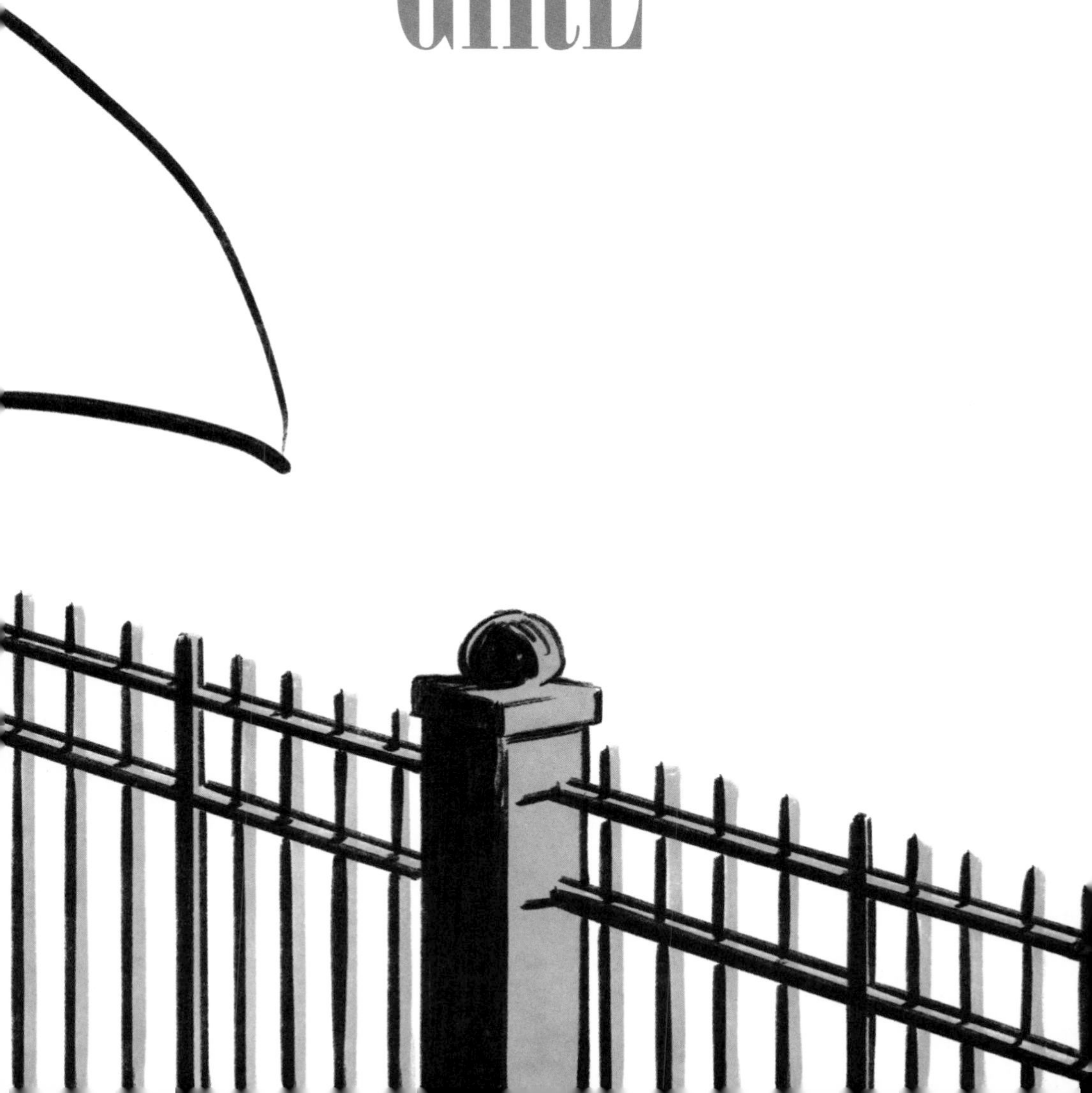

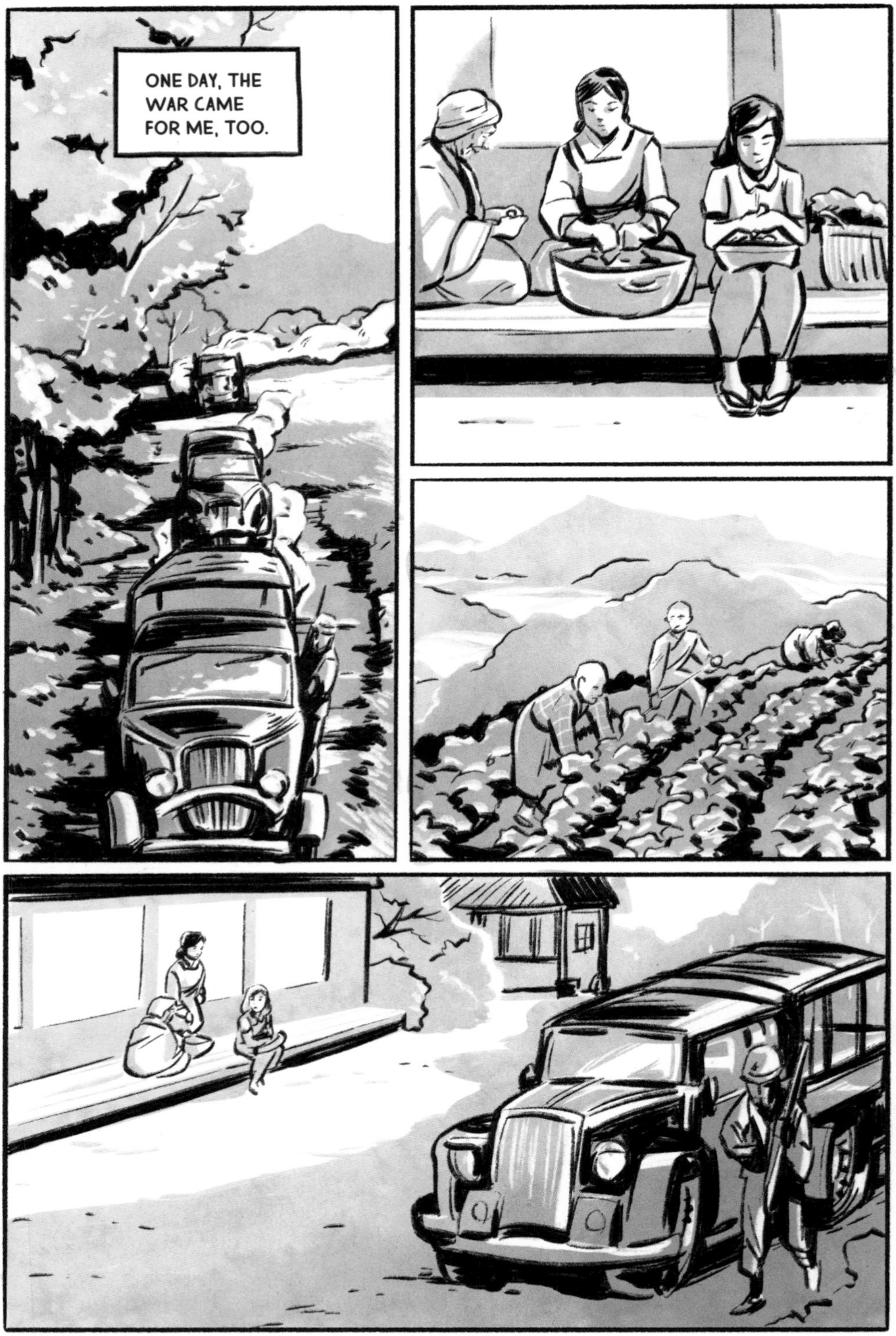
ONE DAY, THE WAR CAME FOR ME, TOO.

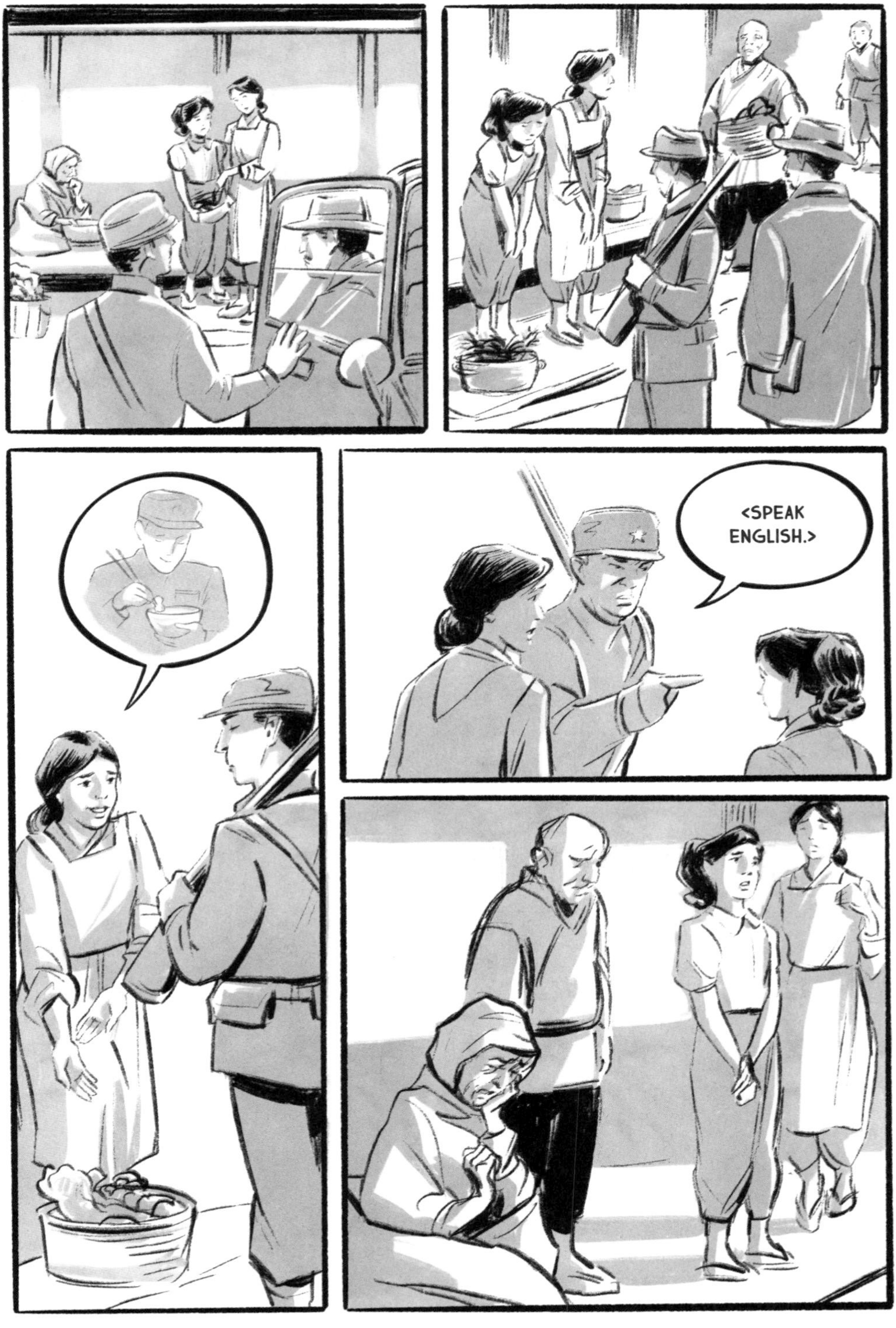
<SPEAK ENGLISH.>

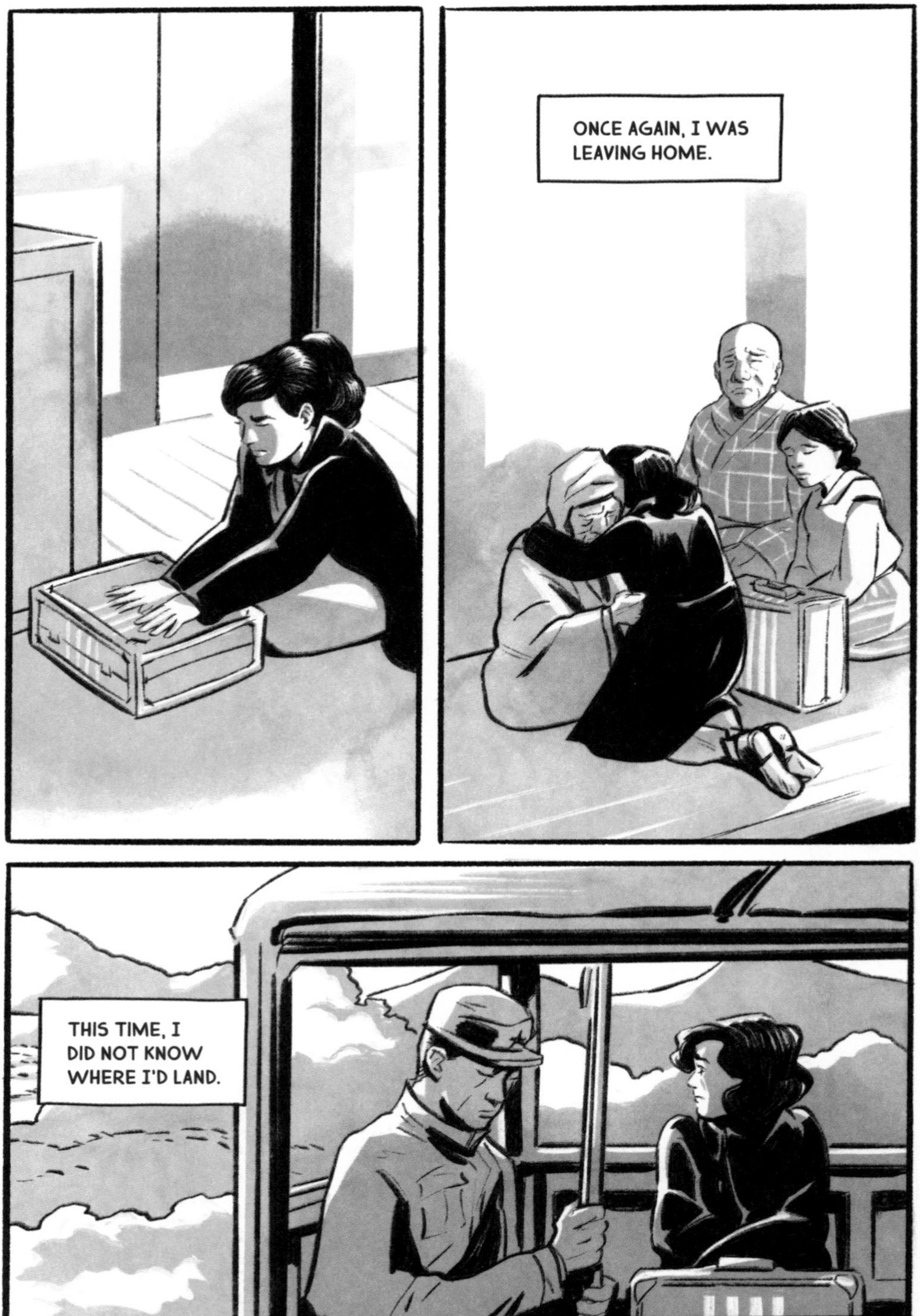
ONCE AGAIN, I WAS LEAVING HOME.
THIS TIME, I DID NOT KNOW WHERE I'D LAND.

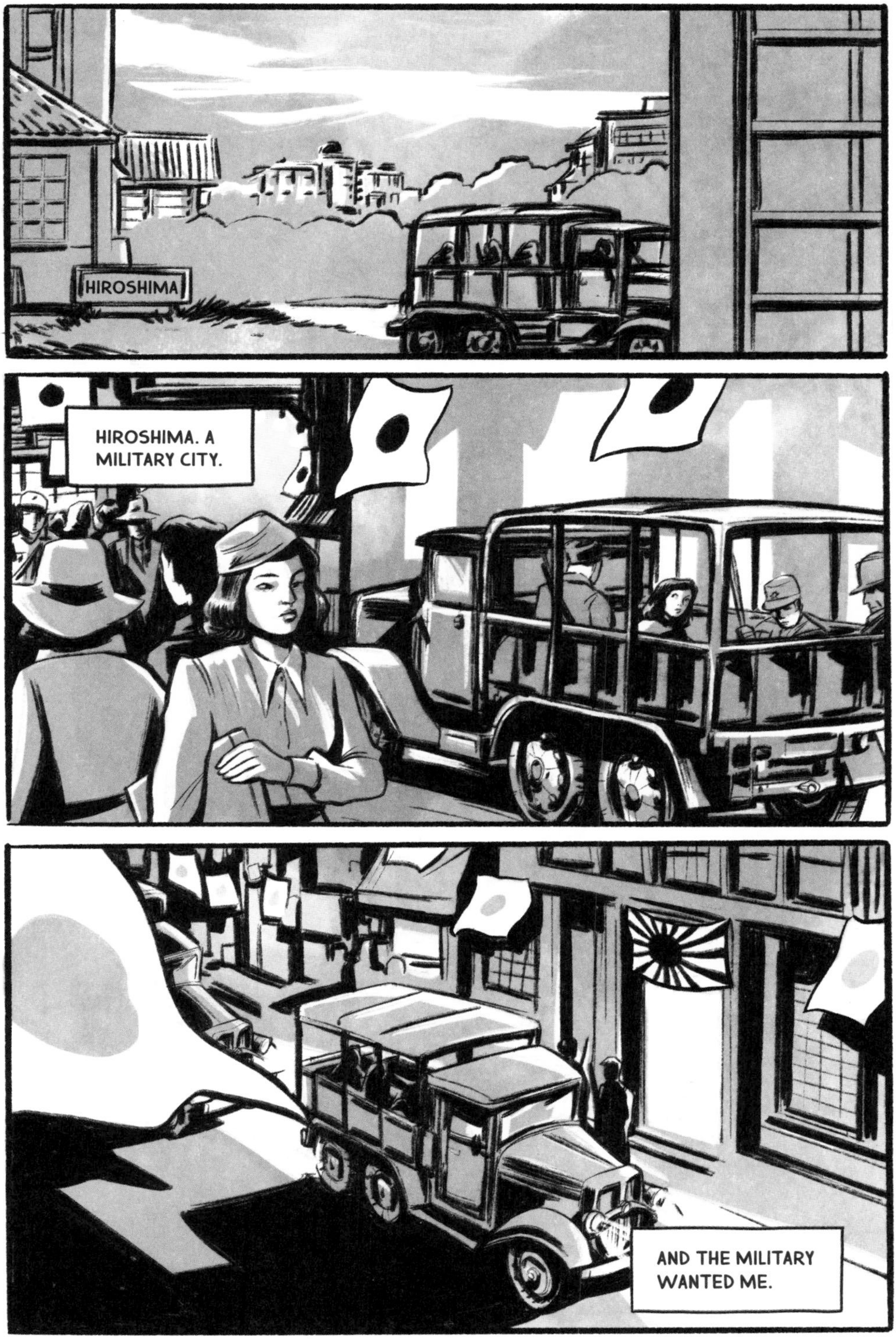
HIROSHIMA
HIROSHIMA. A MILITARY CITY.
AND THE MILITARY WANTED ME.

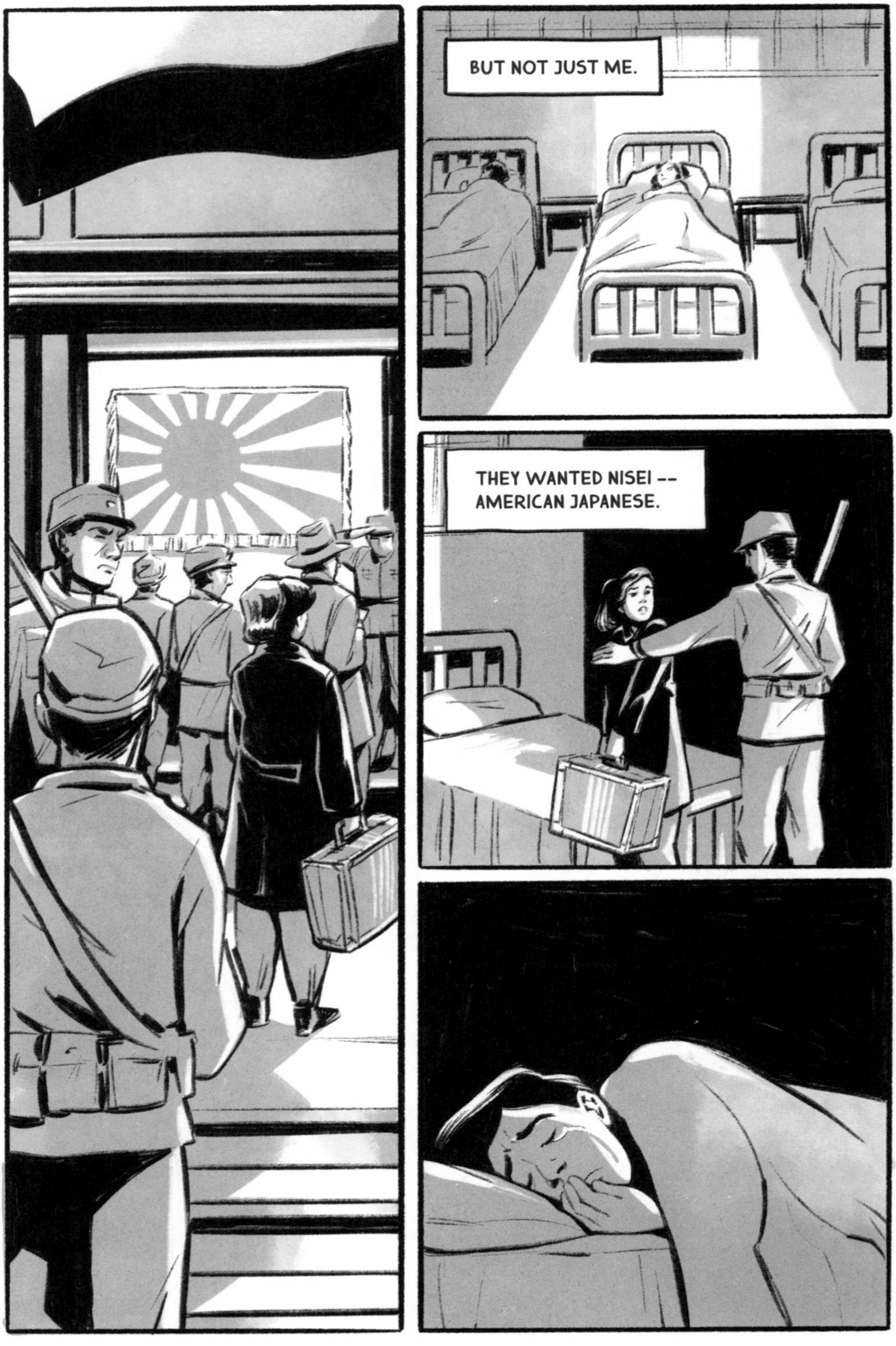
BUT NOT JUST ME.
THEY WANTED NISEI -- AMERICAN JAPANESE.

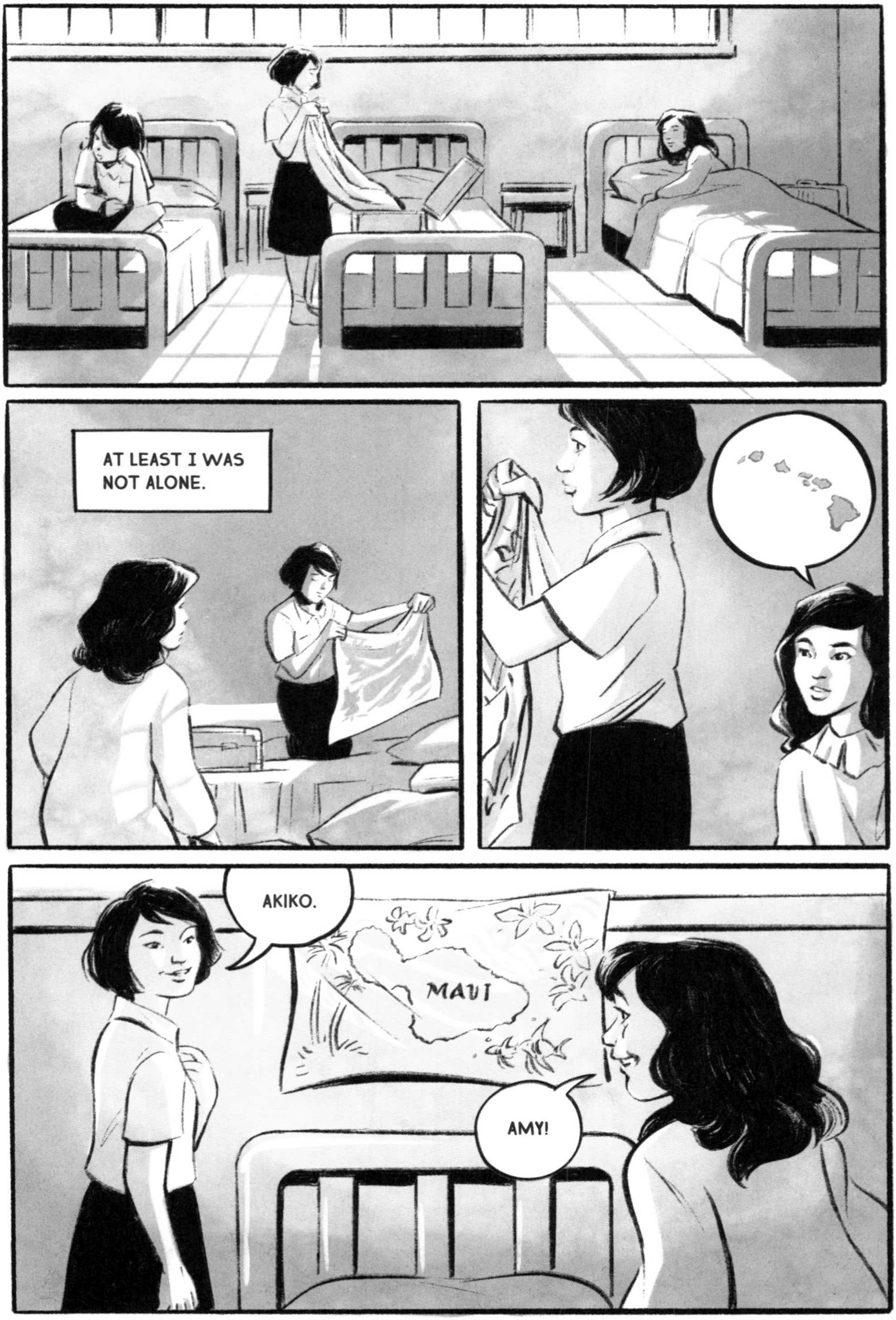
AT LEAST I WAS NOT ALONE.
AKIKO.
MAUI
AMY!

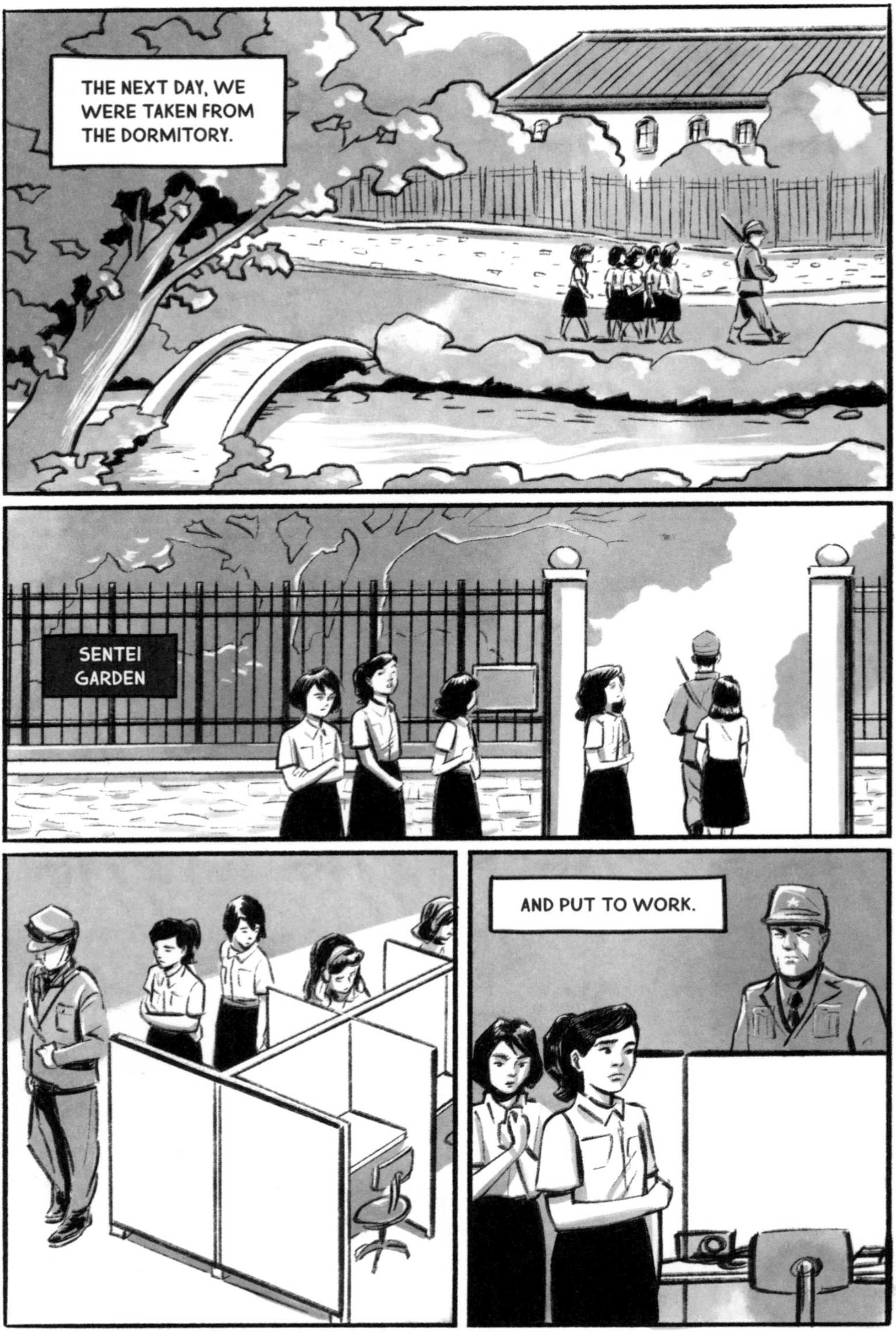
THE NEXT DAY, WE WERE TAKEN FROM THE DORMITORY.
SENTEI GARDEN
AND PUT TO WORK.

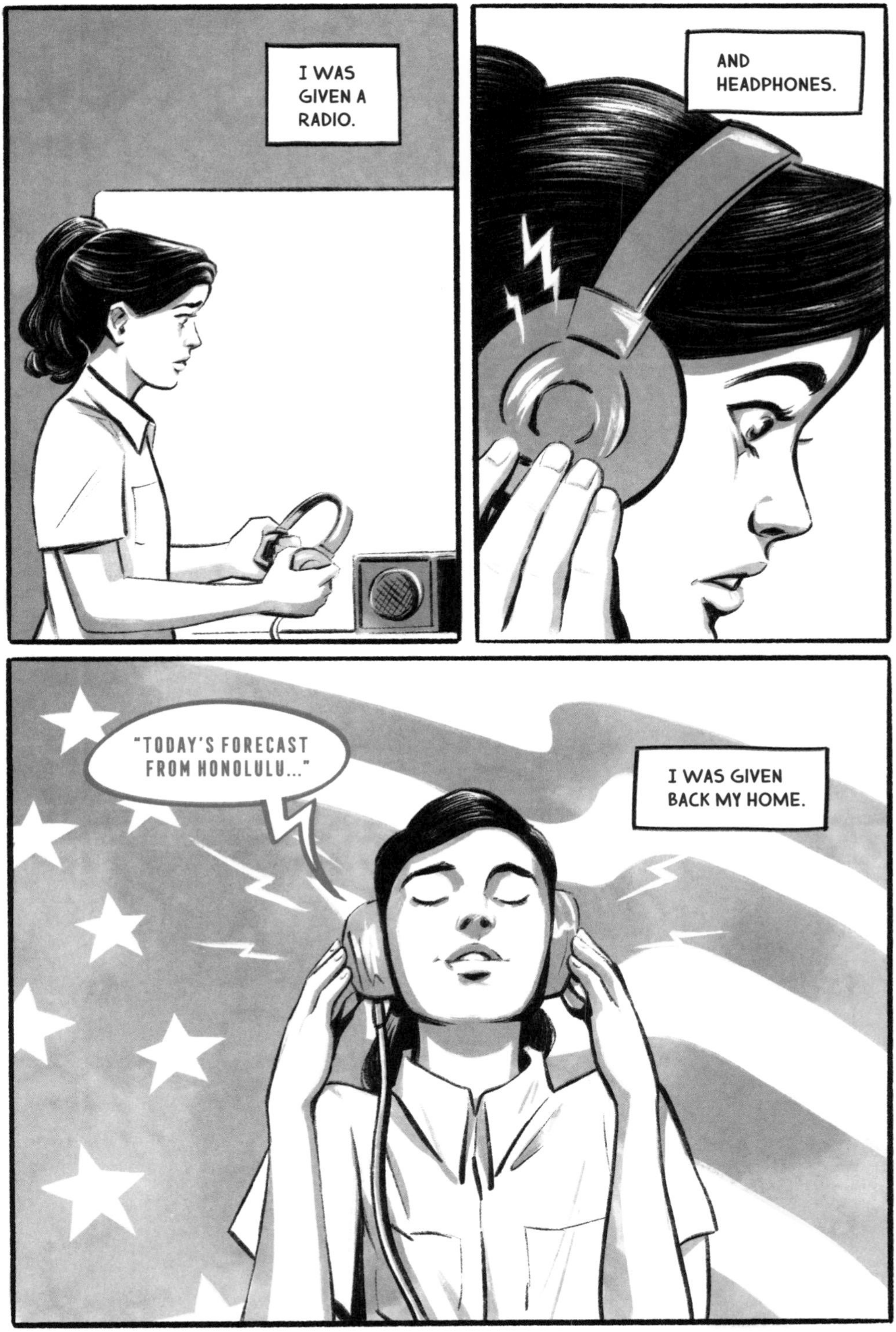
I WAS GIVEN A RADIO.
AND HEADPHONES.
"TODAY'S FORECAST FROM HONOLULU..."
I WAS GIVEN BACK MY HOME.

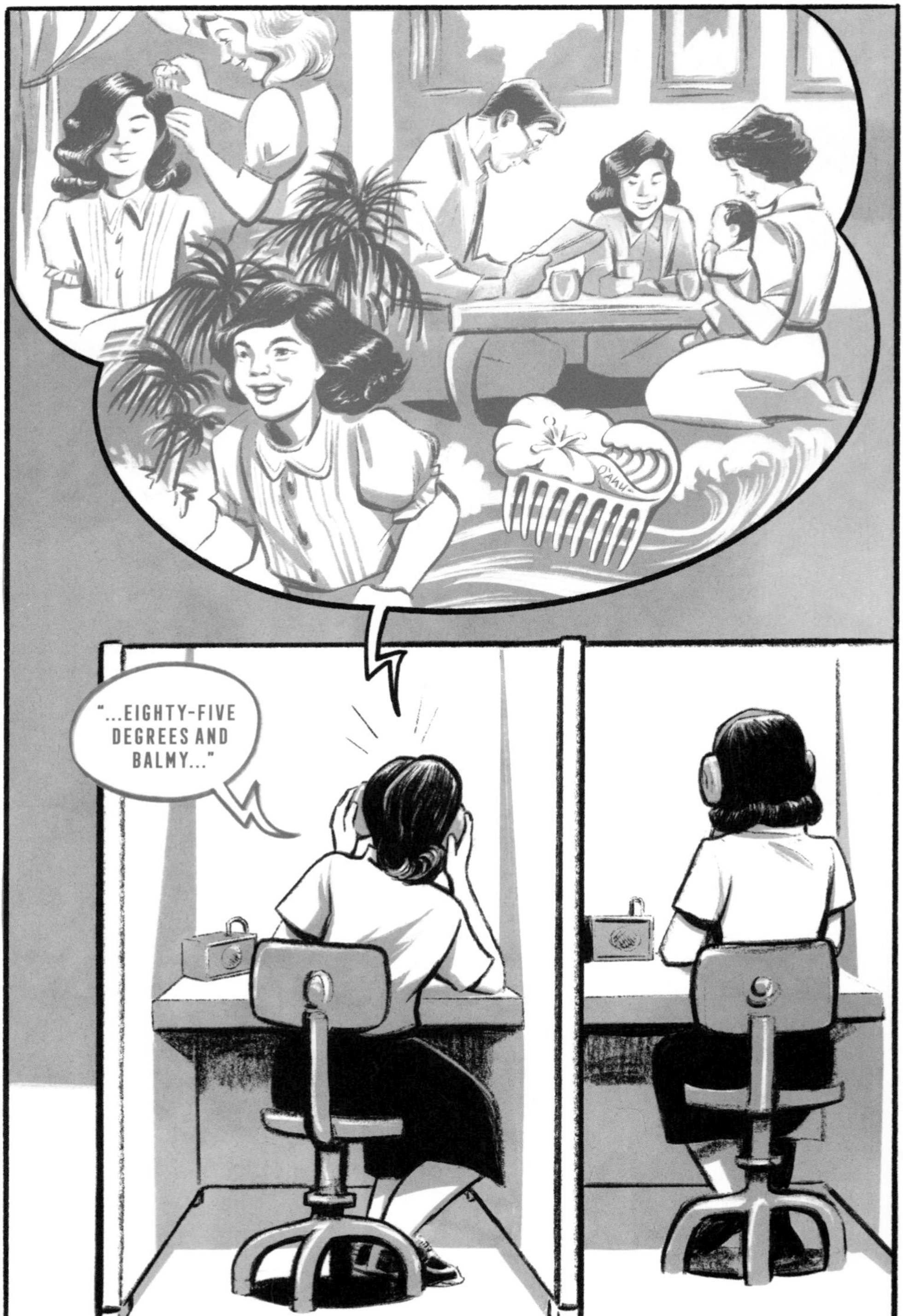
"...EIGHTY-FIVE DEGREES AND BALMY..."

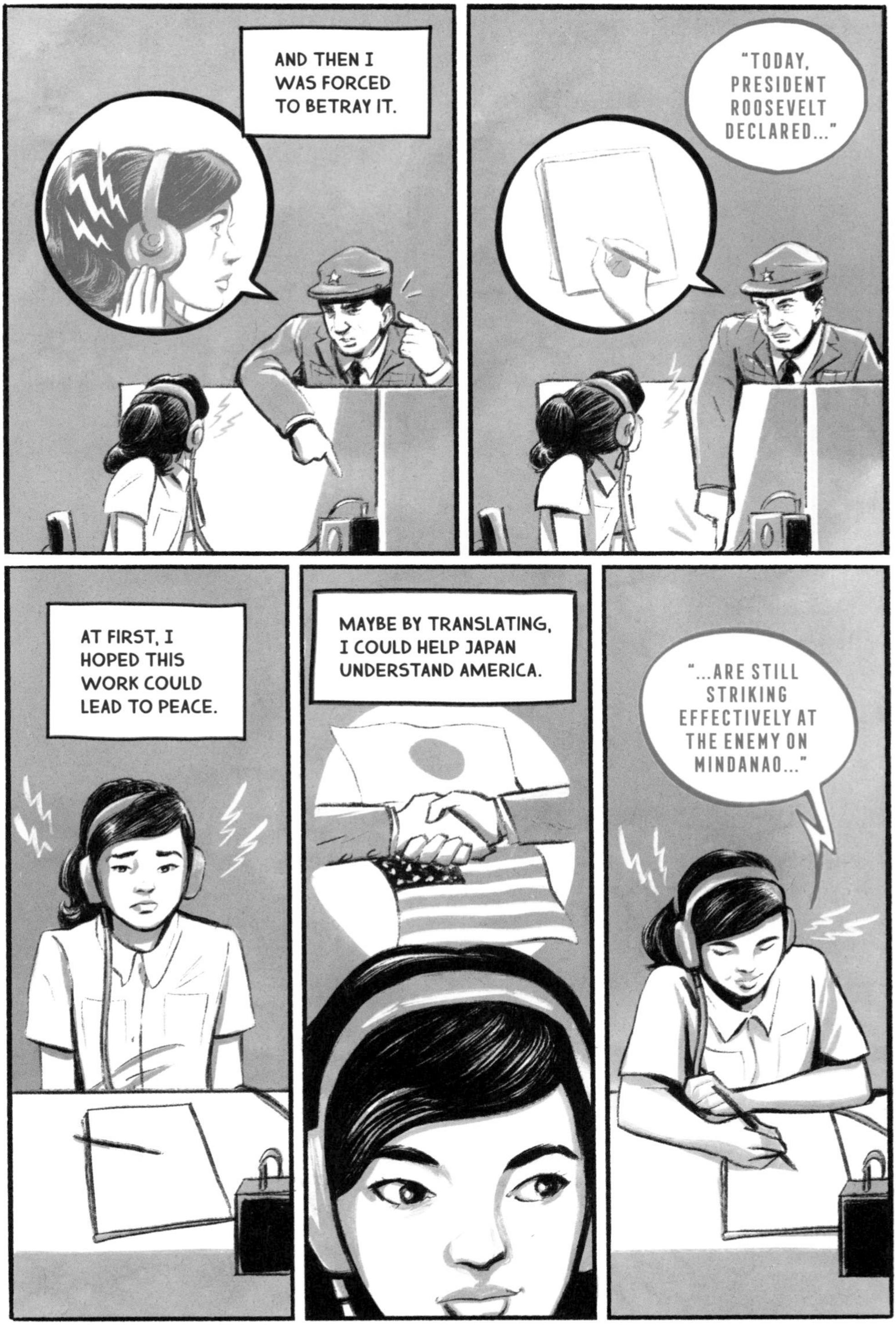
AND THEN I WAS FORCED TO BETRAY IT.
"TODAY, PRESIDENT ROOSEVELT DECLARED..."
AT FIRST, I HOPED THIS WORK COULD LEAD TO PEACE.
MAYBE BY TRANSLATING, I COULD HELP JAPAN UNDERSTAND AMERICA.
"...ARE STILL STRIKING EFFECTIVELY AT THE ENEMY ON MINDANAO..."

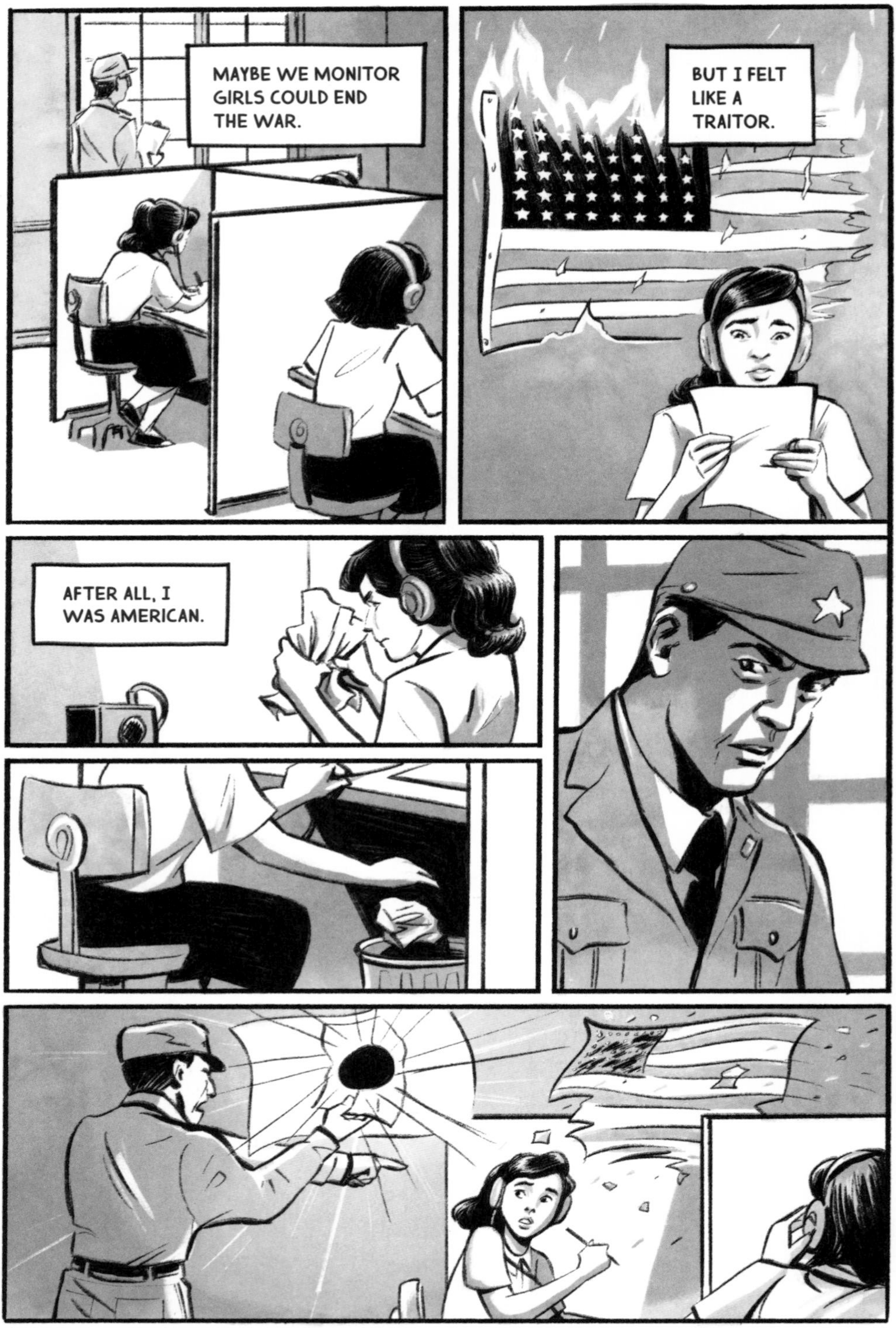
MAYBE WE MONITOR GIRLS COULD END THE WAR.
BUT I FELT LIKE A TRAITOR.
AFTER ALL, I WAS AMERICAN.

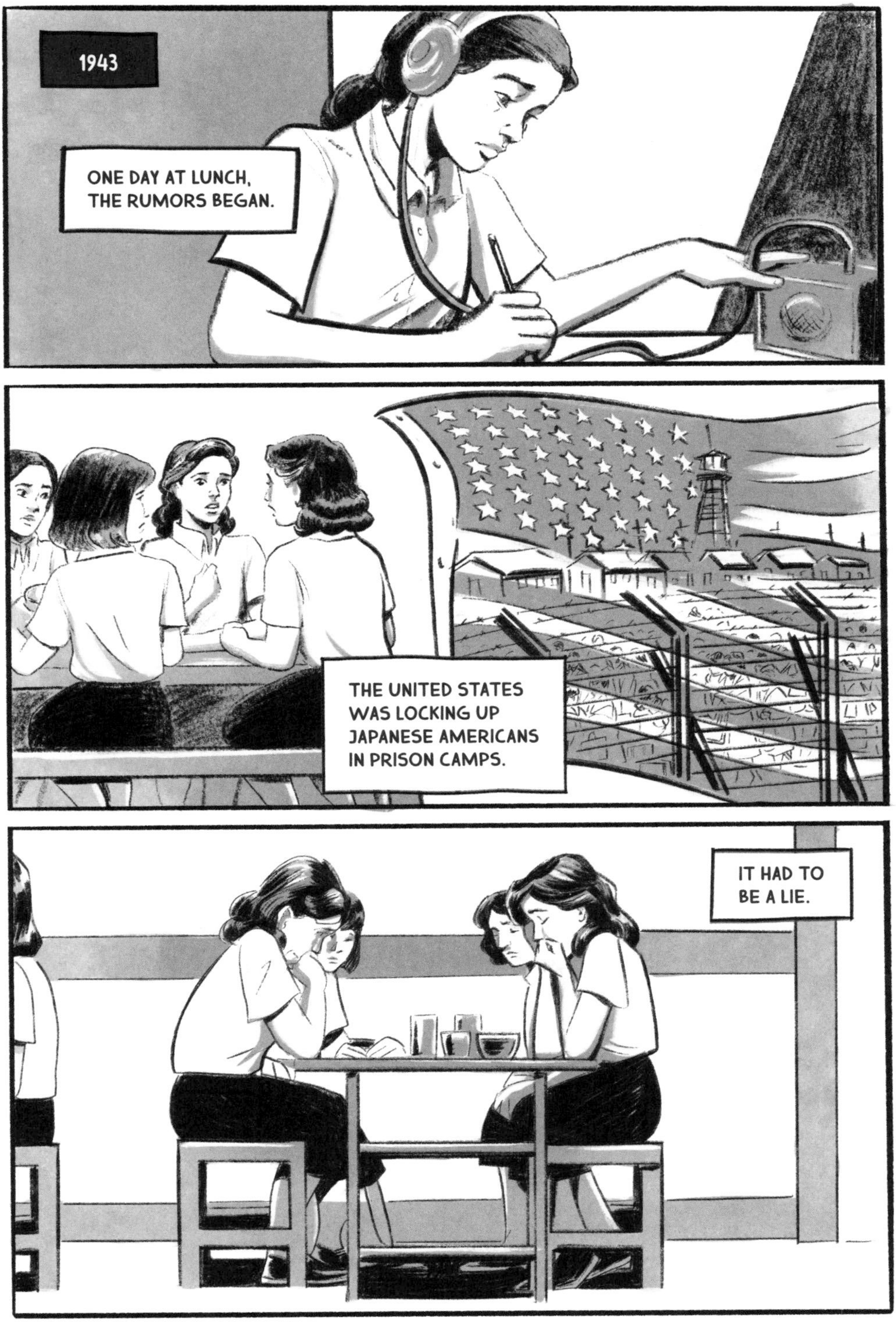
1943
ONE DAY AT LUNCH, THE RUMORS BEGAN.
THE UNITED STATES WAS LOCKING UP JAPANESE AMERICANS IN PRISON CAMPS.
IT HAD TO BE A LIE.

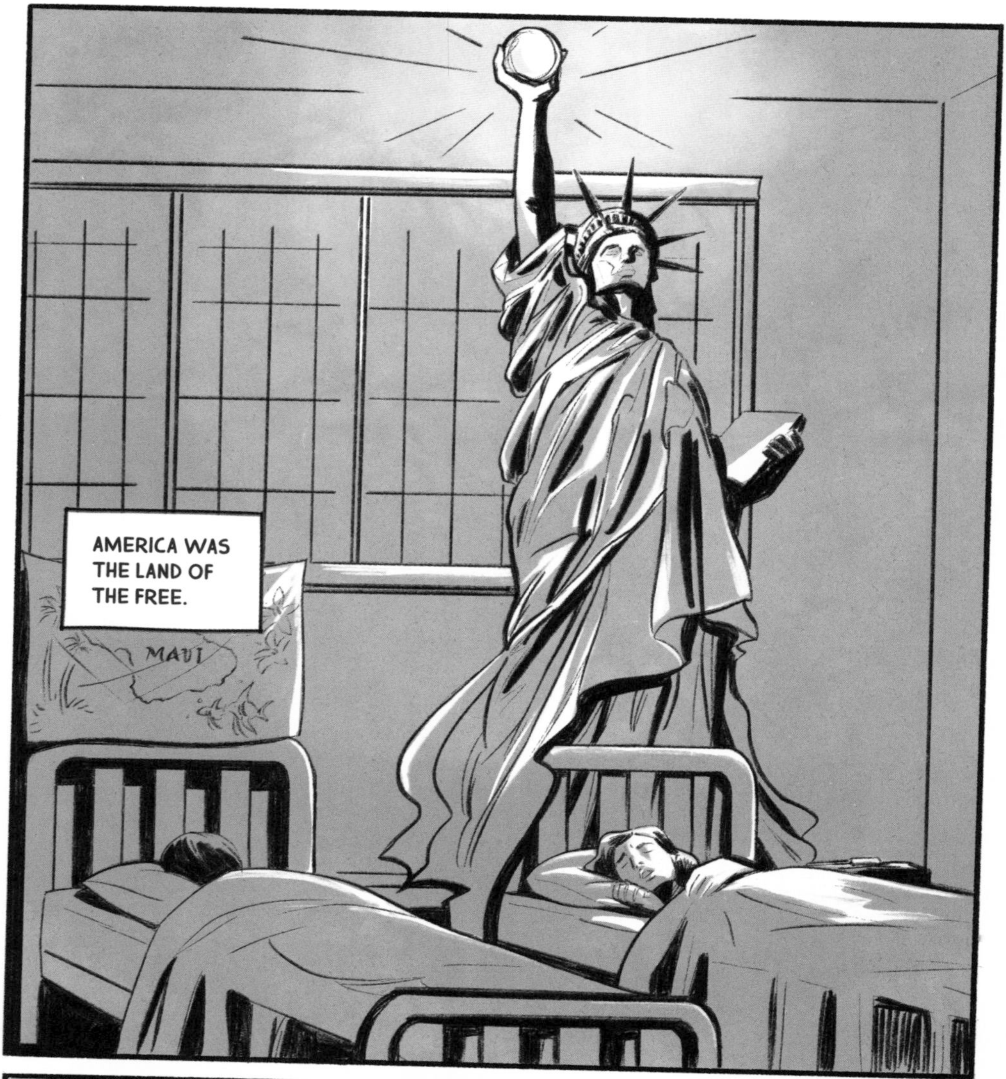
AMERICA WAS THE LAND OF THE FREE.
MAUI

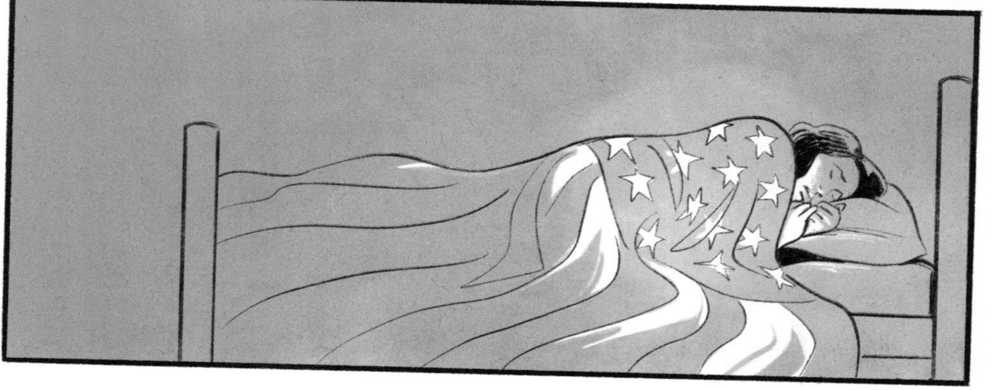

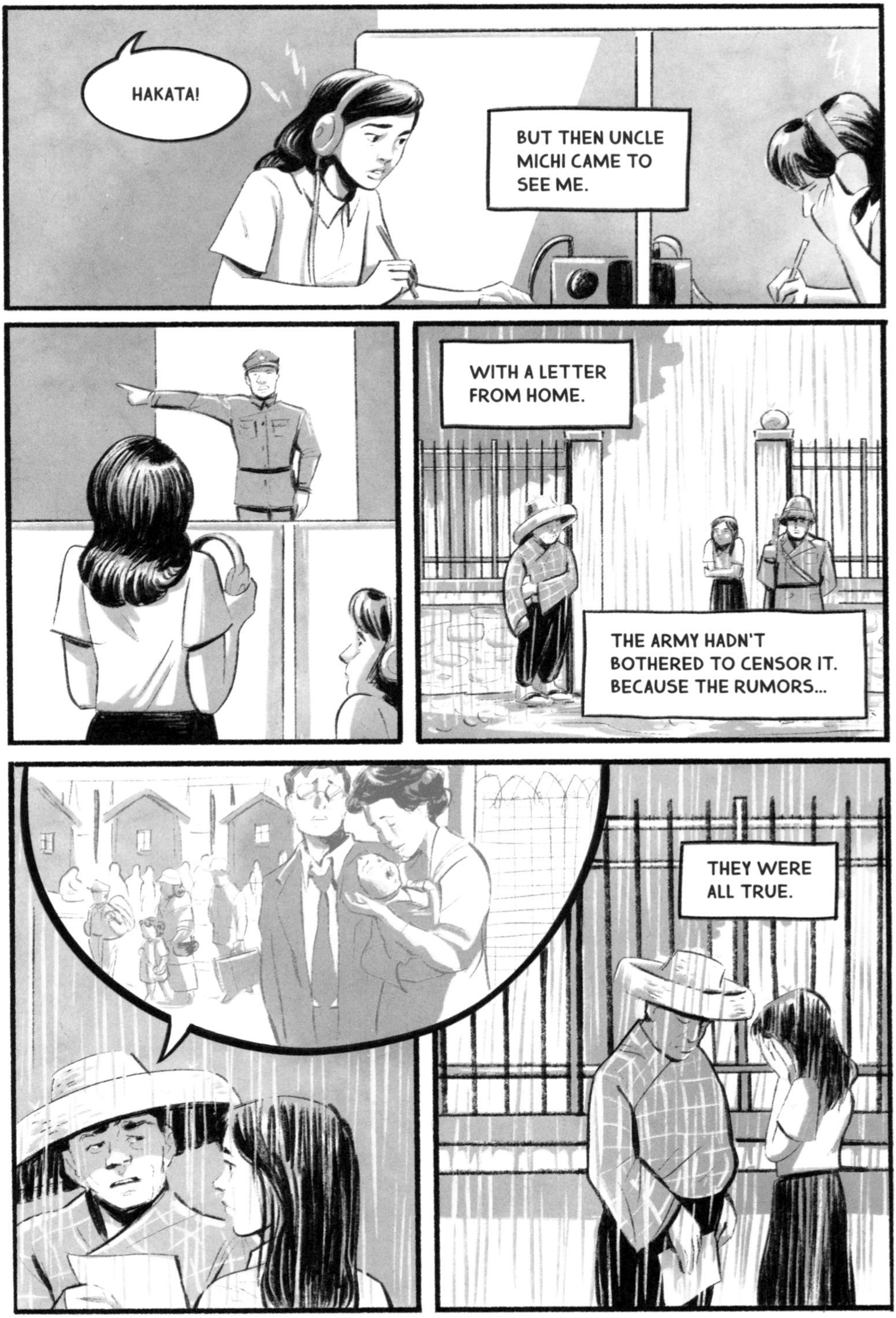
HAKATA!
BUT THEN UNCLE MICHI CAME TO SEE ME.
WITH A LETTER FROM HOME.
THE ARMY HADN'T BOTHERED TO CENSOR IT. BECAUSE THE RUMORS...
THEY WERE ALL TRUE.

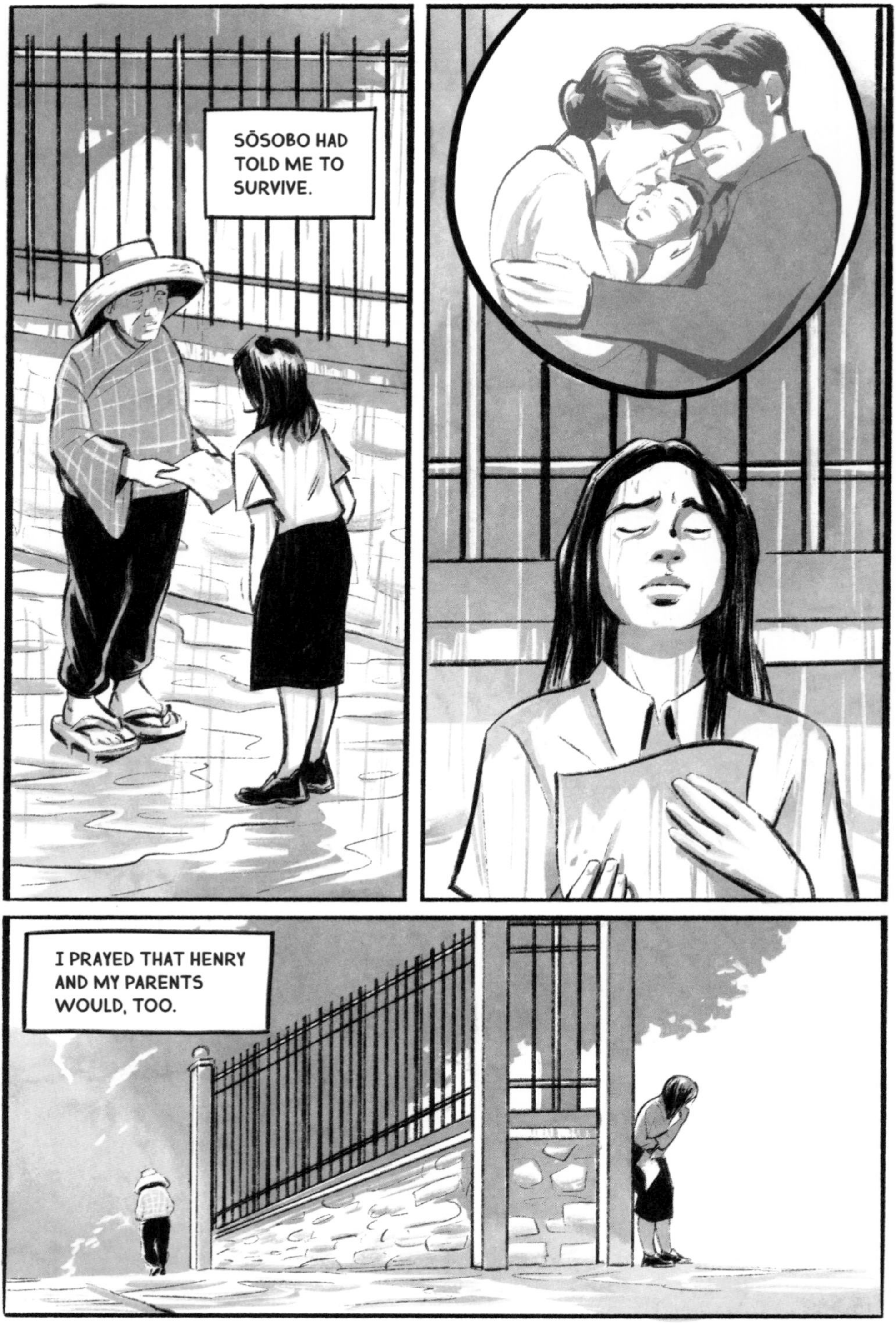
SŌSOBO HAD TOLD ME TO SURVIVE.
I PRAYED THAT HENRY AND MY PARENTS WOULD, TOO.

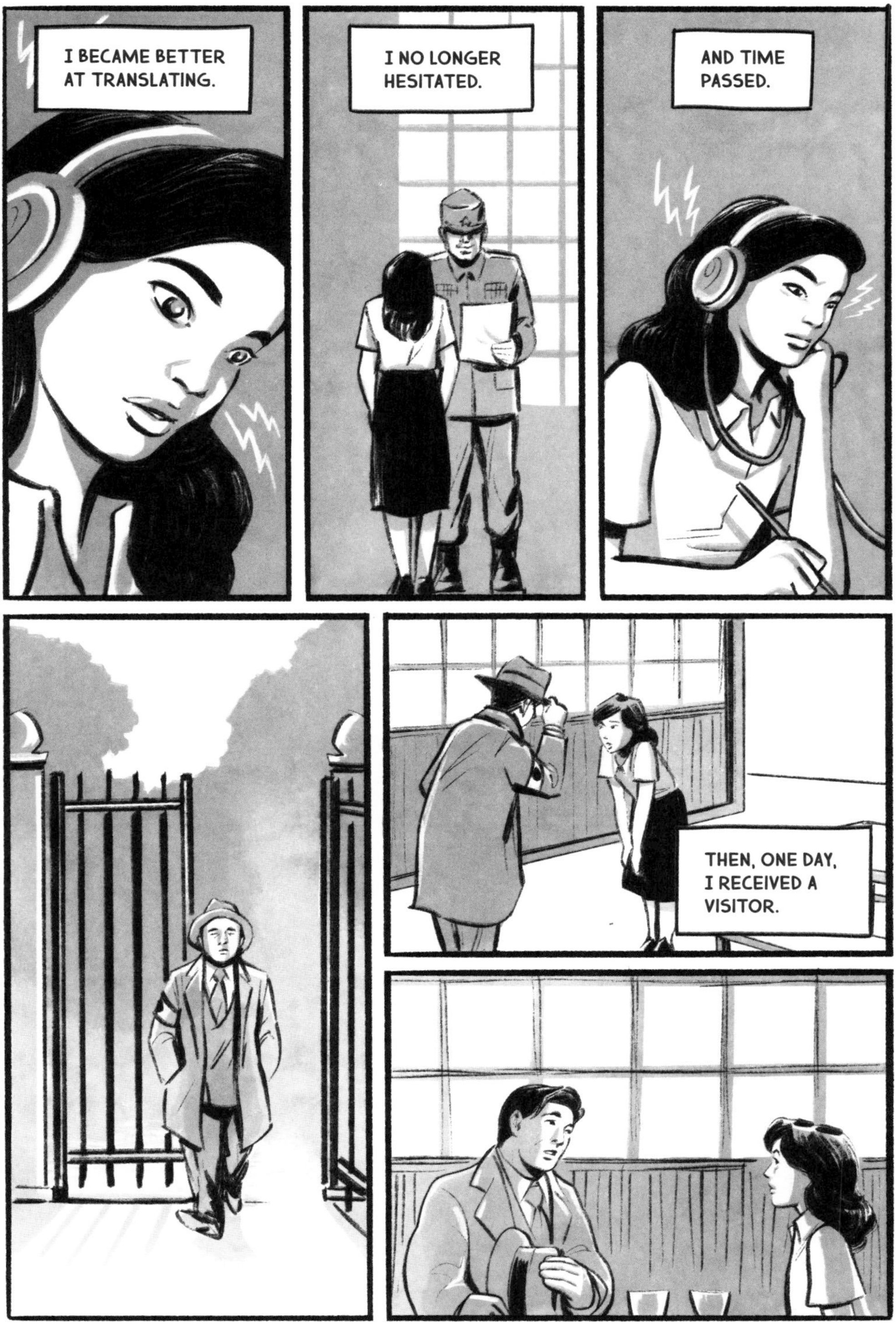
I BECAME BETTER AT TRANSLATING.
I NO LONGER HESITATED.
AND TIME PASSED.
THEN, ONE DAY, I RECEIVED A VISITOR.

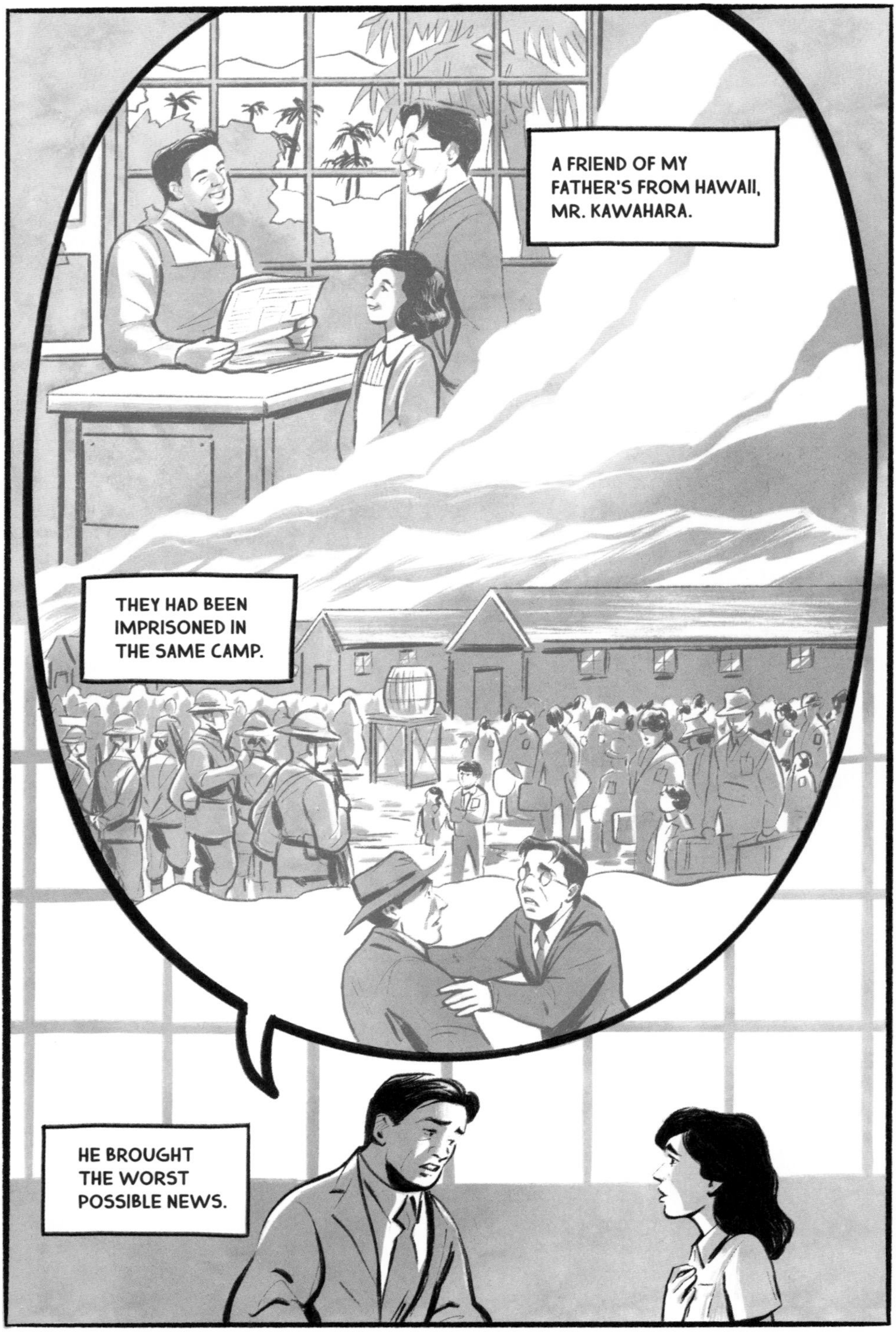
A FRIEND OF MY FATHER'S FROM HAWAII, MR. KAWAHARA.
THEY HAD BEEN IMPRISONED IN THE SAME CAMP.
HE BROUGHT THE WORST POSSIBLE NEWS.

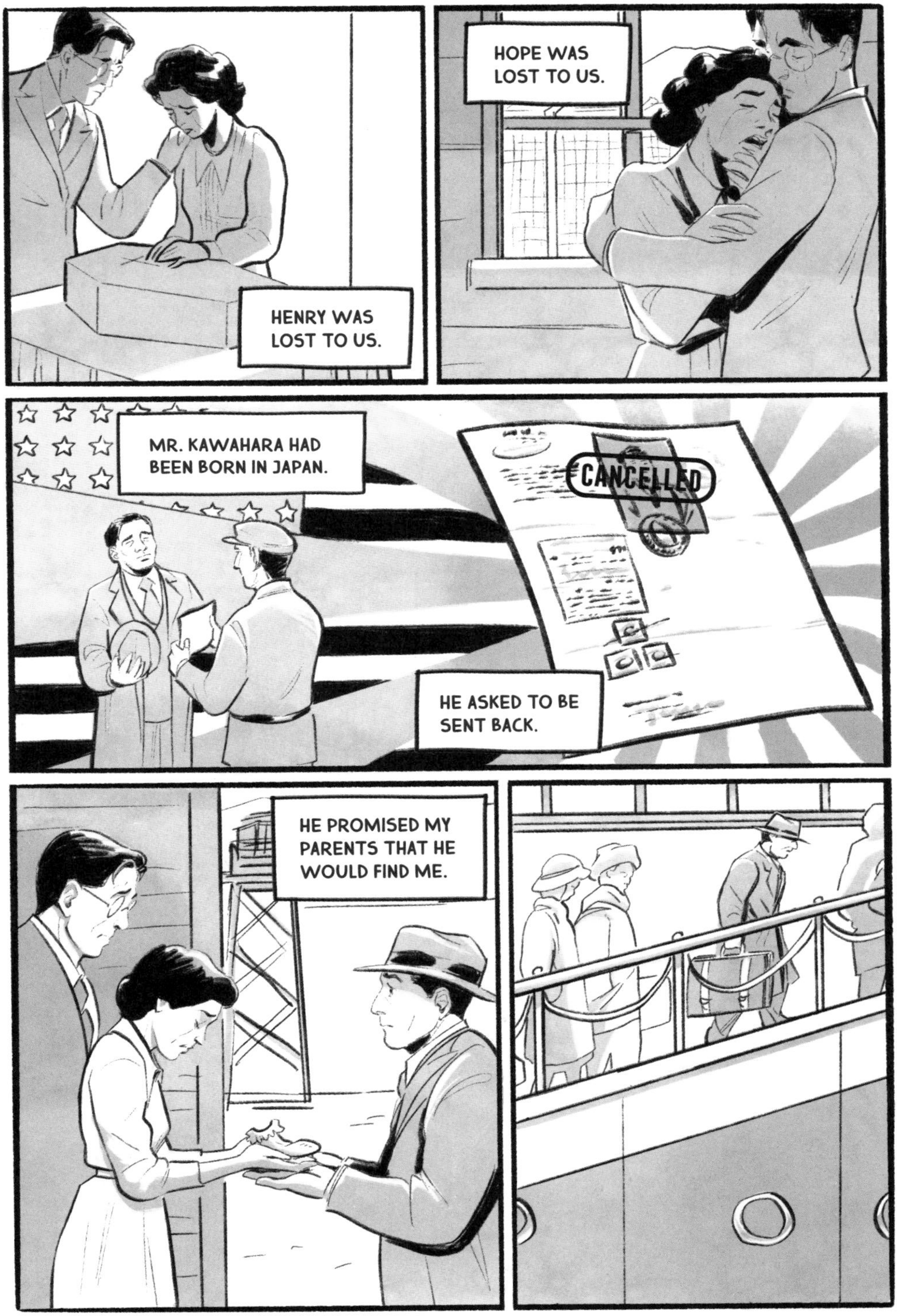
HENRY WAS
LOST TO US.
HOPE WAS
LOST TO US.
MR. KAWAHARA HAD
BEEN BORN IN JAPAN.
CANCELLED
HE ASKED TO BE
SENT BACK.
HE PROMISED MY
PARENTS THAT HE
WOULD FIND ME.

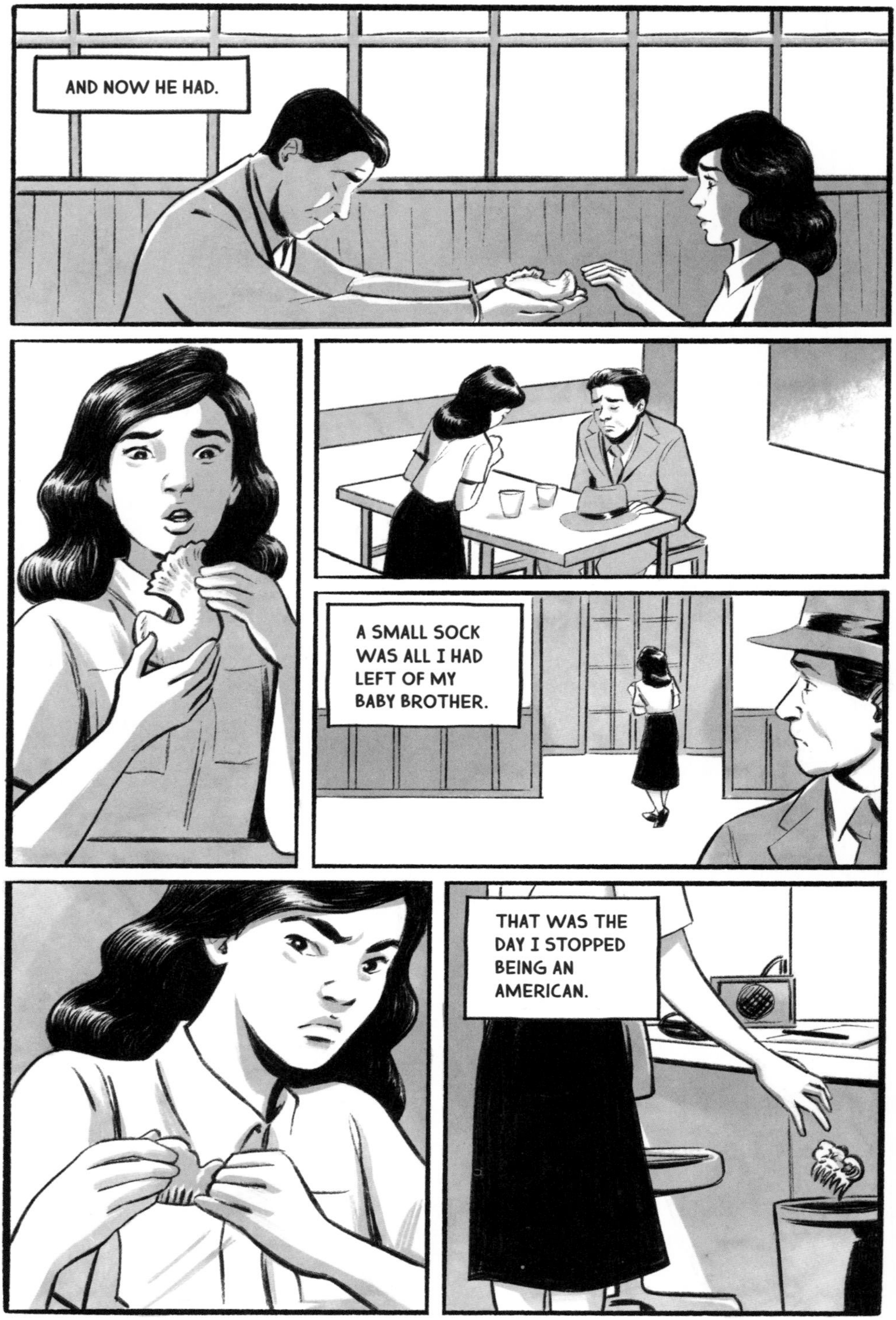
AND NOW HE HAD.
A SMALL SOCK WAS ALL I HAD LEFT OF MY BABY BROTHER.
THAT WAS THE DAY I STOPPED BEING AN AMERICAN.

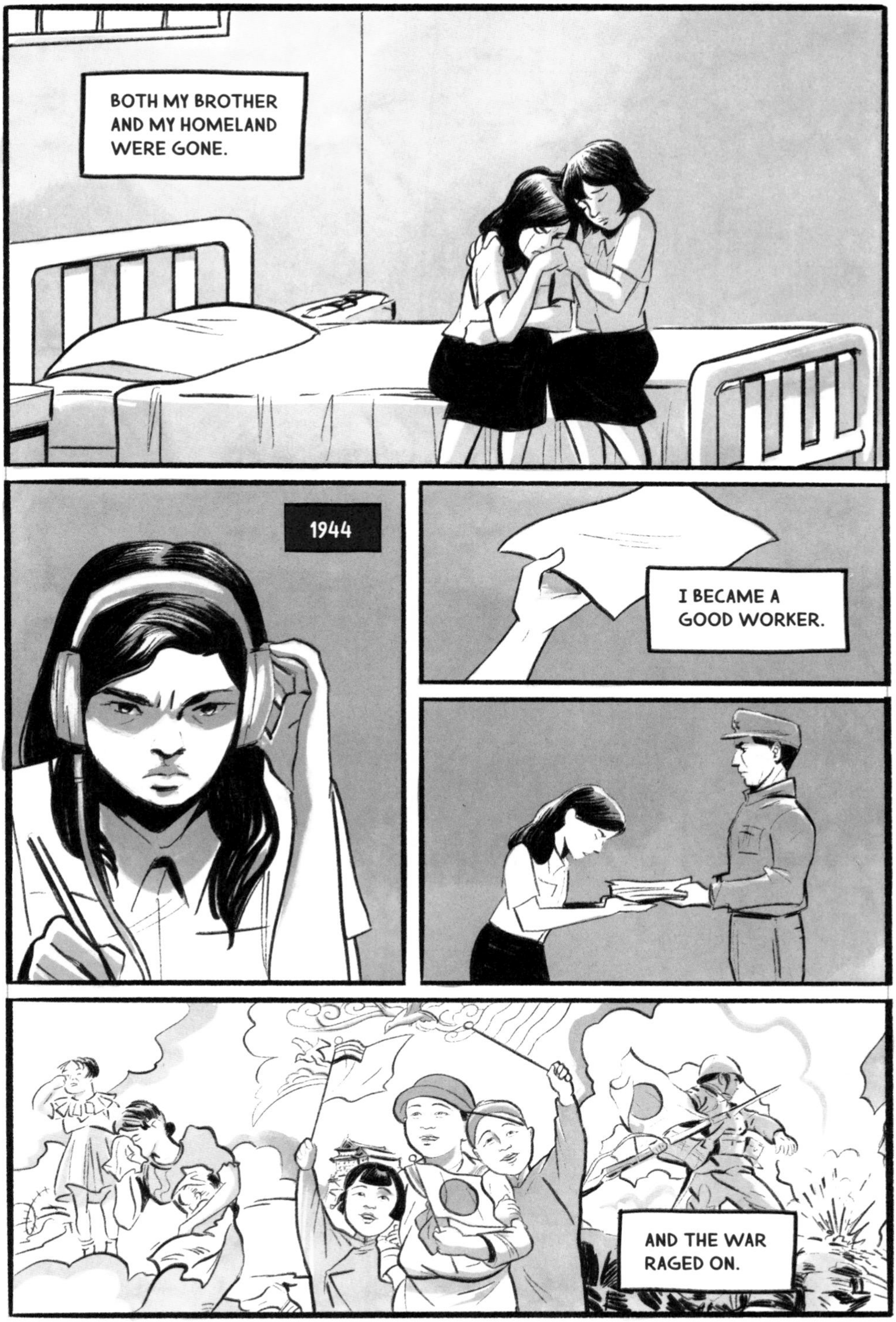
BOTH MY BROTHER AND MY HOMELAND WERE GONE.
1944
I BECAME A GOOD WORKER.
AND THE WAR RAGED ON.

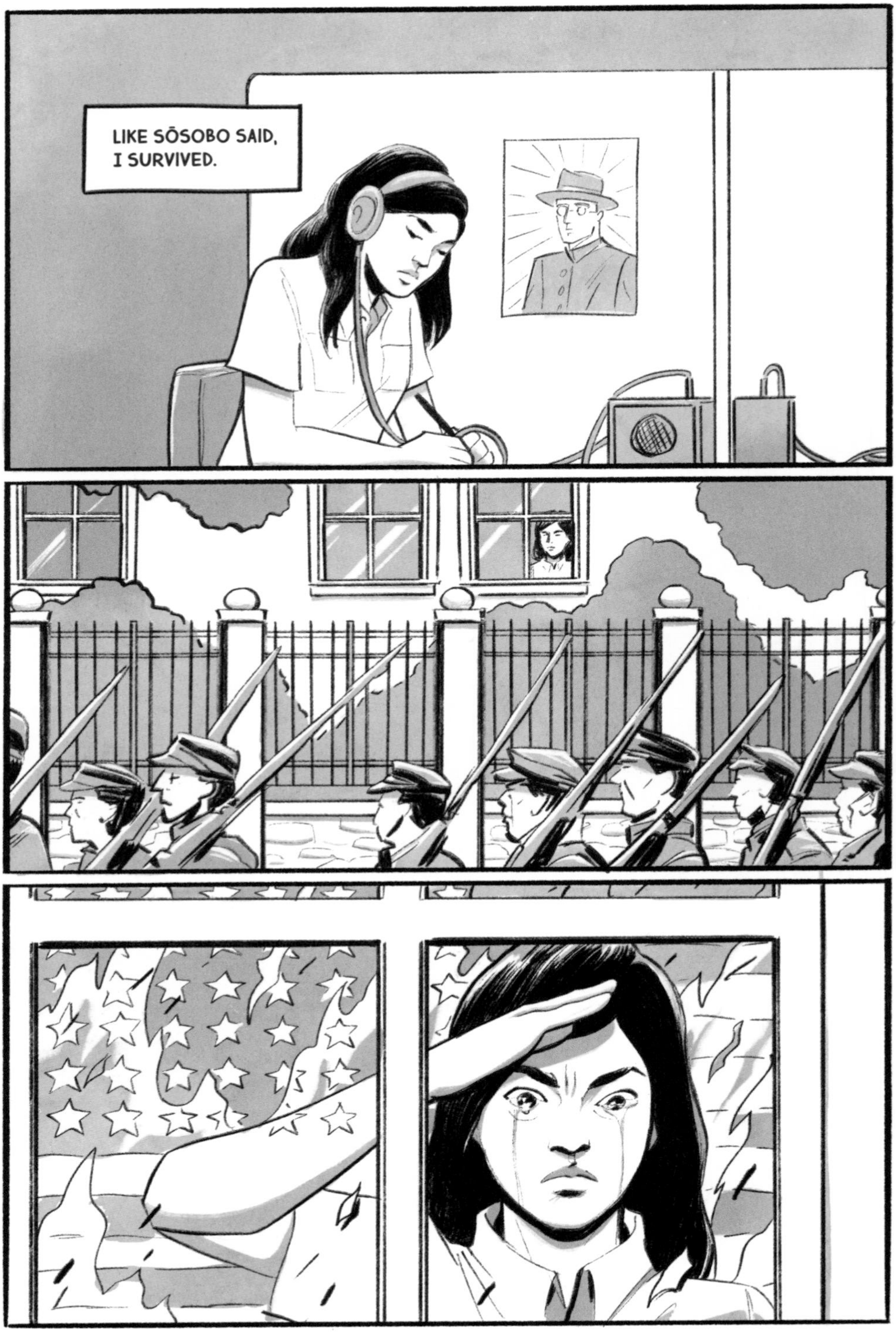
LIKE SŌSOBO SAID,
I SURVIVED.

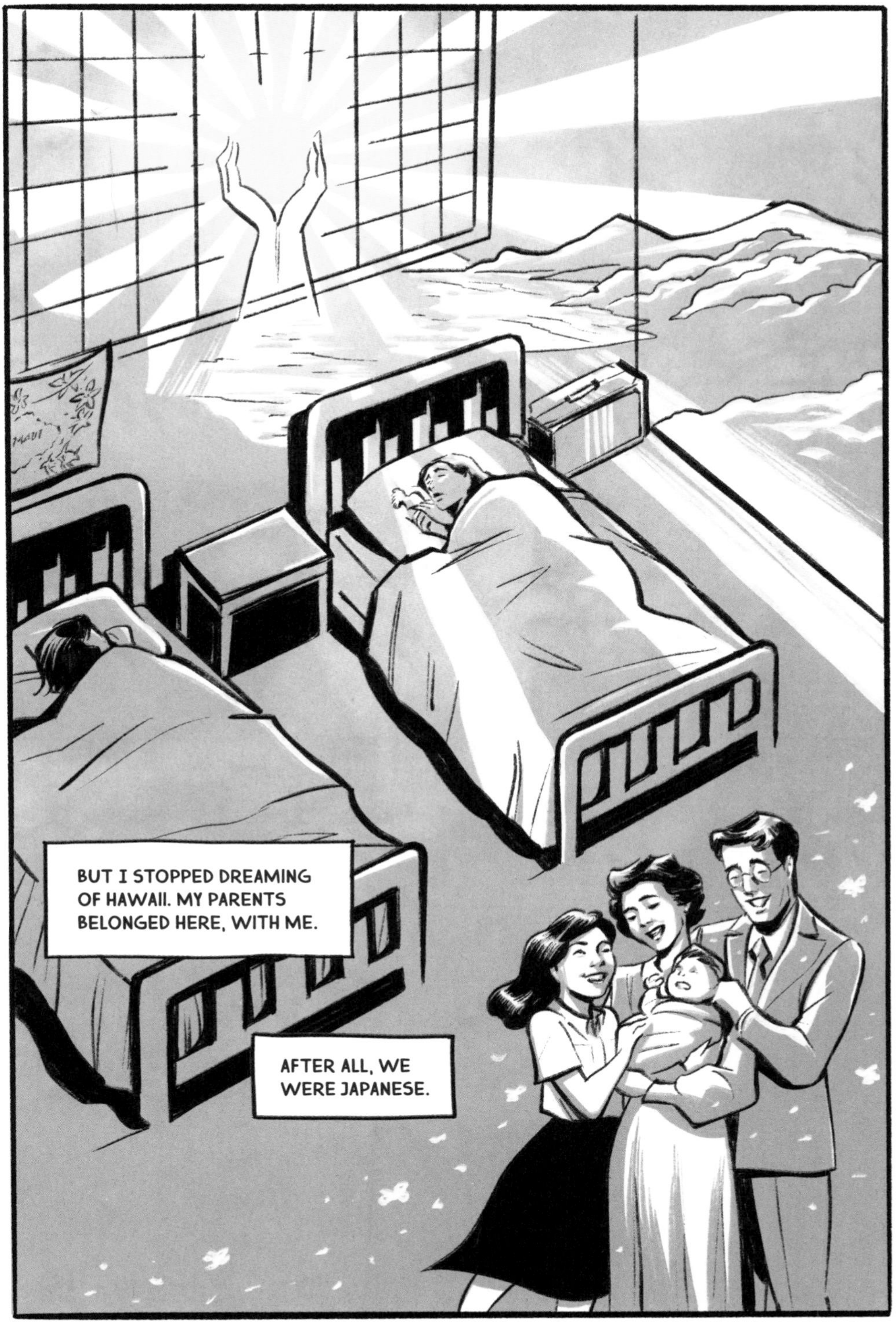
MAUI
BUT I STOPPED DREAMING OF HAWAII. MY PARENTS BELONGED HERE, WITH ME.
AFTER ALL, WE WERE JAPANESE.

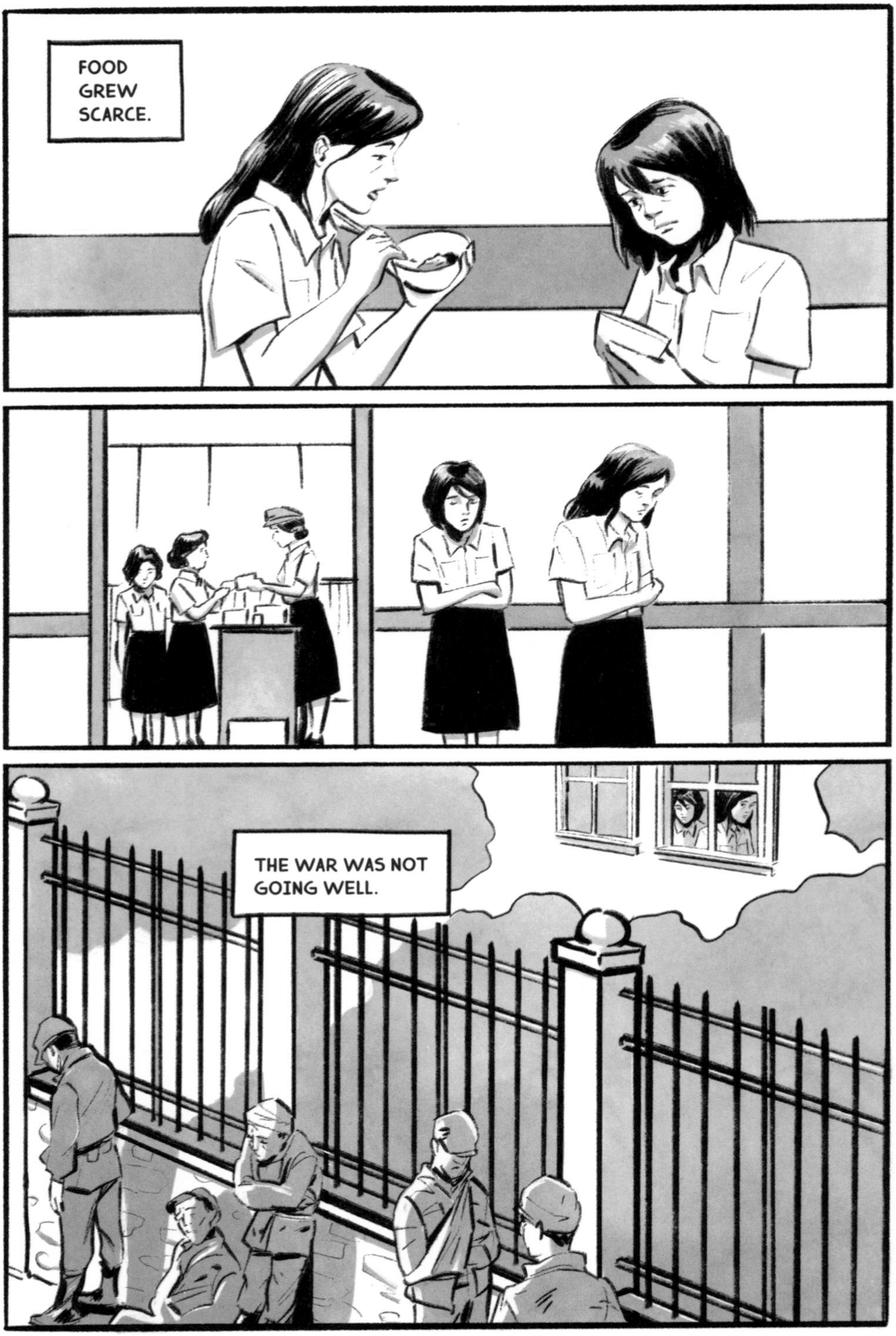
FOOD GROW SCARCE.
THE WAR WAS NOT GOING WELL.

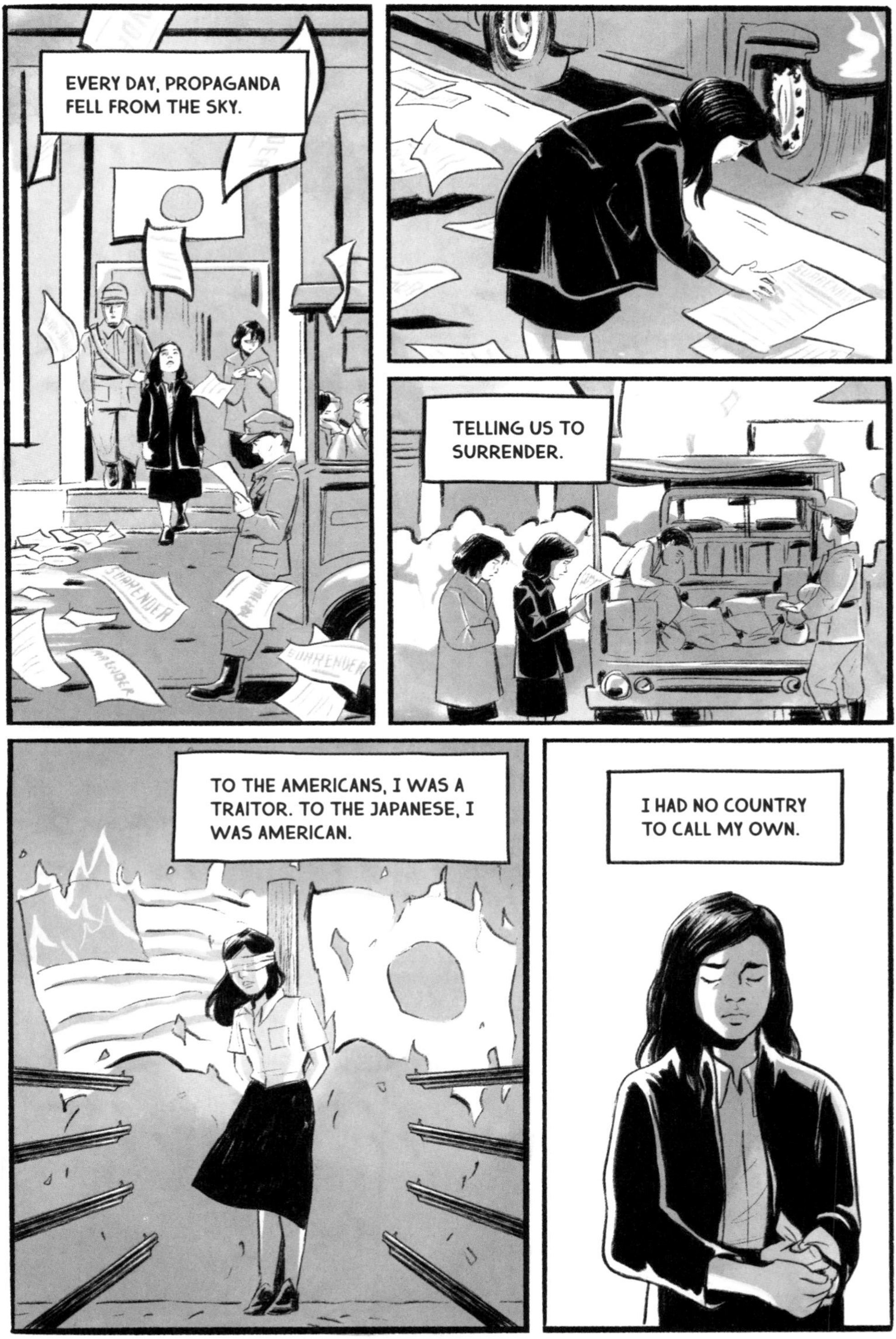
EVERY DAY, PROPAGANDA FELL FROM THE SKY.
SURRENDER
SURRENDER
SURRENDER
TELLING US TO SURRENDER.
TO THE AMERICANS, I WAS A TRAITOR. TO THE JAPANESE, I WAS AMERICAN.
I HAD NO COUNTRY TO CALL MY OWN.

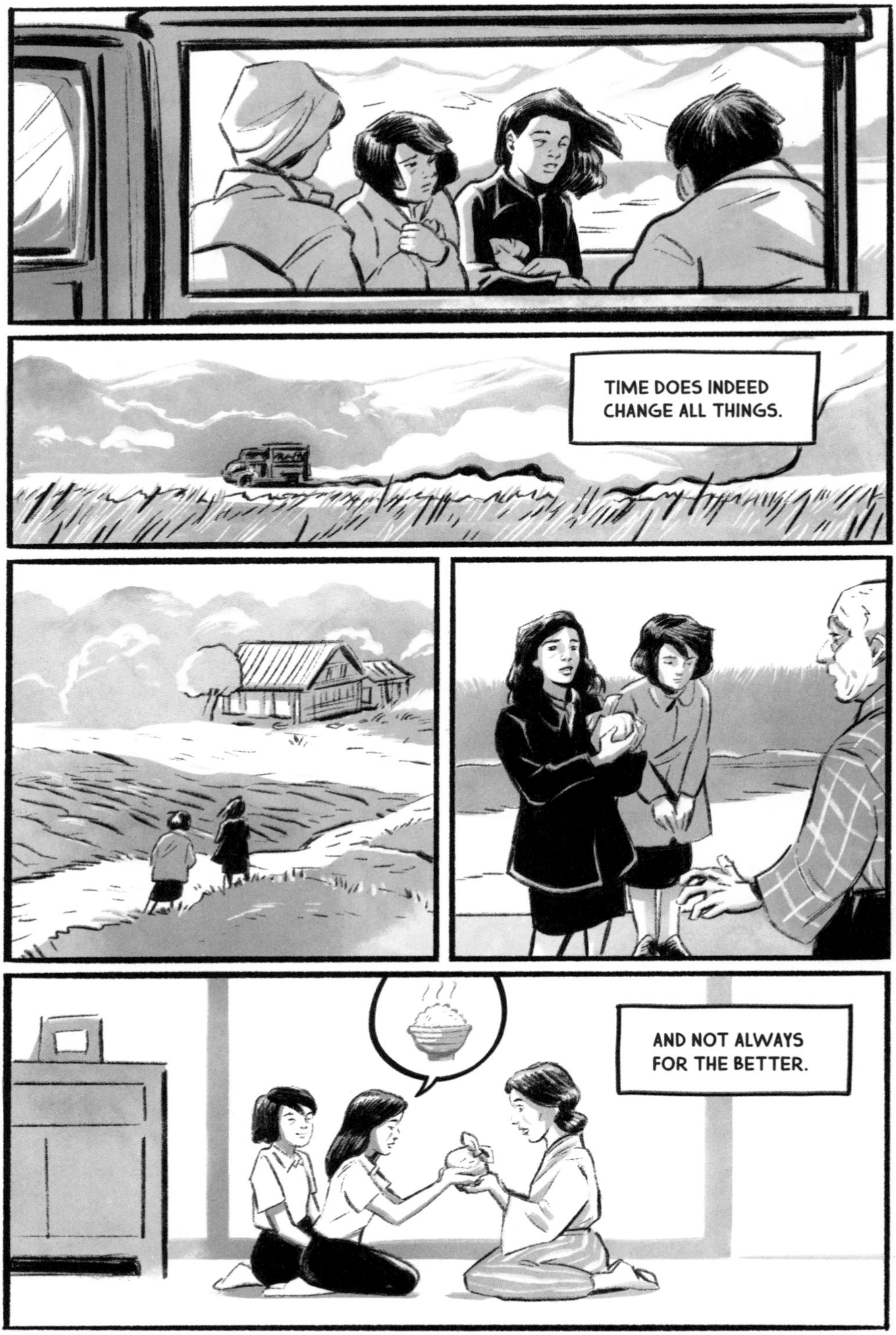
TIME DOES INDEED CHANGE ALL THINGS.
AND NOT ALWAYS FOR THE BETTER.

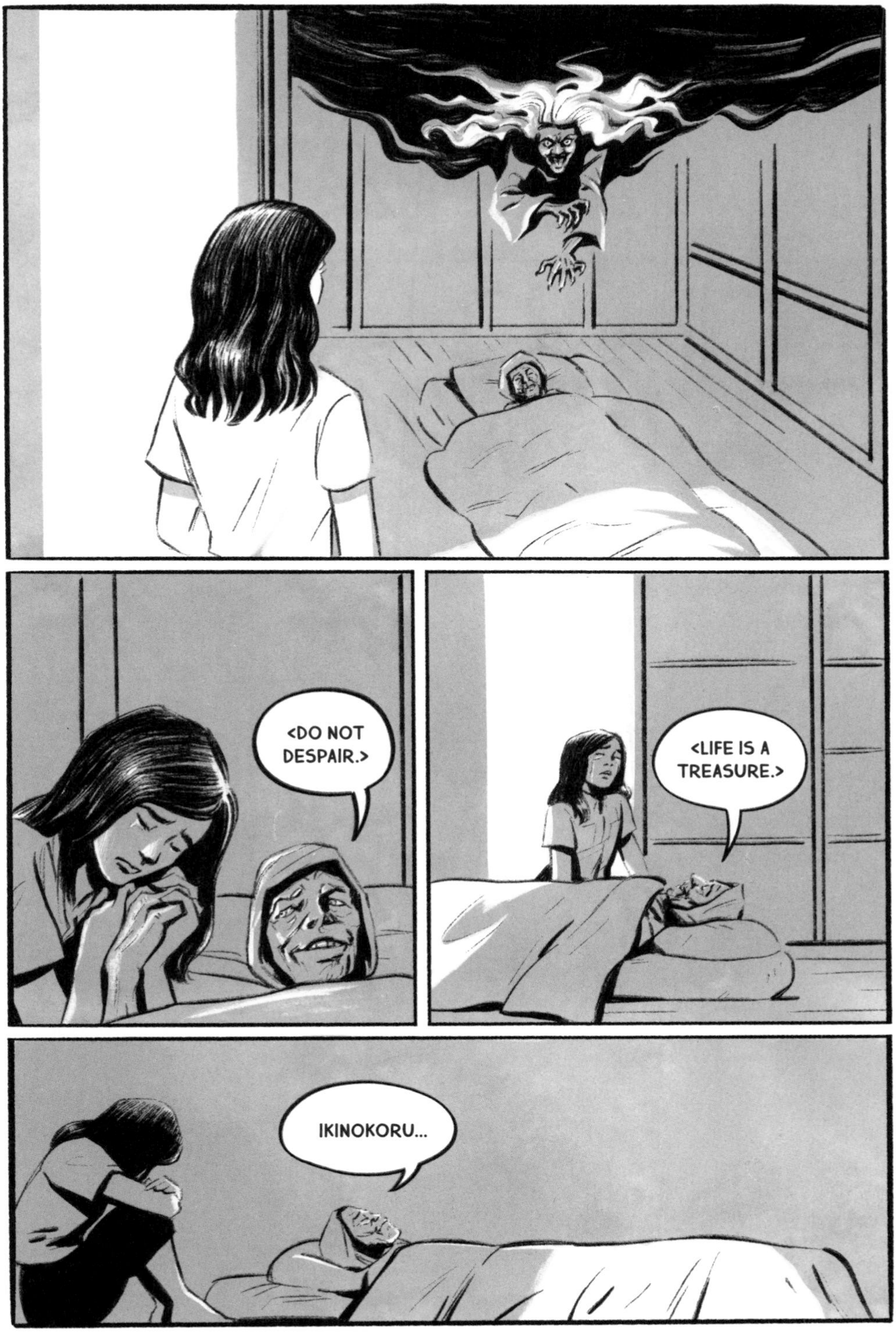
<DO NOT DESPAIR.>
<LIFE IS A TREASURE.>
IKINOKORU...

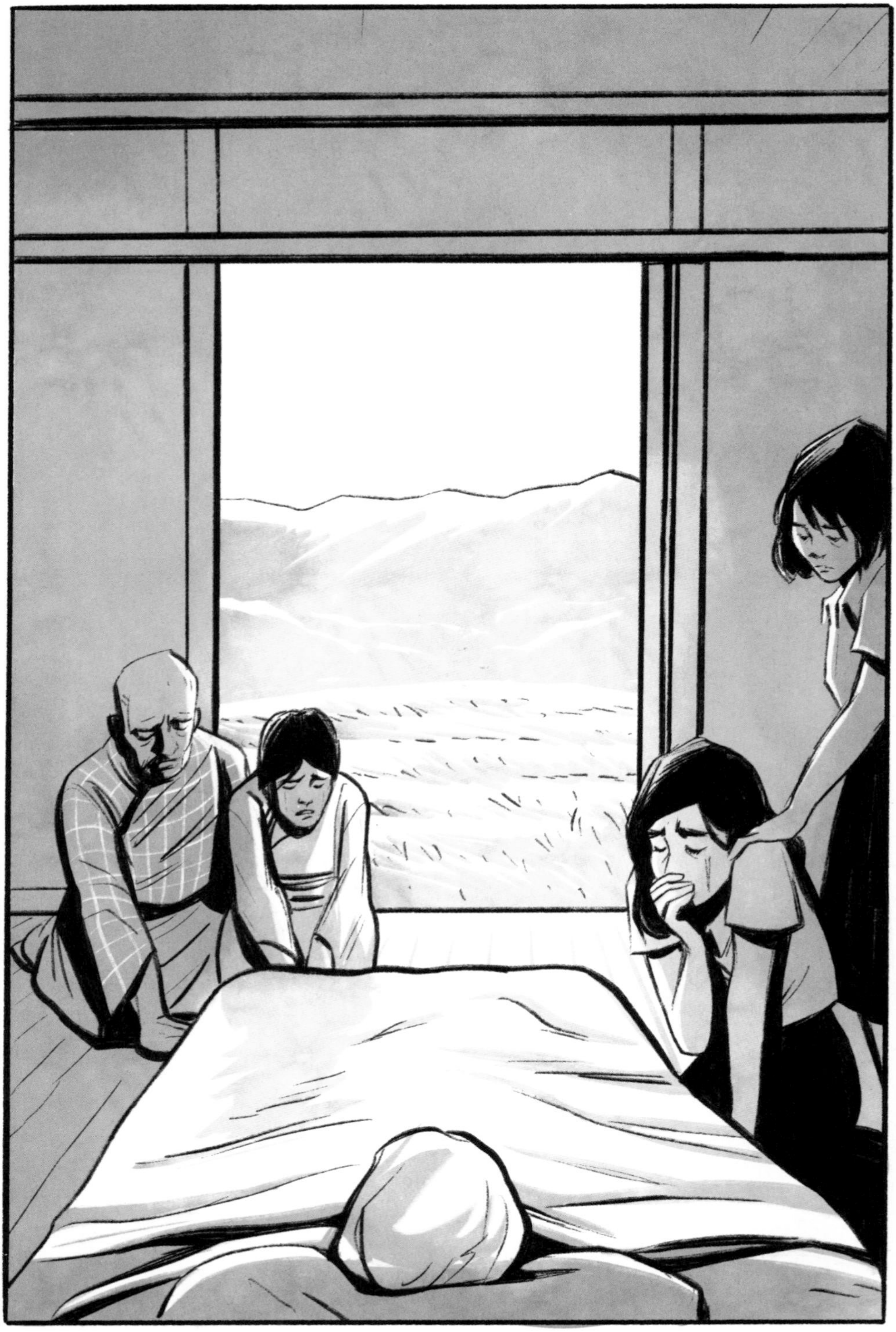

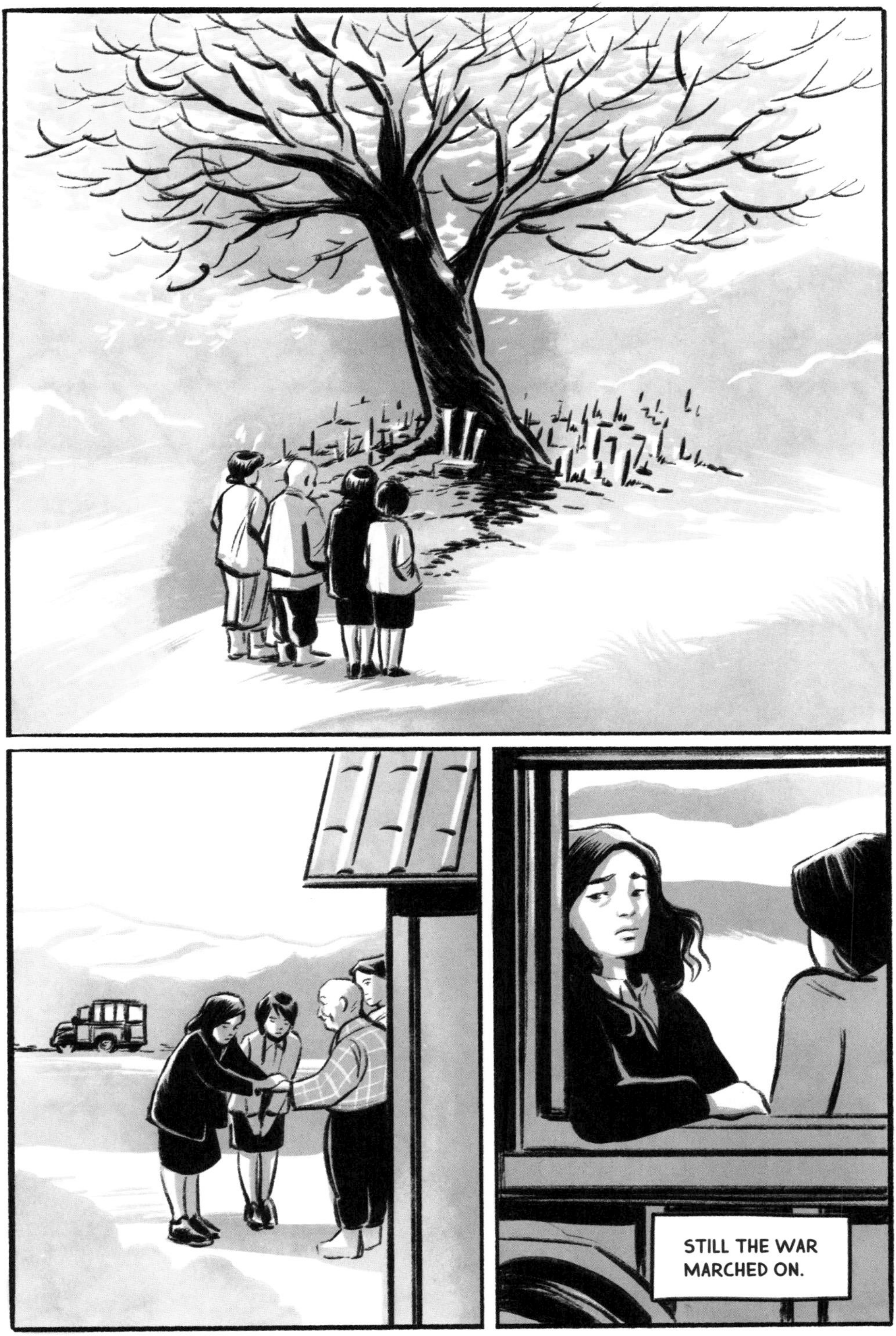
STILL THE WAR
MARCHED ON.

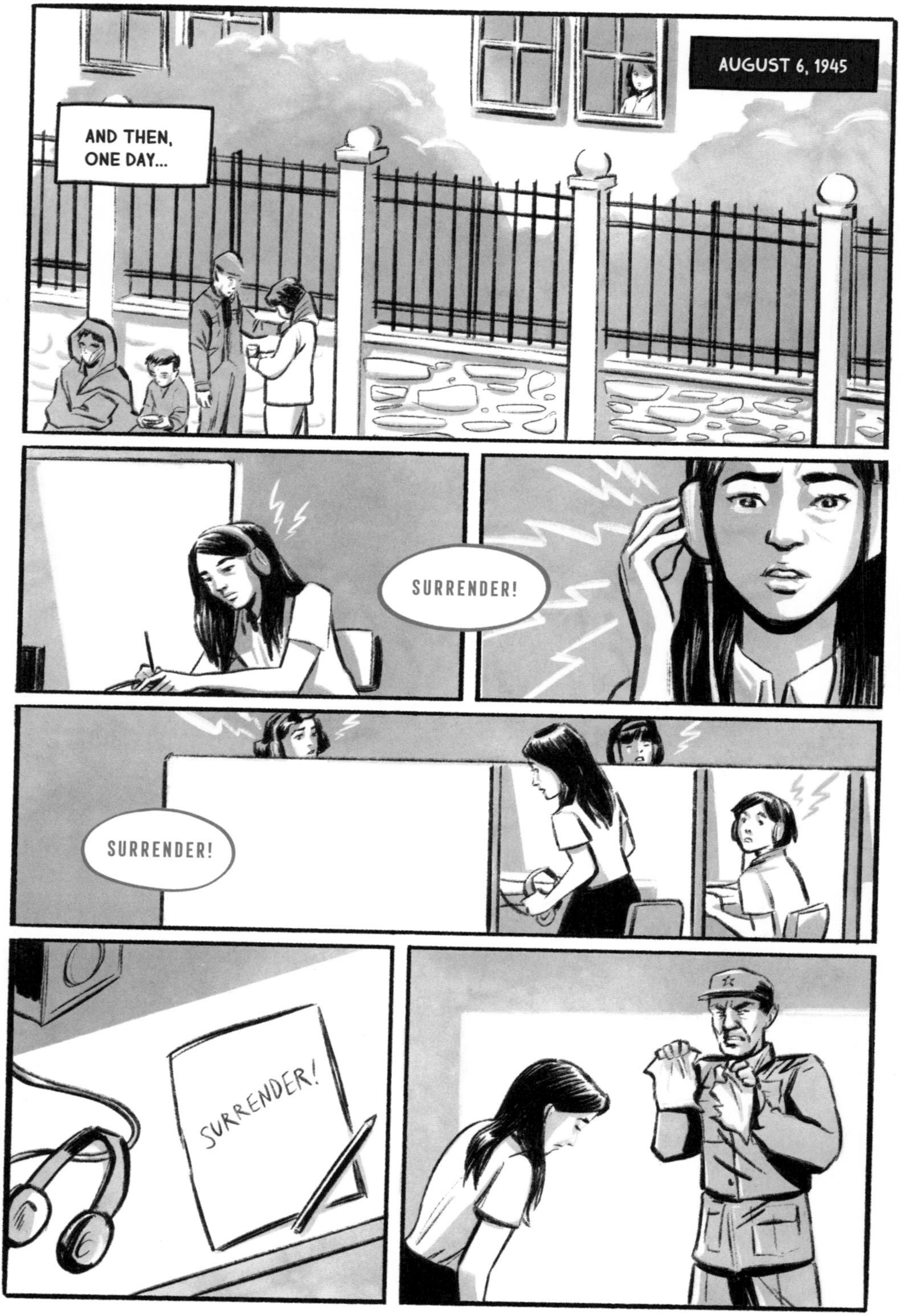
AUGUST 6, 1945
AND THEN, ONE DAY...
SURRENDER!
SURRENDER!
SURRENDER!

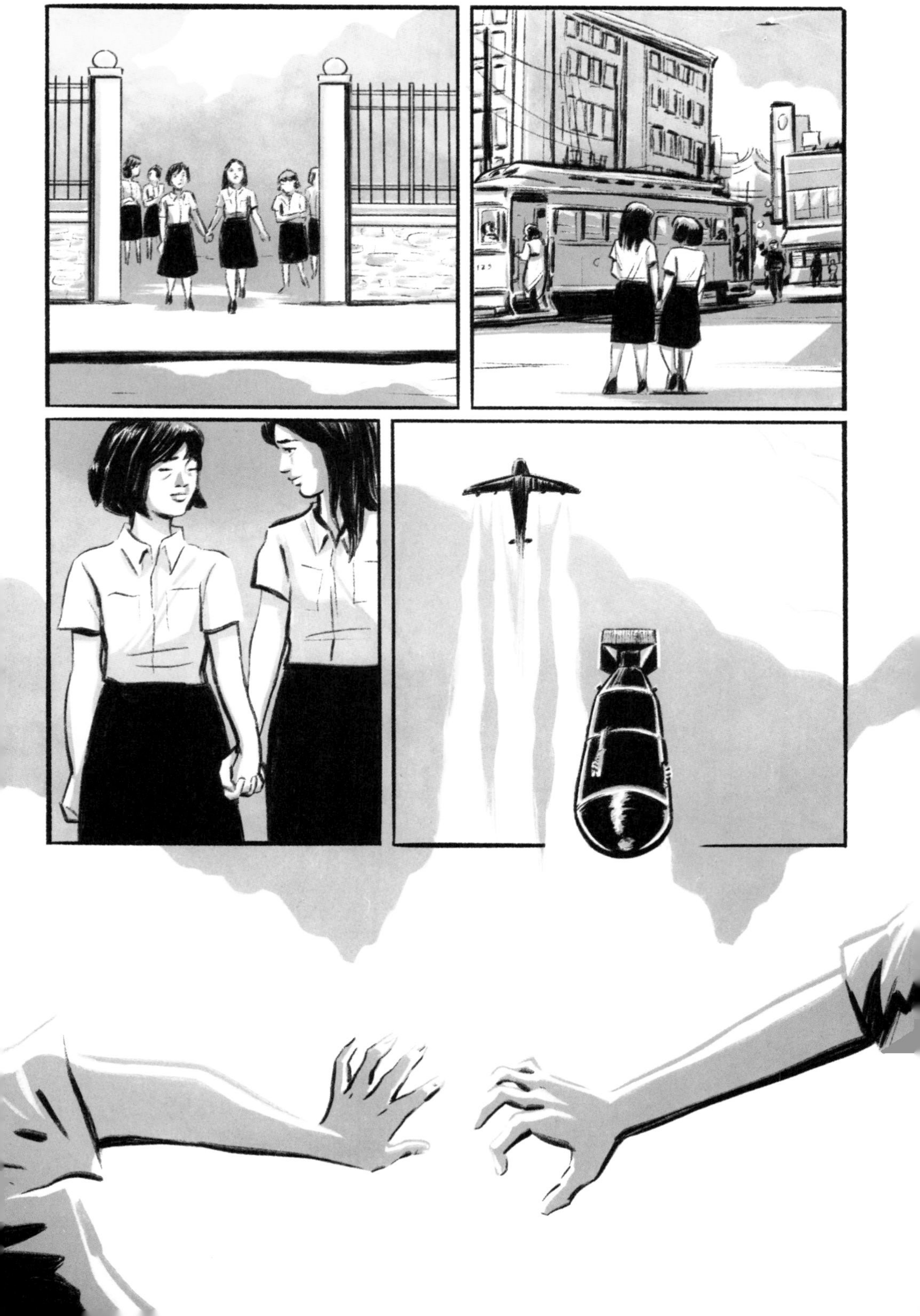

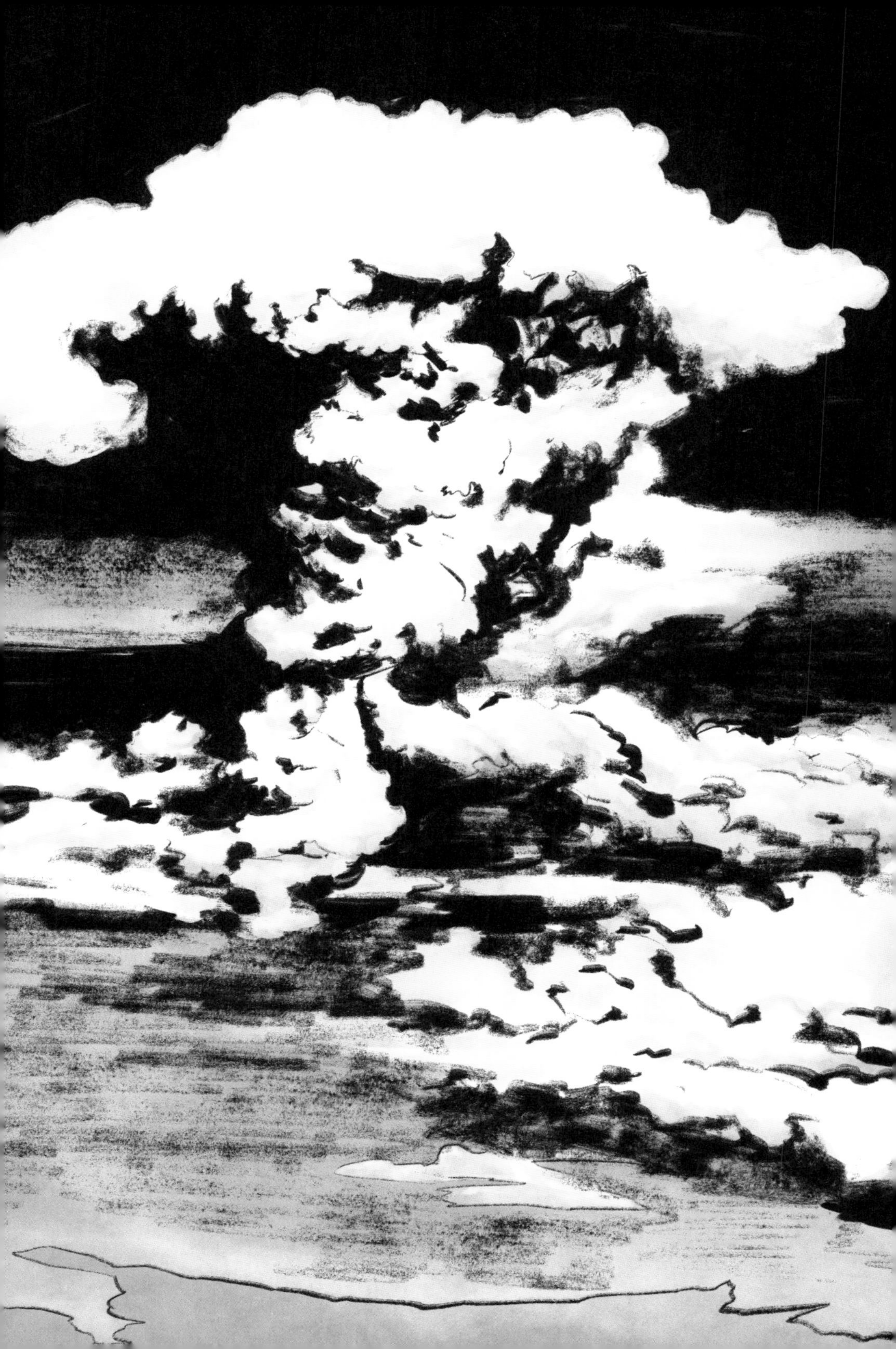

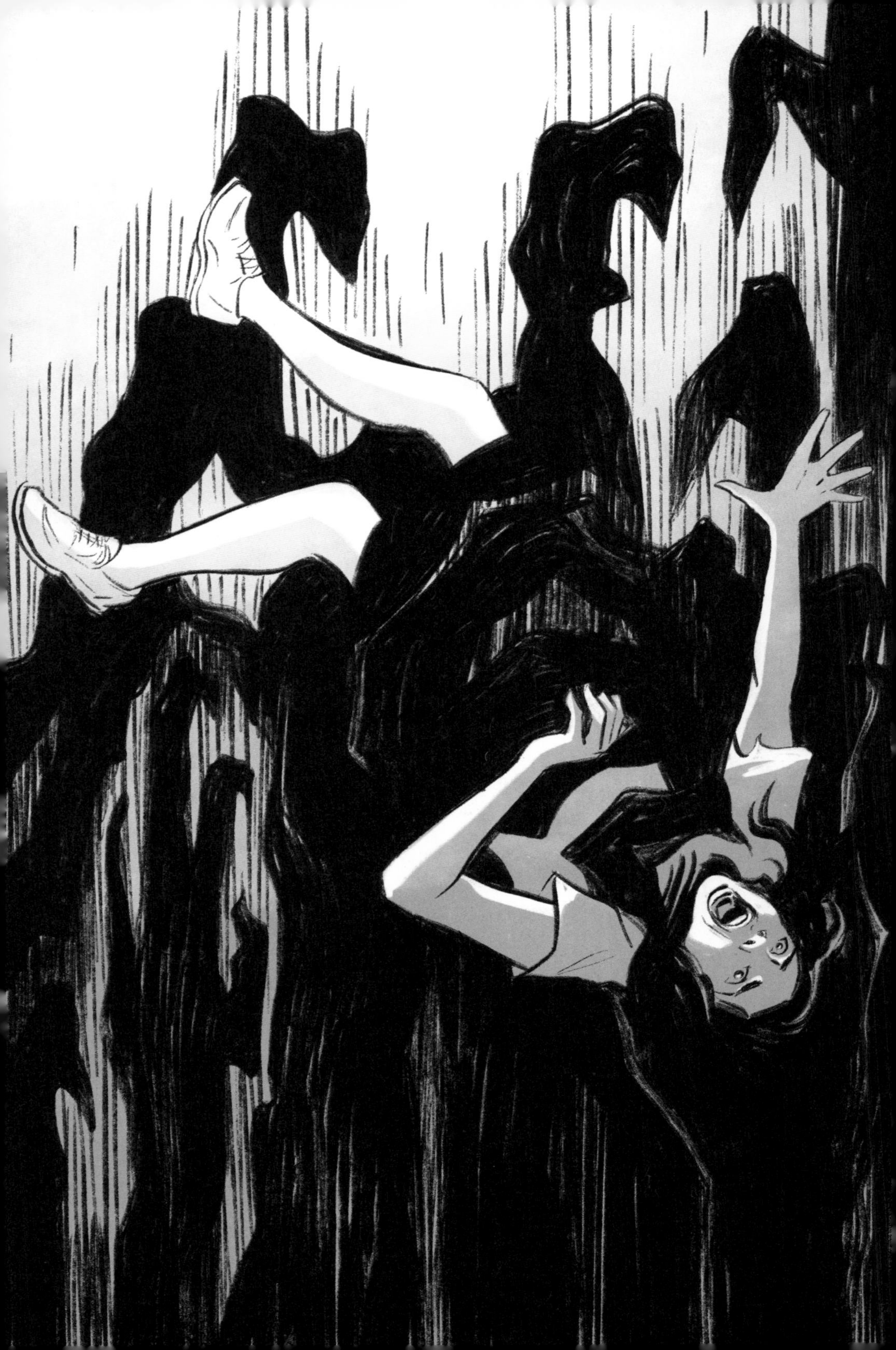

# HIBAKUSHA

SURVIVOR

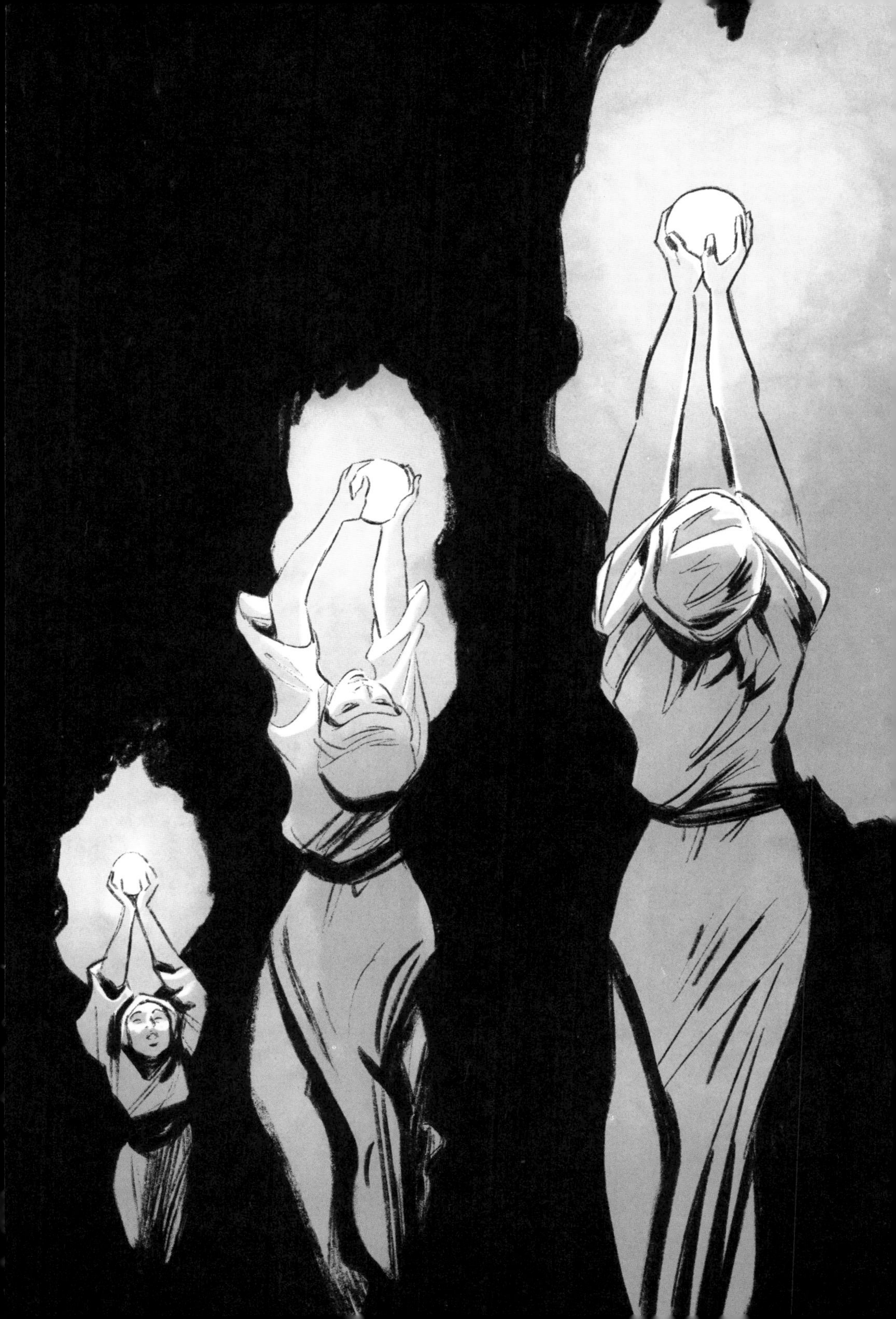

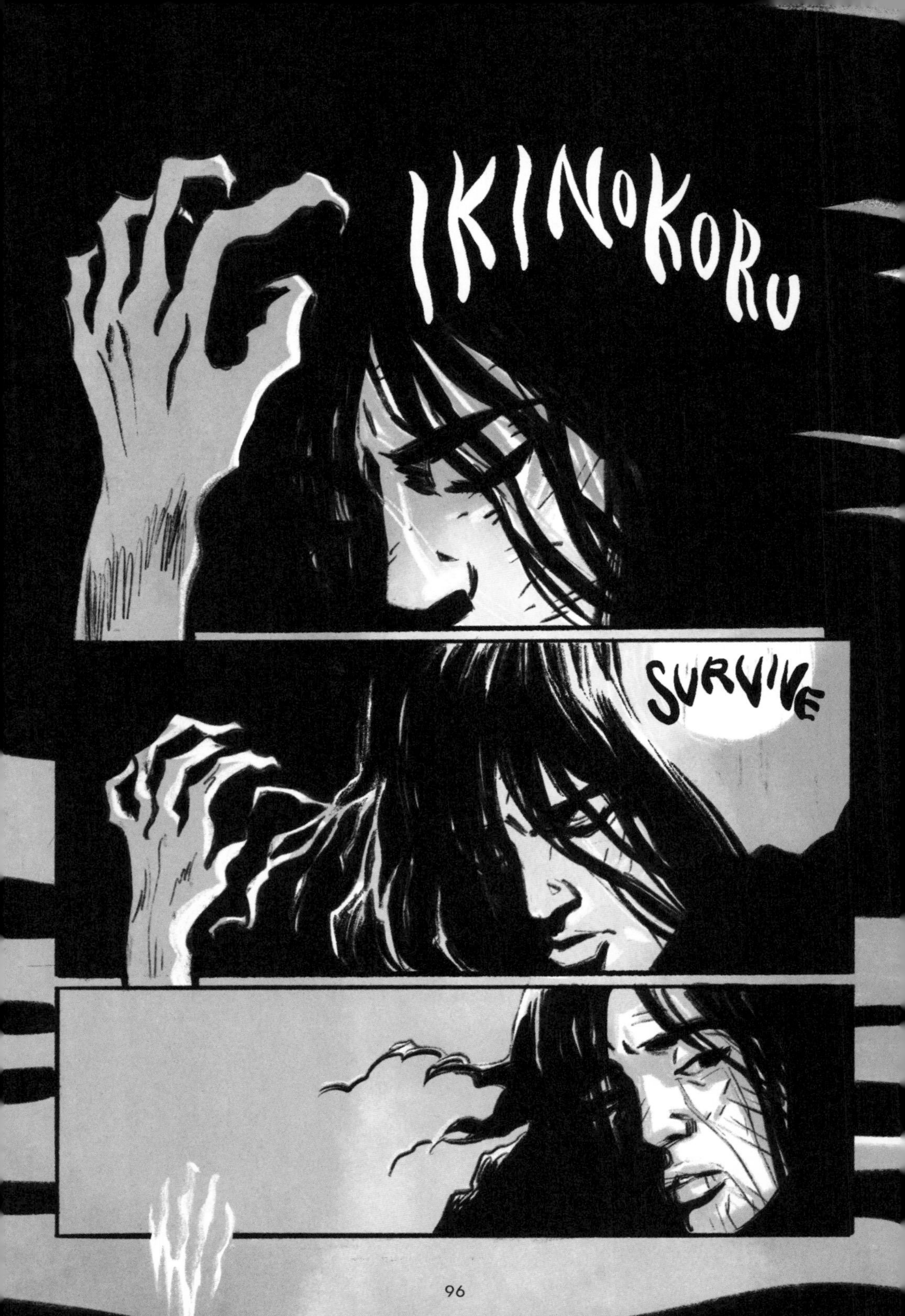
IKINOKORU
SURVIVE

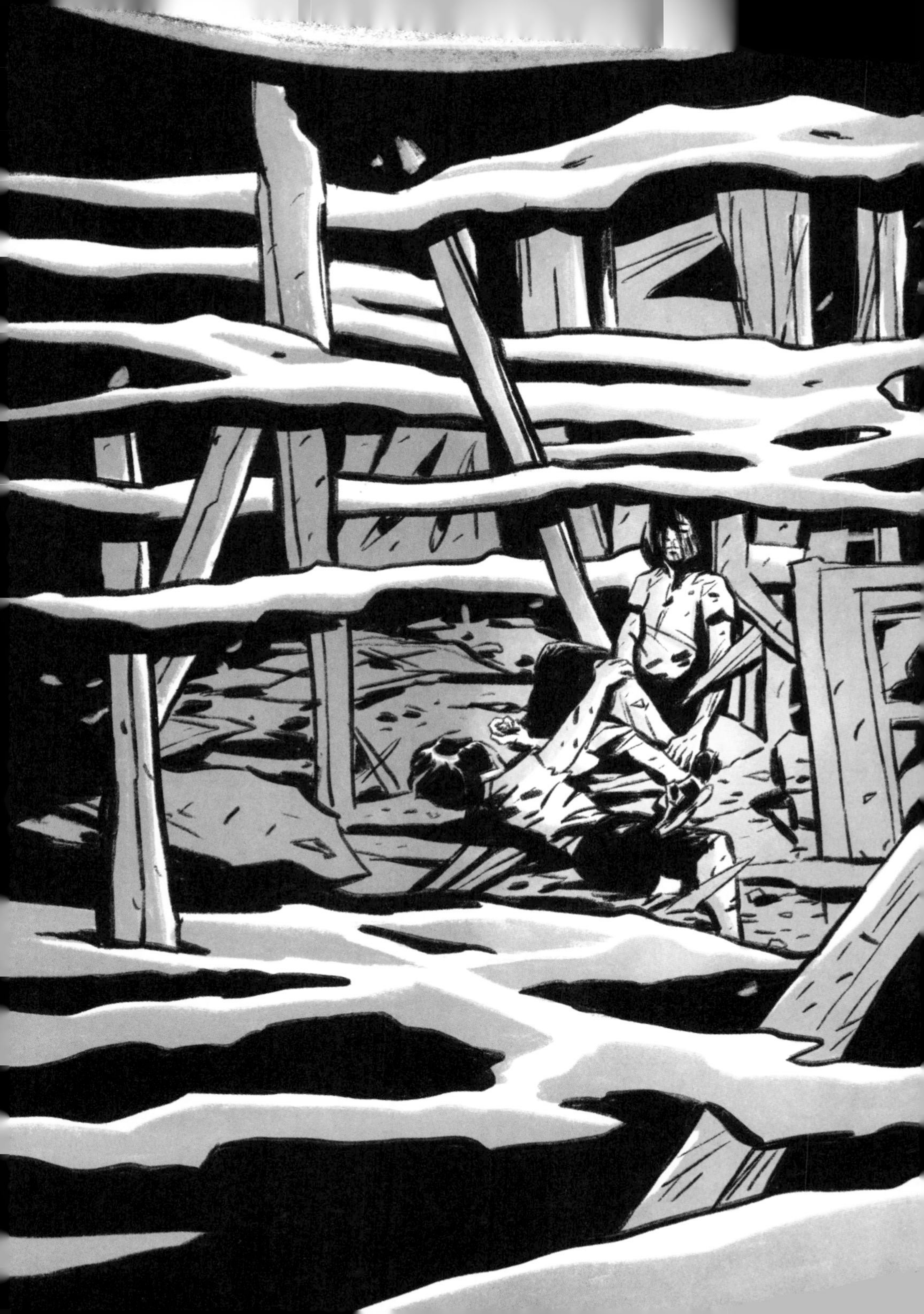

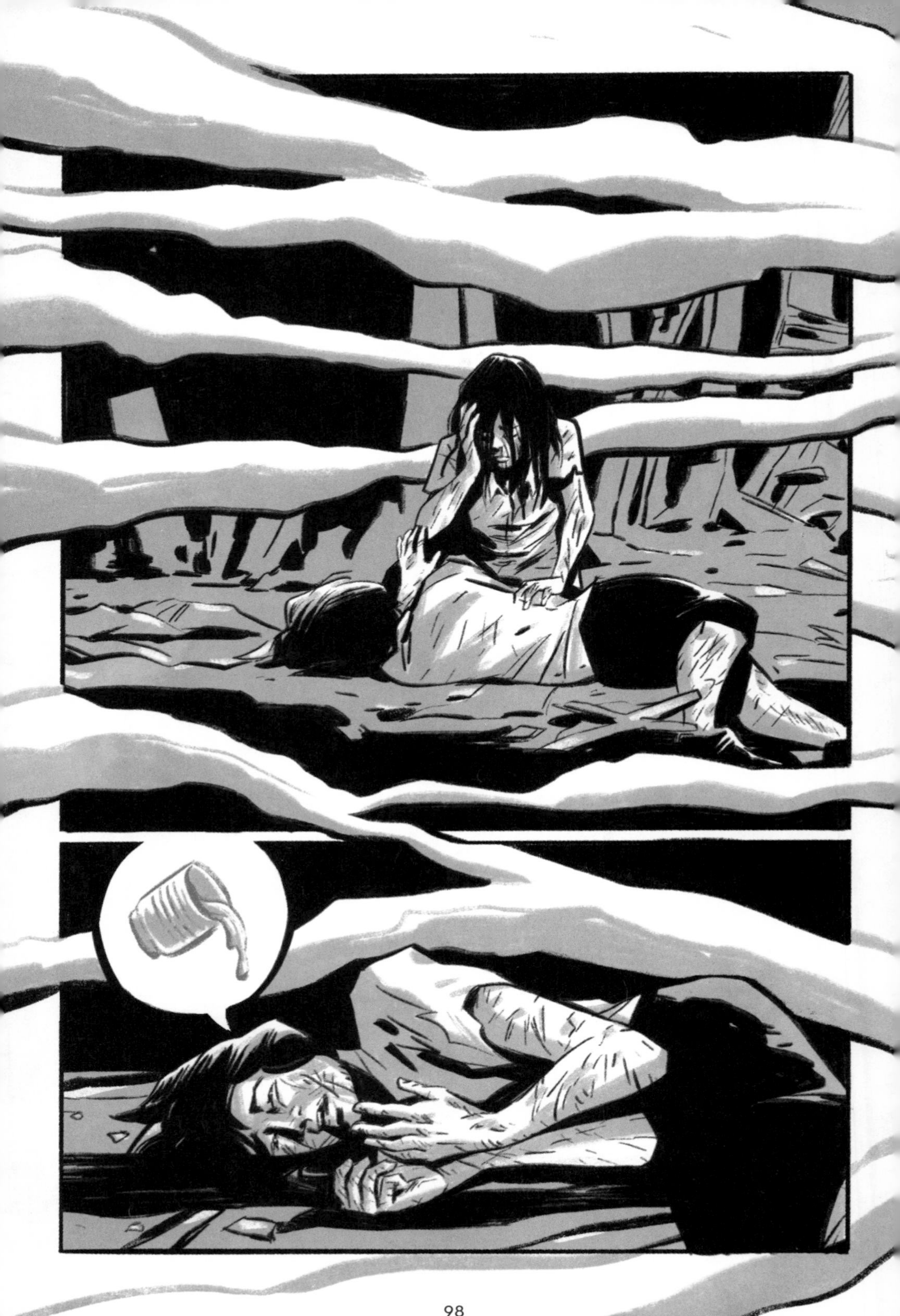

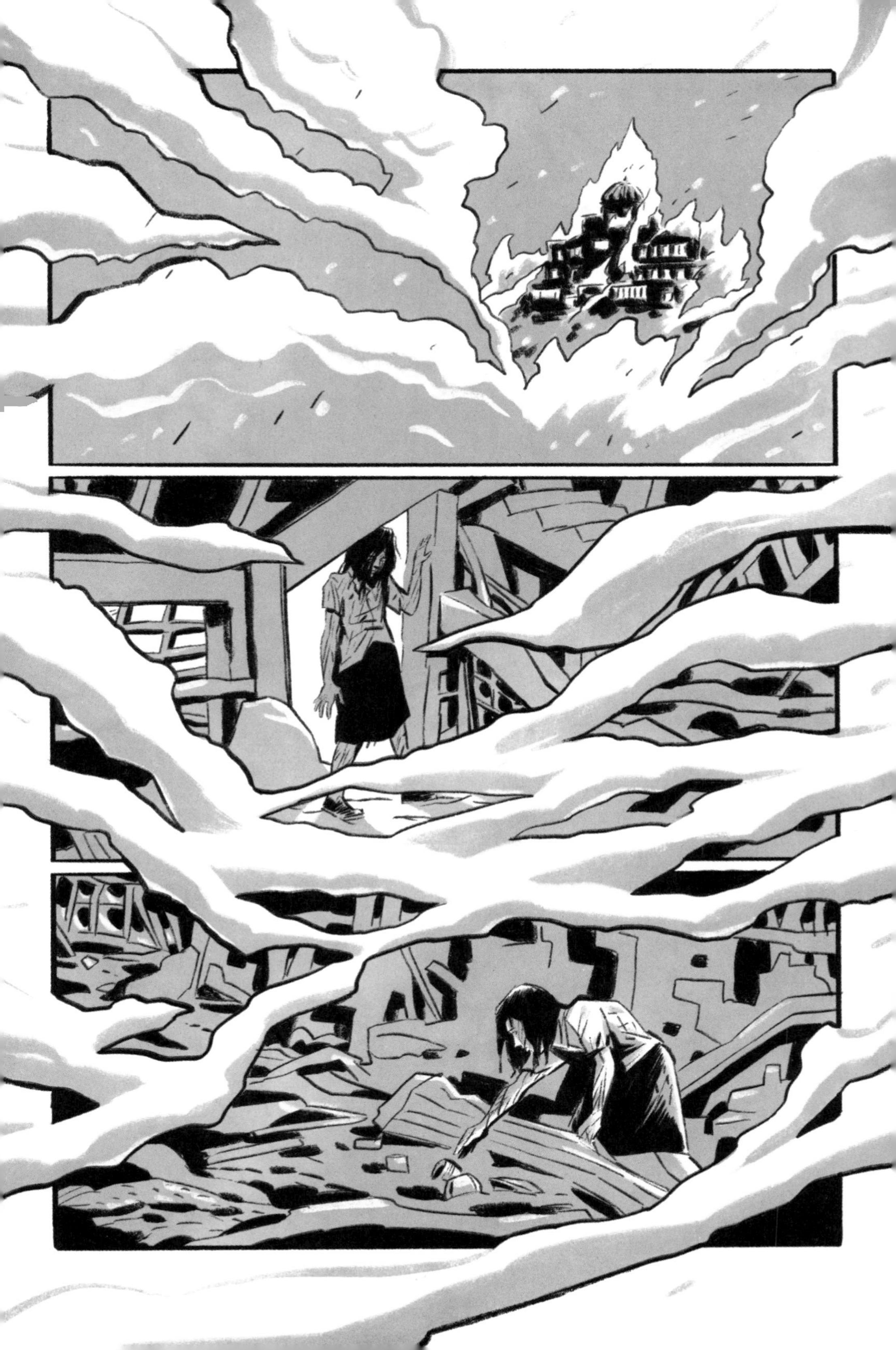

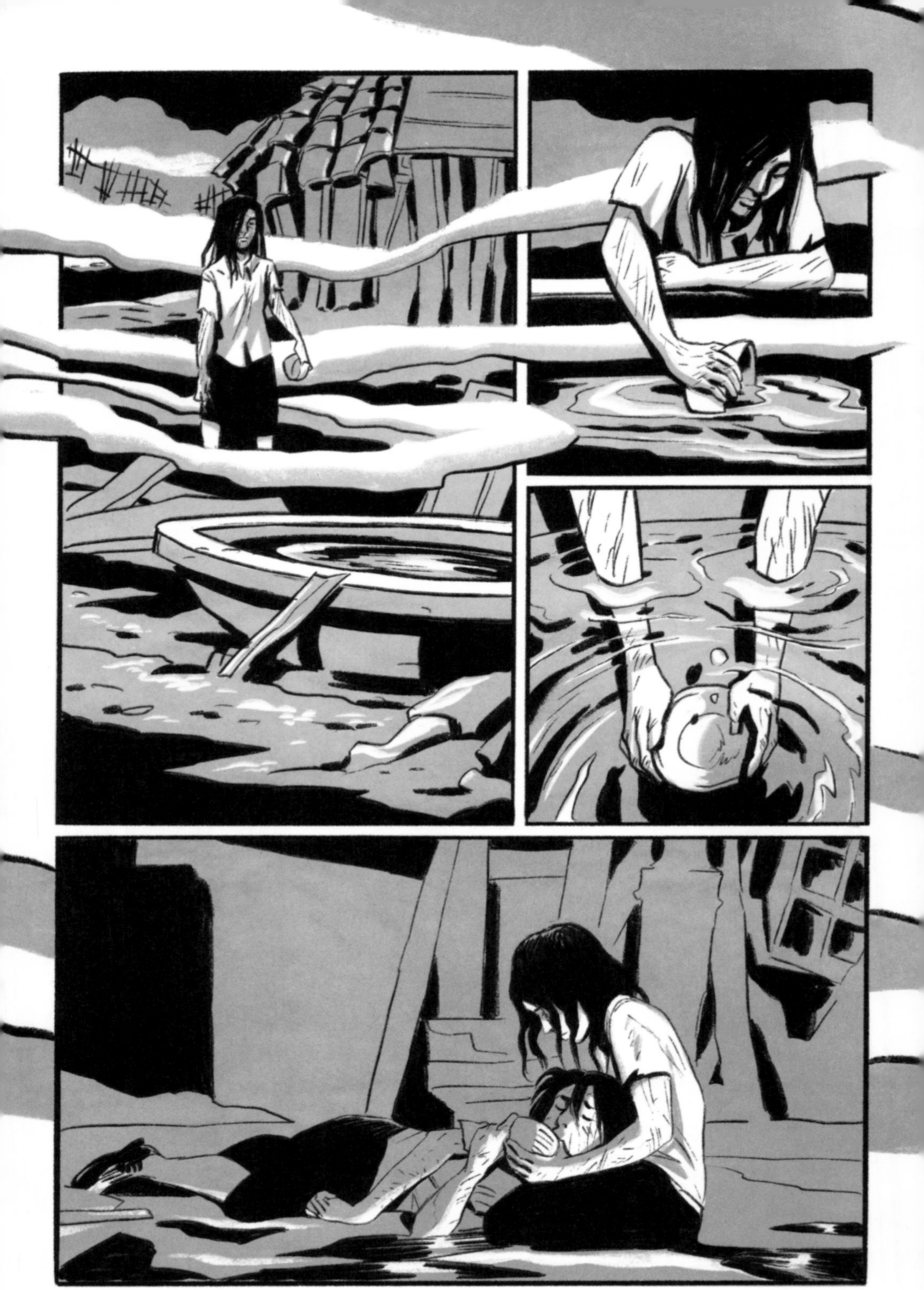

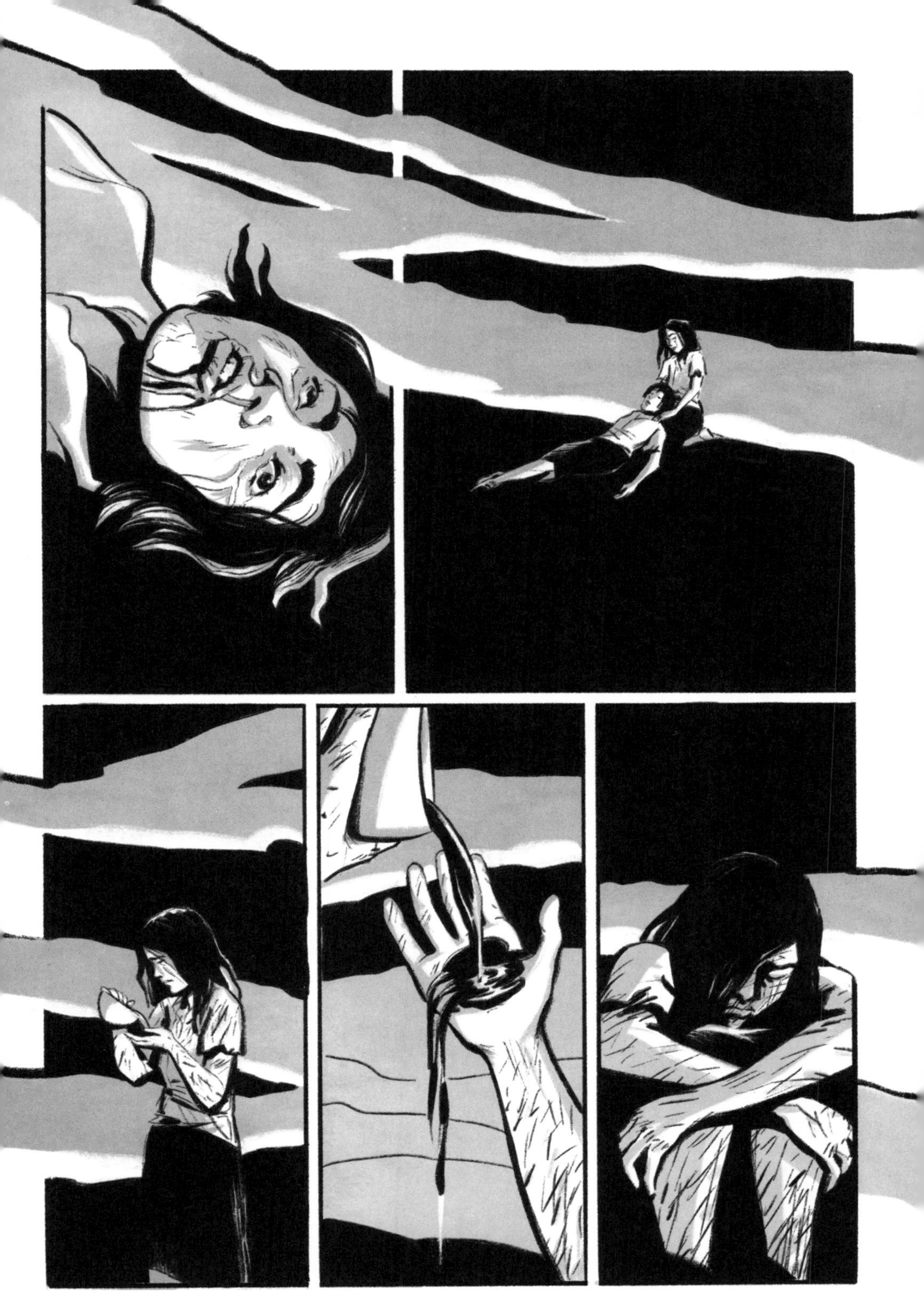

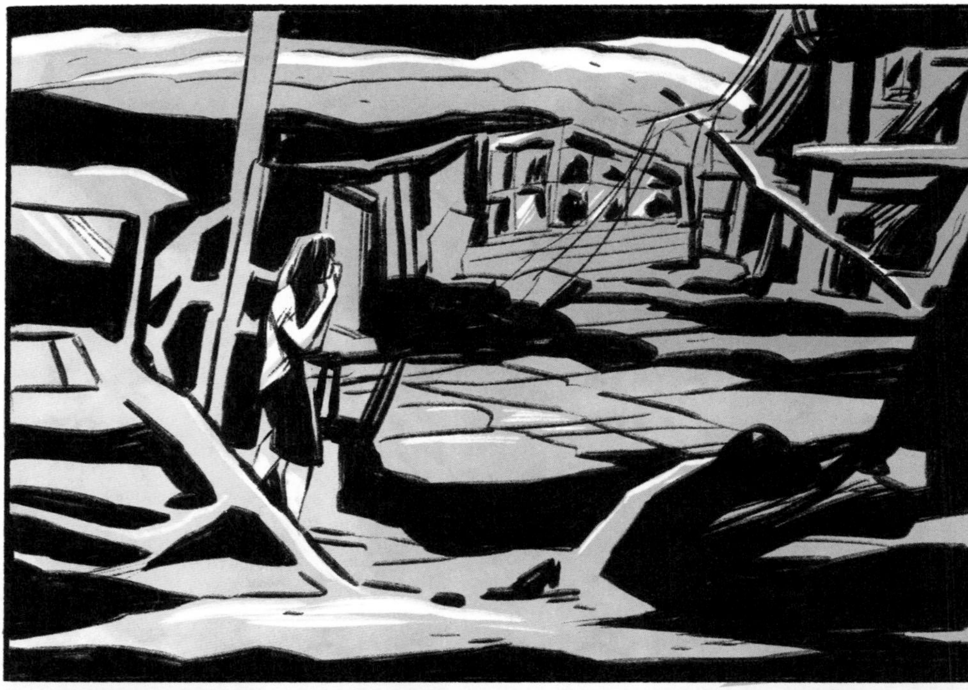

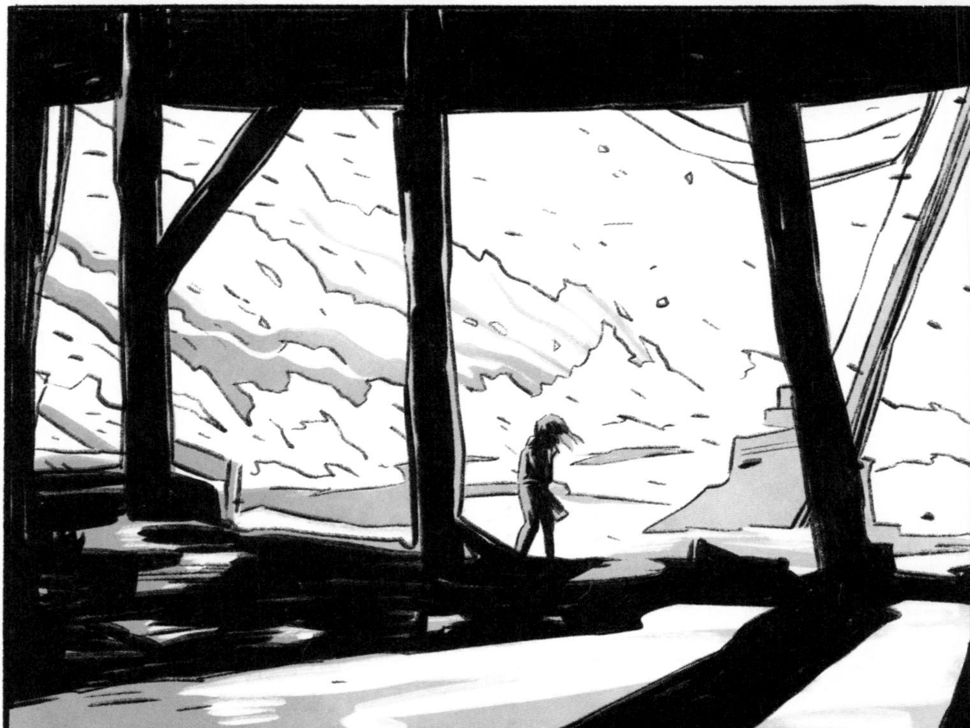

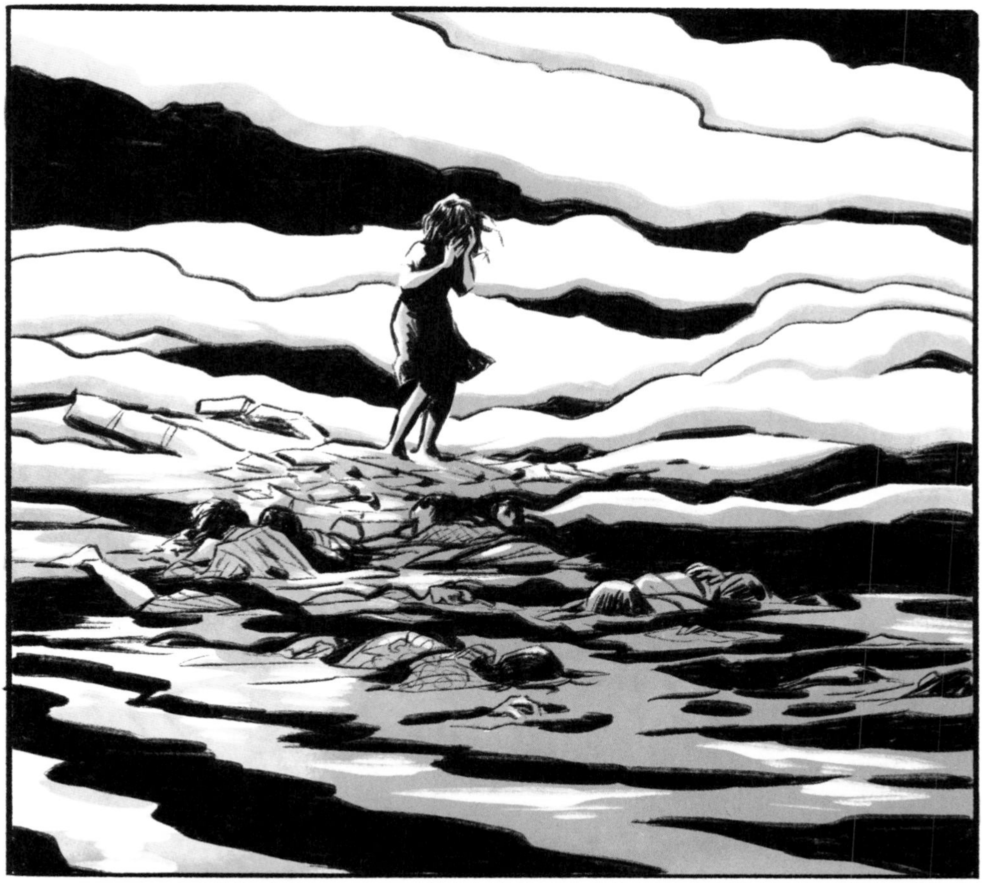

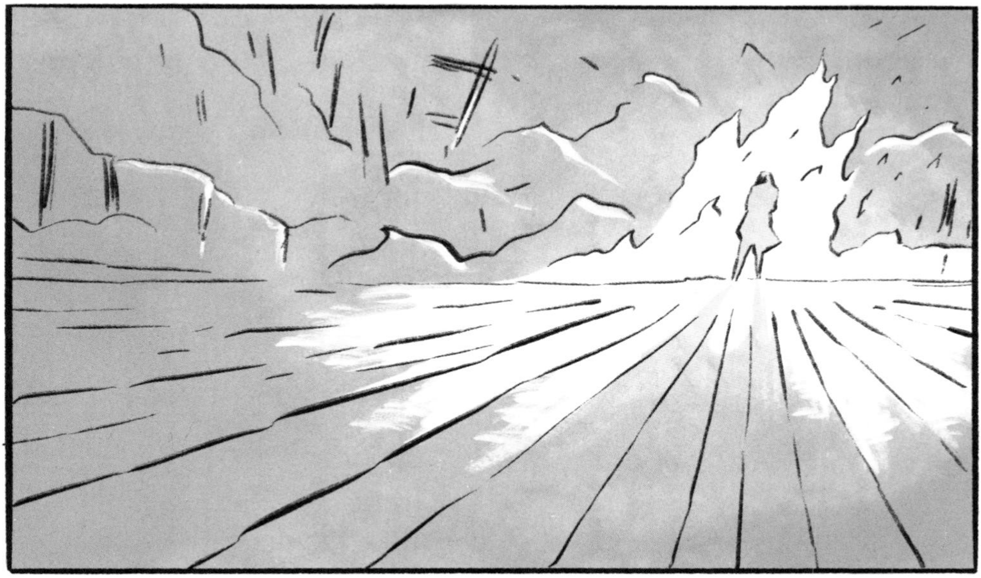

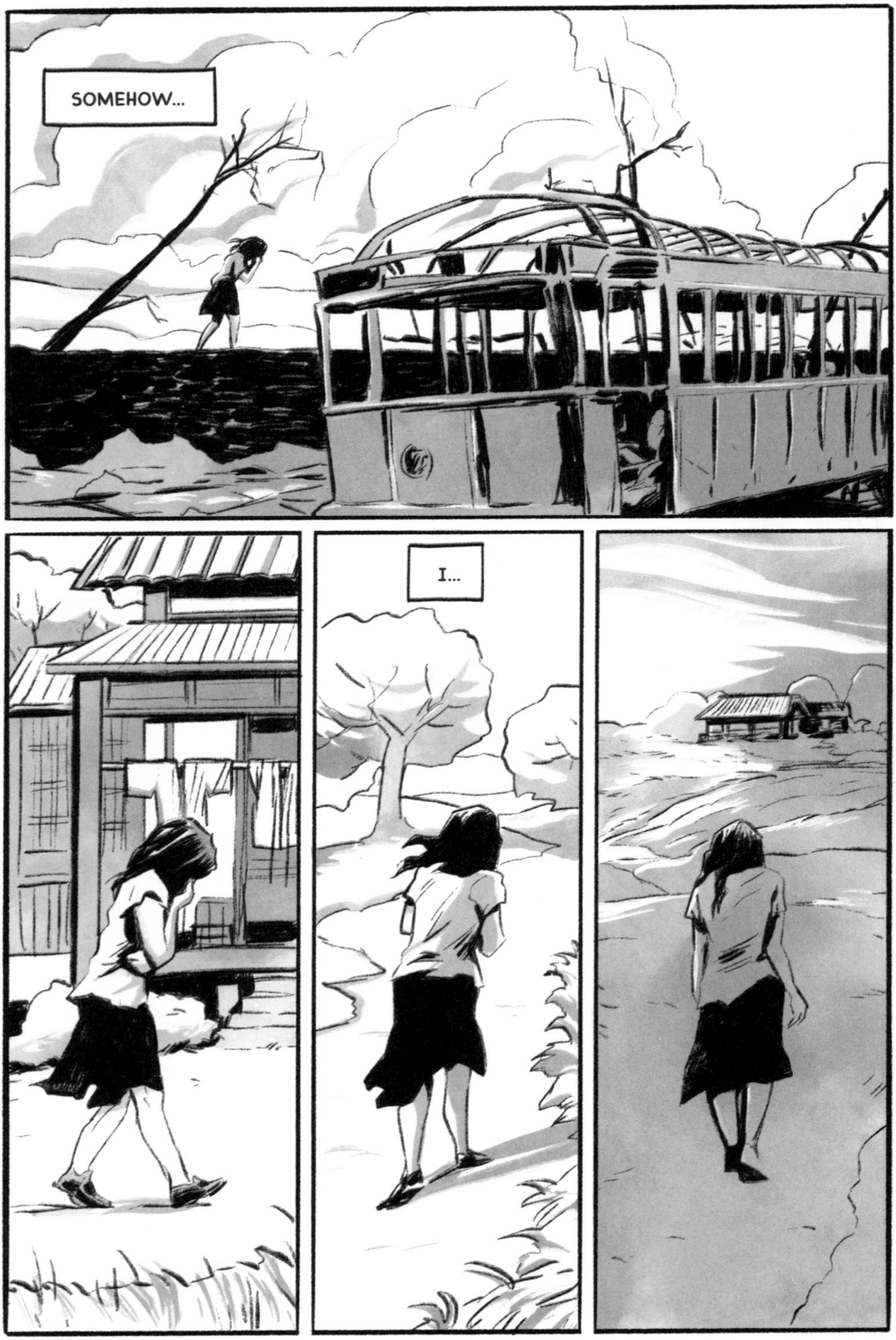
SOMEHOW...
I...

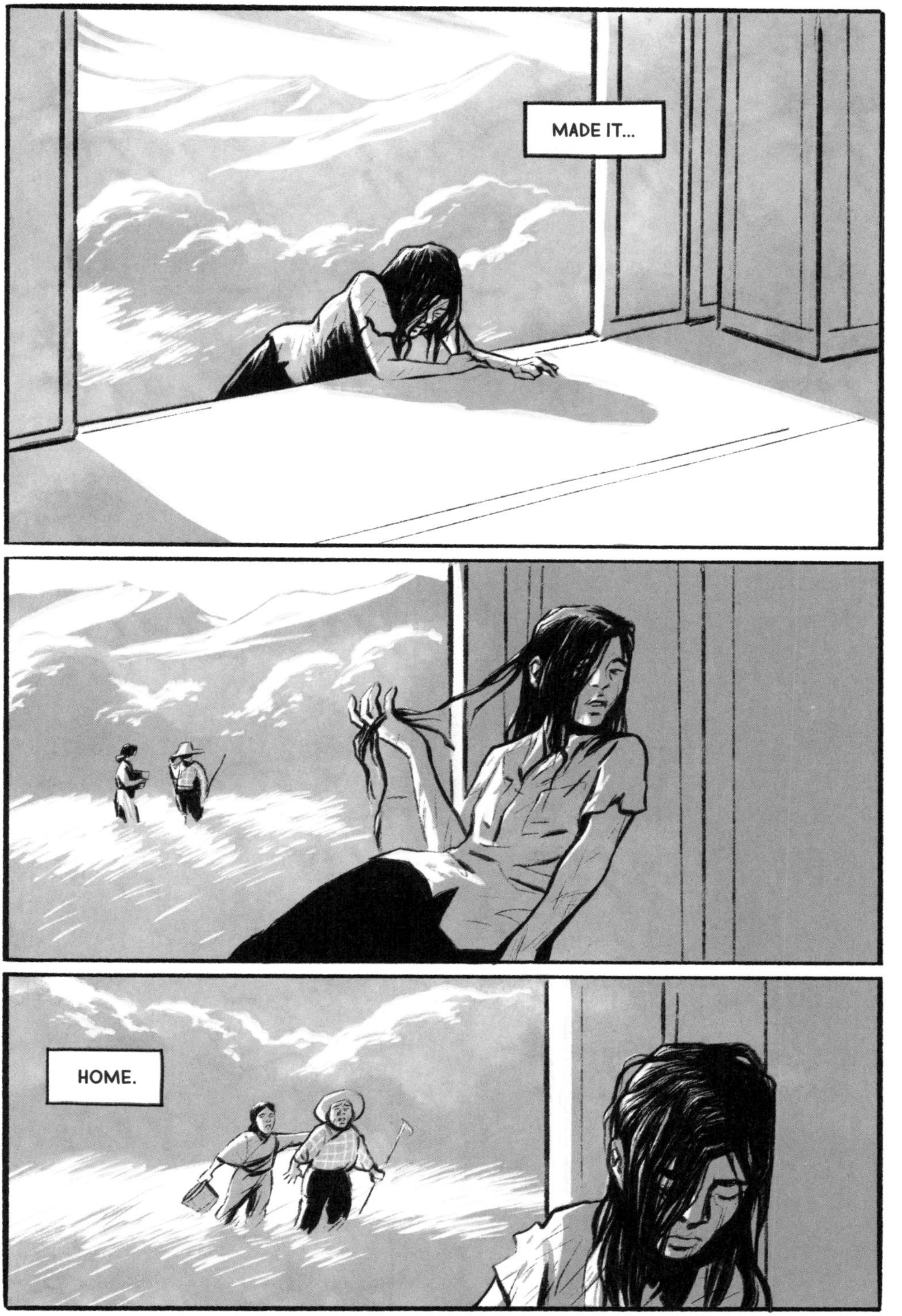
MADE IT...
HOME.

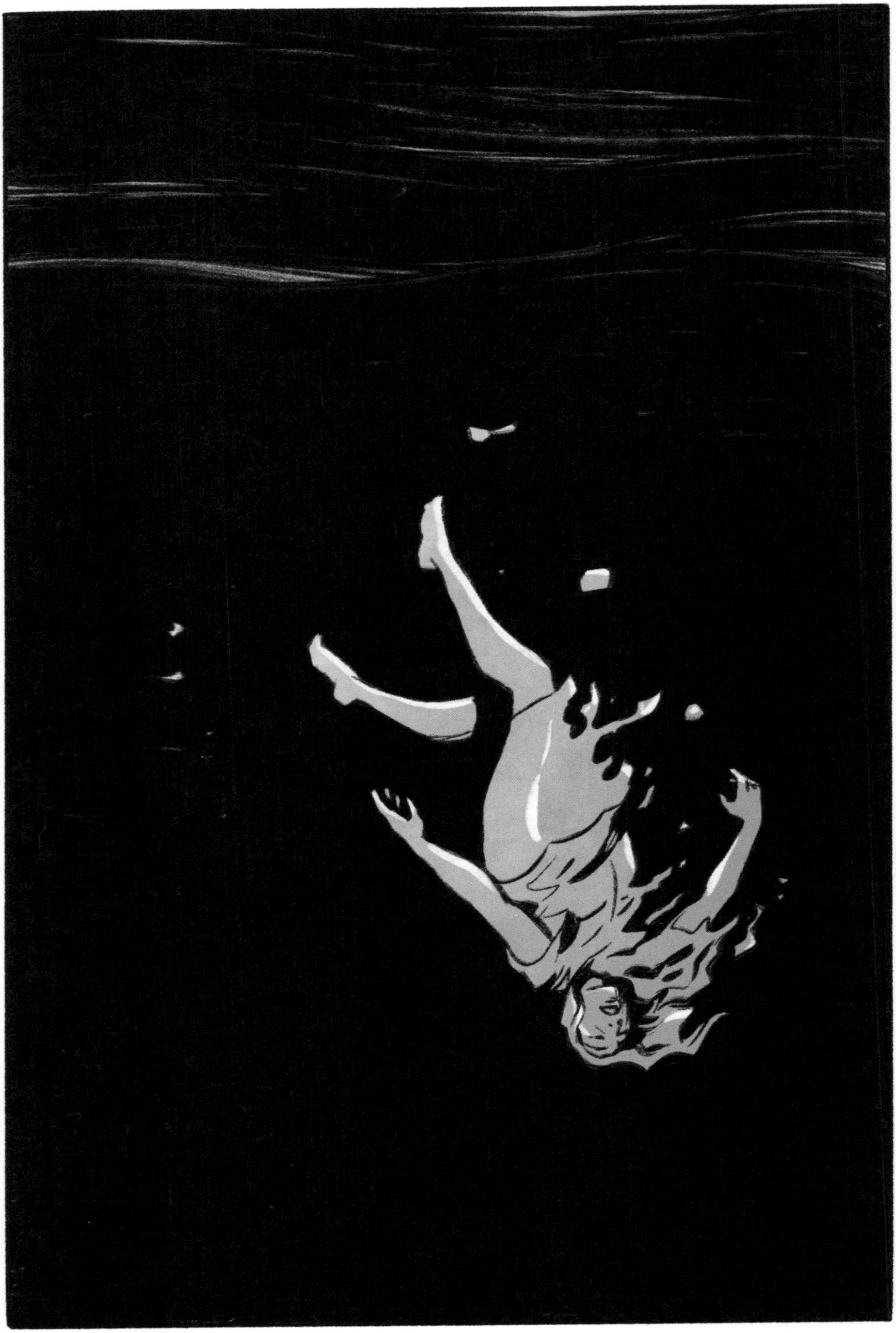

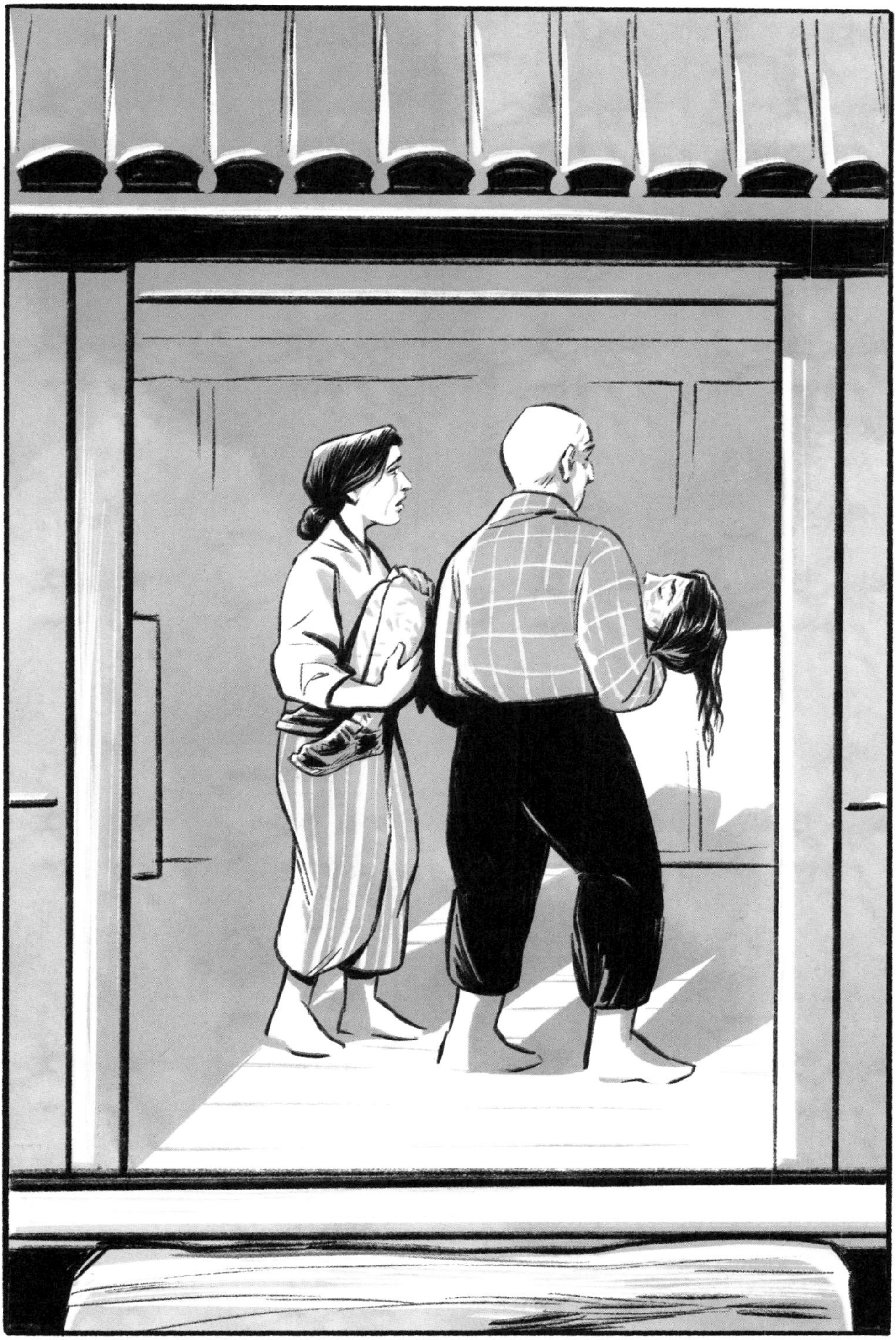

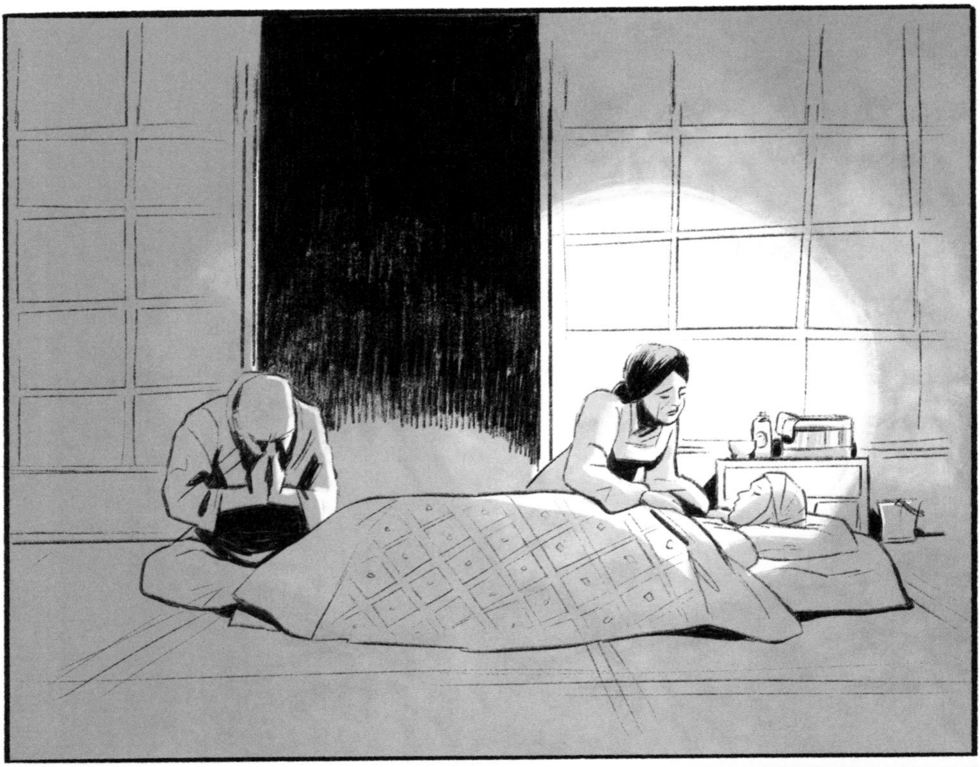

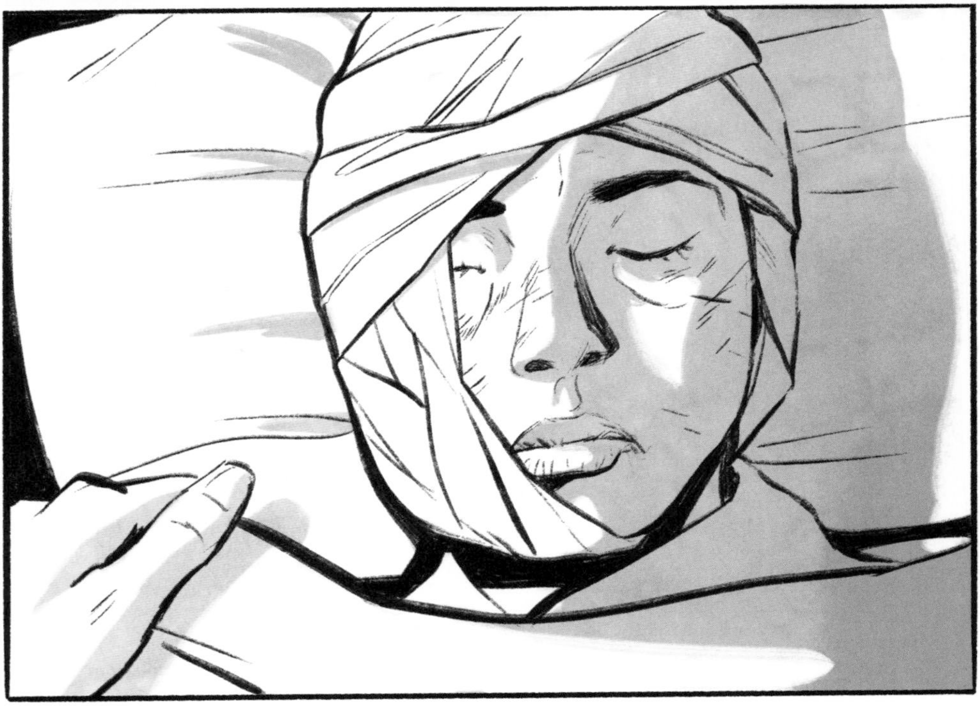

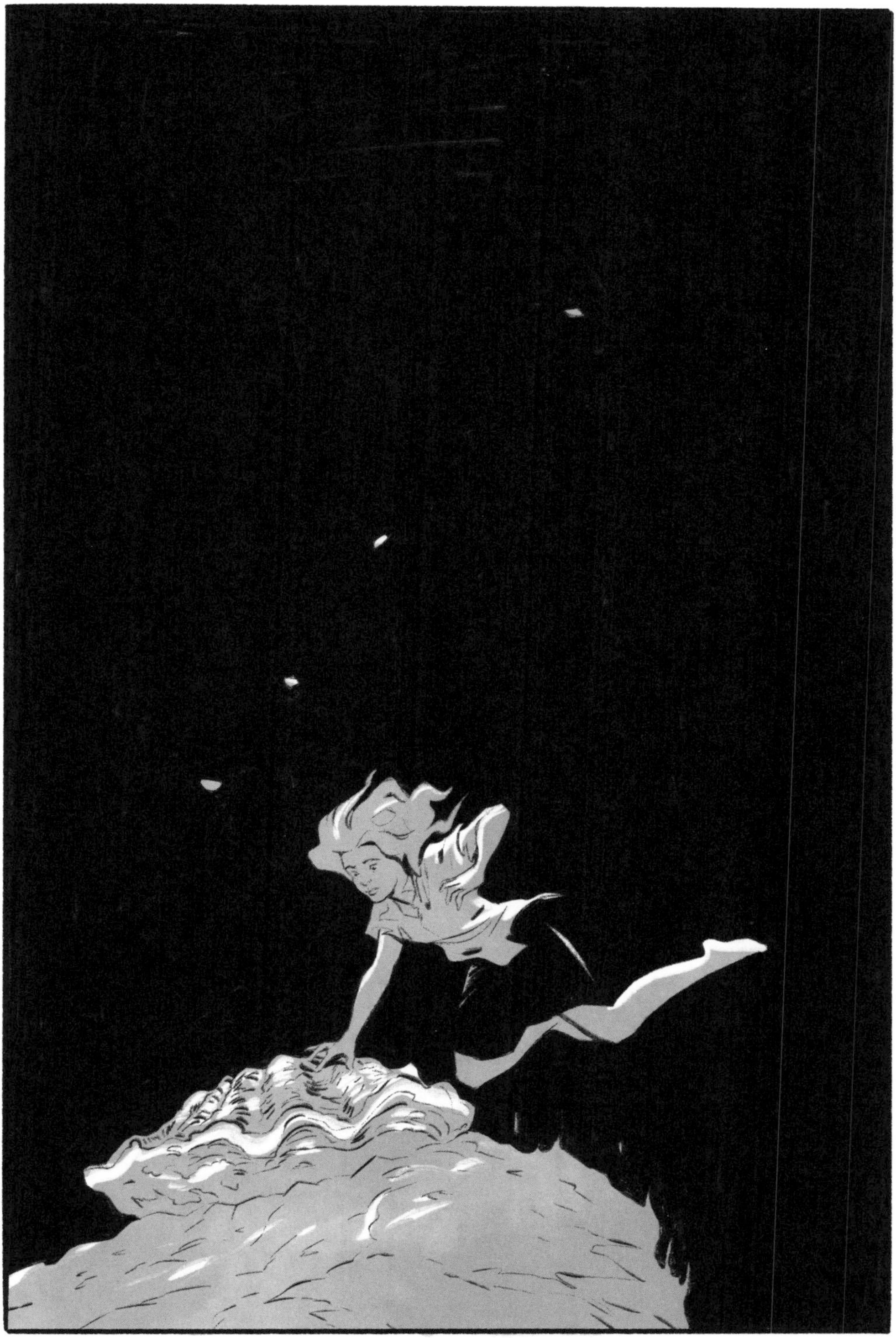

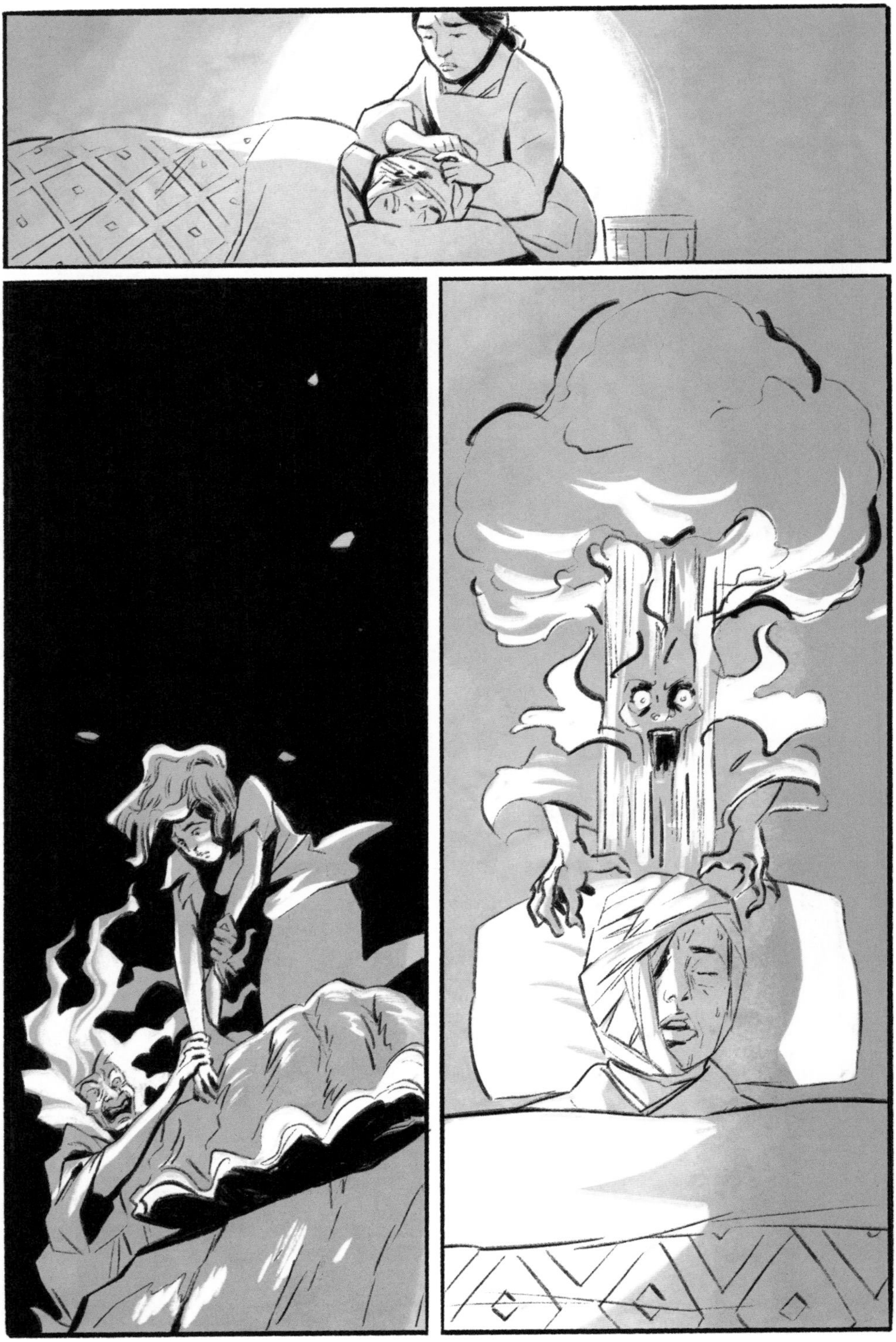

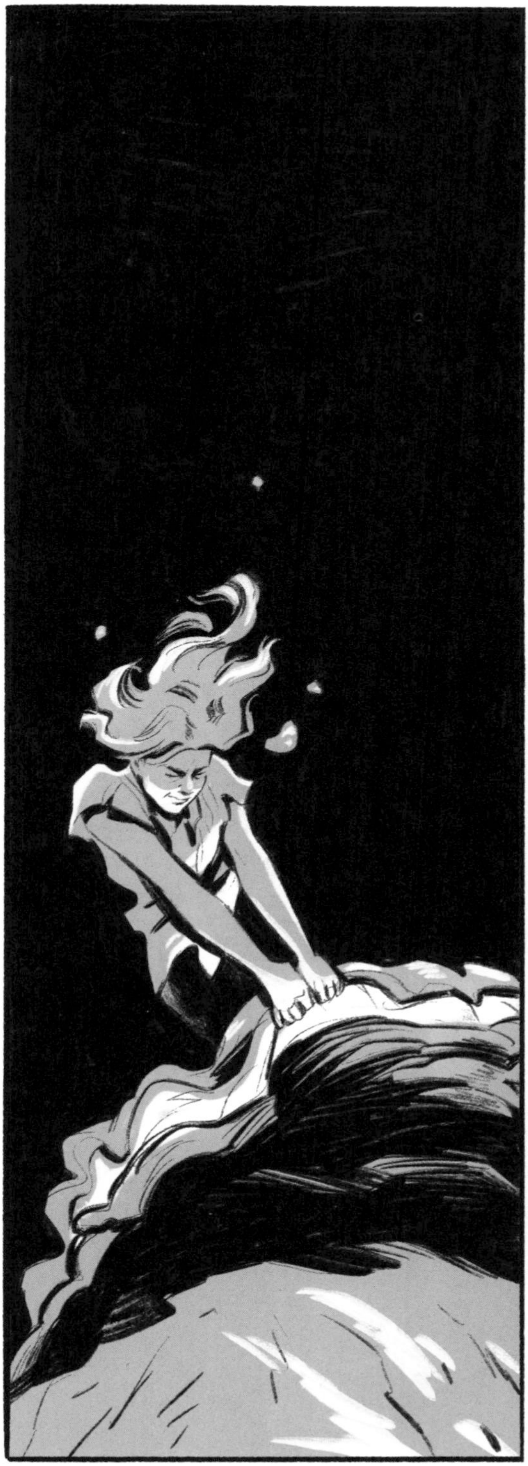
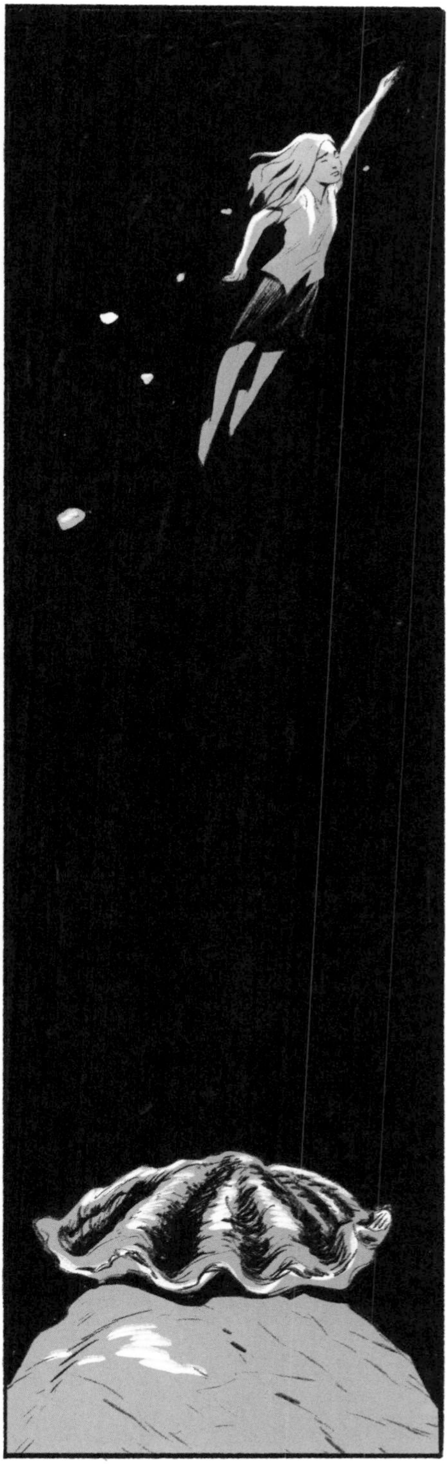

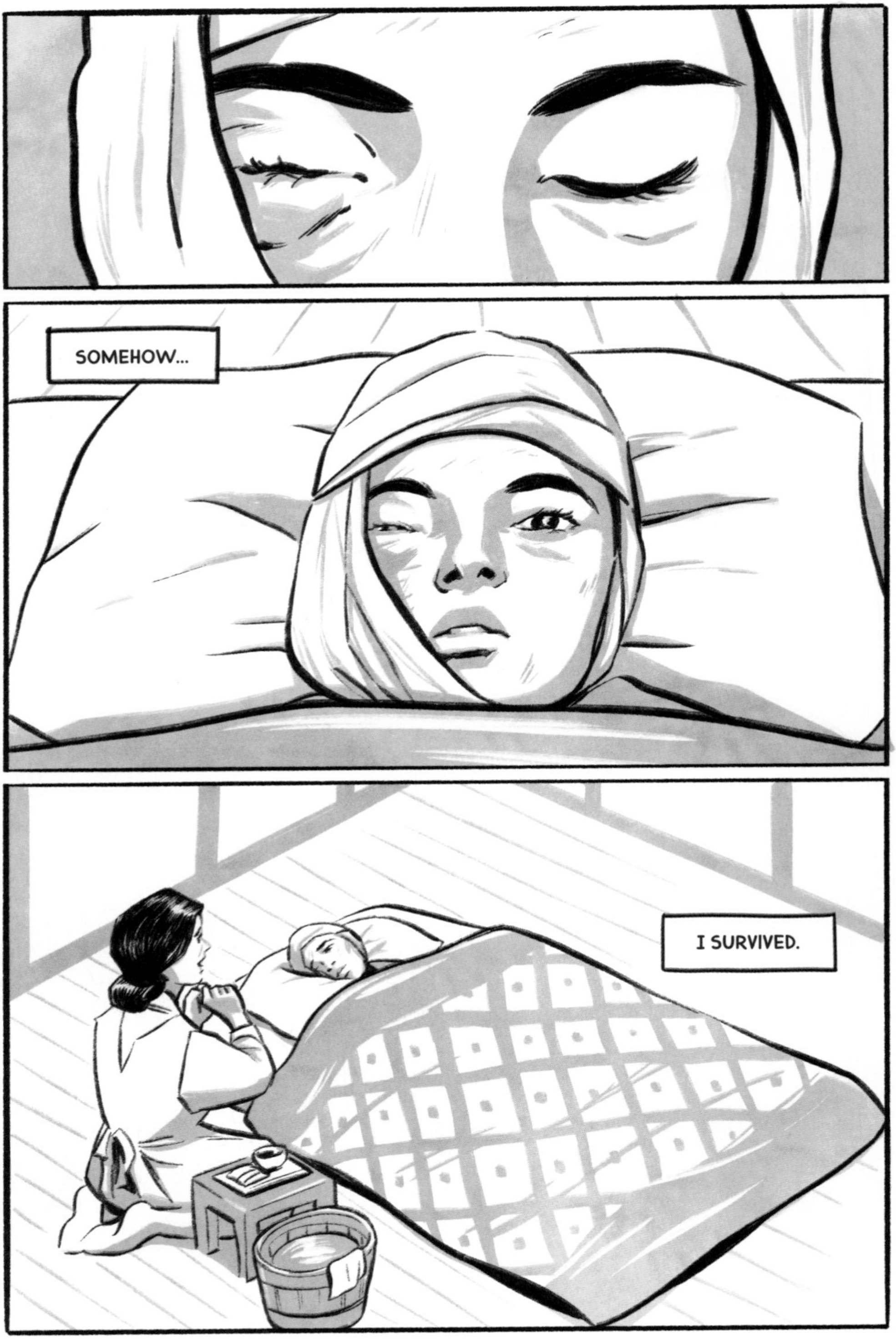
SOMEHOW...
I SURVIVED.

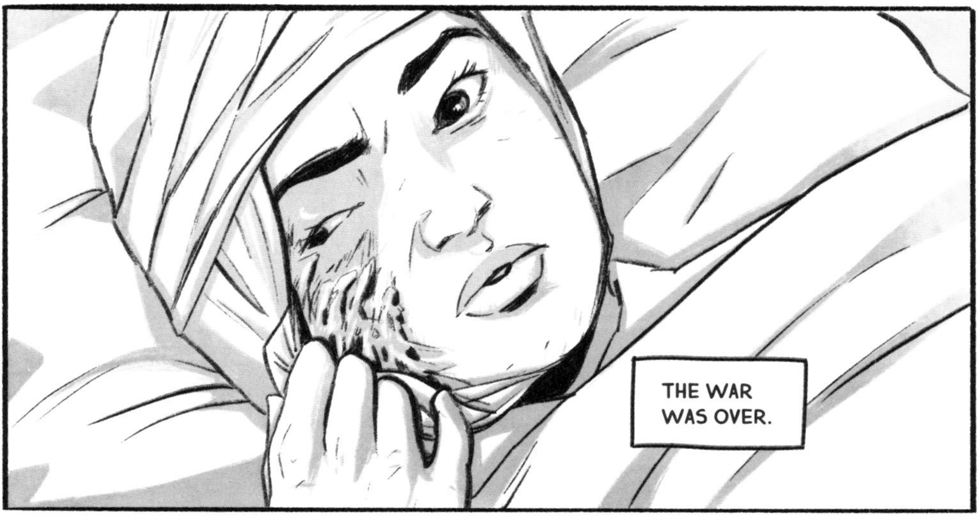
THE WAR
WAS OVER.

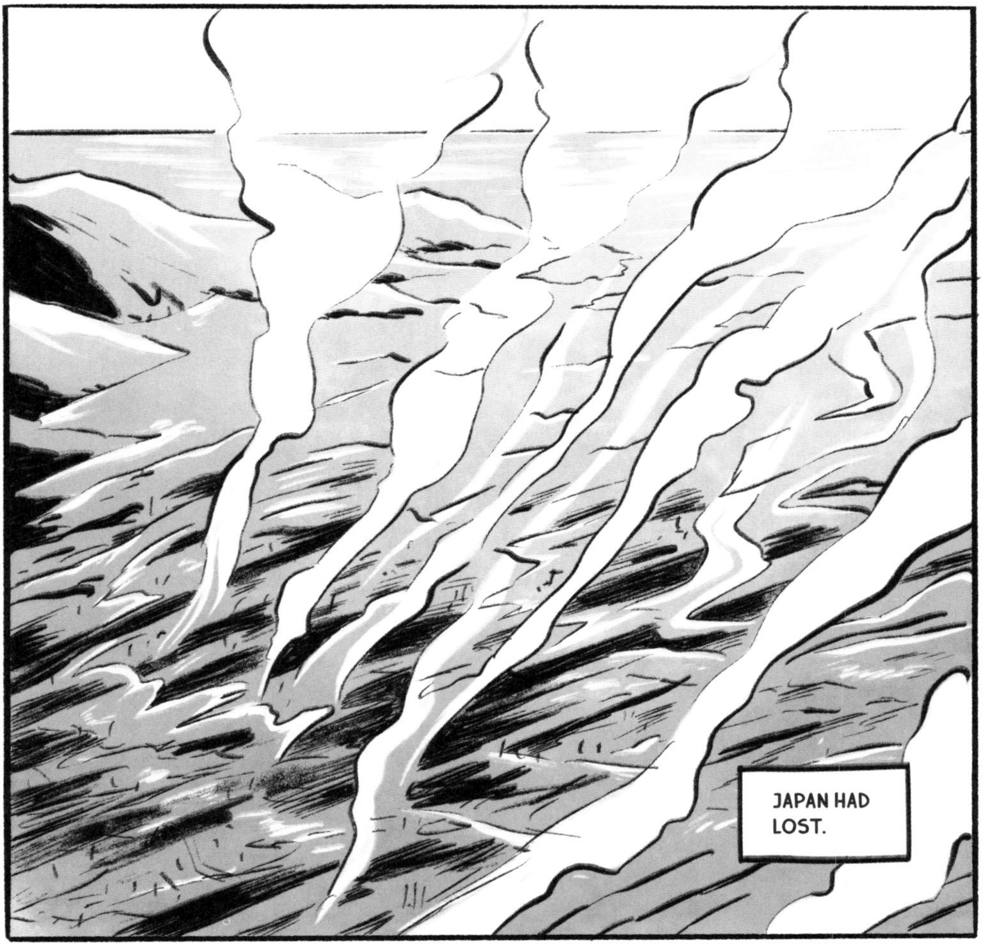
JAPAN HAD
LOST.

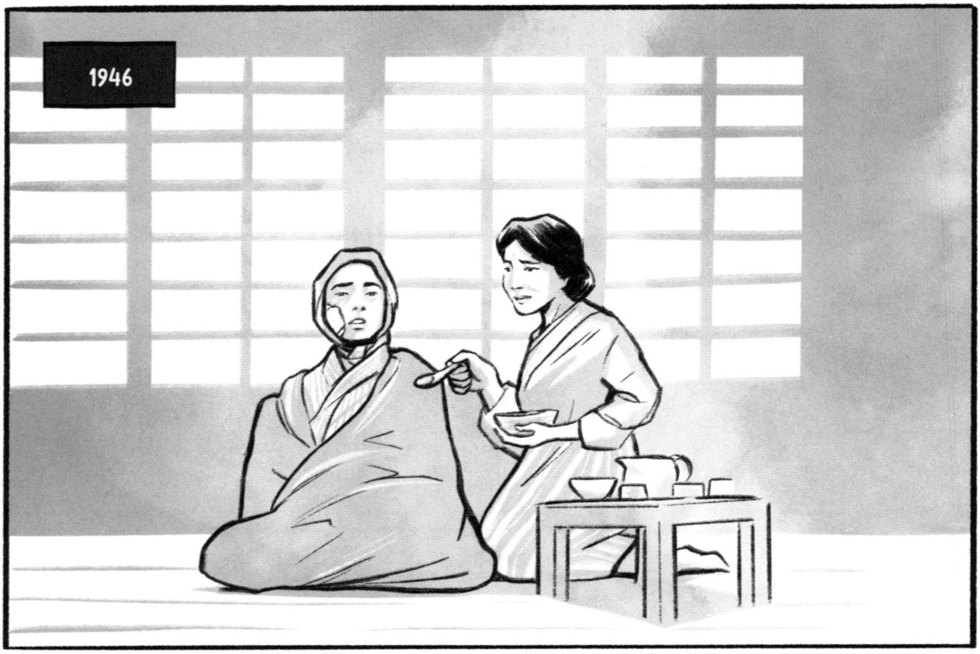
1946

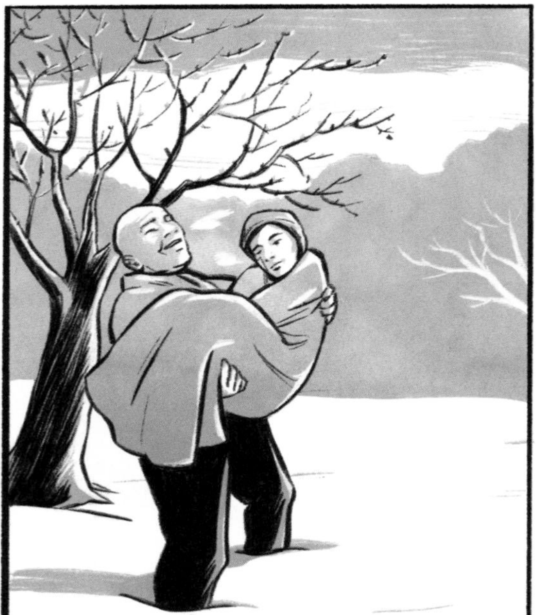

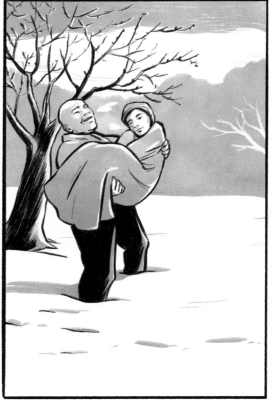

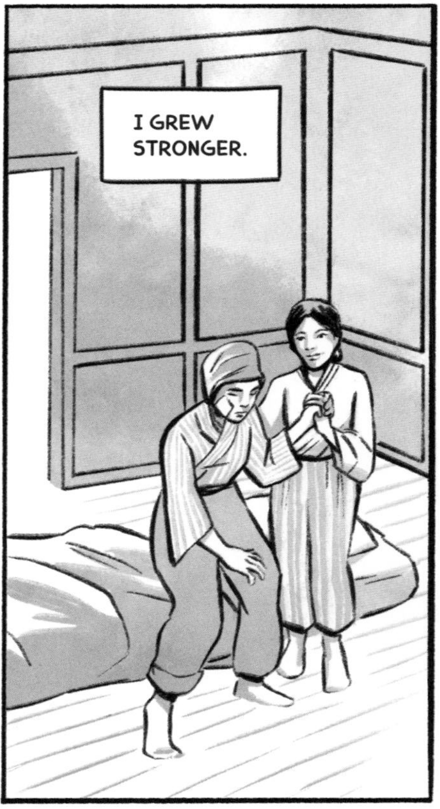
I GREW STRONGER.

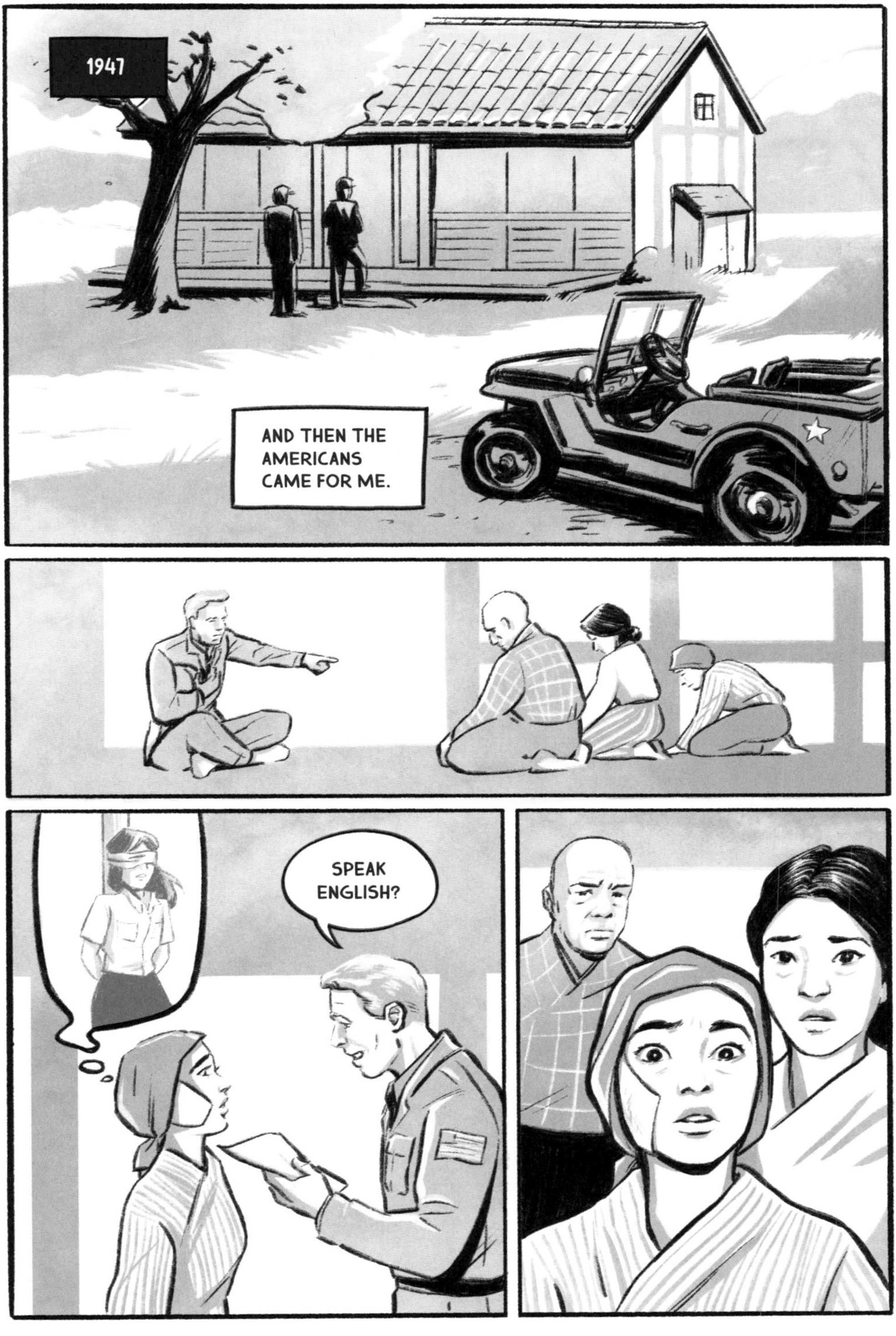
1947
AND THEN THE AMERICANS CAME FOR ME.
SPEAK ENGLISH?

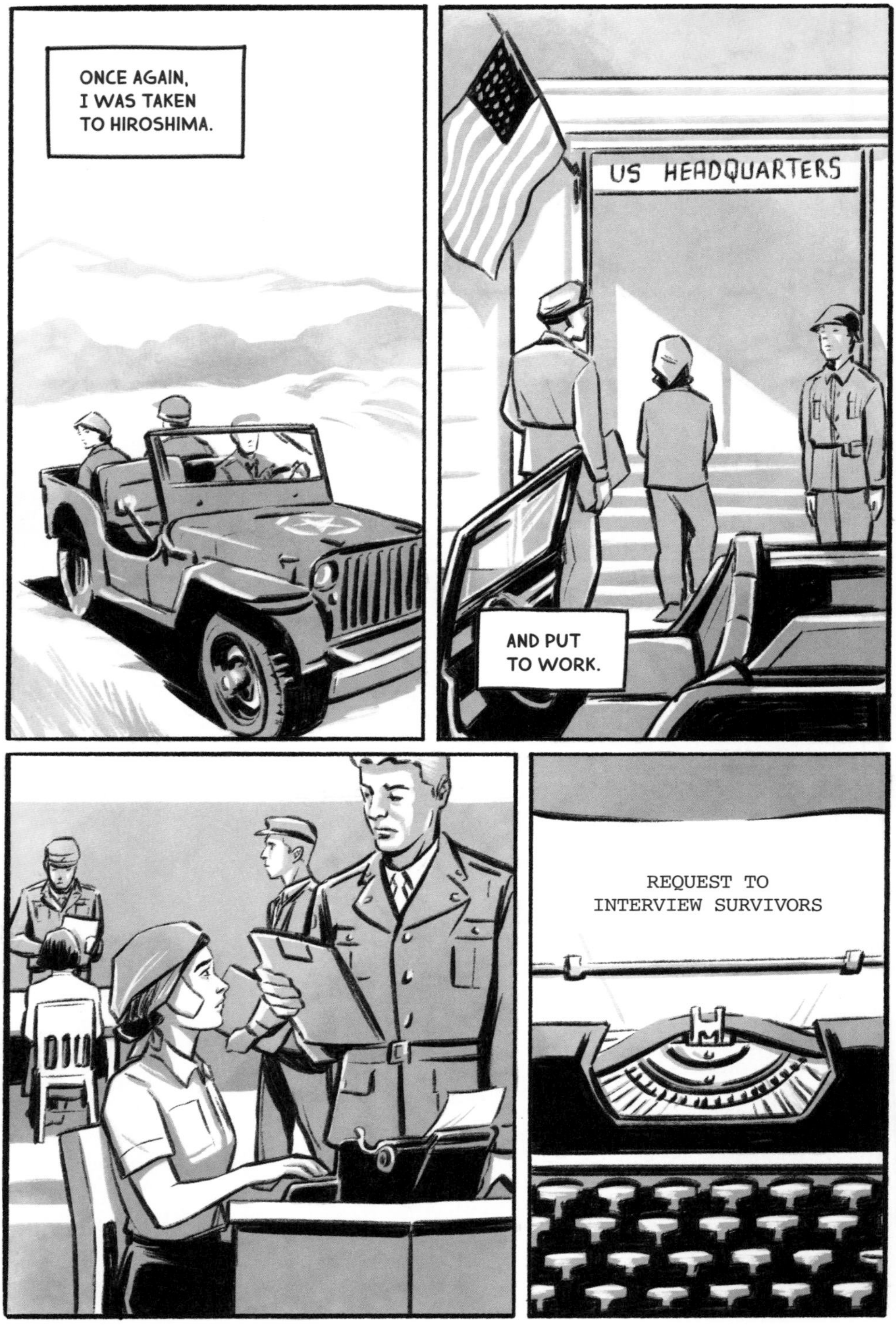
ONCE AGAIN,
I WAS TAKEN
TO HIROSHIMA.
US HEADQUARTERS
AND PUT
TO WORK.
REQUEST TO
INTERVIEW SURVIVORS

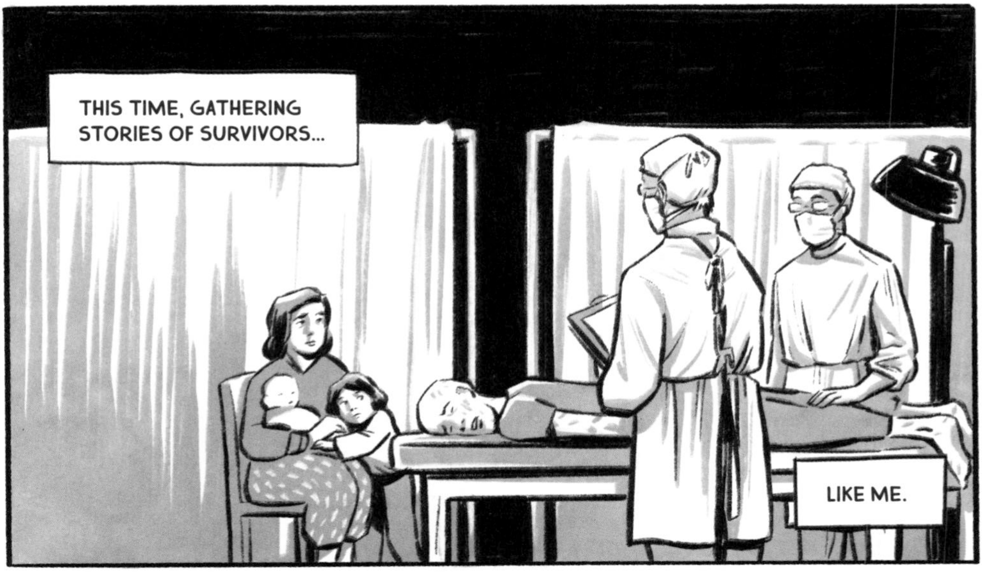
THIS TIME, GATHERING STORIES OF SURVIVORS...
LIKE ME.

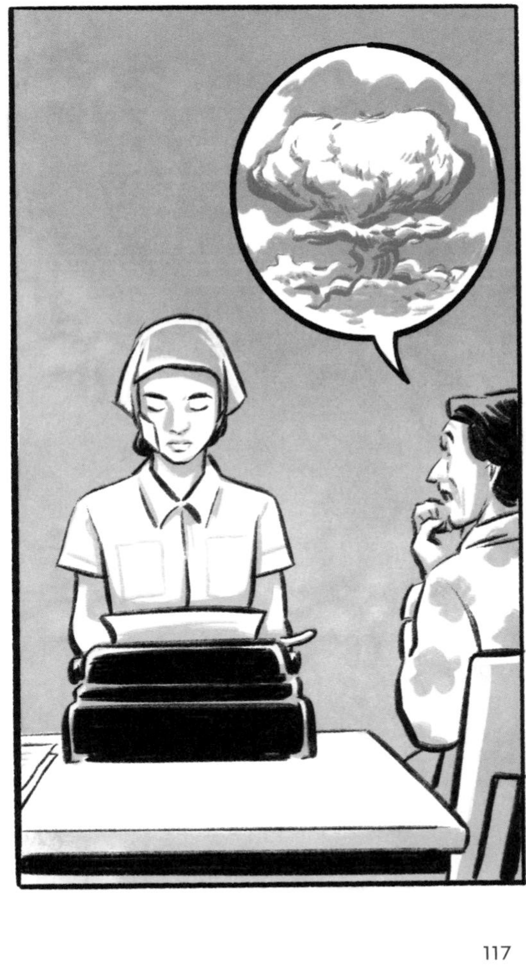

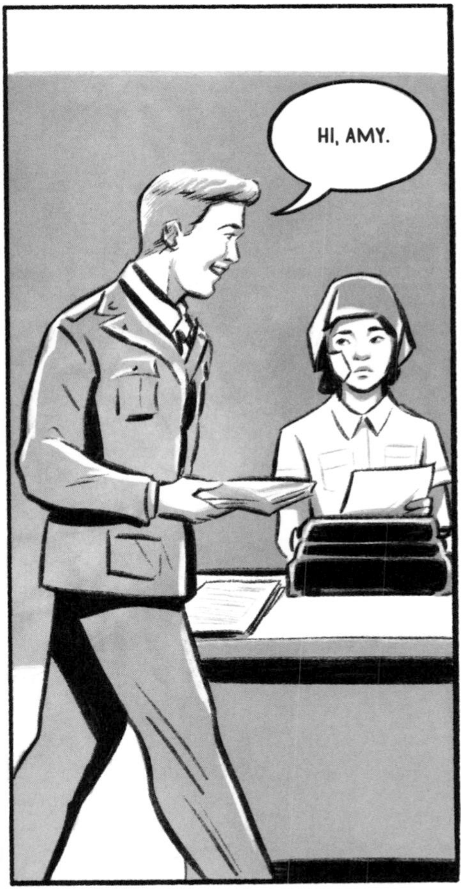
HI, AMY.

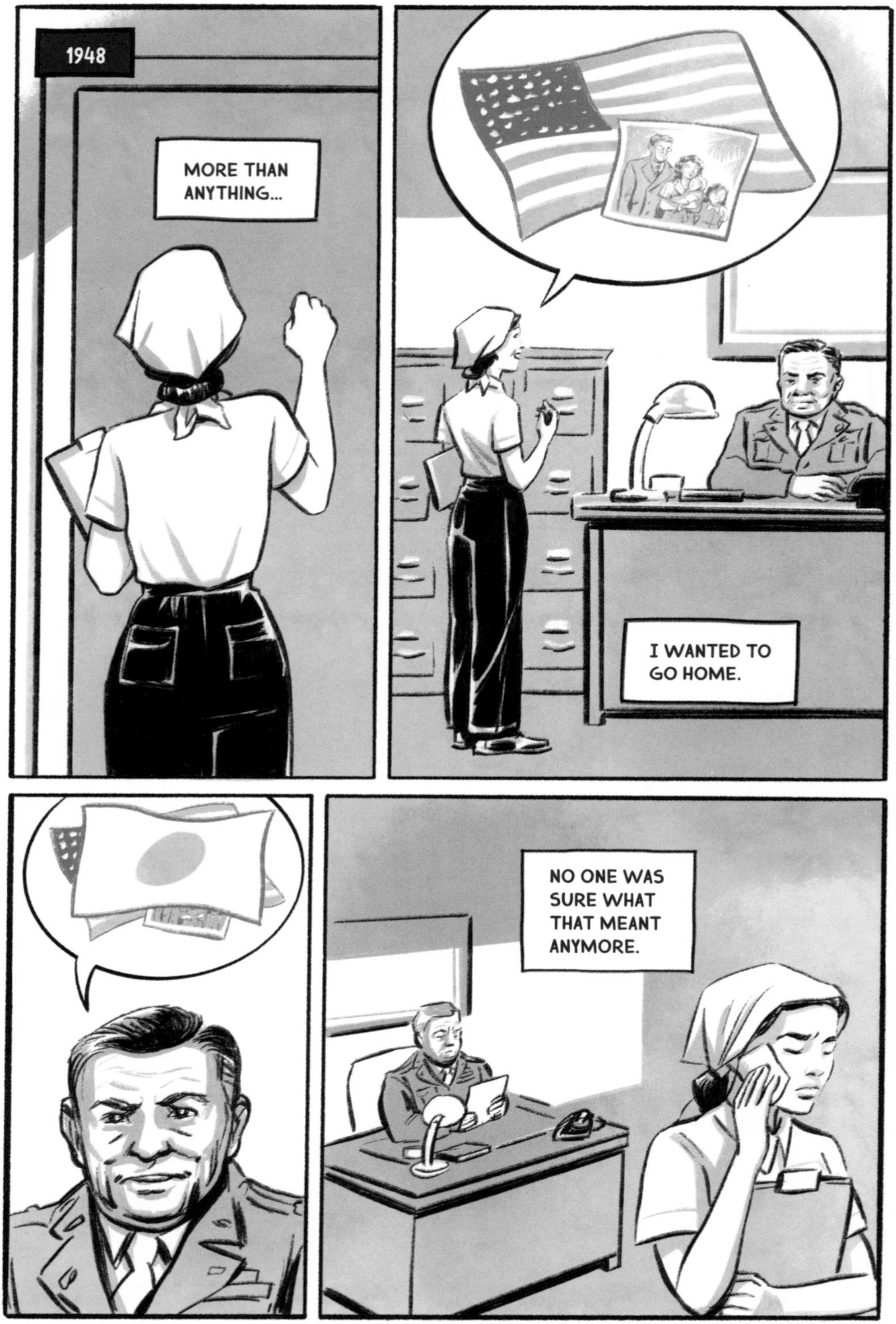
1948
MORE THAN ANYTHING...
I WANTED TO GO HOME.
NO ONE WAS SURE WHAT THAT MEANT ANYMORE.

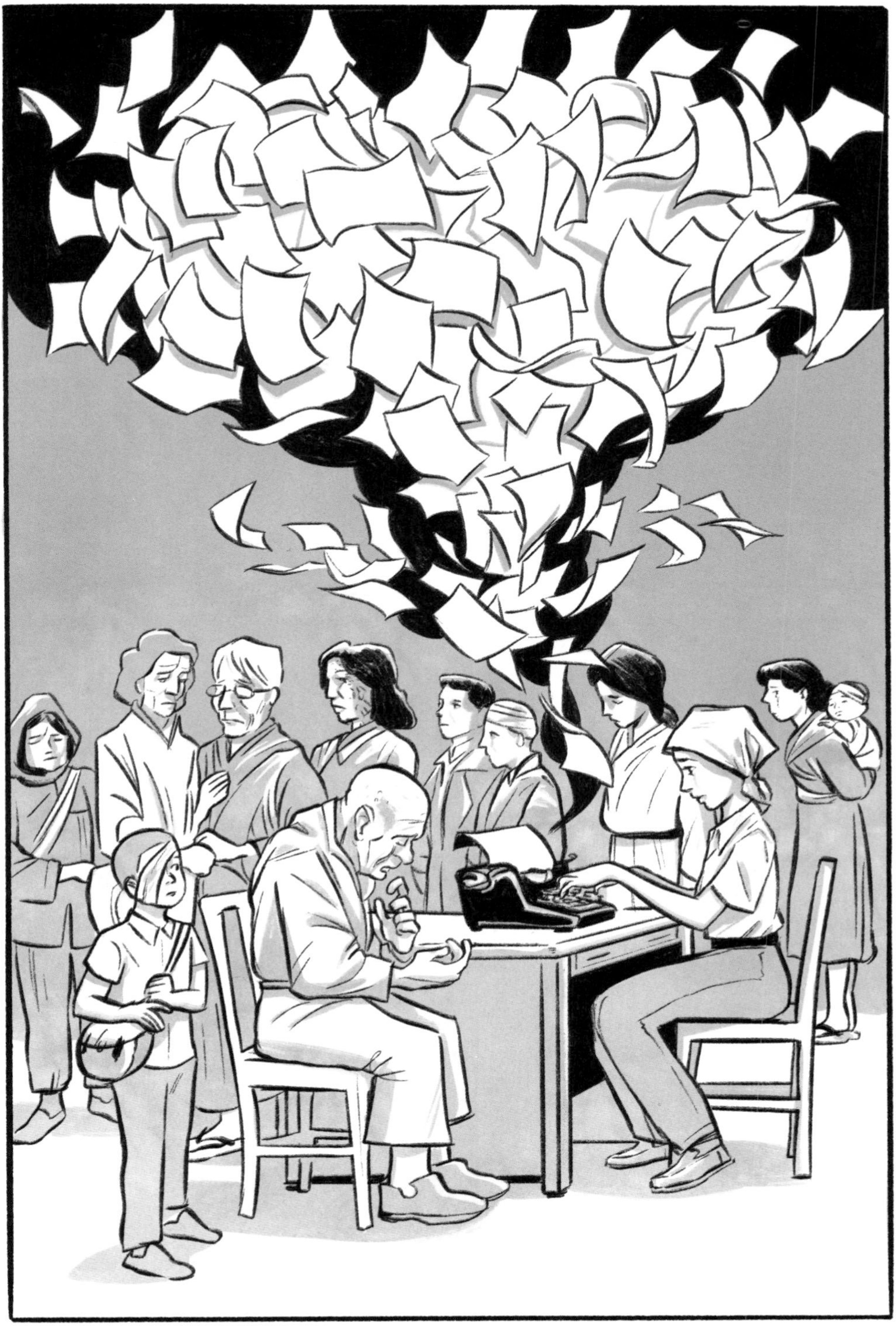

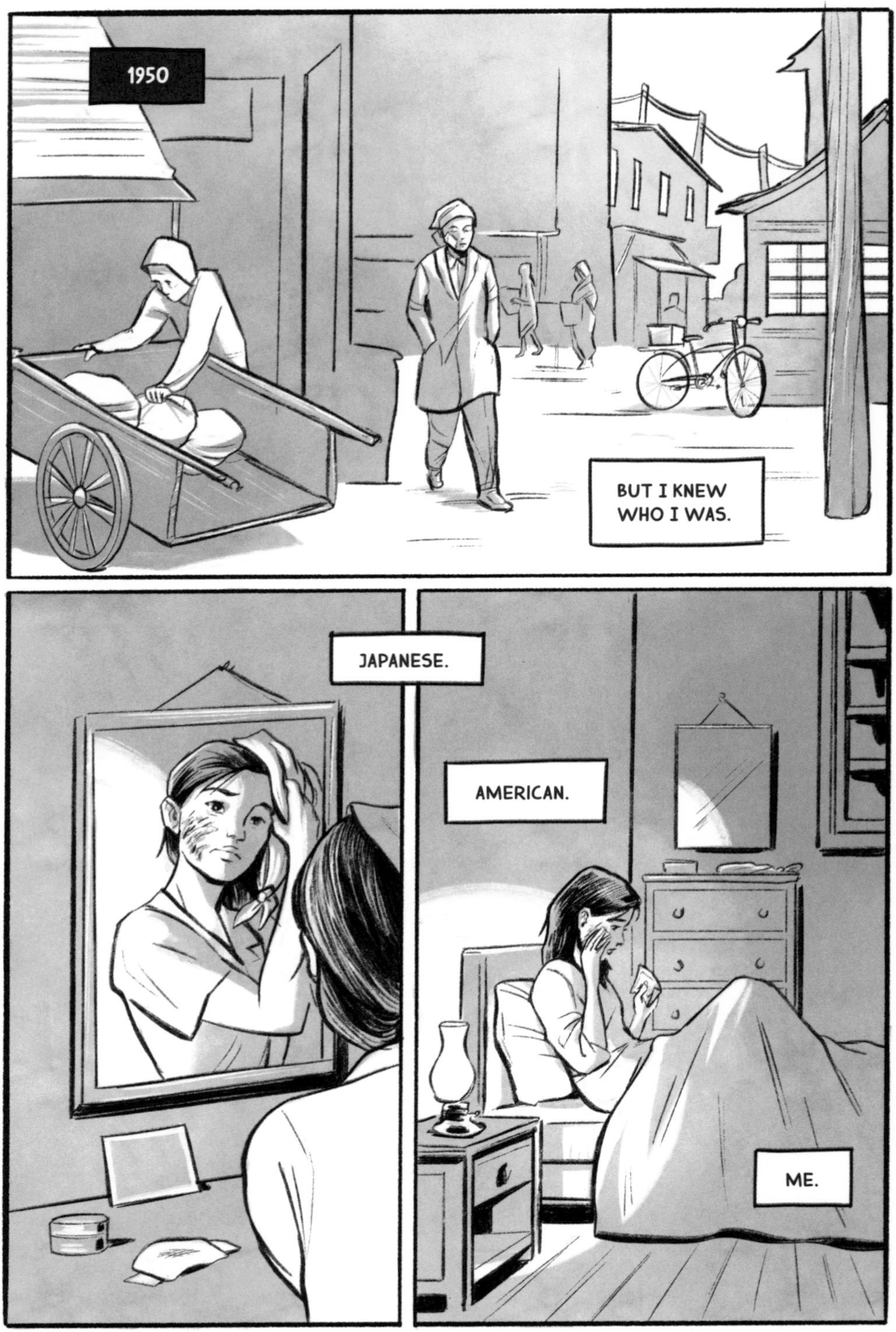
1950
BUT I KNEW WHO I WAS.
JAPANESE.
AMERICAN.
ME.

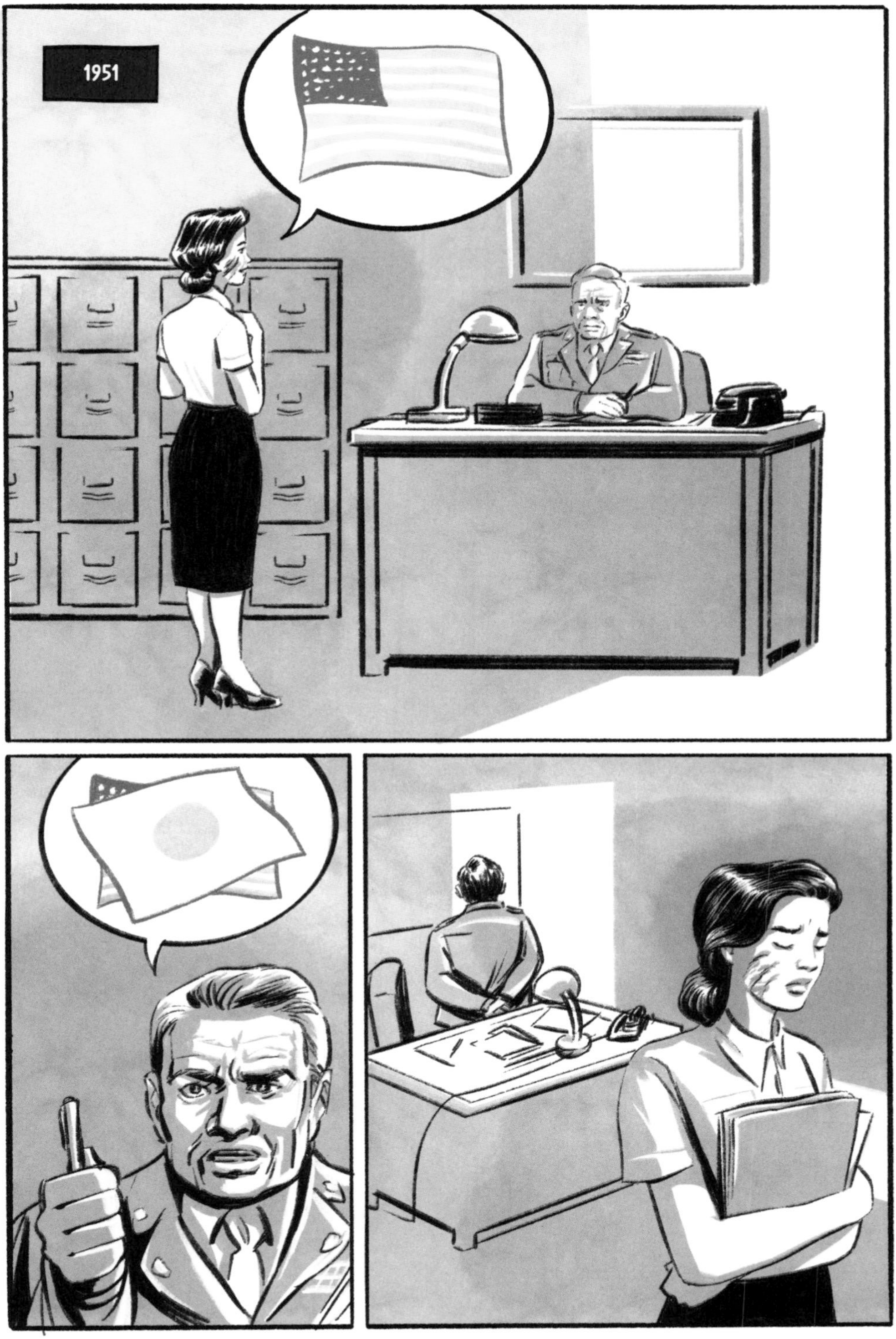
1951

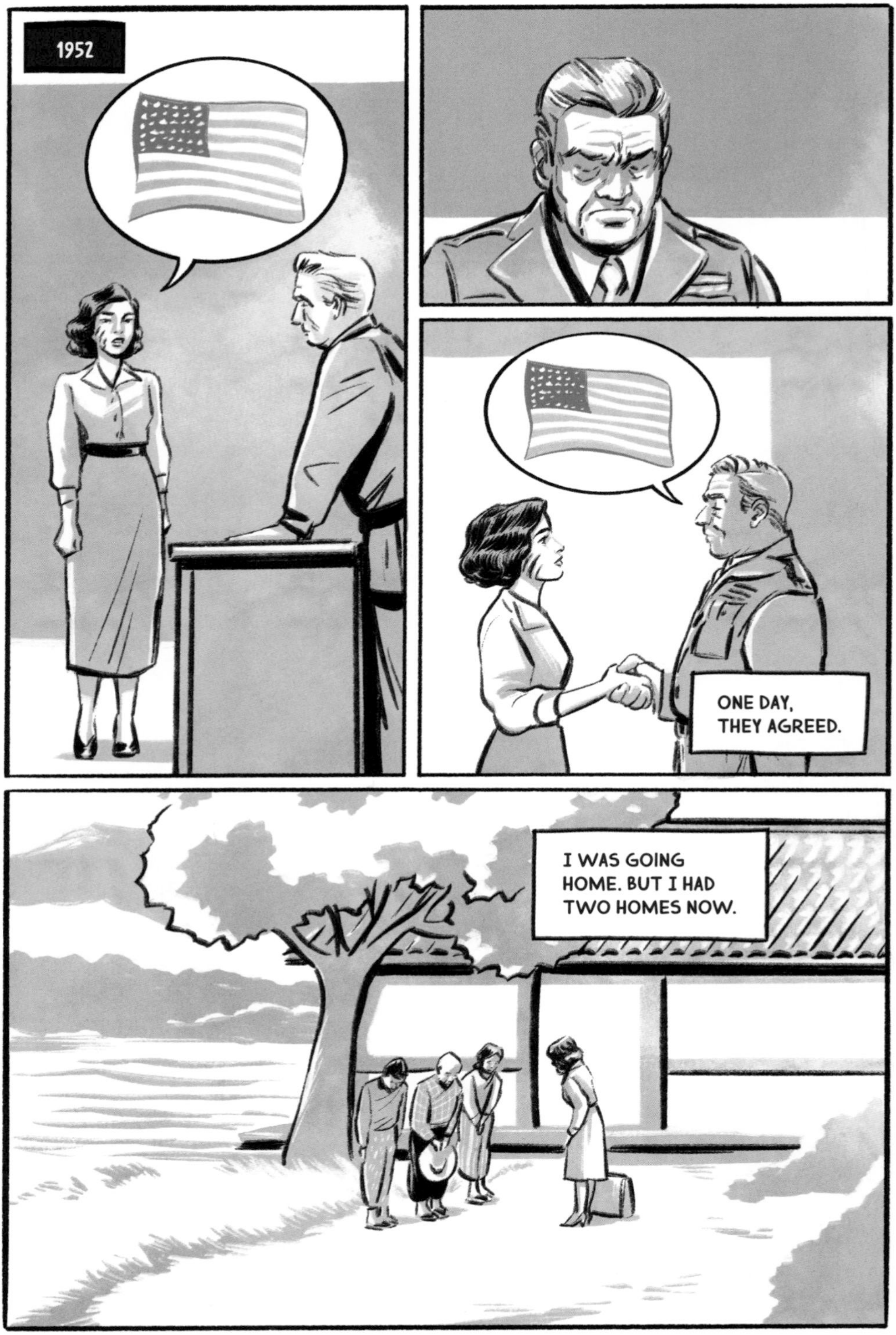
1952
ONE DAY, THEY AGREED.
I WAS GOING HOME. BUT I HAD TWO HOMES NOW.

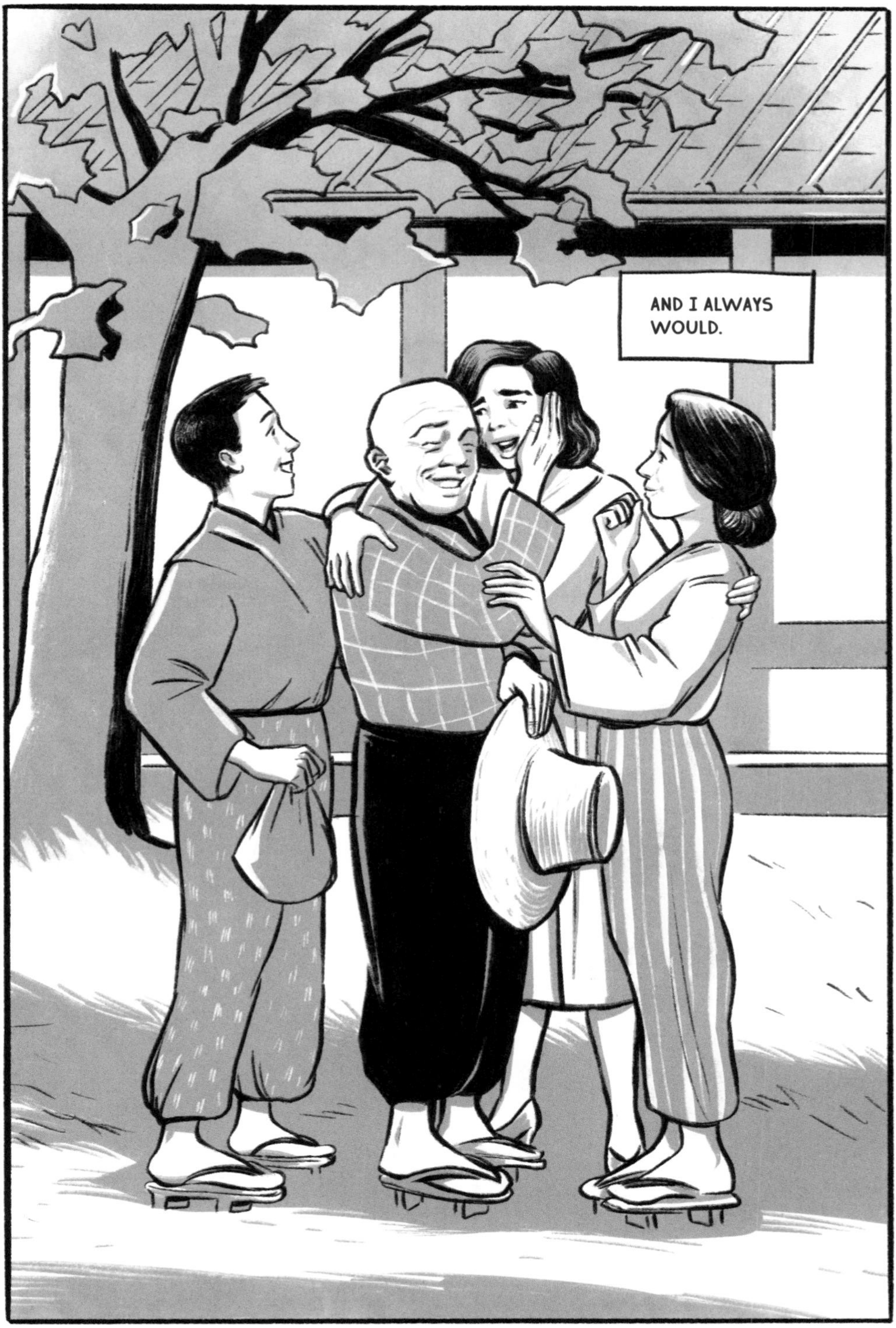
AND I ALWAYS WOULD.

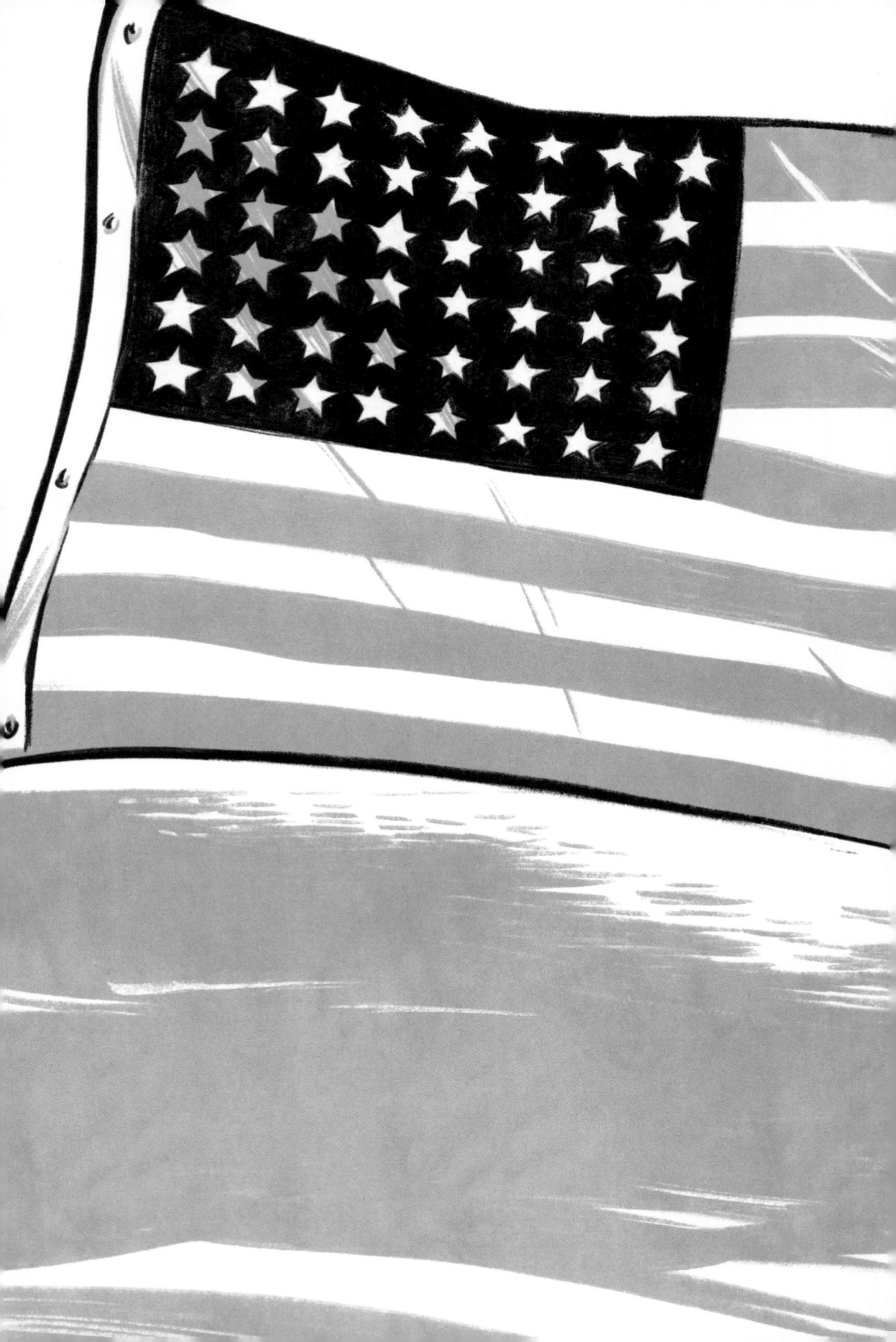

# 1952

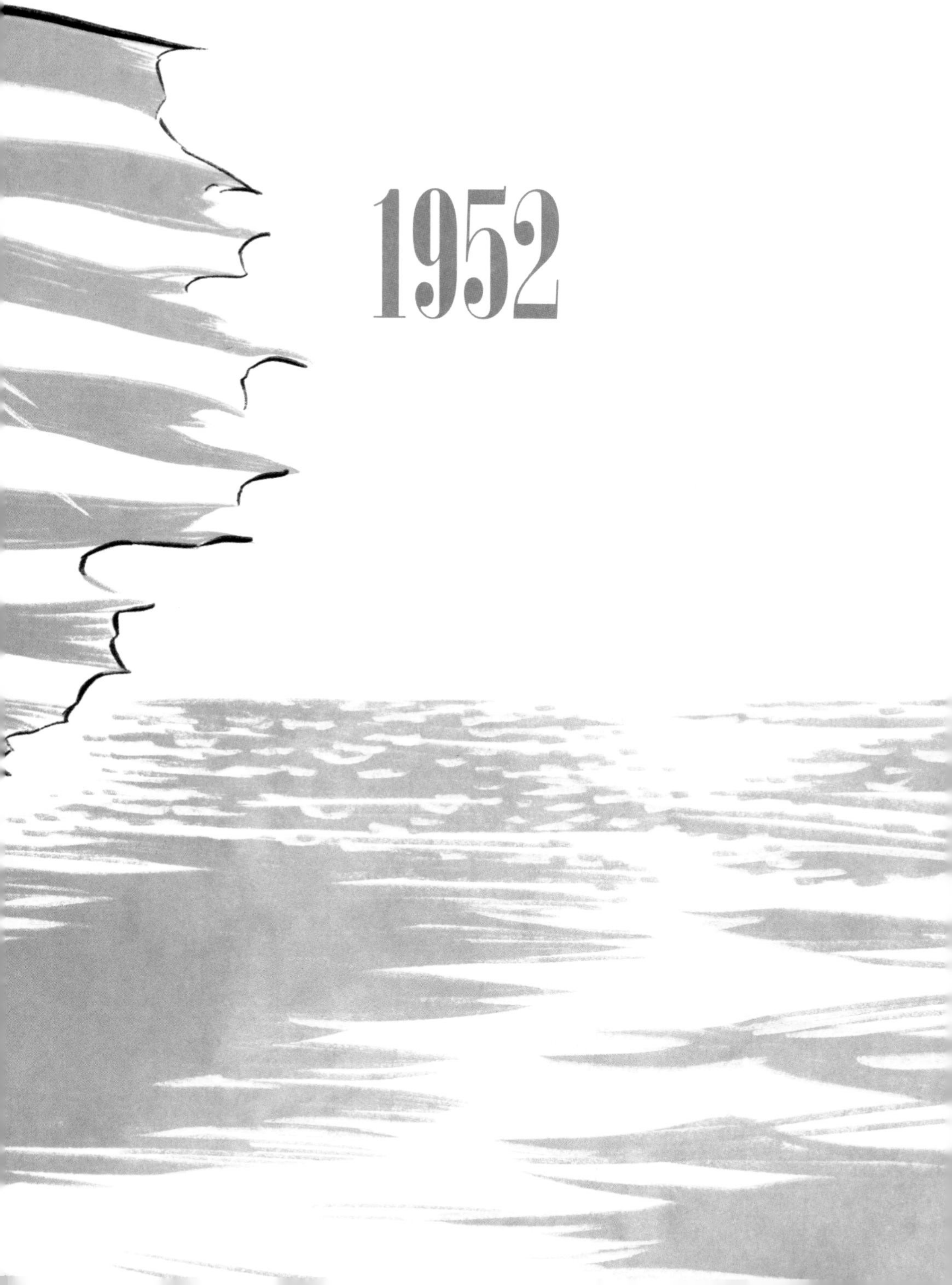

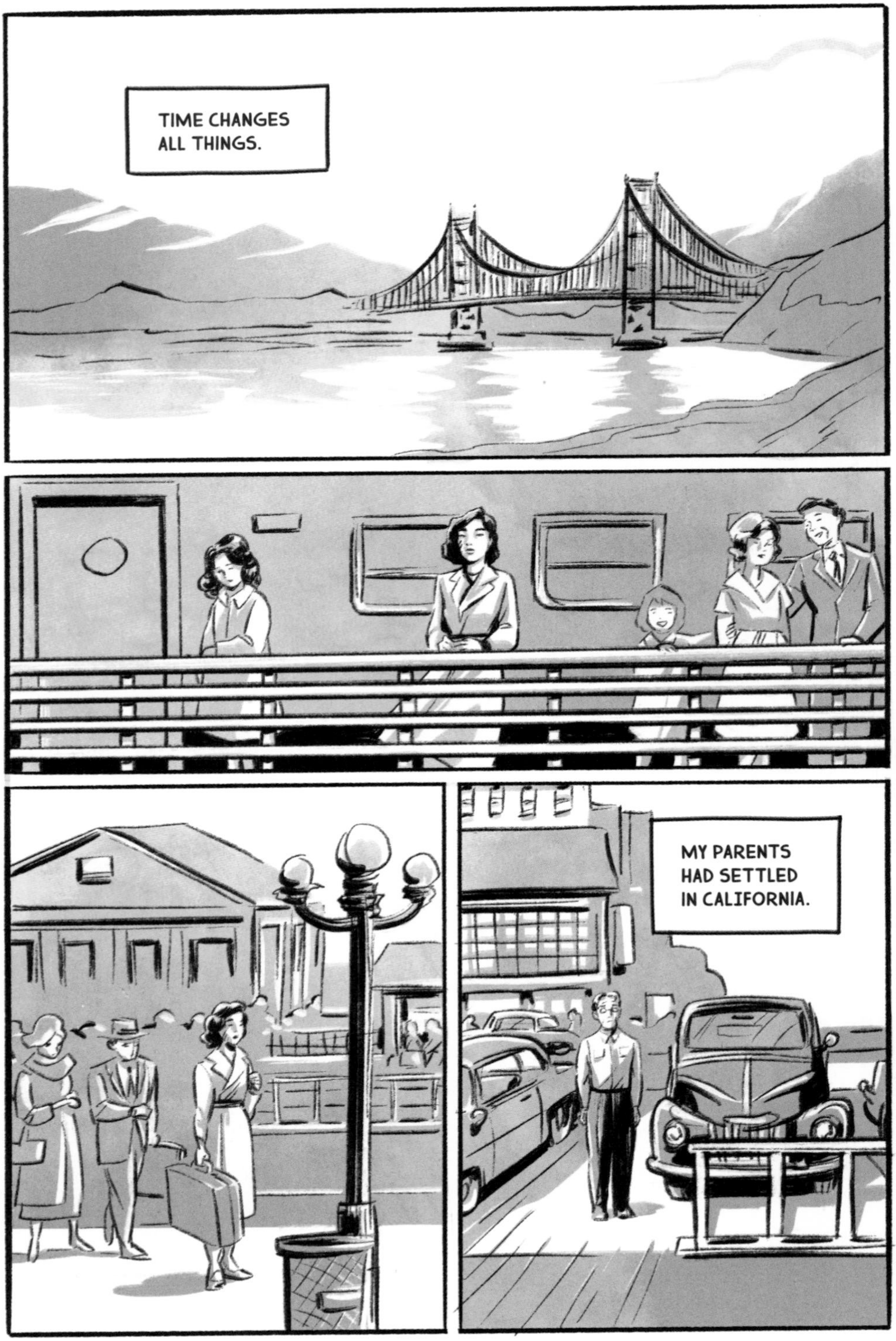
TIME CHANGES ALL THINGS.
MY PARENTS HAD SETTLED IN CALIFORNIA.

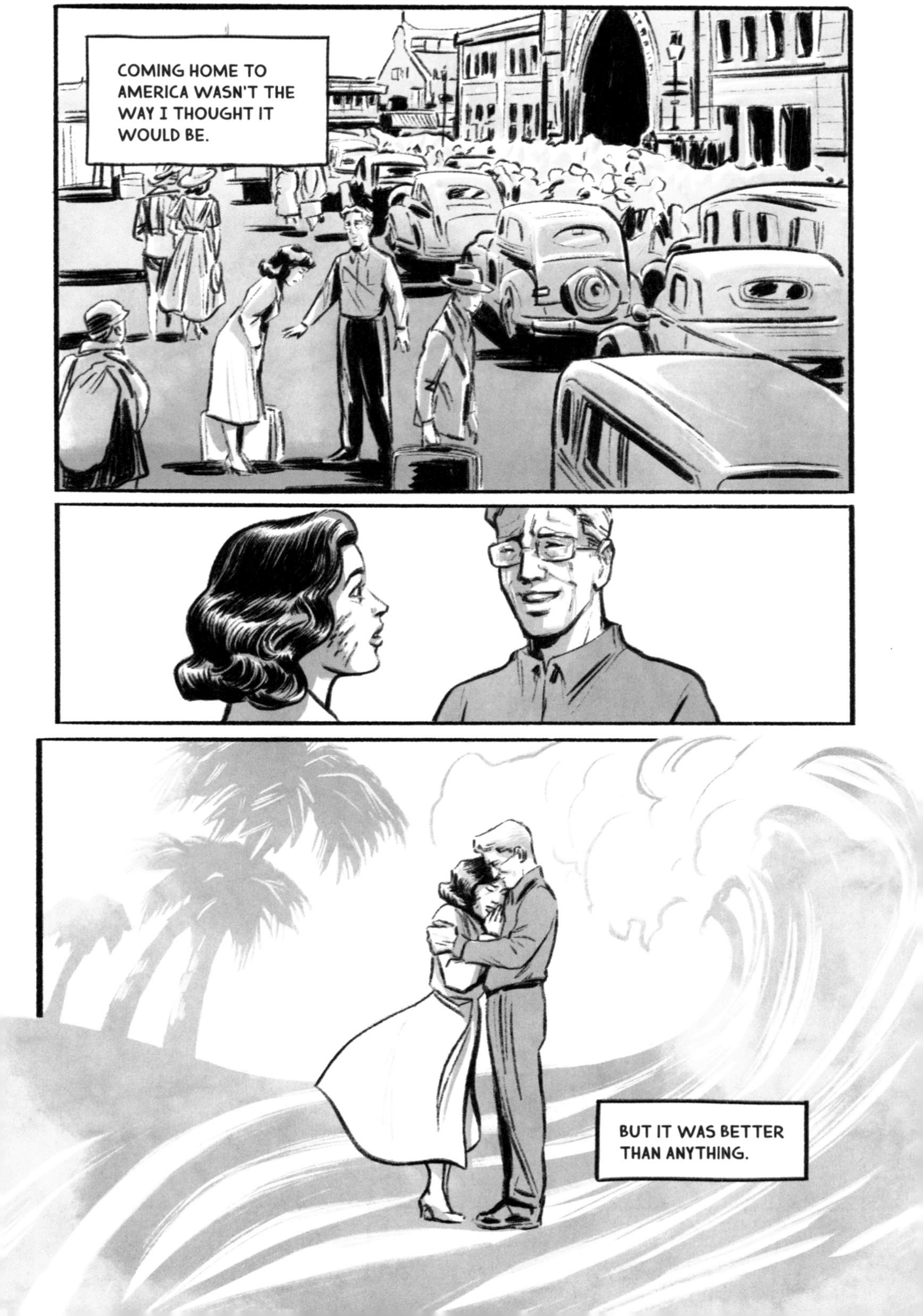
COMING HOME TO AMERICA WASN'T THE WAY I THOUGHT IT WOULD BE.
BUT IT WAS BETTER THAN ANYTHING.

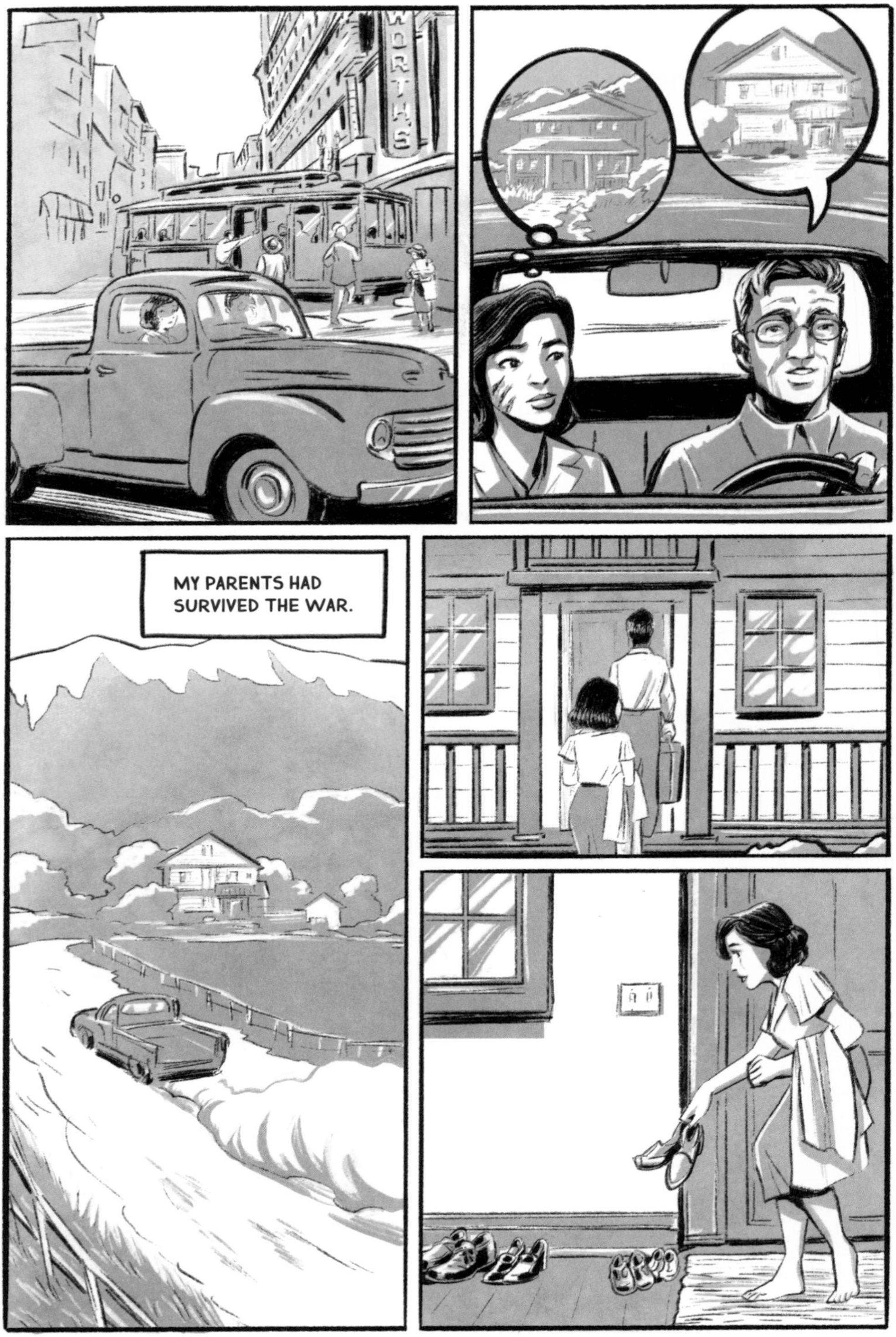
WORTHS
MY PARENTS HAD SURVIVED THE WAR.

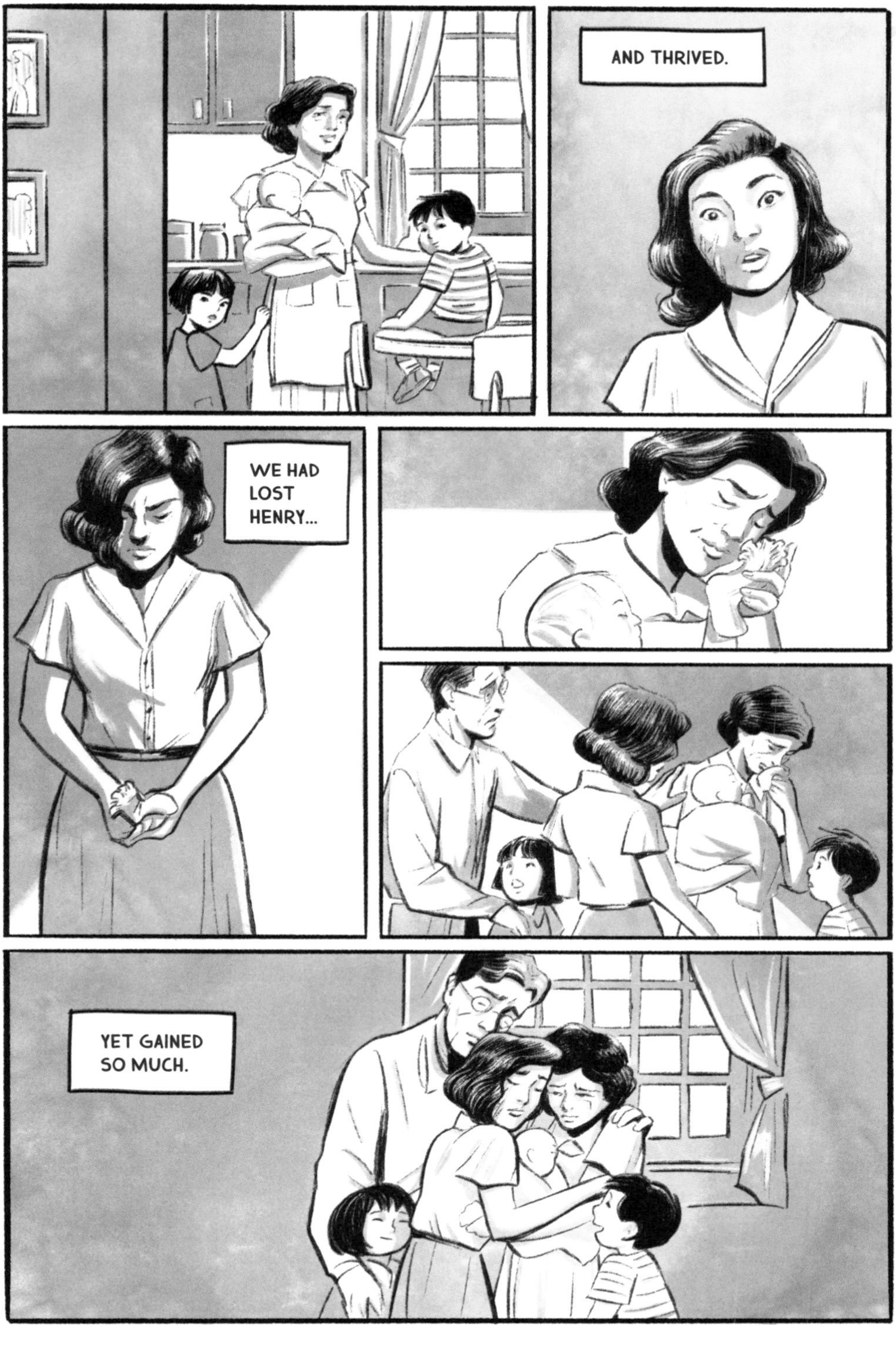
AND THRIVED.
WE HAD LOST HENRY...
YET GAINED SO MUCH.

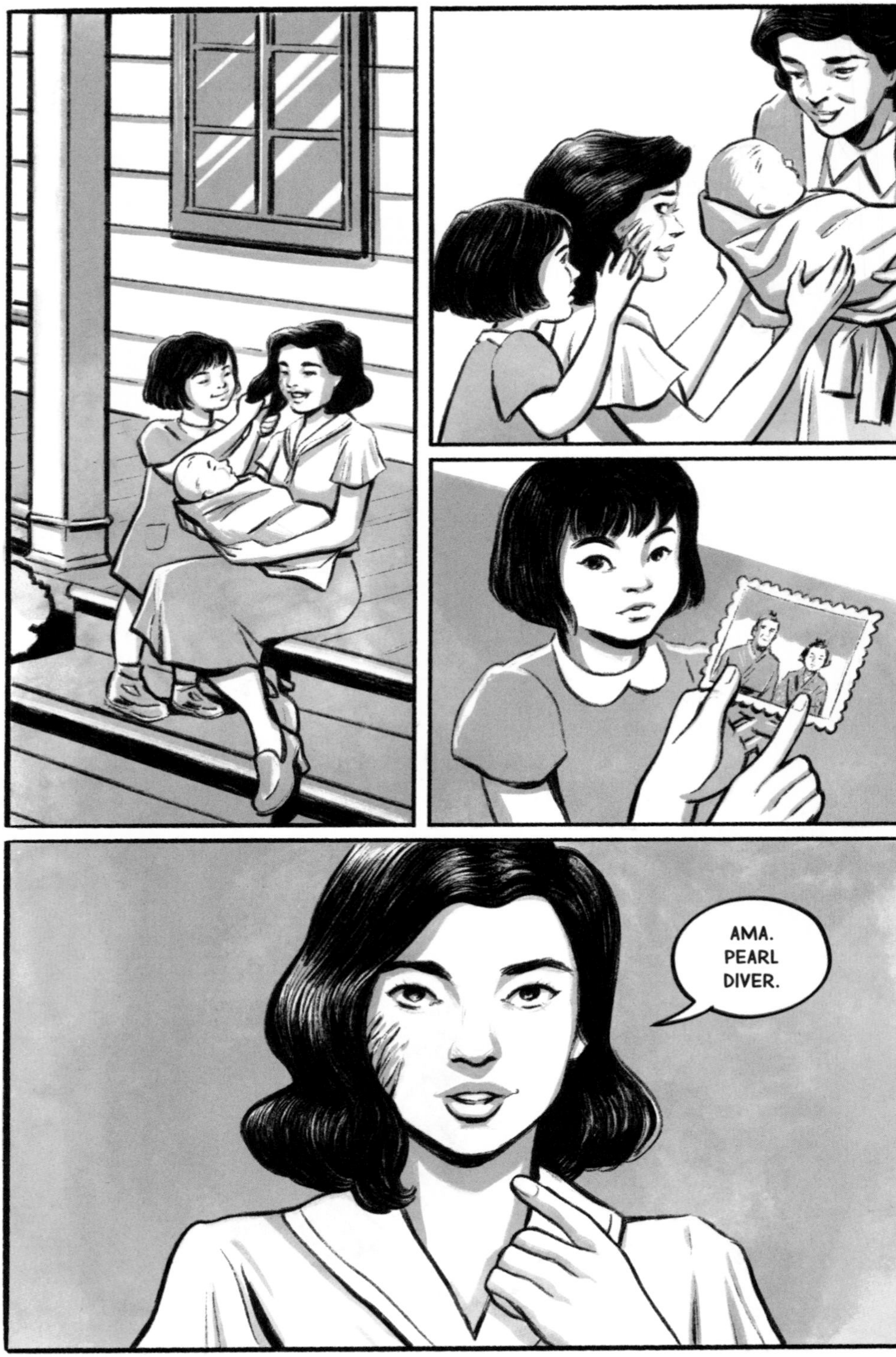
AMA.
PEARL
DIVER.

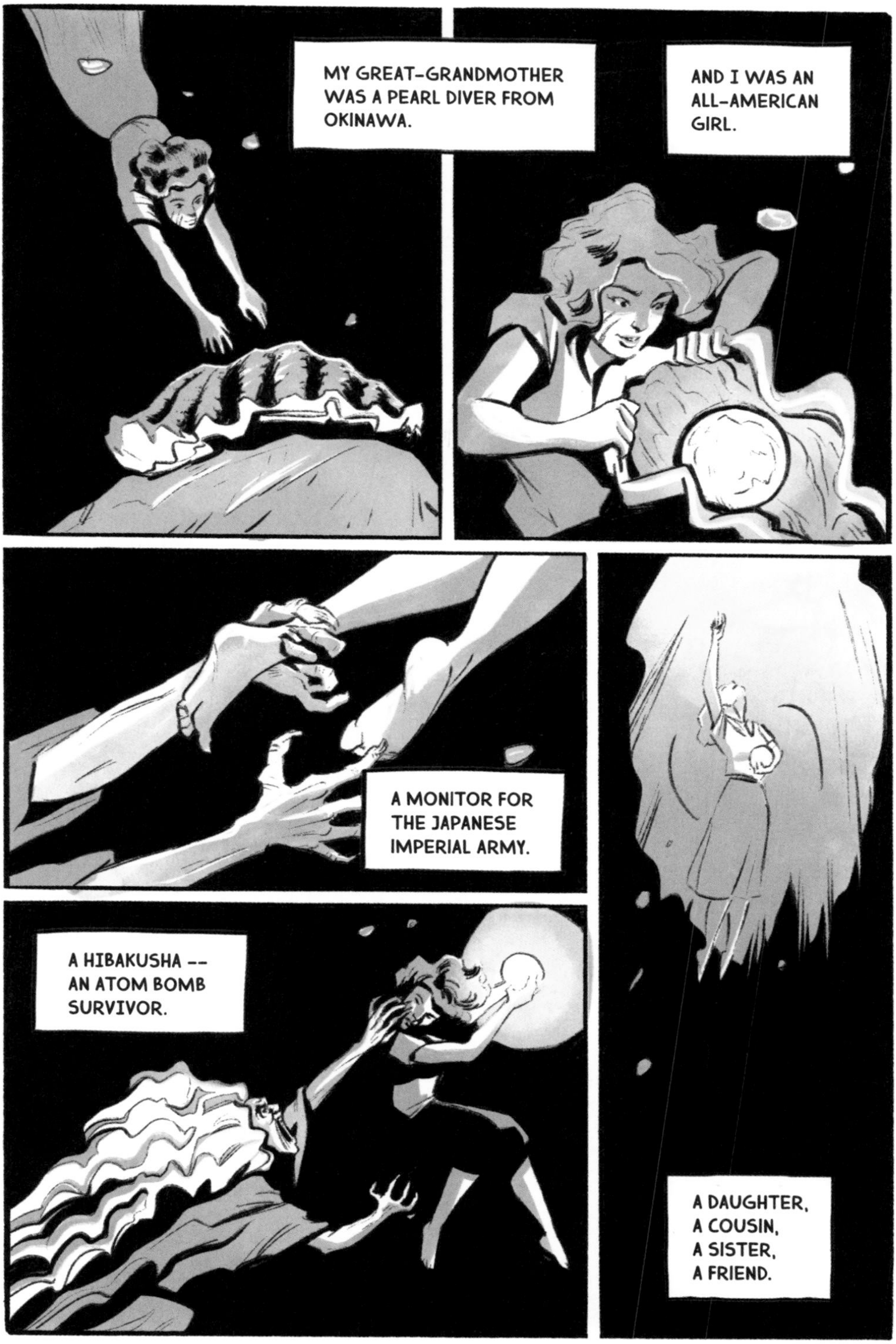
MY GREAT-GRANDMOTHER WAS A PEARL DIVER FROM OKINAWA.
AND I WAS AN ALL-AMERICAN GIRL.
A MONITOR FOR THE JAPANESE IMPERIAL ARMY.
A HIBAKUSHA -- AN ATOM BOMB SURVIVOR.
A DAUGHTER, A COUSIN, A SISTER, A FRIEND.

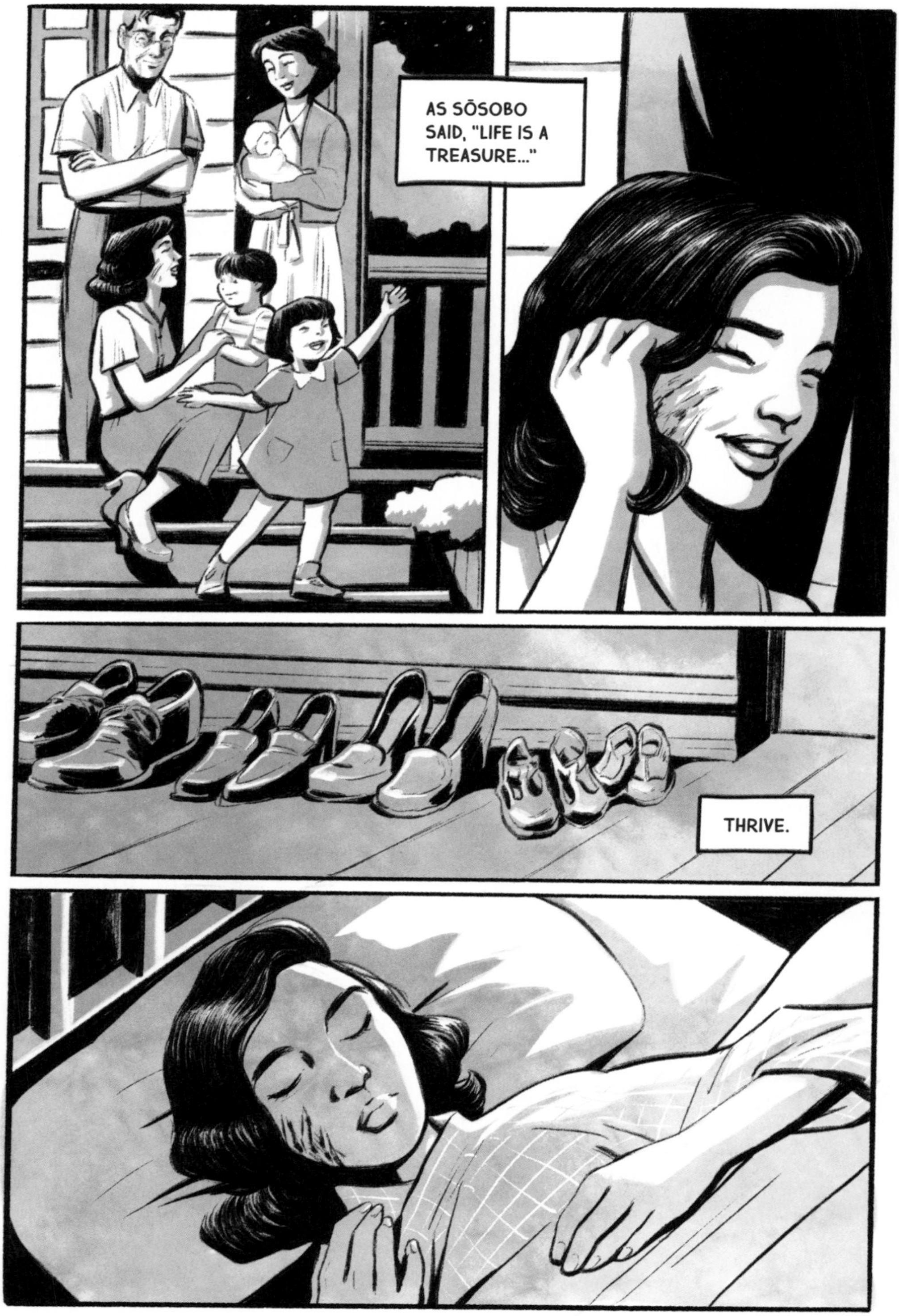
AS SŌSOBO SAID, "LIFE IS A TREASURE..."
THRIVE.

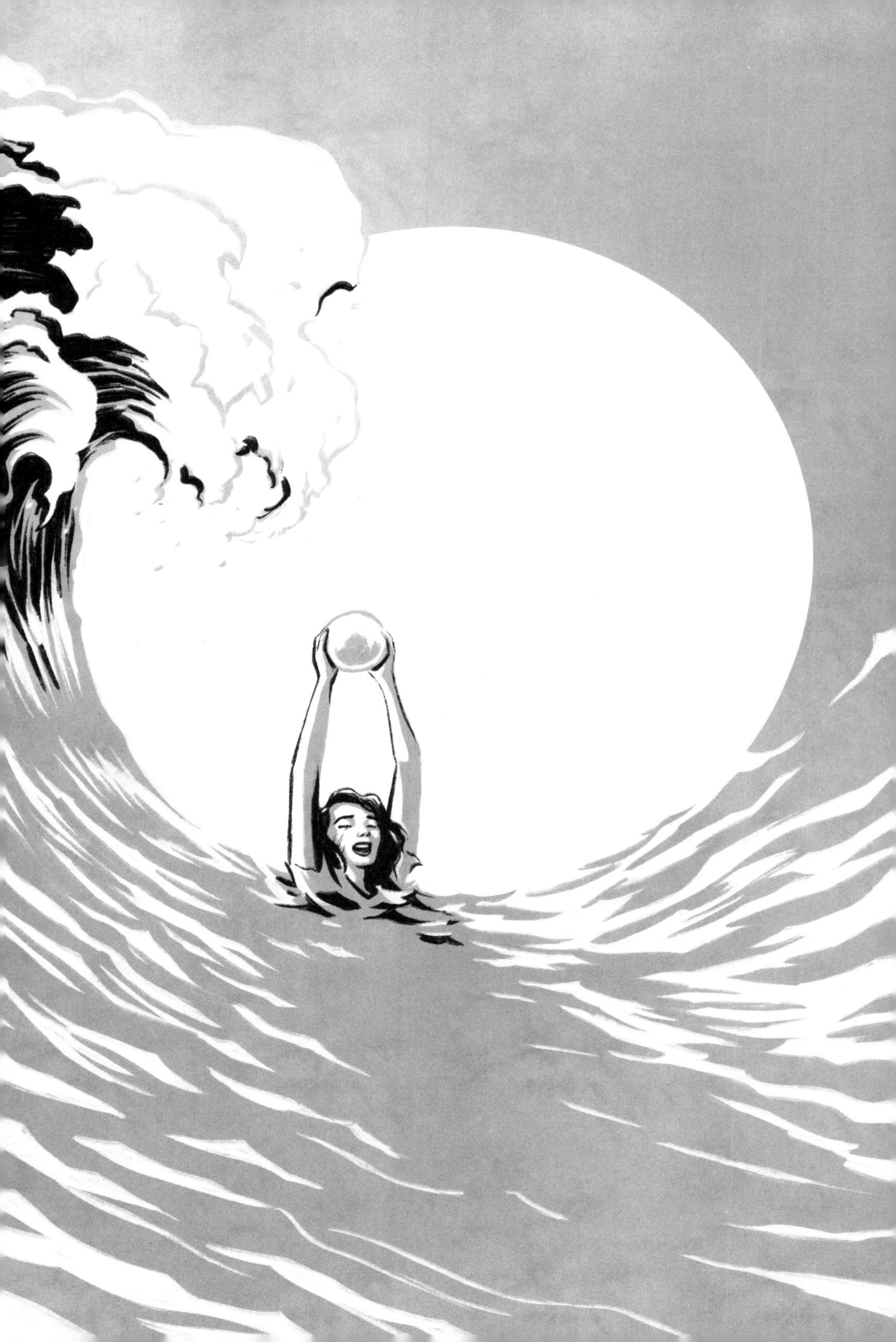

# WRITER ACKNOWLEDGMENTS

They say it takes a village to make a book. This is doubly true for a graphic novel. *Pearl* would not have been possible without the generosity of my friend Rahna Reiko Rizzuto, whose beautiful memoir, *Hiroshima in the Morning,* held the seeds of this story. Her incredible generosity in sharing her research is the reason why this book exists today. My thanks also to Allen Spiegel for insisting on reading an early draft and introducing it, and me, to my editor, Cassandra Pelham Fulton. A special thanks to my guide in Hiroshima, Yoshimi N., who walked the grounds of Shukkeien — formerly Sentei — Garden with me and showed me the scars and the beauty of her city; and to Dr. Yuki Miyamoto, who corrected my Japanese, expanded my knowledge, and gave kind feedback on this book.

**SHERRI L. SMITH**

# ILLUSTRATOR ACKNOWLEDGMENTS

I am nothing but grateful to dear friends and family who carried and supported my work whilst I was at the drafting table, to my colleagues and peers for all the assistance and encouragement, and to the steadfast team of Graphix. My deepest appreciation must also be extended to the communities who kindly shared their insights with me, including the Japanese Cultural Center of Hawai'i, where I came to understand the prelude and aftermath of the horrors of war.

CHRISTINE NORRIE

## ABOUT THE WRITER

Sherri L. Smith is the prolific author of multiple award-winning children's books, including *The Blossom and the Firefly*, *Flygirl*, *Orleans*, and several books in the Who Was series. She has written for *Bart Simpson* comics, James Cameron's *Avatar* comics, and *Wonder Woman*. Her books have appeared on a number of state reading lists and have been named as Junior Library Guild, Children's Book Council, and American Library Association Best Books for Young People selections. Sherri teaches creative writing in the MFA in Children's Writing program at Hamline University, and has taught at Goddard College and Old Dominion University. She lives in Los Angeles with her husband and a disreputable cat. Visit her online at sherrilsmith.com.

## ABOUT THE ILLUSTRATOR

Christine Norrie is a multiple Eisner-nominated artist and writer. She co-created the graphic novels *Breaking Up* with Aimee Friedman and illustrated *Hopeless Savages* by Jen van Meter and Chynna Clugston-Major, and has contributed to the *Black Canary* and *Lumberjanes* comics. She lives on a farm in upstate New York, where she raises hens and maintains a large garden. Visit her online at christinenorrie.com.